Library of Congress Control Number: 2016919467
Book also placed in London's British Library and in Oxford University's Bodleian Library.
ISBN: Hardcover   978-1-5144-9925-2
               Softcover   978-1-5144-9923-8
               eBook   978-1-5144-9924-5

Print information available on the last page.

Rev. date: 02/28/2017

To order additional copies of this book, contact:
Xlibris
800-056-3182
www.Xlibrispublishing.co.uk
Orders@Xlibrispublishing.co.uk
742822

TOKOLOSI

John Skinner

Dedicated to Sonia, to our global family and friends, to all victims of natural and man-made disasters, and to the far fewer who strive to save so many victims' lives and livelihoods.

Contents

Illustrations:

Foreword

Switch on television and, in these troubled times, we too often witness yet another natural or man-made disaster and pitiably tragic suffering. There may be searchers, rescuers, doctors, nurses, police, soldiers, many other helpers, all striving to save lives, protect livelihoods, relieve suffering and whatever else is needed to combat disaster, limit its affects, prevent more fatalities and so forth.

Many parts of Africa are seriously drought-prone. Set mostly in the 1990s within an imaginary sub-Saharan African country during severe prolonged drought, this novel features grave water, food, health-care and sanitation problems, the onset of HIV/AIDS, poor governance, endemic corruption, violence and bloodshed. It also features the revolutionary impact of new technology: cell phones, solar panels, etc., but the world wide web has yet to extend its reach and link laptops with those in, say, America and Europe.

Gwato, a mythical tribe's language translated within this book, projects its people's thoughts, spoken or written words. Its clipped clauses, frequent comma-emphases and word order may seem odd to users of conventional English.

Greetings and best wishes, John Skinner.

Highland Strife

Whoosh as dry tinder ignited. *Thump* when a roof caved in. Fanned by a vindictive wind, a family's home became a raging furnace, and another, then another, and soon the acrid stench of burning thatch engulfed Katama. Men were shouting, chasing other men, fighting, bleeding. Children, too terrifed to cry, huddled close to weeping grandmother's, most with babies in their arms. Grandfathers, parents and older sisters struggled desperately to beat out the fast spreading flames. Older brothers, riding ponies, drove precious livestock to safety; their dogs competing with wild animals to sound warnings of danger.

Within an hour, fires were blazing in the village across the gorge – in vicious, gruesome reprisal.

No words could describe how Katama's headman felt that night. Years of coaxing his clan to live peacefully with hostile neighbours had been destroyed by brainless crimes. Mercifully, no one was badly injured, but seven law abiding families were homeless!

After combing the charred homes for most of the next morning, yet finding nothing of worth, the heartbroken headman and his sombre people gathered outside the café. While praying, a strange noise startled them! Was God coming to punish the guilty? Anxious faces turned heavenwards seeking an answer. The noise became louder! Then something flew fast and low above their heads to their chief's village across the gorge. Most women and young children clung to each other when it flew to their village and landed close by.

Their headman hurried to find out what made so much noise and dust – when he came back, he said a *helicopter* brought the provincial governor and their chief to see the burnt rondavels. Then, before the governor left Katama, he angrily blamed its people for *all* the fires. The headman said there were a few bad men in both villages and asked him to help the seven Kataman families with no homes or possessions. 'You help them!' the governor shouted, so that everybody heard, and their chief nodded his head. Men shook their fists, some called them very bad names. Scared of more trouble, the women tried to stop them.

Many boys wanted to see a helicopter and followed the angry stranger, but he shouted 'go home' and they hid close by. He got in the helicopter, it made a very loud noise, and when all the dust went, they saw it flying above the high peaks.

Every Kataman helped the families with no homes – none would lend their hated chief even a donkey and made him walk home to the village across the gorge.

Although belonging to the same tribe, relations between those two Obangwato clans were so hostile, just trivial squabbles could trigger mischief or unrest. Moreover, they referred to each other never by place names, but as 'the people in the village across the gorge.' The only communities east of the high peaks, their isolation should have bonded them, yet their very solitude had bred such mutual suspicion and distrust, they had grown apart. So many fractious years had nurtured wounds now beyond mending – tormenting wounds inflicted long ago by the spell cast upon the village across the deep gorge.

According to tribal legend, a witch doctor from a country far to the south had come to that village and had laid in front of her feet bits of human bones and small round stones to drive away the evil dwarfs that hid there. She had called the dwarfs, tokolosi.

Ever since then, when believers in curses and evil spirits said the tokolosi still haunted that village, its people accused the clan across the gorge of spreading malicious rumours – "speaking bad thoughts" in their Gwato language. Yet, both clans blamed the tokolosi if vultures perched or snakes lurked close by, if baboons stole food or a baby, if a leopard killed their kinfolk or livestock. The evil tokolosi were blamed for everything bad.

Many Obangwatos, wherever they lived, believed that only the elderly died naturally – witchcraft caused untimely death. The widely used expression 'to be late' meant a person or one of their animals had died. Some believed that witchcraft could stop them dying.

Many still looked to their chief for redemption when drought destroyed their crops, and because he had inherited secret rain-making charms from his ancestors, they took comfort from the belief that the bringing of rain stood high among his duties.

The people of both clans judged their chief on his ability to bring peace. But Katamans said: 'He brings war, all the days and nights. He sent the bad men from the village where he lives, to burn down seven of our rondavels.' Most Katamans said their bad men were right to burn down seven of his village's rondavels, soon after. Some said it was wrong. None blamed the tokolosi – maybe for one time, only, many thought.

Their headman knew he would always feel ashamed of his failure to stop the wicked crimes of his clan's troublemakers. It would blacken his name, always! He solemnly rode to the village across the gorge and found the chief was *not* ashamed of his troublemakers' crimes, but angry that the headman had come to his kraal without permission.

'Ride back to Katama,' he shouted. 'The guilty men are there, unless the cowards have run away.'

'The guilty men are in this village, also. If you were fair to the Kataman clan, fourteen families would still have homes and treasured possessions. Both of your clans must share the scarce pasture and cooking dung, just as they share the precious stream water down in the gorge . . . a gorge that must no longer divide us and our people.'

Rancour and conflict would sadly prevail, thanks to a biased perfidious chief.

It would take more than twenty years, the death of their chief and his son's succession to replace so much fruitless, rancourous, harmful conflict with inter-clan friendliness and a compassionate understanding between people of the same tribe. People hitherto unable to share their mutual tribulations or to live peacefully on either side of the deep, dark gorge. People, sharing a common heritage, who'd been unable to stop blaming each other or the evil tokolosi for virtually everything bad that happened under a relentless sun. A sun that too often brought very bad drought to their part of Africa, where widespread hardship and suffering were commonplace; where every adult and child deserved nutritious food, much better health care, education, governance; far greater access to electricity – enabling them to communicate their problems and what help they urgently required – so that those in a position to help them could respond as soon as possible. Also, the many rich foreigners, who had so much when they had next to nothing, could teach them how to be more self-sufficient. How to test water before they drank it. How to build a small dam to catch the rare rains. How to build and empty latrines, so that they would no longer have to squat where they and their ancestors had always squatted. With even more assistance from foreign donors urgently needed, a vital question remained – was it all far too much to expect?

Katama

High Peaks

Village across the Gorge

Katama and the village across the gorge with the high peaks beyond

The Mashedi Family

Less than forty rondavels clung to a sunny mountainside above a deep gorge. These round thatched sandstone huts were small primitive dwellings, overshadowed by huge boulders, poised as if about to roll and crush all within their path. A café, the only shop, had cinder-block walls and a corrugated-tin roof. Some corrals afforded frail calves, lambs and foals sanctuary. Oil from aloe plants eased winter coughs. This was Katama, a remote highland village in sub-tropical Africa's dusty interior and the Mashedi family's home.

Ten miles away across a deep gorge towered a range of jaggéd high peaks, beyond the larger of the two villages, where their chief lived. The two oldest Mashedi daughters went to school there, near the priest's dilapidated church, the midwife's ramshackle clinic and a spotless police-post, where the postman sorted letters and sometimes parcels – when not drunk in a choice of rowdy shebeens.

The many surrounding mountains reaching ten thousand feet, changed from pale green in summer to burnt-ochre in winter when grass all but died. High in the peaks, a spring fed a life- and crop-sustaining stream which cascaded over rocks before plunging into the gorge. Flourishing in summer, the stream became a trickle or bone dry in winter, unless a storm or snowfall swelled its meagre flow. Then, women and girls hurried down into the gorge and returned with a gourd balanced on their heads, full of precious water, to store in large baked clay pots. Too many years, though, the summer rains never came.

Ngabo Mashedi, a tall smart police sergeant, rode home from Mabela – the provincial capital – every month to spend two days with his family and brought money for his wife to buy cooking oil, sewing thread, soap or medicines at Katama's café.

The thirty miles to Mabela took about eight hours on horseback. For the steep tortuous path, the only path over the high peaks with many treacherous hazards, was just a narrow ledge between sheer rock-faces and deep ravines for most of its highest length. If no rains came, herd boys rode to Mabela on ponies, leading donkeys which carried back sacks of maize meal and sometimes dried beans. When the herd boys were safely past the village across the gorge, they were pleased to see many Katamans waving.

Tsabo Mashedi, a quietly observant six-year-old, sat on the rock close by his family's rondavel to see the sun sink behind the high peaks. He wanted to ride to the high peaks! Matashaba, his eldest sister was eight. She brewed tea and helped their grandmother to cook mealie-meal on the fire. His mother sat with him, feeding his baby sister, Palima, with mother's milk. When his father rode home he sat with them, also, and told stories that made them laugh. If they were sad, Tsabo told a happy story. His middle sister was seven, but Dinea never sat with them or helped people. She walked alone, always.

Self-taught, Ngabo Mashedi had big ambitions for his only son and he told Tsabo: 'If more money comes to me, you will go to the mission school in Mabela, soon after.'

That excited Tsabo, but also troubled him.

Their priest rode from the village across the gorge every Sunday and Katamans went to Mass near the café. One Sunday, the priest said, a herd boy stopped a leopard killing his family's cattle and when he led the cattle back to his village the headman called him a *hero* and the villagers clapped their hands. Tsabo wanted to be hero and stop a leopard killing his family's cattle, and he wanted to go to the mission school also. He and his friend, Mueketso, would be seven at Easter. Mueketso had been a herd boy two years and he wanted to go to the mission school now!

'My angry father said I must stay a herd boy many years to get my mother money,' he told Tsabo. 'My father gives the money I get to the girl he wants to marry. This I know.'

As in most African tribes, being a herd boy had long been glorified, for it was said to enhance self-reliance, courage and much else. But guarding livestock and searching for better pasture, water and food for themselves could prove fatal when predators struck.

Often for months on end, Kataman herd-boys searched daily for water, pasture and their own food, then drove cattle, sheep and goats into one or more of the many corrals scattered throughout the highlands. Although guarded by their dogs the boys rested, rather than slept. A jackal's bark seemed very close at night. A leopard's stealthy prowl caused them far greater fear. Often, herd-boys and their dogs were warned of approaching danger by buck browsing on the hillsides, which leapt into flight at the faintest sound or slightest movement, by baboons squatting on rocks or ledges ready to welcome each dawn, or by circling vultures hoping for early prey.

No trees sheltered Katama from the sun. Everyone was used to the sun but the crops suffered. In good years – rain provided welcome respite and families grew sufficient food to meet their immediate needs, with enough left over to see them through the dry winter months. In bad years – hunger, thirst and illness could bring out the worst in people, for suffering caused quarrels, quarrels led to abuse and abuse poisoned minds. Some people were jealous of those with more water, food, fields, livestock and possessions than they had, yet prided themselves on *not* being jealous. Some believed magic killed evil spirits and smeared witchdoctor grease on sticks stuck in the soil to make their maize and beans grow when no rains came. Some feared the tokolosi since childhood. Drought, witchcraft, magic, evil spirits, rumour, gossip – all maner of fears, taboos, suspicions, prophesies and prejudices which had prospered long in the village across the gorge – were the tokolosi's staunchest allies. Most Kataman men, women and teenagers believed and many said their chief was the tokolosi's best friend.

The women and girls of both villages and of most ages, often with babies strapped to their backs, worked in the fields, mostly steep and narrow, close by Katama. Some in the village across the gorge were bigger and not so steep. The older men talked, drank home-brewed beer and smoked clay pipes. Most younger men worked in South Africa and it took two nights and one day by bus from Mabela to the mines. By faster minibus-taxi the fares were much dearer – the too frequent road and mining accidents far costlier. Both villages had their share of widows and orphans.

Not only did women bear children, grow crops, cook, and draw water from the stream. Farther down the gorge, in separate pools for each of the two clans, they washed clothes, beat them on rocks and laid them out to dry. They sheared sheep and goats, combed and spun wool and mohair, knitted garments and wove blankets for their family or bartered them for the necessities not sold in the cafés. They burned brushwood on cooking fires, but more often burned dung – dung that should have enriched the thin overworked soil of their narrow steep fields – soil that storms swept down the cliffs to clog the stream below. They had to scavenge very far for scarce brushwood. If Kataman women were caught with sticks and bits of bush, the chief's bad men stole them and gave them to women from the village where he and his bad men lived. When they stopped Kataman herd boys grazing livestock on some good pasture, their headman rode to Mabela, hoping his clan's many grievances would receive fair judgement, at last.

'There are no legally binding land use rights,' the provincial governor said. 'So people of both clans may collect brushwood and graze livestock wherever they wish. Ask your chief if you can build fences!' The governor's hurtful laughter echoed while the headman miserably rode home. It still echoed after he told his villagers the bad news.

Discredited by one clan and urged on by the other, their chief was confronted by many protests in Katama. Tsabo's mother kept his oldest sisters at home. Some mothers refused to send their children to school in the village across the gorge because they feared that the tolokolosi, hiding there, were doing evil things, again. Others gave a witchdoctor maize-meal and asked him to mend their chief's shadow – shadow, power and justice being the same word in Gwato.

Widely held in high esteem, Ngabo Mashedi befriended people he trusted, whatever their tribe, clan or race, and was aptly severe with transgressors. When he rode home last month he told his wife and older children to beware of the troublemakers in both villages.

Some bad men from the village across the gorge stole a Kataman man's horse. Outside Katama's café, that afternoon, the headman begged his men not to retaliate. Raised voices attracted more men, as well as women and children, and the protest became riotous.

With her baby in her arms, Ma Mashedi, her son and her older daughters hurried back to their rondavel to kneel and pray. Tsabo asked Jesus to send his father home, quick!

That evening seven rondavels were burned down in Katama and, soon after, seven in the village across the gorge. A helicopter brought the provincial governor to Katama next day and he blamed the people of Katama for *all* the fires. The headman said there were a few bad men in both villages and asked him to help the homeless families. He flew back to Mabela and their clan helped the homeless families. Their chief came, also, but no one would lend him even a donkey and made him walk home to the village across the gorge.

Tsabo's tribal history would years later record: "The provincial governor and the local chief deserved to live unhappily ever after; their reputations and consciences blackened."

Lying awake one night, Tsabo was thinking about helicopters when their rondavel door was unlocked. Standing against the door, his mother shouted: 'Who comes?'

'Your husband comes. I ride from Mabela to guard our village.'

Next morning their headman assembled the villagers and thanked Ngabo Mashedi for coming from Mabela to guard them. But when Ngabo came home from working close by, he sat alone and never spoke to his family. Then one evening he said: 'I will leave the police, soon, and find work in a mine in South Africa, after.'

'Why go so far? Why my husband? Why?' Stay close by and make us happy, again.'

'More money will come to me and Tsabo will go to the mission school in Mabela.'

Tsabo slept on the mat between his father and oldest sister. After his mother blew out the candle, he asked himself: 'Where will I sleep at the mission school? What will I eat? When will I come home?' He was still awake when his mother fed his baby sister and whispered to him: 'The sun comes, soon, Tsabo. You must sleep, now.'

His father answered the questions next morning and his mother went with them to the headman's rondavel. His father said: 'I will work in a mine in South Africa, soon, to get money for Tsabo to go to the mission school in Mabela.'

'Are you happy to hear this?' the headman asked Ma Mashedi.

'I am happy, now. My husband said he and Tsabo will come home at Christmas, every year, and at Easter, also.'

That evening, the headman gathered together his people and told them: 'I have good news. Ngabo Mashedi will leave the police and work in the mines, soon after, to get more money to pay the . . .'

'It is *bad* news,' a miner's widow called out. 'If Ngabo goes there, the chief will send his bad men here, very quick, and the evil tokolosi will come, also.'

'Your sons will guard you and I will help them,' the headman said. 'I have more good news. Tsabo will go to the mission school, soon. You must ride my brown pony, every day, Tsabo, and he will take you to Mabela, when the day comes.'

When the words came, Tsabo thanked the headman and asked if the pony had a name.

'You will give him a good name. This I know.'

'My middle man is Patrick and I will call him Pat.'

'Hero! Hero!' his friends chanted. They sat with him at the Mass when the priest praised the young herd boy who stopped a leopard killing his family's cattle.

'Tsabo is my hero, also,' his mother told them, with an arm round her precious son.

The White Man
Who Smiles

Most days Tsabo rode Pat, a bigger pony than he'd ridden before, up the steep path behind Katama to the ridge and then they climbed to the waterfall at the top of the gorge, and sometimes climbed higher towards the high peaks. They were good friends from the moment they met.

On his last day in the police Ngabo Mashedi rode Pat to Mabela, took off his uniform, left it at police headquaters and put on his best suit. He then went to the Mission to buy his son's school clothes and pay for his son's first term, which ended just before Easter. The next day he rode home and told his family: 'Pat is a brave and strong pony. He will take Tsabo to the mission school after Christmas at the month's end.'

Tsabo's mother wove a blanket in his school colours, green and white. His eldest sister knitted green socks, his grandmother knitted white socks, and his grandfather bought him a new pen at the café. Tsabo had never had so many Christmas presents.

He put his presents in a bag, one week after, and tied it to his saddle. 'Bring me good news of your school work, Tsabo,' his mother said. He saw her tears, but no tears came to him. His father was near! His grandparents and oldest sister and many friends waved when he rode Pat down the path to the gorge, close behind his father's horse. A herd boy rode behind him on a pony, also, and will lead Pat and his father's horse back to Katama. At the top of the steep path from the gorge, they saw all the people waving, still. They passed the village across the gorge and climbed a very steep path to the high peaks. That ride to Mabela would stay long Tsabo's memory.

Some six years later, the nun who taught English, told her pupils to write about their first days at the mission school. Tsabo felt embarrassed when she said his story would be in the next school magazine. He felt much better when she said: 'I corrected your English.'

Newcomers

My home is in Katama, a very small village on the other side of
the high peaks we can see from our school. I came here when I was
seven, like most boys and girls. My father was a police sergeant and
later he went to work in the mines to get more money. He had ridden
Pat, our village headman's brown pony, to Mabela once before and
when he came back he said 'Pat is a brave and strong pony.' I had
often ridden Pat, but never over the high peaks.

Soon after Christmas, six years ago, my father rode his horse,
I rode Pat and a herd-boy rode with us on his pony to Mabela. The
path over the high peaks is very steep and narrow. When will Pat
rest and drink water from my gourd, is my bag of school clothes tied
to my saddle, will we fall into a gorge, I remember thinking many
times. We passed too near many deep gorges and my father called
them ravines.

We were at the top of the path, at last, but Katama was too far
away to see. My father pointed to Mabela and there was only flat
land. I had never seen flat land before. After I had checked Pat's
harness and hooves, he drank some of the water in my gourd and
ate some of the maize-grain in his nosebag. The herd boy made a
fire with dry dung, cooked mealie-meal and gave some to my father
and me. We drank more water from our gourds, because the herd
boy still had three full gourds. They put a stone on a pile of stones
and I did, also, after my father said it will bring me good luck. We
all put a stone on another pile where the path ended and a wider
path began. I could see many houses far below us. 'It is Mabela' my
father said. 'We will get there at sunset, after three hours riding.'

When we got to the mission school, I stroked Pat's head and
thanked him for bringing me there safely. My father tied our lead-
reins to the herd boy's saddle. The herd boy said he knew a good
resting place close by and would start riding home at sunrise. I
remember Pat trotting behind the herd-boy's pony along a dark road
and feeling very sad.

My father took me to a room near the school's gate. The woman
in the room was our school secretary who greeted us. My father said
'Stay well, Tsabo' and ran to find a bus to take him to the mines. He

had gone when I said 'Go well, Father.' I felt very sad again, but not lonely because many children were there.

Our school secretary asked a girl to take me to eat food and she led me into a very big room with many windows and many lights in the roof. We waited in a line of young and older children. A woman gave us mealie-meal and beans in a *china* bowl, a spoon, a *glass* of water and we sat on a wooden *bench* at one of the many long wooden tables. The girl whispered the new words I must remember. At home, my family sat on a rock outside our rondavel. We all took mealie-meal and sometimes beans from my grandmother's cooking pot with our hands to eat them and we talked. At school, I must say nothing.

A woman in a black coat and white hat read out many names and when I heard mine, I followed her and other boys into a much bigger building with more windows, and all the windows had lights in them. At the top of many steps, she told us how to use the *toilet* paper, how to *flush* the toilet, how to fill a *basin* with hot or cold water from *taps*, how to clean our teeth with the *toothbrush* and *toothpaste* she gave each of us, and she told us to wash with soap. After we had washed she took us to a long room, a *dormitory* she called it, and gave each of us a bed. I had seen a bed in a book my sister brought home from her school near Katama. I undressed quickly, took the blanket my mother wove from my bag, wrapped it round me and laid down on a *mattress*. It was much softer than my family's sleeping mat. The woman had no candles to blow out – she made all the lights blow out, themselves. I asked Jesus to guard my family and friends, but I was too tired to remember new words.

The woman woke me early next morning. I went to a toilet, washed in a basin, cleaned my teeth and put on the white shirt, green shorts and black shoes my father had bought me. The woman led the boys in our dormitory down the steps to the room where we had eaten before. She called the room a *refectory*. After breakfast, all the boys and girls at the school stood in many lines outside the refectory. 'Is the woman a priest?' I asked the boy standing behind me and he whispered 'She is a nun.'

The nun said 'Your line is called *newcomers*, and when I speak your family name you must raise a hand.' I was the only Mashedi.

We went into a church. It was much bigger and better than the church near my home. The newcomers sat with the nun on the front benches. Many older children sat behind us and we all stood when a priest came. He looked like the giant in my picture book and he was *white!* I had never seen white people before, but I had read about them. The priest was very tall, had a big grey beard and wore a long brown coat. Newcomers and cassock were words I learned, soon after. He said a prayer in Gwato and when we sang a hymn, the noise was louder than the army helicopter when it landed at Katama. But the singing was not as loud as the noise it made when it took off. I want to be a helicopter pilot.

After assembly the nun took the newcomers to a class room. She was small, black and walked fast. She gave each of us a desk and a chair and told us to sit down. Then the door opened and the white man came in.

'Stand and greet Father Patrick, our priest and headmaster,'the nun shouted.

We all stood and shouted even louder 'Good morning Father.'

'Peace be with you my children,' he said with a big smile. 'Sister Marie Louise is your teacher. She will speak much of this school and your lessons, after. I come to meet you, before, and to ask your first names, also.' He spoke good Gwato.

The nun told the children sitting at the front of the classroom to answer first, and when it came to my turn, I had counted seven boys with the same name as mine.

'I am Tsabo, Father.'

'There are many Tsabos. You have another name my son?'

'It is Patrick, Father.'

'We will speak Patrick all the days in this place. This name I know!'

Father Patrick smiled much more, the children giggled and I remember feeling very happy because my school name was the same as the white man who smiles.'

That was Tsabo's story about his first days at school – now his second ride over the high peaks. Before Easter that year, his father was waiting outside the school with the herd boy who'd led Pat and his father's horse from Katama. On the way home, to bring them luck, they each put a stone on both piles that a teacher had told him were called 'shrines to lost riders' because the riders were buried under the piles. By the time they reached home, his father and the herd boy knew "everything" about the mission school and Tsabo's lessons. And he and the herd boy also knew what Ngabo Mashedi chose to tell them about the gold mine where he worked and the hostel he stayed in. That evening Tsabo and his father had to repeat it all and answer his mother's, eldest sister's and grandparents' many questions.

Next morning they both had to repeat it all again and answer more questions when the headman assembled every villager in Katama that day outside the café. The headman told Tsabo's father: 'I am very proud of you, Ngabo, and your son and my brown pony, also.'

On Easter Sunday, after Mass, the headman untied Pat's reins from the café's tethering rail and handed the reins to Tsabo. 'Pat is your Easter present and you are his present.'

No words came to Tsabo, but he thought Pat nodded and smiled. 'Thank you,' he eventually managed to say to the kind headman.

A week later, on Tsabo's and Mueketso's seventh birthdays, they rode their ponies up the steep path to the ridge behind Katama. There was no snow on the mountains far to the south, but the wind was cold. Mueketso led the way up the path to the waterfall, followed by his mother's many goats and Tsabo. He wanted to see the good pasture Mueketso had found up in the high peaks for all the goats he guarded, every day and night – their ponies liked the pasture and also drank water from a spring above the waterfall, Mueketso asked many questions about Tsabo's school and after they had been answered, he said: 'I will go there, one day, if my father gives your school the money . . . But this I think not!'

'Your mother sells goat milk. Will she give the mission school some of the money she gets? Tsabo asked.

'My father takes all her money and he gives it to the girl he will marry, very soon.'

They each put a stone on a shrine to lost riders and long before it was dark, Tsabo rode back to Katama, thinking sadly about why some fathers were bad, when his was so good.

Thereafter, he would put the same number of stones as his age on every shrine he and Pat saw. He hoped this would bring them even more good luck – and also help Mueketso.

Or maybe it was their guardian angel that protected Pat and Tsabo whenever they had steep and narrow squeaks on their many adventurous treks, back and forth, over the high peaks. Or was it their courage, Pat's skill and Tsabo's horsemanship?

Becoming a Man

Kolokuana Grammar School in the country's capital and both mission schools in the two provincial capitals, all founded in the 1870s, compared favourably with similar British schools in terms of curricula, teaching standards and facilities. In 1968 the country gained its independendence and the Grammar School was renamed the International High School in 1972, retaining a British headmaster and Commonwealth teachers. The mission school in the northern province's capital, Anglican – its southern counterpart, St John's mission school in Mabela, Catholic, which being in a very drought-prone part of the country, had remained food-self-sufficient by keeping pigs and chickens, also growing maize, peas and beans, but the very low water level in Mabela's reservoir had often caused great concern.

Of the five hundred or so pupils at St John's, around three quarters were boys. At the end of their fifth year, the boys moved from dormitories with thirty beds to smaller ones with twelve beds and each had a wooden cupboard to keep their clothes and books tidier. Most girls lived locally and the few boarders slept in the nunnery.

Tsabo's bed in his new dormitory was by a window and when the new day's sun woke him, he prayed for his family's safety, hoped they stayed well, thought about the future and what that might bring. His father would be at work, already, earning more money to pay the mission school. This morning, he would write to the best father in the world.

'Thank you for the letter. You asked me to write in English to help you speak it better. I learn much and hope to go to the university in Kolokuana. After your police friend rode back from Katama last week, he said my mother, grandparents and sisters stay well and hope you are happy. I also hope this. Please send another letter soon. Go well, my father.'

He enjoyed his private time, before the early morning rush began. He wanted to be a history teacher, like Father Patrick. But maybe he would be a lawyer because they earned much more money to give back to his father, sooner. After doing that, he would learn to fly a helicopter, visit Rome, see the Pope, go to London . . . The nun's hand-bell clanged.

'Wake up boys, you are going home today!' she shouted and the dormitory sprang into life. There was even more rushing on going home days.

Tsabo's and his friend Mueketso's birthdays were in April during the mission school's Easter holidays. They would share their thirteenth, just as they had shared most birthdays, riding their ponies. They climbed the steep twisting path to the ridge behind Katama. The mountains farthest to the south were already snow-capped. The high peaks and waterfall to the west shone in the sun. The dark, deep gorge to the north became wider towards the east and ended at the border with another country.

Last Easter they rode east towards that border. Near the end of the gorge, there were "No Entry" signs, many tents and piles of rocks beside many big holes. Soldiers shouted, some fired guns and both ponies bolted back along the ridge, spurred on by Mueketso and Tsabo, crouching low in their saddles and clinging to their reins.

This year they would ride *west!* Their ponies were happily climbing the steeper path to the waterfall when Tsabo saw smoke rising from a valley to the south.

'Who lives there?' he asked Mueketso. 'It is far from a village.'

'It is the initiation school. I am a herd-boy nine years, before. My uncle speaks well of me and my mother's goats. I will go to the initiation school, soon, to make me a man.'

Initiation school was a subject never taught at St John's. It seemed that nobody really knew what was involved, despite the notice displayed in every classroom which informed pupils that "Ignorance Breeds Mistakes" – that had been the original wording!! Whenever initiation school gossip circulated among boys, as it sometimes did, the Mother Superior reminded both boys and girls, at morning assembly, that both forms of circumcision were barbaric tortures. She also took the opportunity to add that all methods of contraception had been banned by every new Pope – a law that every Catholic must obey. A law Tsabo would nearly twenty years later reject as unforgivably senseless when AIDS struck Africa.

'How will the initiation school make you a man?' he asked Mueketso.

'I have no father, now, to tell me. My uncle says, maybe I will stay there with more boys, and our chief's men will teach us. Maybe we will go to to a big palaver, after, and a knife will cut the skin from our cocks. This I think.'

The tops of Tsabo's legs went numb. 'What will the men teach?'

'My uncle said, maybe they will teach the story and the songs of our tribe, and how to make babies, also, and how to beat wives if they do or speak bad things . . . The knife is sharp when my cock comes. This I hope.'

'I am happy not to be a herd-boy,' grunted Tsabo.

'You will not make a man. This I know!' Tugging his reins Mueketso steered his pony into the lead. Most of that year's birthday ride continued in silence.

For the rest of the holiday and back at school next term, Mueketso's words "You will not make a man" stayed in Tsabo's head every day and most nights. Then, after Mass one Sunday, he plucked up courage and approached the priest.

'May I ask you a question, Father?' English had been Tsabo's everyday language at the mission for the past three years. 'Will I become a man?'

'I've heard some funny ones in my time, but that beats the lot. Let's take a walk.'

Tsabo had to trot to keep up. The priest's big straw hat tied under his long beard and his large brown cassock made him look even more enormous. While hurrying round the football pitch Tsabo repeated, rather breathlessly, everything Mueketso said and Father Patrick light-heartedly explained what he called: 'The main facts of married life.'

Before striding away, the priest spoke sternly: 'Concentrate on your studies, Patrick. There will be plenty of time for adventures of that sort later – when you become a man.'

A man – "he who rules" in Gwato – had, from time immemorial, held a place of dignity within his family and tribe – becoming a man, a progression steeped in tradition. Coddled by his mother and sisters from birth, an Obangwato man-child was taught by his father to respect his parents, grandparents and relatives. And to use his eyes and ears, for they had much to teach him. From as young as five, boys would be entrusted to guard livestock, probably overseen by an elder brother or cousin. A lowland boy usually drove livestock home every evening. A highland boy was likely to spend far longer away from home. He would meet other herd boys, spar with them, hunt and trap food, kill a rock rabbit with a slung stone, all the time becoming more confident, stronger and braver. Tribal traditions remained powerful in the highlands; less so in the lowland towns and villages.

Most herd boys aged twelve or thirteen went to an initiation school. The gravity of the long-standing ritual leading to circumcision demanded that it be conducted in meagre isolated huts behind a wall, as it were, of strict secrecy. Female circumcision, now mercifully rare among their Obangwato tribe, usually happened within or nearby the victim's home.

Educated tribesmen, Tsabo's self-educated father and other men, who had been spared initiation school, knew very little with any certainty of what actually went on behind that wall of secrecy. There were rumours, of course. Their chief appointed a senior initiate and some assistants to regulate the ritual, a witchdoctor provided medicine and the herd boy's tasks were made as difficult as possible. Harsh discipline and often flagrant cruelty engendered prompt obedience and strength of mind. After less than a month, every herd boy had been taught tribal lore, history and songs, had a theoretical knowledge of sexual relations with women – and sometimes practical experience of lying naked every night on the dirt-floor of a draughty hut, without moving a muscle. Then, the moment came for the knife-slash, for the boy's cry of pain to be drowned by other boys singing, for the wound to be smeared with the male witch doctor's grease, for the new initiates' arduous exercise to begin and ease the lingering pain. People might hear their distant chanting, might catch sight of them jogging along a remote path, might notice smoke from their cooking fire – much like the plume of smoke Tsabo and Mueketso had seen on one of their pony rides.

Whichever their sex, witch doctors were believed to practise white magic in a desire to safeguard their adherents' physical and moral well-being – sorcerers indulged in black magic (juju), too often inflicting curses or killing a victim. Witch doctors and scorcerers, one a self-styled miracle-maker, the other a charlatan, could well be foes and might fight each other until one fled or died. Both were determined to prove their powers within their permanent or transitory bailiwick, maybe by promoting obsessions, suspicions, prejudices or sanctifying coincidences which many Africans revered as portents of prosperity. Many feared other coincidences, regarded as omens of an unknown, impending misfortune that a witch doctor or sorcerer would help them to avoid. Some witch doctors, but more often sorcerers, made a practice of murdering albinos, whose bones and pale flesh would bring customers good health, financial fortune or both.

Since most schoolteachers were Christians, very few boys who had attended a "pagan" initiation school were allowed a conventional education. Many boys, unable to read or write, joined earlier Obangwato initiates in such far away places with strange sounding names as Johannesburg and Kimberley. They fed well in their miners' hostel, had regular health checks and at the end of their contracts went home, not always healthy or wealthy, for proflicacy, prostitutes and sexually transmitted diseases could have taken their toll.

In common with most fellow-tribesmen, retired miners tended to regard ploughing and growing crops as women's work. Yet the more livestock they owned and the more herd boys they employed, the higher their standing within their tribe.

Wrapped in colourful patterned blankets, wearing smart trilbies and riding their own horses, more than a few former miners saw out each day chatting, drinking, playing cards or womanising – oblivious to the hardships of family life and all the erosion surrounding them. Unmaintained mountain paths were fast becoming gullies which cleaved the scarce pasture, scarcer arable land and arid slopes. And when rain next pelted down, loosening more rocks and what soil remained, the gullies, like so many others before, would widen, deepen and lengthen relentlessly. But welcome and often long-awaited rain would barely dampen so much desolation before escaping – un-trapped, un-conserved, simply wasted.

Only the government had money, equipment, materials and skilled labour to prevent or repair such extensive damage, build small dams, fit gutters and pipes to roofs, and so on. Fields were too few just to let them disappear. Rainwater too precious just to let it run away. The challenging problems were so widespread that far more than the government's limited resources were needed, though too much external aid could discourage self-help.

Another compelling problem faced the government – indeed, African governments in general – pitifully inadequate sanitation! As with stemming erosion, belatedly improving sanitation in urban and rural communities depended heavily on resource availability, as well as education, enforcement and scrutiny which had rarely been a matter of concern or priority to colonial administrators in former times, nor to present-day politicians.

St John's mission school's many toilets were always kept clean and had paper, but at home Tsabo had to squat in the open, where most Katamans had always squatted, which for some people was almost anywhere. Most went behind one of the big rocks, too near to their village, when they wanted to squat. His mother and sisters went there before sunrise, but it was difficult to see where they were walking and what they were walking on, which the many rats and dogs ate. His family always washed when they got home. Some people cleaned themselves with a rag without washing their hands.

A doctor had told St John's pupils at assembly: 'Bad sanitation and bad hygiene causes chronic diarrhoea and typhoid. There must be enough toilets because, if some people still squat in the open, they will probably get these diseases, pass them on to more people and many may die. If they get cholera, very many may die!'

In the letter pupils took home the doctor repeated in Gwato what he'd told them, with among the translated words: *ksolli* instead of chronic diarrhoea and typhoid; *matsolli* and *bhoddo* instead of cholera and feaces. Drawings showed how and where to build a toilet, how to empty it and what to do with the *bhoddo*.

After riding home, Tsabo gave the headman the letter, which he read to the villagers, and Tsabo explained the drawings. Some women wanted to know how to get money to buy wood to build toilets and tools to make holes in the rocks on Katama's mountainside. The men present, most of them retired miners, agreed that only power-tools would make holes in such solid rock. Expecting them to avoid hard work by opposing change, their headman nevertheless rode to Mabela and asked the provincial governor for help.

'Why do you want government money to buy wood and tools?' he asked. 'Our tribes-people have always squatted in the open and must do what their ancestors always did.'

The headman had asked the governor for help after the rondavels were burned down and after their chief stopped Katama's herd boys grazing livestock on better pasture, both times without success. Now he miserably rode home to tell his clan he had failed to help them, again.

More than twenty years would pass before Tsabo could afford to provide his clan, and the clan across the gorge, each with four ventilated, improved, pit-latrines – "VIP" latrines.

The Mysterious
Second Prize

Tsabo had good reason to be proud of his second name, since Father Patrick towered over everybody at St John's and in so many ways – mentor, motivator, confidant – masterful at infusing his charges with common sense and fair play – skilful at instilling in them faith, hope and wisdom. A heavyweight in all respects! Obangwato people were generous with praise names and "The White Man Who Smiles" fitted the jovial Irishman perfectly.

Teaching history was his specialility, extolling the spread of Christianity his passion, tutoring sixth formers his challenge. They inveigled him on one occasion into describing his island birthplace where, he claimed, plentiful rain nurtured bountiful crops; where the rich pasture, the gently undulating hills and even the mountains, were always a glorious green; where hard-working folk had something to show for their labours.

'Is there such a place?' Tsabo inquired. Mabela had been waterless for months. Unless it rained within the next few weeks, the town might as well not have a reservoir.

'There most certainly is such a place,' Father Patrick proudly said. 'Very soon, I trust, the Lord will shine His light upon you, my friends, then you will have something to show for your labours, and so will your families for that matter.'

This reminded Tsabo of his father's infrequent homecomings, now only at Christmas. His father always asked to see his children's school reports and after reading each one he repeated, without fail, the same four English words: 'Well done. Thank you.'

Tsabo was thankful, too. Their father had something to show for *his* labours and so had their mother. But life was never easy for them. Matashaba, their eldest daughter, had married a classmate from the village across the gorge requiring a dowry of ten cows; then twenty sheep were sold so that Dinea, their younger daughter, could go to the big hospital in their country's capital, Kolokuana, to train as a nurse.

Only Tsabo and his youngest sister, Palima, remained at school and he would soon be leaving St John's. Having passed Kolokuana University's entrance exam with distinction, he agonised over committing his parents to still more hardship and self-denial.

Remembering much about his final speech day would be difficult, Tsabo realised that, though he knew his family would be thrilled to see him being presented with the coveted Headmaster's Prize for his year as the school's senior prefect. But now, apparently, he'd receive a second prize. When asked why, all Father Patrick did was *smile!*

Most of all, Tsabo wanted his parents and sisters to enjoy that December Saturday, the only speech day they had been able to attend. Two of his sisters, Dinea and Palima, had ridden to Mabela before. His mother and Matashaba had never been to this town or to the school he'd told them so much about. If he felt nervous, how must they be feeling?

His family were staying with one of his father's police friends, but there was no time to check if they had all arrived safely. He was too busy positioning a refectory table and more benches in the church, printing two hundred copies of the programme and ensuring his successor knew what to do before next year's speech day. The clock struck eleven. He rushed out to the gate, ready to greet his family and to meet his newborn nephew.

He had reserved them a bench near the front. His mother, clearly overawed by the size of the church and congregation, insisted on sitting at the back near the door: her grandson might cry and must be fed. Matashaba obediently began to unbutton her blouse and, all of a sudden, her embarrassed brother found something extremely urgent to do.

Father Patrick showed the provincial governor and other guests to their places at the refectory table which now separated the nave from the chancel, and after a rousing hymn, the Mother Superior recited the Obangwato prayer of friendship. All appeared to be going well, though Tsabo was surprised to see a white stranger among the guests, even more so when Father Patrick launched forth with an *un*-programmed speech.

'Peace be with you, ladies and gentlemen. I am happy to welcome a visitor from far to this place. I will speak English, next, and Gwato again, after. This is a momentous day in the history of our blesséd school and in my thirty-seven years at St John's. It gives me the utmost pleasure to announce on behalf of everyone who teaches and officiates here that a pupil has won a scholarship at Oxford University in England. Our first award of its kind.' Turning to face the senior prefect, sitting at the far end of the table, the priest proclaimed: 'This is a truly magnificent achievement, Patrick. Many, many congratulations!'

The Gwato translation ended, the applause exploded, and Tsabo's family craned their necks to catch sight of the boy called Patrick. But he was hidden from their view by many bobbing and weaving heads, all trying to do the same.

Prize-giving began and the first name the secretary called out was lost in a hubbub of chatter. She beckoned Tsabo. Rising unsteadily and bracing himself just enough to reach the centre of what seemed a very long refectory table, he could muster only a jerky bow, when the provincial governor handed him a wobbly pile of books. Somehow, he returned to his chair without dropping any and still dazed by Father Patrick's revelation.

After a queue of pupils, stretching the length of the nave, had received their prizes the national anthem, sung in harmony with great gusto, brought proceedings to a resounding close. Tsabo had been far too breathless to pay homage to his homeland and was about to engineer a stealthy exit when the white stranger waylaid him and introduced himself.

'The British high commissioner in Kolokuana recommended your award. He has sent me to convey his congratulations and best wishes, to which I add my own.'

Tsabo thanked them both, lost for more words. He could not have said that accepting the award was *impossible!* The moment the mystery of a second prize had been solved, he realised he must make that decision. A decision he had shrunk from contemplating and knew he would regret, forever.

Following Father Patrick into the sacristy, he was explaining that his parents could not afford to send him to a university overseas, when a letter appeared from within the depths of a voluminous brown cassock. Dumbfounded by its contents, he embraced the startled priest, rescued his prizes from the floor and raced off to find his family. Dinea, his middle sister, had gone. He wasn't surprised. She'd never been interested in anything her family did and more than probably would rather have not come to the speech day.

'Your many books make us very proud,' Tsabo's father said in Gwato and then asked: 'Who is this boy, Patrick? The boy who will go to the university in England, soon.'

'Your son!'

Tsabo's mother and other two sisters stood on tip-toe, threw their arms round his neck and tears drenched the front of his shirt. Moved by the passionate scene, a finger dabbed under his eye to remove a fly – or so Father Patrick imagined. Judging it time to greet the Mashedi family, the priest disclosed in their language the letter's heaven-sent tidings.

'A white man worked in Mabela, before, and he gave much money for Obangwatos to study at Oxford University, after. He will pay for Patrick's room, food and journeys, also. No bills will come to you. This I promise.'

'A miracle,' croaked Ngabo Mashedi, looking mightily relieved.

'There are many miracles,' hooted Father Patrick. 'This I know.'

Clasping the priest's hands, he held them tightly as he spoke. 'There are many dreams, also. This *I* know. I think all the years, Tsabo will go to the university in Kolokuana. You make him clever, now, and he will go to a better place. Thank you, my brother.' He could pay the priest no greater compliment than to address him as my brother and then, by way of an admonishment, he asked: 'Why is it you call my son by his middle name?'

Before Father Patrick could answer, the provincial governor barged aside the people pressing around the young man, who had brought their tribe merit and would surely bring it fame. The governor, the principal guest and a very important person in his own right, let it be known that he had taken grave exception to being ignored because an upstart had fooled the examiners of some foreign, probably bogus, education establishment.

'Where are you from?' he abruptly asked Tsabo in English.

'Katama, sir.'

'Huh!' he scoffed. 'I had to fly there once, after some fires, to sort out the villagers.'

The gentleman was left to an affronted priest's tender mercy.

A meal in the refectory preceded a brief tour of the mission's pig and chicken sheds, a lengthy visit to the school's library and, as a final treat, what remained of Tsabo's family climbed many steps to his cosy little bunk. Its tidiness even impressed his mother. To her, electricity was magic! She was fascinated by the kettle that boiled water; the table lamp she kept switching on and off, until Tsabo stopped her, in case the fuse blew and plunged the whole building into darkness. It had often occurred before – the generator objected to the table lamps and kettles prefects secreted in their dormitory-end bunks. But his mother was thankful for electricity, whilst descending all the well-lit steps from his bunk, before returning to the police friend's candle-lit rondavel and his wife's cooking fire.

The form Tsabo signed next morning accepting the place at Oxford also confirmed his arrival in the following September and indicated his preference to read law.

'The deed is done,' Father Patrick chuckled, licking the envelope. 'Because you'll be sure to need a smart suit, a thick raincoat and all the rest, for that matter, the archbishop's offered you a job in Kolokuana. You should be aware that he very strongly endorsed the applications St John's made to three of Oxford's many colleges.'

Ever since Tsabo had arrived at the mission, he had been determined to repay the huge debt he owed his father – not just money, a debt of gratitude, as well. His family had gone without too much, so that he could have the education they were denied. He would never be able to repay everyone at St John's, especially Father Patrick, or the white man who'd given money to enable him to study at such a famous university. Yet nothing could lessen the exhilaration he felt on approaching a second, even more momentous, challenge in his life. Then, typically, Father Patrick threw down a third challenge.

'Do you remember asking me all those years ago if you would become a man? Now is the time! Go well, my son.'

'How could I forget trying to keep up while you raced round that football pitch? Stay well, Father.'

Ngabo Mashedi rode ahead, his wife and two of his daughters behind him, chattering endlessly, Matashaba's baby slept or was fed on the move, Tsabo at the rear of the line – alone with his questions. Will Oxford's professors and students accept me? Will I be the only black person there? What will happen if the money runs out before I get my degree? I should have asked Father Patrick that! And why didn't I have the courage to contradict that arrogant provincial governor? The chief had caused those terrible fires. It was he who ought to have been sorted out, *not* the people of Katama! But now the chief was late, and some of his clans-people said a witch doctor had given him bad medicine.

Tsabo and his father again stood side-by-side at that special place – the sharp bend in the track. With Mabela basking in the midday sun far below, they placed many stones on the shrine to lost riders and did likewise on the shrine up in the high peaks.

Tsabo's mother and Matashaba refused to ride down the steep path. On the way to Mabela all the narrow ledges close by deep gorges had scared them. They walked down the path, Palima and Tsabo rode in front of them, leading the ponies the headman had lent them. Their father walked with them, leading his horse.

It was late afternoon when Matashaba gave them refreshing tea outside her rondavel in the village across the gorge. The sun had set by the time Tsabo led his parents and Palima in a prayer of thanksgiving for reaching home safely. A much-loved, familiar home he would all too quickly be exchanging for the intimidating unknown.

News travelled fast. No sooner had he arrived than all the villagers were summoned to the café. Having described, as bidden, the previous day's events, albeit hampered by his mother's elaborations, Tsabo was honoured by being invited to share the headman's mug of home-brewed beer. Men roared approval, women ululated delight and children clapped their hands. Would Tsabo or his father one day take the place of their childless headman, villagers asked each other, but before they found answers, the brew got them singing and dancing. One sip of that oily grey liquid had been too much for Tsabo. Unlike Mueketso, who'd swallowed a mug full in two gulps and was queuing for more. No longer Katama's oldest herd boy, Mueketso, was learning to read and write and hoped to become a farrier.

For the past three years, Tsabo had ridden one of the headman's horses to and from St John's. Pat, the brown pony the headman had given him, had taken Palima to school in the village across the gorge and had waited patiently to take her home. He had also taken her twice to Mabela and brought her back safely. But Pat would always be *his* pony! Just as a reminder, an unforgettable muzzle forced its way under a memorable armpit.

They both escorted Tsabo's hobbling grandparents back to their rondavel, where by custom and privilege, Pat graciously accepted the remnants of the evening's mealie-meal.

'Where is it you will go?' a hushed voice asked.

With a gentle smile, Tsabo bent low to soothe a troubled brow.

'Sleep well, grandfather. I will tell you in the morning.'

Early on Christmas Day, Matashaba, her baby son and husband, his relatives and friends, the priest and the late chief's eldest son and successor, started out from the village across the gorge to Katama, some on horseback, others on foot. After countless fraught years, members of both clans joined in harmony and praise at the baptism of Sekiso Patrick. They also witnessed their new chief, Katama's headman and Tsabo vowing to be caring godfathers. Roasting ox-meat on the fire, every woman joined in unison with preparing a feast worthy of such a joyous occasion and Tsabo felt free to celebrate at last. No longer would his parents have to scrape together his school fees, term after term, year after year, and that alone was reason enough to rejoice. There were other reasons, too. He could help his mother and Matashaba look after his grandparents, could ride to Palima's school and return with her. He could spend much more time with Mueketso and their many friends.

He could also read his prizes, brought home in his saddlebags – Gibbon's *Decline and Fall of the Roman Empire*; Fisher's *History of Europe*; Churchill's *History of the English Speaking Peoples*; Harrer's *Seven Years in Tibet*; Dickens's *Great Expectations*.

A book on Tibet and another entitled *Great Expectations* might be two more of Father Patrick's crafty challenges, Tsabo reckoned.

Three months short of his nineteenth birthday Tsabo rode back to Mabela and had supper with Sister Marie Louise, his very first teacher – Father Patrick was resting after the day's teaching. Having stayed overnight at St John's and said many farewells, he spent the next day sweltering in an over-loaded minibus taxi before seeing his country's capital, at last.

Very much to his disappointment, though, Kolokuana turned out to be nothing like the thriving city he'd always imagined. Apart from the main street, it was a squalid shambles, ridden with poverty, crime and violence. With the Catholic seminary his temporary home and a classmate training to be a priest, a watchful companion, the farthest Tsabo strayed most weeks was to the British Council, a two-storey building in the main street, where he did a computer course, borrowed books, read newspapers and listened to the BBC World Service News.

When September finally arrived, he had catalogued the cathedral library, read late into every night and sent most of his earnings to his father. Wearing a carefully pressed brown suit, spotted in a market, with his passport and wallet inside his shirt, a heavy rucksack on his back and the archbishop's thick raincoat over an arm, he boarded the airport bus, flew to Mavimbi on Africa's east coast and spent that night in a passenger jet before reaching somewhere he'd hoped yet had never expected to reach – England!

Surmountable Hurdles

Tsabo arrived at Oxford via London's amazing underground railway and Victoria coach station. Threading his way through streets full of busy people and double-decker buses, he eventually found himself gazing up at an imposing fortress of similar size and style to several others he'd passed. This had to be the college. On venturing inside, the window in a wall suddenly slid open, making him jump, and a man's voice asked: 'Yes?' Once the name in his passport had been matched with the name on a list, he was sold a black gown, led across a yard, called a quadrangle, and left to climb three lots of stairs to a room no bigger than his school bunk. His head, now in a whirl, had scarcely caught up with his feet when a short elderly man, almost hidden behind a large green apron, arrived with a bucket of coal. Because of his stoop, the man raised his chin before speaking.

'Me name's Ron Simpson. Oi'm yer scout,' he said and lit the fire. 'Wasn't no central 'eatin in them days. Oh, no! This quad's bin 'ere close on seven 'underd years yer know.' He cleaned both hands on the apron and inspected the newly purchased gown. 'A young gen'almun can't wear this! It's got 'oles. Oi'll swap first thin termorrer.'

Tsabo had read that college scouts were more than friendly and helpful cleaners, they made students feel welcome and responded if encouragement and support were needed. After showering down in the basement, he curled up in bed and the next thing he knew a curtain was drawn back. Ron hung a replacement gown on a hook behind the door, put a mug of tea on the chair beside the bed and handed Tsabo a card with the college's address printed in gold lettering.

'Dr Macauslan's yer tutor,' Ron reverently disclosed.

'Welcome,' the card read. 'Mr Simpson has told me that you arrived yesterday. I look forward to our meeting at breakfast in Hall. Dermot Macausland.'

'Better wear a suit . . . 'av yer got wun?' Peering in the wardrobe Ron found the brown suit, bought in a market, which Tsabo had pressed so carefully before leaving Kolokuana. Ron held it up, shook it, spread it on the bed and tried to smooth out all the creases.

'I wore it getting here,' Tsabo explained, apologetically.

'These yer shoes?' Ron rubbed them with his apron. 'Oi'll give 'em a good polish an press the suit later. Best not keep Dr Macauslan waitin. 'As ter 'av 'is mornin tea at six o'clock, sharp. Bit ovva clock watcher, 'ee is. Top notcher, though. Oh, yes!' Standing by the window, Ron pointed to a building as big as a church. 'That's where yer gotta go.'

Tsabo slung on the suit, scampered down the stairs and across the quad into a long, wide refectory with portraits on every wall. A middle-aged man, the only person in there, was sitting at a table near the door. 'Dr Macausland? I'm Tsabo Mashedi,' he said rather breathlessly. We shook hands and the tall, slim, young African sat down next to me.

'May I call you Tsabo?' I asked. He smiled and nodded. 'All the tables will be full and overflowing within a fortnight. My set's on the same stairs as your room. Set is Oxford speak for study, et cetera. I eat in Hall most weekdays and go home at weekends, if my wife's not abroad. The academic progress and social well-being of every student, here, is monitored by a moral tutor. I shall remain your moral tutor throughout your time with us. All your first year tutorials will be conducted by me. In your second and third years, you will likely go to other tutors, as well. You will be encouraged to attend a wide range of lectures, to take part in debates and to make good use of the many facilities the university offers. You'll need a hearty breakfast after all that rigmarole . . . *essential* rigmarole.'

A waiter took our orders: mine scrambled eggs on toast; Tsabo shyly chose the same. We had some good laughs about his journey and arrival here, which helped Tsabo relax.

After breakfast and Ron's conducted tour of the precincts, he showed Tsabo his secret cupboard full of 'gen'almun's leavings' in Ron's words. Tsabo returned to his room with a dark blue blazer, three pullovers, a black bow tie and an expensive-looking grey suit made, according to Ron, in a very posh London shop called Arley

Street. Duly impressed, Tsabo searched inside the jacket for the suit's label.

'Don't take no notice of labels. Oi've gotta jacket wiv Buckinum Paliss in it. Oi sewed the label in its collar meself . . . Ain't shiverin, are yer? Oi'll go an get some more coal.'

At the Freshman's Dinner on the first Friday of Michaelmas Term, the Fellows filed into Hall and stood behind their chairs at High Table, while a student chanted the Latin grace Tsabo had chanted at St John's. But *not* in a gown and bow tie! He sat next to the middle-aged graduate of the college whom he'd met in his tutor's study before dinner. Harry, Dr Macausland's cousin, was surprisingly interested in Tsabo's country, all of its mountains, the Mabela plain, and not in the least put out when asked about his own background.

'Born in Northern Ireland, educated in England, joined a management consultancy in London, worked in the United States, married an American dress-designer, then we spent twenty years in the Far East, where I specialised in business organisation and logistics,' Harry rattled off. 'I retired, aged 48, when my firm was taken over earlier this year,' he gloomily added. 'All I have to keep me busy are hobbies . . . learning to fly's the latest.'

By the time they left Hall, Tsabo had decided that a helicopter pilot's course was way beyond his means and had been assured that a good law degree was a worthy objective, should he be seeking a lucrative career. He'd also been invited to stay with Harry and his wife at their home in the Cotswolds. 'An area of outstanding natural beauty!' Harry had proudly said, 'under an hour west by train.'

Most Freshers on first coming up to Oxford, with an aura all of its own, would admit to feelings of bewilderment, at times alarmed bewilderment! The Freshman from an African mission school would generously claim, however, that it was his tutor's patient guidance which had greatly helped him to clear such seemingly insurmountable hurdles.

As his tutor, I would counter-claim that it was Tsabo Mashedi's God-given strength of character, not just his proven intellect, which had enabled him to settle smoothly into a roundly fulfilling new life, and to use his talents and time to best advantage. Unlike many first-year students, he arrived with no preconceptions, no prejudices, no hang-ups of any kind. His ability to cut through the peripheral bone of every subject we discussed to get at its innermost marrow struck me as quite exceptional.

We grew to value each other's company, invariably an ideal scholar-tutor relationship. In Tsabo's case, it led to him spending Christmas with my wife and me in our London flat. Between sight-seeing jaunts, he described his childhood and when I'd dug out one of my father's albums, he was *dumbstruck!* Staring him in the face, were photos of Mabela, St John's Mission, its priest and its school's headmaster – Father Patrick, the surrounding area, even one of Katama, all taken in the early 1960s, prior to my father's retirement as governor of the southern province. Before those chance revelations, I had no inkling of Tsabo's precise roots, nor he of my indirect link with his homeland.

To cap this uncanny coincidence, several years later, Father Patrick would tell me that my father's retirement bequest had funded Tsabo's Oxford scholarship!

Library research, note-taking, typing essays, attending lectures, debates and twice-weekly tutorials made for a hectic schedule, yet Tsabo found time to thumb an occasional lift and visit Harry and his American wife, Belinda, in the Cotswolds. They were great hosts.

To his family and friends, Tsabo sent picture-postcards of impressive Oxford exteriors and interiors, some within just a stone's throw of his room. With his first letter to Father Patrick, he enclosed an aerial photograph, indicating his own and other colleges, libraries, museums, science laboratories and the courts where he'd taken up playing squash.

In his reply, the priest disclosed that the aerial photograph had so impressed Professor Matanya, the vice chancellor of Kolokuana University, that she intended to visit Oxford during her next trip to Britain in late August. She hoped Tsabo would have time to show her some highlights. 'The penalty of fame!' was Father Patrick's enlivening postscript.

Having spent too much of his earnings, as a Saturdays-only menswear shop assistant, on an excellently illustrated Oxford tourist brochure, Tsabo sent it to Father Patrick with his college's telephone number, a note saying he would be pleased to show the professor around and enclosed in the envelope 'a few hurried jottings' as he described them.

'In early medieval society, sons of poor families could penetrate an all-powerful elite only by attending university, taking holy orders and then seeking advancement, secular or pastoral, and often both. Lecturers (priests, friars later) and scholars (ordinands) had been drawn to Oxford since the eleventh century and the first recorded foreign student arrived in 1190. The growing number of students needed big lecture rooms and decent places to eat and sleep. More students brought more friction between "Town and Gown." A violent affray in 1209 caused some Gowns to flee to Cambridge – "the other place." In 1214, a chancellor of Oxford University was appointed. Fifty years later three colleges had been founded, by 1571 another nine, 36 at present. In 1230, the chancellor had delegated the running of the university to a vice chancellor, who for many years, has also supervised its development as a leading seat of learning and working with among many others: masters, provosts, wardens or whatever a college governing body chooses to call its elected head.'

'In round figures, the university has 4,000 academic staff of the highest distinction and 18,000 students of both sexes – 3,000 from overseas. Post-doctoral courses prepare men and women of many nationalities to contribute significantly to the university's acclaimed scientific and medical research. Oxford has produced more than 50 Nobel Prize winners, 24 British prime ministers, several from other Commonwealth countries – also the prime minister of the former Cape Colony whose vast mining profits still fund Rhodes Scholars from the Commonwealth, United States and Germany. They share a unique experience of attending the world's oldest English-speaking university.'

Typing that piece brought home to Tsabo how fortunate and privileged he was to be part, a miniscule part, of a place where no hour or day was alike, no moment expendable, no missed opportunity recoverable. It was impossible to pay too much homage to such a renowned institution on a single page. He sealed, stamped and posted the envelope to two other renowned institutions: Father Patrick and St John's Mission, in far away Mabela.

What with researching essays and preparing for next term, Tsabo had to make time to go on one of Oxford's official tours. His guide, a postgraduate anthropology student well versed in their university's architecture and traditions. As a bonus, Jill happened to be an African antiquities buff. She agreed to accompany him and his African guest, then helped reduce his over-long short-list of highlights to their mutually agreed Top Ten Gems.

Tsabo met Professor Matanya at the train station, they walked to the University Church of St Mary the Virgin and climbed up to the balcony at the base of its spire. This afforded an ideal all-round view, an opportunity for him to point out the profusion of landmarks, and for the professor, once she'd recovered her breath, to orientate herself. After coffee with Jill, in the church's café, the trio set forth at a fairly brisk pace on their tour – some Gems had required special permission to visit. The Queen's College's *Upper Library*, serenely outstanding among a host of worthy competitors, was their first port of call. Then to *New College*, its glorious chapel reredos, dining hall and garden bounded by the old city wall. Next came *The Divinity School*, Oxford's oldest lecture rooms. Its grand perpendicular architecture contrasting in style with the Sheldonian Theatre and the Clarendon Building close by. *Duke Humphrey's Library* followed, the medieval predecessor of the Bodleian with its immense and ever-increasing collection of ancient and modern published works, linked by underground book conveyor to the New Bodleian Library. The elegantly domed *Radcliffe Camera*, a seventeenth century edifice resplendent in its square, with yet more books and manuscripts, Tsabo their frequent peruser. Five more Gems to go.

After lunch in one of the posher pubs – the professor paid – she wandered entranced through *Magdalen College's* cloisters, its deer park and watched Beaux punting Belles on the river, but Jill's idea of hiring a punt, she politely scotched, being a non-swimmer, like most Africans. She loved everything at *Merton College*, one of Oxford's oldest. A short step took them to Christ Church, its largest college, and among the many portraits lining the walls of its magnificent *Great Hall* hung one of a 19th century mathematics tutor, the author of Alice in Wonderland and its sequel. In the nearby Cathedral, she listened in awe to Jill decribing the life of *St Frideswide*, a seventh century nun. Finally the *Ashmolean Museum,* which so captivated a now flagging professor, that only Tsabo's offer of a nice cup of tea in his College Hall would tempt her away. There Tsabo's tutor presented the professor with a leather-bound account of the University's long history – inscribed on its fly-leaf: "To Kolokuana's Vice-Chancellor from her Oxford counterpart, with best wishes from all of us here and with personal regret at being unable to meet you today." The professor was speechlessly overwhelmed! Another cup of tea worked wonders.

Outside in the street she asked Tsabo, in a weak moment he'd later assume, to address her students and staff on returning to his home country.

'I sincerely hope you *will* return,' she added, her quizzical glance darting from Tsabo to Jill. 'Thank you both for a wonderful day. And it didn't rain!' Having hailed a passing taxi with her pink parasol she gave it to Jill. Before the bemused recipient could muster a grateful response, the professor had eased her weighty self onto the seat beside the driver. 'Drop me at the train station please.' To her guides, she said: 'If I find a good typist, I'll send your vice chancellor and both of you a précis of all my university's exciting plans.'

'Great' was all Tsabo had time to say while Jill waved a pink parasol farewell.

During Tsabo's second year at Oxford, the academic pace accelerated, which I know he found stimulating. Although the last person on earth to brag about his achievements, he won a university prize for his essay on the continuing importance of case law in Britain's former colonies and dependencies. His newspaper article about external aid to developing countries drew plaudits from pundits, also from prominent politicians, within and beyond

Britain's shores. I could go on, but will spare his blushes and dodge his rebuke.

Meanwhile, his extra-mural activities multiplied: acting in an amateur dramatic club's performance of Shakespeare's Othello, serving at ecumenical communion in our college chapel and twice-weekly squash practice. In addition to his Saturday job in the menswear shop, he proof-read for publishers in his "spare time". With his pavement now paved with coppers, he hitch-hiked to Paris in the springtime, then back-packed through Italy at the height of its summer and managed to catch a glimpse of the Pope whilst touring Rome.

His third year would be devoted to unremitting revision within the confines of his lofty garret – a resolve suddenly shattered by a chilling turn of events, triggered by Ron doing his damnedest to deliver an urgent message, just as quickly as his creaking knees and his highly polished brown boots would allow. Tsabo thanked him, ran to the porter's lodge and phoned his middle sister.

'Come home,' Dinea wailed. 'Our father is hurt *bad!*'

'How badly? Where? When?' The long-distance line made his frantic voice echo.

There had been an explosion in their father's mine, he was in a Johannesburg hospital, Dinea had no money to travel there. She had told Tsabo the hospital's number, but all his phone calls went unanswered. With his tutor abroad he rang Harry, whom he'd met at the Fresher's Dinner and several times since. He explained what had happened, and because his father must be properly cared for, he must fly home. Harry suggested he keep trying to contact the hospital and find out how serious his father's injuries were, before deciding what best to do.

Harry and his wife arrived at Tsabo's college within an hour. Belinda sympathised: 'It must be doubly distressing to feel so distant and out of touch.' Never one to shrink from taking charge, Harry insisted that Tsabo went back with them and used their telephone.

Within another hour, Tsabo was standing in their hallway. International inquiries had confirmed that the number was correct – but there was still no reply! In desperation, he called the Johannesburg police. They knew of an explosion at a local mine and that some miners had been killed, and then blandly informed him that "blacks-only" hospitals never answered their phones at weekends. This made Tsabo all the more determined to ask the college bursar to lend him the airfare. 'Lord Amighty. Help!' he cried out disconsolately.

The following day he was able to tell his sister that their father was recovering and his right leg had been saved! He promised Harry he would stay longer next time. A promise fleetingly kept when, a fortnight later, he and his chauffeuse called in for a quick cuppa. Blonde and rosy-cheeked – a strapping lass reared on a Cumbrian farm – Jill had helped Harry conduct an African professor round Oxford and had just submitted a doctoral thesis on some aspect of anthropology so esoteric its title left her hosts mesmerised.

Once they had left, Belinda said: 'So Tsabo now has a very good incentive for staying the course. I trust he's not over-smitten by the Jill bug, with his final exams only ten short months away. What say you, Harry?'

'The boot's on the other foot, Jill's the one who's smitten, I could tell that a mile off! Anyway, what's anthropology if it isn't the study of man as an animal? One must assume that Tsabo is proving an energetic research vehicle . . . during silent hours, of course.'

'Do you know something? You can be deliciously crude if you really put your mind to it. Come, animal, my research laboratory awaits upstairs.'

Belinda was tugging at a sleeve of his gardening overalls when her ardour-dampening mother rang from America which meant he'd have loads more time to do lots more weeding – by torchlight! One day, he reckoned, they'll name a particularly virulent strain of convolvulus after me and I'll get a second-career knighthood for services to pest control.

Wearing a white bow tie and black gown, a rosebud in his buttonhole and a mortarboard perched on his head, Tsabo joined friends to celebrate the end of 'schools' – final exams in Oxford speak. With the champagne polished off, cider prolonged their revelling until, by dawn's early light, he happened to stumble upon his college and eventually his room. When Ron brought the morning tea he suddenly noticed, even with badly blurred vision, that some wretch had vomited all over the shoes he'd just taken off. He quickly shoved them under his bed, but Ron's acute sense of smell and surprisingly deft footwork made very short work of retrieving them – even though he had on the highly polished brown boots he always wore. Their clunking up the stairs usually warned Tsabo of his scout's approach, but this time he hadn't heard Ron coming. Perhaps he was going deaf!

'Better wear them shoes in the shower. Bin sick on anythin else?' Ron asked, sniffing round the room. 'Where's yer socks?'

Tsabo shrugged his shoulders. 'It wasn't me who was sick,' he feebly protested.

'All gen'almuns says that . . . Yer won't be wanting this.' Ron drank the tea, opened the window as widely as possible and crept out. He must have taken the shoes.

With a throbbing head and churning stomach, Tsabo staggered down the stairs to the toilet and discovered why his socks were missing. The stinking things were on his feet!

The rosebud had died in its buttonhole. A fellow-reveller returned his white bow tie and mortarboard, their sale might help to pay his "battles" – college bill. His gown would remain a treasured reminder of an extra-special scout, an unfailing adviser, the loyalest of friends and a very great deal more.

What to give Ron as a parting present? Having wracked his brains to no avail, Tsabo phoned Father Patrick. He said he would send an Obangwato chief's patterned blanket. On arrival, its label read 'Woven in England' which made it all the more acceptable to Ron. He showed the blanket to all the college scouts, everyone in the butlery, the kitchen, the porter's lodge and anybody who asked what he was carrying. From then on, it would take pride of place on the humble camp bed in his cramped back-street digs.

When invited to visit his digs, Tsabo was permitted to sit on the camp bed if he didn't spill his cocoa on the blanket. Perched on the only chair, Ron recounted his life-story: following in his father's footsteps, he had been a scout since leaving school, apart from his army service throughout the second world war. He had no relatives – the countless students he'd scouted for were his family. All their picture postcards, covering the walls, Tsabo would soon add to. He and Ron ambled past the track where Bannister had run his record mile, over Magdalen Bridge and along The High. When back on home-territory, Ron proclaimed: 'They'll 'av ter 'av plenty'a cart 'orses ter get me coffin outta 'ere. The best college in the 'ole worl. 'Tis yer know. Oh, yes! So you remember that.'

Self-effacing and no limelight-seeker, Tsabo unobtrusively took his place among the very best of his Oxford peers. An avid reader, a gifted writer and challenging debater, his first class honours came as no surprise to me, his tutor, or to his scout. I overheard Ron telling his mates down in their shoe-cleaning room: 'Oi knows a good'un when oi sees one.'

Belinda and Harry were invited to the conferment ceremony, held in the Sheldonian. A balcony afforded an excellent view of proceedings – but Jill, standing between them, would keep dabbing her eyes. When a hood was draped over Tsabo's shoulders, the poor girl insisted on sobbing and the resplendently attired dignitary, enthroned on the podium, momentarily stared up at the culprit before nonchalantly glancing elsewhere.

Tsabo, his whole being electrified with joy, led the way to The Randolph. Not that he was recklessly splashing out, Jill had insisted on investing in one of its lunch tables. The cost of one of his favourite affordable midday snacks, vegetable soup, was enough to turn Tsabo off the joint. He chose some posh kind of salad, but Belinda asked the waiter in penguin-attire to delay taking orders. He bowed and drew her attention to the wine list.

'A suggestion,' Belinda said. 'You treat Tsabo to a celebration this evening, Jill, and Harry will stand lunch, won't you darling.'

Harry winced from a sharp kick on a shin. 'Absolutely,' he meekly replied, though he hadn't expected his guests to be so hungry or so addicted to such expensive claret.

'Delicious steak,' Tsabo enthused. 'If only my parents could have been with us today.'

'Never mind. Just think how happy they'll be when they hear your wonderful news,' chirruped Belinda, at her most consoling.

'Will you be called to the bar in London?' Harry asked, at his most pressurising. He would have recommended the Inner Temple had his wife not re-kicked his shin.

'I'll decide what to do after seeing how my father's leg is progressing.' Tsabo thought for a moment. 'But if I tell him how much a barrister can earn, he'll stop limping and do a somersault instead.'

'Please come back soon,' Jill whimpered, squeezing his hand.

Reflected in her tearful eyes were twin images of the white-man-who-smiles, then that unforgettable Irish voice said: 'You've done well, my son.' Those few words were worth more to Tsabo than all the books in the Bodleian.

Harry and I are cousins, born within a year of each other in the same Ulster village. We attended the same schools in England and the same Oxford college. When Harry scurried off to be a management consultant, I stayed on to teach law. We also shared a common bond with Africa. Our maternal grandfather might have died there and my father had seen out his working days there, when a British crown colony's provincial governor.

Now Tsabo was returning to Africa, anxious to be reunited with his injured father and his family, yet reluctant to leave Oxford and keen to come back whenever possible. Even though there were farewell parties to attend, he set about editing my foregoing chapters.

He wrote most months. With his father recovering, now the killer-drought threatening to decimate his tribe was his overriding concern. I told Harry and sensed what was in his mind. Frustrated, to say the very least, at being deprived of the top job when his firm was taken over, he hankered after any action anywhere and reminded me of his availability. A reminder I immediately faxed to Tsabo. Shortly afterwards, a Whitehall colleague phoned and asked me to outline Harry's career and achievements. The jungle drums had beaten!

Before leaving, Harry read the edited chapters and hoped a record of his experiences in Africa would provide useful material for additional chapters. We were both intent on helping to rectify the dearth of books describing in practical terms disaster prevention and relief efforts relentlessly underway in many of the poorest parts of a disaster-prone world.

And it could prove handy to have Harry on-the-ball in the African country causing my handlers and part-time me mounting concern. Then another phone call from the Whitehall colleague despatched me to Heathrow, overnight to Mavimbi Airport, next day a conflab with the Mavimbi's British ambassador, before an under-cover flight to Kolokuana.

An African army officer briefed me. 'A few white mercenaries based in the neighbouring country attacked before sunrise today. None of my soldiers guarding this site were killed, fortunately, and nothing was stolen or damaged. The only mercenary captured was flown by helicopter to the hospital in Mabela. If he survives, you may get some useful leads.'

Mabela was fifteen minutes flying-time and I needed to fly there early next morning. The officer spoke on a radio. A helicopter would come soon after dawn he said and then offered me a bed and a meal, an offer gratefully accepted. I'd been locked in a bed-less, food-less aircraft hanger in Kolokuana's army barracks the previous night and most of that day waiting for a helicopter to fly me here. I now knew why. When it came to defending a site coveted by many more than the neighbouring country's hard-up rulers, a part-time itinerant evidence gatherer's transport requirements were way down the batting order.

Before dawn next morning the radio confirmed the inevitable, no helicopter available. I was lent a horse and two soldiers armed with rifles, not because they expected to shoot anyone, leopards had been spotted in the mountains between us and the casualty I had to question. With a soldier leading and another behind me we rode for about half an hour up a stream at the bottom of a gorge, it was easier than following an unkempt path. Then, up on a plateau, we skirted a village, with another on the opposite side of the gorge that my map indicated was Katama – Tsabo's home-village.

Towering beyond us, a jaggéd wall barred our way. 'It is the high peaks, with one path over,' a soldier told me. The higher and steeper the horses climbed, the stronger the wind and fiercer the sun. The narrow path soon became a succession of even narrower ledges, clinging to sheer rock. Although an experienced rider, I feared the horse would falter and we'd both end up at the foot of a deep ravine. Too many were beckoning us! Faced with such an unappealing prospect, one was supposed to grit one's teeth. Mine had hopped it on the very first ledge.

When the path widened, we watered and rested the horses, checked their hooves and harness, then drained three of the water bottles in the soldiers' saddle bags. The scarcity of resting places meant that, by the time we reached the pass, around halfway to Mabela, we'd been riding almost continuously for five hours, with fifteen miles and some three hours to go.

In the welcome shadow of a dome-shaped pinnacle, we repeated the horsecare routine and fitted their nose-bags. They'd certainly earned a good feed. Producing sticks from his saddle bag, a soldier re-heated a stodgy lump of mealie-meal in an army mess tin over a fire and I helped my couple of handfuls down with thirst-quenching water. Only then did I notice three stripes on the arm of one of the soldier's camouflaged shirt – his younger colleague stripeless, yet equally alert and helpful.

My attention was diverted to a large pile of stones, supporting several plastic crosses. 'It is a shrine to lost riders,' the sergeant told me and I nodded apprehensively. He added a stone to the pile. 'My brother will hear the stone,' he said and mumbled what sounded like a prayer. So I added a stone and prayed – its content escapes me, now, but could well have been morbidly faint-hearted. What I do recall, however, was wondering whether my father had stood at the summit of this pass, at well over ten thousand feet, surveying a part of his domain while a colonial era governor of this country's southern province. One thing for sure, he would have had no feeling of dominance over the many thousands of people who'd welcomed his reforms. Yet cynics in this country's capital had accused him of giving imperialism a good name, when he'd hated the word and questioned its concept.

Break over – time to press on. The private had cleaned his rifle, and the sergeant's. No leopards encountered, not even a passer-by of the human species, just barren moonscape.

We descended a long winding path, rode down a track with vehicle tyre marks in the dust and passed a second shrine to lost riders with fewer crosses, which cheered me. Far below us was Mabela, my parent's bungalow where I'd proposed to my future wife, and just beyond it, the hospital we'd reached slightly earlier than the estimated three hours.

The white mercenary was dead but his identity disc had survived. Whatever his crime or crimes there were likely to be grieving mourners and they must be pitied.

I thanked both soldiers and patted the borrowed horse – paltry expressions of gratitude for getting me there alive. We stayed overnight at the army camp in Mabela and I itched to walk up the road to St John's Mission and ask if Father Patrick, of whom Tsabo had told me so much, was available to meet me. But I was honour-bound to stay under-cover.

We rode back to the site next day, where another repulsed attack provided four white mercenaries to photograph, interrogate and record my questions and their answers. Next morning I had only their mug-shots and my record of unanswered questions locked in my briefcase, chained to a wrist. After helicoptering back to Kolokuana, at midday I boarded the same flimsy, single-prop, eighteen-seater aircraft back to Mavimbi where I would be invited to share cups of tea and buttered teacakes with the British ambassador prior to divulging my evidence – dissapointingly skimpy for me, though avidly acceptable to him.

There was plenty to mull over during my flight to East Africa where my archaeologist wife was assisting with further research into the hunting and gathering capabilities of *homo sapiens* who apparently first settled on the shores of Lake Rudolf, later renamed Turkana.

The problem with being married to a practitioner of my wife's calling was that her husband wouldn't become interesting until he

47

himself was a relic! The trick was to look scruffy, haggard, and hobble when walking with her and seek the help of one of her arms, which could lead to opportunities to prove that he was yet to achieve relic-status. Wendy was waiting at Nairobi Airport and asked why I looked so decrepid.

More Coincidences

Belinda could see his new rubbish heap from the kitchen. Harry was shifting the damned thing and thinking how poignantly such drudgery symbolised retirement when he heard Belinda call out: 'Telephone! Someone important wants to speak to you!' He sped across the lawn, stumbled down the steps, shed his gumboots outside the front door and a sock chose to stay in a boot. After all that, a pompous London civil servant had the temerity to ask if he was fit and available.

'Extremely fit,' Harry replied, gently easing himself up from another painful attack of gardener's stoop. 'Available for what?'

'This enquiry relates to a possible short-term assignment abroad, principally involving logistics, apparently one of your many fortés. That is all I am permitted to say at present. You may hear more in a day or two.'

'Absolutely understood,' smarmed Harry. 'Many thanks for contacting me.'

'Who was he?' The question came from the kitchen.

'Oh, just some minor functionary updating his ruddy computer.'

Leaving it there for the time being, but hopefully for no more than a day or two, Harry recaptured the sock, pulled on the gumboots and resumed his more zestful menial labour.

That night he found himself deplaning in a crumbling Yugoslavia, then re-directed via Afghanistan to take on what remained of the Khmers Rouges and bury their bloodstained rubbish heaps. Honest humanitarian endeavour all mixed up with putrefying garbage, lost shovels and missed flights – a ghastly mess! Just as the frenzied ordeal seemed about to give way to pacifying slumber, his bedside phone rang and a UN chap, with a cultured English accent, told him he was calling from some place in Africa. Africa? Africa hadn't featured in his nocturnal odyssey and Harry couldn't figure out why. Nor had he expected such a rapid response. Drowsiness caused him to ask the chap to spell his intricate name.

49

'London has suggested I phone you,' Mr Suleiman al Rashid went on to say. 'We are into the second year of this country's worst drought within living memory, and urgently need a logistics expert for six months, to help plan and co-ordinate much needed drought relief. Should this interest you, I can offer a competitive salary plus expenses.'

Drought! He had never tackled drought. Other problems began to stir in Harry's thick head – wife, grandchildren, flying lessons, the local choral society, governorship of his old school. Even so, by working in Africa he might well be able to solve, once and for all, the family mystery stretching back almost a century.

'When do you want me to start?' Harry quietly asked. His wife's ears were flapping.

'Would immediately be too soon? . . . . . . Hello, are you still there?'

'Yes, still here. I was wondering if you'd call me this afternoon, after I've had time to speak to the boss.' If he'd said that he and his boss were in bed together, the caller might not have rung back or maybe he'd have stayed on the line. One never knew, these days.

'Your boss!' the Arab exclaimed. 'I thought you were retired.'

'Self-employed, actually. We'll talk later, then.'

Belinda's question was nicely put. Harry had striven for half of his forty-eight years to emulate her light touch. His strengths, she often reminded him, were not consulting her before jumping in with both feet, lining up cutlery, and never putting the dustbins out on Fridays. Settling back against the pillows he delivered one of his more concise briefings, only to be subjected to one of Belinda's most riveting ploys – the disquieting lull.

Eventually she said: 'Now that trying to fly a funny little airplane has further impaired your hearing, and in view of your obvious boredom with domestic chores and gardening, going to feed millions of starving Africans might shame you into losing some weight.'

Unsurprised by her familiar routine, he found her compliant attitude nicely warming, right down to his cold hot-water bottle. He went to the toilet, lest she changed her mind or asked which country so urgently required his expertise. In his dozy state, or perhaps in his excitement, he'd forgotten to ask its name.

When the Arab rang back, Harry duly corrected the omission and agreed to fly there in a fortnight. Meanwhile, he tried in vain to tell Tsabo of his imminent arrival, underwent an exhaustive medical check, had his blood tested and exposed his biceps to six jabs.

In the darkest corner of a Heathrow multi-storey car park Harry kissed Belinda farewell, while his daughter resolutely loaded his luggage, plus both of her children, onto a trolley. Hating goodbyes, particularly family goodbyes, he had tried to persuade them not to 'see him off' – an unkind expression on so upsetting an occasion – just a bout of stupidity he staightaway dismissed as yet another of his Virgoan pernickety fads. True to his Star, he was a perfectionist, obsessively so, his wife maintained. His brain worked in "threes" or their multiples, particularly 33, whether it was repeating inconsequential mannerisms, or jotting down things to be done, or deciding on the number of paragraphs in an important paper he planned to type. Meticulous planning was just one of his many passions. He also straightended things – cutlery, lawn edges, rows of chairs – and to his wife's rising bile, he'd invented the perfect method of loading a dishwasher. Moreover, as he'd often been reminded during a long, successful career in management consultancy, he never suffered fools gladly. Sadly, it showed! How would he react to the young lady who'd weighed his luggage and was frowning at the result? He surprised his wife, and himself, by paying the exorbitant extra-baggage charge without demur, and then hugged his two grandchildren, his daughter and last, but by no means least, hugged Belinda. She never let him kiss her in public. He was inclined to go overboard a bit.

The overnight economy-class jet flight to Mavimbi was very cramped, yet uneventful. The daily departure to Kolokuana was delayed five hours. A queue of liverish passengers was waiting to board a rather flimsy looking prop-aircraft, when the pilot moved along the line apologising for any inconvenience. By briefly recounting a few of his more daring aerial exploits, Harry secured a seat on the crew-deck – whereupon an eavesdropper, apparently the aide to a cabinet minister, demanded that they be given precedence, as a matter of protocol. With the jumbo-sized minister now wrestling with the aircraft's steps, there was no way the cockpit could provide fitting accommodation, the African pilot humbly and amusingly submitted. And only a cabinet minister's aide, intent on securing an early seat in the cabinet, would have refuted such foolproof evidence.

Approaching Kolokuana, extreme turbulence and minimal visibility forced the pilot to circle until a raging dust storm had abated. Because they landed late, the passengers carried their baggage to the terminal building. Harry had to make two trips. A helicopter whisked the minister and his aide away and less prestigious transport collected everybody else – everybody else except himself! With his sole means of escape flying back to Mavimbi, he cursed himself for ever agreeing to set foot in such a godforsaken place.

'Excuse me, sir. Are you coming or going?'

Harry spun round and couldn't believe his eyes. They thumped each other's back and laughed so much they had to bend forward to catch their breath, altogether a performance that would have generated not a little consternation, had such frivolous hilarity occurred within the hallowed precincts of their venerable Oxford College.

With Harry's 'Belinda sends you her love, I tried to ring you, what are you doing with yourself these days?' done and dusted, they were soon passing acres of gruesome shacks, teeming with humanity. By the roadside men, women, children, even toddlers, begged for help, with the police unmercifully and too brutally moving them on. But where to?

'Not a pretty sight,' Tsabo dolefully commented. 'Thousands of hungry, thirsty, sick, diseased and penniless people have to exist without electricity, mains water or sewerage. Yet nothing's being done to remedy this or to tackle their poverty and squalor. Relief aid will be directed only to subsistence farmers in the southern province, even though most of the capital's slum dwellers recently left there, to escape the threat of famine. It's a terrible dilemma . . . and a shameful tragedy.'

The traffic became more congested, with Saturday shoppers blindly sauntering across unlit streets. Undeterred by a surfeit of near misses, Tsabo resumed his commentary.

'You asked what I'm up to. On returning from Oxford, my grandparents had died, my father had no job, and my mother and youngest sister had joined him here, in Kolokuana. Our village is ravaged by drought! They were lodging, and still are, with my father's sister in a shanty-suburb like the ones we passed. My mother works but her meagre wage won't pay for my youngest sister's schooling or their keep. So I've taken a temporary UN job as the assistant drought relief co-ordinator. Your assistant as it's turned out.'

'That's handy.' It's a godsend! Harry reckoned. 'What about your father's leg injury? Does he get a pension?'

'Having slogged in that mine for twenty-three hard years, he still hadn't qualified for a pension. He had no insurance cover, either, and our social welfare people are hardly flush with money, or beacons of propriety. But I'm chasing compensation!' Tsabo manoeuvred the UN duty car across a deeply cratered parking lot. 'Here we are, moderately safe and sound. This is the only hotel hereabouts semi-worthy of the name. I'm afraid it'll have to do until we find you somewhere decent to rent.'

A fluorescent sign with some dud letters blinked their arrival at the Horseman's Rest. A tethering rail beside a mounting block at the single storey hotel's entrance, plus several pick-up trucks parked nearby, awaited their riders noisily ensconced in the bar. It would have made a passable setting for a cowboy movie but for a figure shuffling towards them. Enfolded in an army greatcoat, concealing both ankles and both hands, he also wore what appeared to be a Russian tank crewman's leather helmet, though being on the small side, it had sprung up and slipped sideways; its dome dented and earflaps splayed. He smiled a friendly greeting, gallantly grabbed Harry's monster case and dropped it on both of his unmilitarily shod feet. His string of expletives required no translation.

Tsabo led the way, lugging two holdalls. Harry followed, carrying his briefcase and a plastic bag of duty-frees: pipe tobacco and whisky. The porter lagged behind dragging the case. Tsabo had vetted the accommodation and also had the key to unlock the gate in the lofty wooden fence topped with barbed-wire surrounding rows of round, thatched huts. Rondavels, Tsabo called them. He unlocked one and they dumped all the impedimenta inside. Having received a generous tip, the porter put his Russian tank-crewman's leather helmet back on his head and his outsize army greatcoat shuffled off contentedly.

With time only for a wash and a change of shirt, Harry was shunted back into Tsabo's UN car and driven to the UN club – a larger rondavel than the one they'd just left. There he met Suleiman al Rashid, the voice from Africa, apparently the UN's chief of mission. Of medium height, slim and dapper, his well-groomed wavy hair greying at the temples, the chief of mission looked the urbane type on whom a leather jacket, slacks and trainers seemed out of place. Not all that much younger than himself, Harry reckoned. Having bought Harry and Tsabo a glass of beer each, plus an orange juice for himself, Mr Rashid briefed Harry on the national emergency, his terms of reference as the UN's "designated drought relief co-ordinator" and ending up with the political set-up.

'The president is a figurehead,' he explained sardonically. 'There is no prime minister, as such. The finance minister runs the country.'

'Will this top-level, high-powered, drought relief team you mentioned be just Tsabo and me?' Harry asked, feeling a tad vulnerable.

'I'm assured that a retired senior civil servant will join you both shortly. It will then be up to the three of you to decide who else to co-opt. If you need advice, consult me. Now transport. Tsabo will collect you tomorrow morning in a UN land-cruiser which you will use for official purposes, charging my development budget for its diesel fuel and always parking it securely. Vehicle theft is a common occurrence.'

Having work to attend to, Tsabo excused himself, and Mr Rashid answered just a few of the many questions Harry's harassed memory, usually calmly reliable, ought to have reminded him to ask.

Whilst driving Harry back to the hotel, Suleiman suggested they use first names. Born in Syria, he'd majored at London University's School of Oriental and African Studies and had managed UN grass-roots development projects in various parts of the world for more than twenty years, before taking up his present post four months ago.

Worn out by the overnight flight, Harry gave supper a miss and had an early night, but his brain went into overdrive. Clearly an experienced and shrewd diplomat, Suleiman had struck him as a person he could work with, relate to, seek guidance from. Someone who, if necessary, would intervene swiftly and decisively. At least, that was what Harry hoped would happen. Pitched into a demanding situation in an unfamiliar environment, he, the UN's designated drought relief co-ordinator, would need all the help he could get!

And Tsabo? Harry had read that "Coincidences are powerful in Africa and never to be taken lightly." Had he and Tsabo been reunited by fate, a stroke of great fortune, or sheer coincidence? Then there was his uncle's provincial governorship in this very country. His Grandfather's grave could be here somewhere, too. The mystery had lasted long enough.

Sleep was engulfing him when he heard a knock. He jumped out of bed, unlocked the door and when he opened it a smiling African girl asked if he wanted company. He slammed the door shut and re-locked it. But that familiar voice inside his head refused to let him sleep by repeating: the Horseman's Rest's a knocking shop. The sooner you find a decent place to rent, the better.

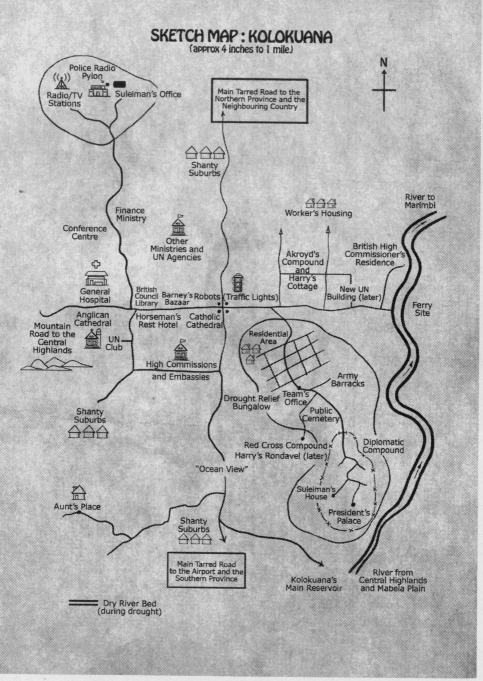

SKETCH MAP : KOLOKUANA

(approx 4 inches to 1 mile)

N

Police Radio Pylon

Radio/TV Stations

Suleiman's Office

Main Tarred Road to the Northern Province and the Neighbouring Country

Shanty Suburbs

Worker's Housing

River to Marimbi

Finance Ministry

Conference Centre

Other Ministries and UN Agencies

Akroyd's Compound and Harry's Cottage

British High Commissioner's Residence

General Hospital

British Council Library

Barney's Robots Bazaar

(Traffic Lights)

New UN Building (later)

Ferry Site

Anglican Cathedral

Horseman's Rest Hotel

Catholic Cathedral

Residential Area

Mountain Road to the Central Highlands

UN Club

High Commissions and Embassies

Army Barracks

Shanty Suburbs

Drought Relief Bungalow

Team's Office

Public Cemetery

Red Cross Compound
Harry's Rondavel (later)

Diplomatic Compound

"Ocean View"

Aunt's Place

Suleiman's House

President's Palace

Shanty Suburbs

Main Tarred Road to the Airport and the Southern Province

Kolokuana's Main Reservoir

River from Central Highlands and Mabela Plain

Dry River Bed (during drought)

Kolokuana's streets, roads and buildings featured in this novel

The Bringer of Rain

Mr Richard Riddington, the British high commissioner, drove Harry around Kolokuana next morning. Its shopping centre compared in size, but not in quality, to that of a small Cotswold market town's. The capital's population now exceeded half a million due to the thousands of squatters who'd fled the drought-ravaged, famine-threatened southern province, Harry was reminded. The itinerary excluded shanty-suburbs, for security reasons!

Richard Riddington's colonnaded residence emitted more than a sniff of fresh paint and furniture polish. Large ornately framed portraits of his feather-hatted, moustachioed predecessors graced a Regency staircase. Photos of their more recent, less ostentatious successors lined the corridor to the marble-clad gentlemen's lavatory. Once the pre-lunch informalities had been dispensed with, Richard led his guest through a spacious reception chamber, festooned with Victorian memorabilia, and out to a veranda overlooking a wide, dry, river bed. A turbaned, Indian butler served an iced lemon-barley aperitif, followed by cold roast beef and salad, rounded off with cheese and coffee. A pukka Sunday snack.

About the same age as Suleiman, yet lankier and greyer, Richard said he'd just arrived in the country and his wife would be joining him later. He'd worked in Africa previously and appeared keen to impose foreign solutions on local problems. Only plausible, Harry reckoned, if the problems were similar and their solutions apposite. Whether they were or not, was far too premature for either of them to judge. Richard came across as one of Her Majesty's more thrustful envoys, very much the type never to rub up the wrong way, but cultivate as an ally. He was about to reveal his helpfulness.

He took Harry to meet a white couple, who lived in a bungalow near the town centre. Dennis Akroyd, who spoke with a South African accent, matched Harry in build, height, age and facial hair. Angela, petite and very English, looked quite a bit younger than her husband and seemed a lot livelier. They were thinking of re-letting their guest-cottage.

The front door, in the bedroom, opened onto the street. The living room had a single-ring gas stove, small 'fridge and sink. The bathroom basin, shower and toilet were clean. The back door led out to the Akroyd's large garden, with parking spaces near a guarded main gate. Reasonably equipped and furnished, the cottage would satisfy Harry's needs, when spruced up. And it had a corrugated tin roof. The hotel rondavel's thatch smothered him, his clothes, bed and belongings with bits of itchy straw he'd suspected were fleas.

Violent thunder woke him that night. Drawing back the curtains, rainwater streaming down the window obscured all but a rapid succession of brilliant lightning flashes which lit up the hotel compound. He fumbled in his diary for Monday 20th April and scribbled: '4 am – first rain for over a year – book a return flight.'

He could see Belinda's smile as he squeezed himself and all his luggage through their back door, her eagerness to lend him her wiping-up cloth while she fetched his gardening togs, her scorn after he'd mounted their bathroom scales.

The thunder drifted away, the deluge stopped as instantly as it had started and the sun urged him to close the curtains. He tuned in to the five o'clock BBC World Service News on his portable clock/radio before withstanding a cold shower. A chatty waitress brought tea and mealie-meal which she said Africans liked to eat and hoped he would like it, also. It wasn't a case of liking the bland porridge, he had to eat the stodgy stuff or starve.

With pools of water hiding its numerous potholes, the road climbed a steep hill, now a muddy torrent, to a flat-roofed three-storey building about a mile from the hotel, wherein Suleiman would brief them further on the way ahead, Tsabo said. While he searched for a parking space, Harry grappled with three over-complicated arrival forms and then signed for that rather ancient land-cruiser the UN was lending him, his driving licence, insurance certificate, mail-box key and a plastic bag bulging with spare-time reading.

Tsabo had warned Harry about Suleiman's secretary – a middle-aged African woman of imposing stature and disagreeable demeanour, whom the staff called Madam Thelma. Apprehended by her on the top floor, she said Mr Rashid was not available.

She opened a door, ushered Harry through it, but excluded Tsabo. Having shut the door, she let Harry know that Mr Rashid was lending the drought relief co-ordinator his deputy's room, only because Mr Ping was on home-leave in South Korea, conveying the distinct impression that she totally disapproved of the arrangement. Perhaps she hadn't been consulted.

Settling into a high-backed leather armchair at an expansive mahogany desk, Harry lit his pipe and amongst the sheaves of paper in the plastic bag he'd been entrusted with, he discovered a copy of the local UN's "Welcome to Station Notes."

"Kolokuana, the capital, is situated near to the centre of the country at 7,000 feet. The southern province varies in altitude from 8,000 to 13,000 feet. Both enjoy a temperate climate.' He underlined enjoy! 'Daily temperatures range from below zero to the upper twenties Celsius in the dry winter months and from zero to the upper thirties in the wet summer months, October to April. The northern province is predominately flat, low-lying and agriculturally productive. Its climate is tropical and temperatures remain in the low forties with generous rainfall evenly spread and humidity high throughout the year."

A smiling little lady in a neatly pressed white overall brought coffee and a biscuit. She spoke in her language and Harry thanked her in his . . . Then he remembered Tsabo!

'Would you know where I might locate Tsabo?' Harry meekly inquired.

'Which Tsabo?' snapped Madam Thelma, her eyes riveted to a computer screen.

'Tsabo Mashedi.'

'Junior officers are on the bottom floor. With the clerks! Please refrain from smoking. I'm allergic.'

Allergic to my pipe or to me? She'd meant both, Harry decided, whilst searching the bottom floor. He and Tsabo were planning their first week's work when the phone rang.

'Her dragonship's pining for you upstairs,' Tsabo chuckled, arching his eyebrows.

Upstairs Madam Thelma re-directed Harry downstairs, which was good for his figure, where Suleiman was waiting to take him

59

to meet the finance minister who, according to Suleiman's Saturday evening briefing, also ran the country.

A gleaming UN-pale-blue-flag-flying black limousine, driven by a pale-blue-liveried-peak-capped chauffeur, purred out of Suleiman's office compound and glided down the steep hill, no longer a muddy torrent. The pools of water which had earlier concealed a plethora of potholes had evaporated under a cloudless sky – re-dampening Harry's spirits.

'I thought last night's rain would hasten a decent spell of wet weather,' he grumbled.

Suleiman shook his head. 'Dust will soon prevail again,' he muttered, his lips pursed.

They entered a palatial sandstone edifice, took the lift to the penthouse and followed a secretary into a spacious inner office where Suleiman introduced Harry to Mr Mboko, the finance minister, and a retinue of senior officials. By coincidence, the minister happened to be the Sumo-sized step-wrestler who had flown with Harry from Mavimbi. Launching into an elaborate welcome, Mr Mboko proceeded to extol the virtues of a time-honoured custom whereby *useful* expatriates were given a Gwato praise name. *Useless* expatriates were appropriately nick-named.

'Your's means the Bringer of Rain in English,' Mr Mboko proclaimed. 'We've had no rain for nearly two years until last night's thunderstorm. Maybe you're a good omen.'

'The compliment is entirely undeserved minister,' Harry felt compelled to say.

With sunlight penetrating every window, Mr Mboko graciously stepped forward, as he must have done on many a grander occasion, to pin a plastic namecard to Harry's lapel.

Delighted with his act of welcome, and that everybody present was also delighted, he touched upon 'my main drought problem' before hastily conjuring up several remedies.

Suleiman intruded, very politely. 'May I remind you, minister, that your drought relief workshop is due to start in your conference centre at nine o'clock tomorrow morning.'

'I'll fly there . . . If the bringer of rain lets me sit next to the pilot.'

'What was that about?' Suleiman asked on the way down in the lift. Harry shrugged his shoulders. Only on leaving the bank, later, did he realise why the male teller had kept on smiling at him. The plastic rain-bringing namecard was still pinned to his left lapel.

More than one hundred civil servants, representatives of non-governmental organisations and members of the two political parties were milling about the conference centre next morning. Harry met a Scots water engineer who'd lived all of his working life in Africa and exuded an air of resigned pessimism. Suleiman joined them and introduced Harry to a very short and tubby, rather elderly man, his facial features partially obscured by a pair of dominant horn-rimmed spectacles with thick pebble-lenses.

'Mr Makoneshi Tsamanachimone,' Suleiman pronounced with commendable ease and aplomb, 'has been confirmed as your local counterpart.'

Counterpart? An unsuitable title, Harry reckoned – but what about the man's handle?

Clearly impervious to the vacant stare when foreigners were told his name, he beamed pugnaciously and reached up to shake Harry's hand, locking his fingers in a vice-like grip and contriving to extract a visible wince.

'Call me Jack,' he disarmingly suggested. 'Everybody does.'

The conference centre had filled to capacity by nine o'clock. Harry sat at the back, next to Alistair Croft, the depressed water engineer. Suleiman, the workshop's sponsor, and Jack, who'd lead for the government, took their places at the front. The third chair remained vacant as minutes, then an hour ticked by. The assembled throng appeared not in the least concerned by an ever-lengthening delay, indicating to Harry that although the difference between GMT and local time had been fixed long ago by global convention, here it was manifestly movable by custom, habit or whim.

The *counterpart* concept still bothered Harry. His pocket dictionary, always kept in his briefcase, defined it as: "a duplicate – a person or thing forming a natural complement to another." Nothing wrong with duplication, if he and Jack deputised for each other, though complementing each other would more than likely provoke continual bickering over who had the final say when it came to difficult or controversial decision-making.

It was past ten o'clock when everybody stood while the finance minister progressed to the front, accompanied by a harassed-looking Tsabo and a hyper intrusive television crew. Once all the hearty handshakes and gushing greetings were in the can, the camera focused on Mr Mboko who frequently stumbled over a script he might not have previously read.

'This is my nation's most important workshop, ever,' he stressed before progressing to the back and out through the door with the television crew still in fawning attendance.

Numerous speakers and a buffet lunch later, Jack chaired a discussion. Sparks flew in every direction and the tenor of the many interventions from the floor and the temper of Jack's ripostes dismayed Harry. He began to have serious misgivings about the motives of most participants, let alone their ability to cope with the drought crisis. Suleiman stood up, welcomed the UN's newly-arrived relief co-ordinator and invited Harry to comment.

'Thank you, Mister Rashid. We shall achieve an effective response to this emergency by good teamwork, by assessing the genuine needs of drought victims, then by planning relief, bottom-up. An effective response is not likely to be achieved by basing urgently needed relief on top-down assumptions and priorities made here, in the capital of your . . .'

A woman, much in the mould of Madam Thelma, rose to her feet, turned to glare at the speaker she had succeeded in cutting short and turned again to address Suleiman.

'Tell this newcomer that *all* the southern province has bad drought. *All* Obangwatos have genuine needs. Therefore *all* must receive water, food and medicines, immediately.'

The woman strode towards the door, basking in sustained applause, leaving Harry for dead and the workshop in irrecoverable turmoil.

'Mr Mboko's sister was echoing what her brother told parliament recently,' Suleiman explained to Harry. 'Tribal chiefs and priests are saying much the same.'

'Everyone wants a free meal,' Jack chipped in. 'That's why so many turned up today.'

Suleiman was not amused. His rural development budget had bought the buffet.

In Mr Ping's room, Jack kicked off the relief team's first meeting by alleging that the UN had always been useless at dealing with emergencies. Only to contradict himself by claiming that, because the five UN bosses with offices in Kolokuana were well aware of the many drought problems, they must get overseas aid quickly! This ingenious solution prompted Tsabo to read out the prescribed procedure:

"As rainfall in the seven African countries currently experiencing severe, prolonged drought may not normalise for several months, their governments are invited to submit a detailed and fully justified appeal for donor assistance to UN headquarters by May 16th. They are to follow this up with a formal presentation, explaining their aid requests, at a conference in London during the following week. Having considered every appeal, the international donor community intends to mount a collective, sustainable response."

With Jack immovable and Tsabo unable to convince him that the UN procedure was binding, something had to snap. It was Harry's patience.

'It's impossible to know what to include in an appeal, until we have made a relief plan and the government has approved it. But we cannot make a relief plan, until the genuine needs of drought victims have been assessed. That's a logical sequence of action.'

'If the UN wants an appeal for donor assistance within a month, I'll have to circulate the draft for comment beforehand,' Jack retorted. 'That's a *realistic* sequence of action.'

'But how can we draft such a vital document without knowing relief requirements?'

'By asking people who know. That's how! I will tell the water, food, health and agriculture ministries to send their chief planners here at eight o'clock tomorrow morning and someone must come from the NGOs, also.'

'I'll go and phone them,' Tsabo said, visibly keen to escape the noxious fug of Jack's cigarette-smoke unhappily blending with Harry's marginally more bearable pipe fumes.

'You mentioned NGOs, Jack. Which non-governmental organisations are likely to get out on the ground and assist with relieving drought?' Harry asked.

'A few international and national charities. The local Red Cross society's director is their spokesman. He was the big shot who criticised the lack of government commitment at that useless workshop. NGOs always controlled relief during previous droughts.'

Harry preferred not to pursue that for the time being, despite his skill at adding new fissures to existing fault lines – a handy management consultancy tool. He must help to prevent a debacle, not create dissension amongst relief agencies. Even so, he'd learned to be wary of NGOs that strove to provide image-boosting aid without first finding out what disaster-stricken people actually needed. Changing tack, he asked Jack: 'Is serious drought a frequent occurrence?'

'Roughly every ten years, but nothing as bad as this one.'

'Have you been involved with relief previously?'

'I worked nearly thirty years in our agriculture ministry, so I was very involved. I was appointed its permanent secretary soon after the last drought crisis and I criticised all the ad hoc relief measures. But, looking back, nobody realised it was so critical in the south until water supplies and crops had already failed, pasture had died and hundreds of people and livestock were starving. The same happened this time, until the cabinet was forced to declare a national emergency and now wants old-timers, like me, to jump into action with no plans, no resources and nothing ready.'

Harry had encountered a surfeit of lack of readiness during his twenty years in the Far East. Part of his task had been to advise governments and businesses how to alleviate the affects of earthquakes and floods. Drought and its problems were brand new to him, and the time for advising other people had passed. Now he and his colleagues would be *doing* the work – urgently needed, life-saving work, in double-quick time.

'When will we get to meet some drought victims and find out what their actual needs are?' Harry asked. 'Not what we think they might be.'

'After you have drafted the appeal and if the army lends us a helicopter with a pilot.'

Jack clambered, knees first, onto a chair and removed his spectacles. 'Up there,' he stretched to indicate on the wall map. 'The northern province is the largest. A lot of good pasture and arable land and no drought. Down here, in the south, subsistence farmers and livestock suffer too often. If it rains, parts of the central and southern highlands, and the Mabela plain between them, can become fertile. We Obangwatos come from the south. Another tribe's in the north.' It sounded like a scathing afterthought.

'Then why doesn't the northern tribe help suffering Obangwatos in the south?'

'That's a long story'. . . Having got down from the chair, safely, Jack said: 'There are six districts in the south, eleven in the north. Most district administrators are un-elected politicians with no administrative experience. They report to a provincial governor in the south. They've got one in the north, also. Water engineers and the other district officials report to their ministries, here. The two provincial governors report to interior minister.'

'I get the picture.' Harry's picture looked horribly confused.

'All problems are solved, here. If they're not, ministers and their senior officials lose face. That's why we've got the job.' Jack dismally lit another fag.

'In a crisis as life-threatening as this one, surely everyone must be geared up. District teams of relief workers must ask drought-stricken communities what their relief requirements are and report those they cannot meet to the southern province's governor or to his staff, who report them to us, bottom-up.'

'Nobody knows what you mean by this bottom-up. We're all top-down, here.'

Biting his tongue, Harry moved on. 'Isn't there any legislation stipulating the duties of civil servants, the police, the army and other key people in a national emergency?'

'There's no act of parliament that explains and enforces government responsibilities in a crisis, if that's what you mean. Civil servants and others haven't been given emergency duties or been briefed on drought relief, and there's no money to train them.'

'Then we'll have to find money and start training, once we know relief requirements. But we won't know relief requirements, until we've got the results of needs assessment surveys and made a plan. So, we're right back at square one, and you're going to say, we haven't got time for all that. We've got to make time!'

More crucially, Jack had run out of fags and borrowed a bit of Harry's pipe tobacco, but left the door of Mr Ping's room open when going to the toilet to get some loo-paper within which to roll the tobacco. Madam Thelma rapidly detected an infringement of her smoking ban and both counterparts suffered a withering tirade. Muttering about bloody women, Jack shut the door, opened the window, lit the prefab fag and had a coughing fit.

Back in the rondavel Harry decided to type the record of his experiences in diary form on a laptop and fax it to me, his cousin Dermot, weekly. Having recorded his account of that day's events, he must have been galled to have to add such a depressing after-note: 'A start that couldn't be worse! Maybe tomorrow morning's meeting will make amends.'

But no chief planners turned up next morning and Jack accused Tsabo of not phoning them, which didn't go down well with Tsabo, who'd spent ages trying to contact them or persuade them to come. The Red Cross operations officer came. So did Alistair Croft, the dispirited Scots water engineer Harry had met at the workshop. Deciding what to do first and then allocating priorities had its excitements – agreeing the six guidelines Harry had drafted proved less contentious.

- Speed and efficiency are vital to save drought victims' lives and livelihoods.
- Obtain and deploy the means of carrying out relief, such as sufficient internal and external aid, money, transport, equipment, leaders, paid and voluntary workers.
- Monitor water sources and supplies in the south regularly; build a static tank in all water-less communities; keep the

tanks replenished from reservoirs in and around Kolokuana and from any smaller reservoirs; find productive springs and disused wells; deepen boreholes and sink a great many more.

- Register every person vulnerable to starvation due to drought (not self-inflicted poverty or neglect) before distributing food – thereby hopefully avoiding a free-for-all with just the fittest or chosen few benefitting.
- Under-nourished children need extra food and nursing care; acutely malnourished children, often prone to mental as well as physical stunting, need a high-protein diet and specialist medical/nursing care.
- Government involvement and input are essential when agreeing more guidelines, planning the way ahead and reviewing progress.

The government's chief planners would attend future meetings – only if one of them was made chairman. Jack refused to step down. Suleiman backed him and circulated the relief team's six guidelines to those he knew or hoped would comply with them, the rest would have to be trained. He also made sure the helicopter his secretary booked had a pilot.

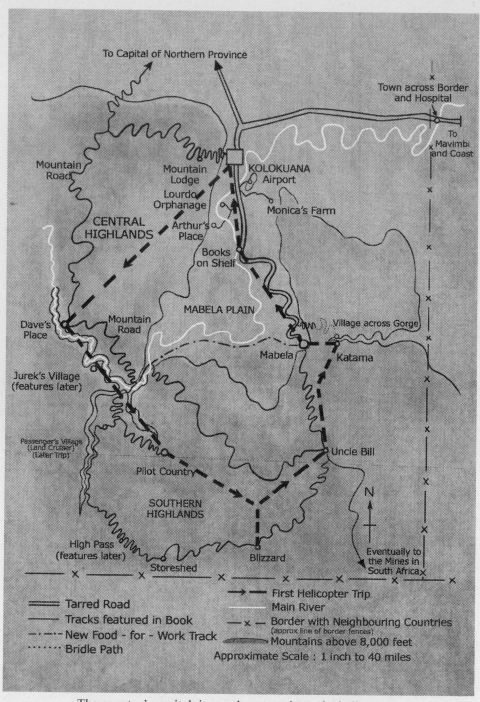

The country's capital, its southern province, the helicopter's
route, locations of later events and so forth

68

Seeing's Believing

Once they had gained entry to the army barracks, a captain, trained to fly helicopters in Germany, strapped them into their seats, fitted their headphones and showed them how to work the intercom. Jack and Tsabo decided that sitting in the back would be a safer bet, enabling Harry, beside the pilot, to monitor the aircraft's dials and follow the route on his latest bundle of large-scale maps. He never went anywhere without lots of relevant large- and small-scale maps. He'd also described to the pilot, prior to their emplaning, just a few of his many aerial exploits, careful to add that he'd only flown a fixed-wing aircraft – in case an in-flight emergency required him suddenly to become a helicopter pilot.

 Headng south-west, they climbed steeply to 10,500 feet, to clear the mountains over-looking the capital – and there were the central highlands! Range upon range, gorge after gorge. Awesome topography! Spectacular scenery! Perfect weather! Had a cloud, even a high wispy one, dared to invade that early morning sky, it would have been a diary event. Within a trice, they'd been elevated to another world. However, on closer inspection, few riverbeds had pools glinting in the sun. Most were bone dry! No sign of cultivation, no pasture, no trees or other vegetation, just an occasional whirling dust plume, glimpses of livestock wandering an arid wilderness, isolated groups of huts, a truck trailing dust on a lonely serpentine track and now and again riders astride irreplaceable horses.

 'I used to live down there,' Jack bellowed into his microphone. 'It took three hours to walk to school and eight hours later I walked back. That's why my legs are so short.'

 Within an hour they landed on a narrow ledge, high above a yawning chasm. A bitter wind gnawed their bones as they followed the path to the district office. The discussion there, strong on drought problems but weak on solutions, took a turn for the better when a charity worker, a middle-aged Yorkshireman called Dave, decided enough was enough.

'I'll write out a list of what's needed and send it by Wells blooody Fargo,' he promised.

Aside from that and Jack's hearty reunion with a classmate, the district administrator, Tsabo's and Harry's march back to the helicopter would be wordlessly despondent, with Jack's school-shortened legs working like pistons to keep pace with two six feet plussers.

Now flying south-east, in half an hour they circled above another desolate but larger settlement. The pilot's birthplace, the intercom informed them. There the meeting took a different form. Some thirty men filed into the small room, old and young alike wrapped in a blanket. Handed paper and a pen by a woman, they sat on the floor, anguish carved deeply on their wind-chafed faces, desiring though not expecting a miracle. They nodded the strangers a cautious greeting and with heads bowed prayed aloud in Gwato.

Most were clan headmen, many had ridden far to attend this palaver, all hoped to return to their people with a morsel of comforting news that might bring a modicum of respite from the effects of a crushing, ruinous drought. Jack briefed them on relief plans, such as they were, but the men wrote nothing and asked no questions. Instead, they relied on their spokesman to describe in English: villages stricken by thirst, hunger and disease, families with no money to buy food or medicine, no fodder for livestock, no crop seed or fertiliser if the rains came. He begged for help and Jack said help would come as soon as possible. Following the national anthem, sung in harmony, the men filed out in dismal silence, gave back the pens and paper, and kept their thoughts to themselves. Mounting emaciated horses, they rode off in various directions, some singly, others in pairs or groups.

For Harry, the whole encounter had been profoundly moving. The grim surrender of pens had epitomised the dire circumstances of those proud men and, through them, their suffering people. There, at the sharp end, the urgent necessity to provide rapid, effective assistance could not have been more painfully obvious, yet the district administrator only quibbled and had to be galvanised into "contemplating" action.

Close to the country's southern border, dense cloud suddenly engulfed the helicopter. By a combination of pilot-skill and divine intervention, the tented camp emerged where the aircraft would be re-fuelled and guarded overnight.

A soldier's waving arms guided the pilot down – in a *blizzard!*

'You get freak weather down here sometimes,' Jack revealed authoritatively, trying to disguise his manifest relief at being back on terra firma.

Their discussion with the district administrator did little to raise their morale, nor did the post-meeting night in a truck drivers' hostel, where candles replaced electric fires and light bulbs at 8 pm, but failed to thaw the water to wash with ten hours later. Jack's freak weather required his two unsuitably clothed colleagues to help soldiers in thick parkas to dig the helicopter out of a snow drift, watched by barefooted children each protected by a threadbare blanket and probably little else.

'If this is freak weather, how can those children survive a real winter?' Harry asked.

'Not all of them will.' Tsabo shook his head and looked forlorn. 'Clambering through snow with both feet bound in rags is one of my earliest memories.'

'I did plenty of that,' Jack chipped in, not to be outdone.

While flying north, past white peaks sparkling in the sun, the scale and impact of this crisis, that had assumed arctic dimensions, began sinking in. 'This is no joy ride,' Harry muttered under his breath. 'Though time spent on reconnaissance is seldom wasted,' he optimistically reminded himself.

'Won't snow help solve the water shortage?' he feebly inquired via the intercom.

'Obangwatos need all the water they can get,' was Jack's ear-splitting response.

'If you speak a little quieter sir,' the pilot suggested, 'we'll still be able to hear you.'

The next district administrator, known as Uncle Bill to all and sundry, told Harry he'd worked in the mines most of his life, adding philosophically that he'd now been given a far tougher job to keep him occupied. In fact, Uncle Bill was no philosopher or political hack, but very much a practical man, superb at his job, hard to please, yet an encourager who always helped others to give of their best. Harry had also heard that Uncle Bill was a wily combatant who applied a boot to deserving backsides, whatever their status or size.

With the three visitors seated on one side of him and the principal chief on the other, the eight members of his drought relief team occupied designated chairs, arranged in a semi-circle facing him. When the Red Cross food aid co-ordinator assigned to his district, a prison superintendent, a Catholic and an Anglican priest, a representative of women's charities and three headteachers had all briefed him, Uncle Bill left no error uncorrected, no omission unnoticed or loose end untied. Impressive leadership and teamwork for other district administrators to emulate, though would they travel long distances just to listen to a retired miner and his equally keen colleagues telling them what to do and how to do it? Thankful farewells, time to move on.

Since returning from England, the emergency had prevented Tsabo from visiting his village, otherwise he would have been spared the shock that awaited him. On their way north, he asked the pilot to fly over Katama, which turned out to be just one more abysmally dry, pitifully run down, highland community. Landing was out of the question. Lack of fuel obliged the pilot to steer the helicopter westwards, clear a jagged range of high peaks and begin the steep descent to Mabela's airstrip, Tsabo said nothing until they landed, and even then, his anguished voice was barely audible.

'The police keep telling me my eldest sister and her family are well. But I must see for myself how she's coping, help her, help my clan to . . .' His voice petered out.

Although they were expected, no vehicle collected them. After the long trudge to the provincial governor's office, he greeted them with extravagant conviviality, filched one of Jack's fags, inquired how their tour had gone and demanded immediate assistance.

'What assistance?' Jack asked.

'Finding out that is your job!'

To avoid more questions, the governor scarpered, unaware that his pacing around the yard chain-smoking was visible through a window. His deputy, a younger brother, proved equally evasive and unhelpful. While the visitors were preparing to leave, the governor's secretary, his sister, hoped they would have a safe journey without bothering to ask where they were going next.

'Not the most impressive performance by a provincial governor,' Harry commented at the Mabela Hotel while tucking into a hot meal, his first since leaving Kolokuana.

'That fool has done nothing for years in case he disgraces his family's name,' sneered Jack. 'And who made all of his forefathers the Obangwato tribe's, my tribe's, paramount chiefs? The British imperialists!'

'I've read that the majority of paramount chiefs were good men,' Harry countered.

'The provincial governor's speciality is presenting school prizes,' Tsabo said icily and described how rude and arrogant the man had been at Tsabo's last speech-day.

They flew north-west to their final meeting. The district office, like most in the south, was a dilapidated colonial relic. From its veranda Harry could see, through the district administrator's open door, some leather-bound books gathering dust on a shelf. In their guardian's absence, he stole into the room and took down the bulkiest volume, printed in 1886. The text of "Her Imperial Majesty's Regulations for District Commissioners" bore the quaintly elegant stamp of yesteryear, so detailed yet also so precise, it was difficult to imagine anything going amiss in Victorian times. A touch different nowadays!

While filling his pipe, Harry visualised a latter-day district commissioner riding in from a gruelling session with a distant governor, before immediately riding out to settle a dispute closer at hand. His vision of that bygone era sharpened when Jack, twitchy and exhaling cigarette smoke, told him the district administrator – the former district commissioner's present day quasi-equivalent – was trying to pacify quarrelling clans and wouldn't return for maybe a week. Harry smiled. It was ever thus. Some things never change. And this he found strangely comforting.

During the flight north to Kolokuana, he reflected on the many challenges ahead. Ever since Sulieman had phoned him at his home he'd scarcely paused for breath, yet all he'd achieved to help the multitude of local drought victims was to start drafting an appeal for estimated donor assistance on a lap-top, with one hand tied behind his back. Now he must start earning his keep by putting theories into practice. That spokesman's plea for help was not only made on behalf of the headmen who'd handed back their pens, his villagers and all the people of the district he knew best, but this country's *every* drought victim.

Back in the Horseman's Rest rondavel that persistent voice inside Harry's head kept repeating 'not a joy ride' while he battled to get some sleep.

Within half an hour of take-off next morning they were in northern province air-space. In another thirty minutes they were flying over mile upon mile of lush savannah grass, abundant cultivation, herds of cattle, tree-shaded settlements, each with a full dam. An hour later they landed alongside a wide fast-flowing river, swollen by the rainstorm the helicopter had been chasing. Instead of the anticipated meeting with district officials, the governor of the northern province walked them to a safari-lodge and suggested they have an afternoon rest before villagers came to entertain them. After the singing and dancing, the governor, his visitors and their entertainers gathered around a log-fire and enjoyed an ox-meat supper and canned lager. Not the home-brewed beer very occasionally on sale in the south which had so attracted Jack, but both of his travelling-companions had shunned.

The fiercest wild animals seen during that day's flight had been zebras, wildebeest and the odd giraffe. Now menacing roars frayed their nerves throughout a hot, clammy night cowering under mosquito nets.

At breakfast, the governor said that the resurgence of malaria and tuberculosis in his province, as well as a growing number of people tested HIV-positive, meant that no food could be sent to drought victims in the south. Although he hated South Africa's apartheid policies, he had contracted to sell its government his province's surplus food at a much higher price than the civil servants in Kolokuana had offered. This would pay for treating his tribe's very sick men, women and children, especially those with AIDS.

'The UN in Mavimbi is funding specialist medical treatment for all AIDS victims in this region. What is happening to that money?' Tsabo inquired, his tone coolly courteous.

The governor ignored the question. 'Famine threatens Obang - watos because nothing is done to help them. Corruption is bad in the south, also. This I know.'

'What's happened to the UN's AIDS money?' thundered Jack. 'This I *don't* know.'

'It's being used to treat the very sick, too.' The governor, in a fluster, sought to defend himself by reminding Jack that all their country's senior appointments in the judiciary, army, police and civil service had always been set aside for Obangwato Catholics to fill. If the northern province's many Anglicans had equal opportunities they would be happier to send water and food to their southern neighbours.'

'Their *starving* southern neighbours,' Tsabo added in frustrated disgust.

Harry wrote in his notebook: 'Charity begins at home and the northern tribe intends its largesse to stay there or sold to the highest bidder. During that first drought relief team meeting, I asked Jack why the more affluent north didn't help the drought-stricken south. His reply 'that's a long story' had closed the lid on a can of spiteful worms. It's now wide open! But at least I know that most northerners belong to the Kasodi tribe.'

They were back in Kolokuana in time for Happy Hour – the UN clubroom's version of the global Thank God it's Friday revelling. The bar was packed with expatriates of most colours and creeds, plus local people of various shades of black and brown, all trying to make themselves heard above the blaring pop-music. Harry's index-fingers dug into both of his ears and with contra-screwing motions deactivated his hearing-aids. Mystified, Jack insisted that Harry crouch, in a crowded bar, so that he could see the tiny sunken gadgets better and watch them being switched on and off, several times. Before long, however, Jack's oily-looking locally brewed beer was wreaking such havoc with his knees, as well as his speech, that Tsabo borrowed a car and drove him home.

Harry investigated the clubroom's compound, unearthed a second rondavel and duly enrolled as a novitiate member of the Friday night pool gang. He was vanquished by an Eritrean garage mechanic and annihilated by a Goanese man, the international high school's "senior" maths master, though Harry outwitted a purveyor of colourful phraseology from down-under . . . Frank – Fozz to his mates – sunk Foster's when not sinking boreholes.

Fozz had apparently hauled his wife, six lively daughters, the eldest only twelve, and their bare essentials from Queensland to Uzbekistan, Azerbaijan and places Fozz couldn't remember, prior to alighting in Kolokuana. On Mondays, he said he parked where a track ran out, swapped his pick-up for a horse, rode to a work-site and then brought a week's worth of grime back on Fridays, quenched his thirst and played pool. Yet the more Fozz strove to quench an evidently unquenchable thirst, the greater his difficulty with hitting balls, let alone the correct one, and the more frequent his use of the F-word. He certainly brightened Harry's evening, though the Goanese maths master seemed un-impressed and the Eritrean garage mechanic compensated for not understanding what anybody said by grinning a lot. Then Marge turned up and lugged Fozz off home to have yet another go at fathering a son or that was how she might have described the process in kosher company.

One pool-playing Friday evening Fozz didn't show up. Harry phoned him and Marge said he was crook. She told Harry to drop round, so he drove to their bungalow. Fozz was lying on a camp bed on the front veranda cuddling his youngest daughter and surrounded by the other five, plus a stack of empty Foster's cans. His wife was hanging out laundry.

'Marge!' he shouted. 'Harry's here! Get some more Foster's! You go and play,' he told his daughters. With his supply replenished and having poured a canful down his gullet, he remembered to say: 'Have one yerself, mate.'

Harry's sympathetic enquiry about the prone invalid's health presented Fozz with the perfect excuse to resort to his customary F-words.

'Last week a .... horse kicked me in the goolies. Marge has a look now and again and reckons they're coming on good. That's a .... relief!'

Early next year Marge would produce a seventh daughter and Fozz named her Cyril, after his old man back in Queensland.

Happy Sam

Berney's Bazaar, a covered market off Kolokuana's main street, was jammed full with all manner of goods and chattels. The freezer cabinets, lining most aisles, were stacked with imported food. It would have been even more of a squeeze along the aisles for the expat customers if there'd been more than just a few African shoppers – perhaps because they much preferred local food or more likely they couldn't afford to buy what was on sale. This had its compensations: there were no queues at the check-out counters and none of the check-out women were telling nearby counterparts what they had done on their day off. If they had one! The check-out women in Harry's local Cotswold supermarket invariably spent ages telling nearby counterparts where they had been and what they had done throughout their most recent holidays, which their nearby counterparts then endeavoured to surpass in activity quantity and quality, while lengthening queues irritably had to listen to it all.

A beaming, ill-kempt, street urchin was quick to offer to carry Harry's "plastics" – the suffix "bags" superfluous. His name, Sam, a six-year-young apparently of no fixed abode or family – but was he one of the many glue sniffers who slept rough in the town centre? From Harry's scant knowledge of such things, Sam appeared to be *clean*. Whether he was trustworthy remained to be seen. Taking a chance, Harry said: 'You here. Next Saturday. Same time.' The boy nodded, beamed even more, and cupped grubby palms above his snub nose to receive a reward. "Happy Sam" scampered off, waving and skipping, to join competing street-boys-cum-plastics-carriers queuing at a stall with 'Ma Honesty's Cheap Bread' advertised in white paint, which had dripped down its khaki awning. Pa Honesty most likely wore a khaki uniform and had *borrowed* the awning.

After two weeks at the Horseman's Rest, Harry moved into the Akroyd's cottage and spent most of that weekend, like the previous one, holed up with Tsabo. Producing a draft appeal for donor assistance was all the more pressing after their trip to the south. Jack had criticised the former ad hoc relief efforts, yet Tsabo and

Harry still had to best-guess the needs of an unquantified number of drought victims. Yet they must persevere! To delay would surely cost countless lives, and were donors to respond best-guessed requests for estimated assistance, it would take at least two months for their aid donations to arrive by sea and be transported by road from Mavimbi's docks.

Without glancing at their draft appeal, let alone discussing its contents, Jack circulated copies for government-only comment, stating in the covering letter that he had done most of the work. Tsabo and Harry let it pass, as if unnoticed. However, they soon realised that whatever they did, or attempted to do, Jack suspected them of ganging up on him. He had probably thought Harry was just an enthusiastic amateur keen to teach local, experienced, civil servants how best to deal with a drought emergency in their own backyard – Tsabo a renegade Obangwato and Harry's over-educated stooge. Worryingly damaging stuff, but the rift mustn't widen. It had to be rapidly narrowed, then firmly and amicably shut.

While nibbling a slimmer's banana Harry tried to ignore the pungent dish Jack called a "plate" he'd bought from a street vendor. Shared lunch breaks were a vital, if insufferable, ritual – otherwise he'd have seen very little of Jack. Neither the morsels deposited about Jack's person, nor the stains he left on letters and documents, detracted from the necessity of shared lunch breaks. Indeed, letters and documents thus soiled provided irrefutable evidence, much akin to a rubber stamp, that they had touched Jack or vice versa, though he'd nevertheless swear he'd never seen whatever it was, and on no account admit to having read it.

At one lunch date they agreed a helpful division of work. Jack would chair meetings, chat up chums, clinch deals and fix things. Harry would read, write and remember things, and together with Tsabo, would attend to the constant grind of planning and co-ordinating relief. If Harry aimed too high or if Jack got irritated, Tsabo would make an ideal moderator or peacemaker. However, their agreement to keep each other informed of their respective intentions, actions and whereabouts would survive only until that afternoon when Jack took possession of an empty bungalow, a second-hand government truck, five newly-recruited staff, a lorry load of part-worn furniture and office equipment, a borrowed electric kettle, some used mugs and rusty garden tools, a brush and a broom, but no vacuum cleaner – in Jack's book, women did the sweeping.

That evening Harry would discover what had been going on in that bungalow and also what Tsabo had been told to pass on. Harry could see he was on edge. 'Jack wants me to move there, but wants you stay here in Mr Ping's room,' he said, expecting a broadside.

'Divide and rule,' was Harry's restrained comment in that evening's diary.

They bade Madam Thelma au revoir, thanked the little lady in the smart white overall for numerous cups of coffee and Tsabo drove down the hill to the finance ministry.* Joining the road from the central highlands which became the main street, passing the Horseman's Rest and Berney's Bazaar, he obeyed the robots – traffic lights – that taxi drivers ignored, especially when red. The signs indicated right to the airport, Mabela and the south; left to the northern province and the neighbouring country; straight on to the redundant ferry.

Taking the river road, he turned right and climbed the hill to a suburb, known as the Residential Area: a paved grid of bungalows popular with the local middle-class and expatriates of equivalent status. But it did have drawbacks, apparently. Water and electricity supplies failed far more often and for much longer than in the utility workers' lines. Also, telephones were notoriously unreliable, if they happened to be connected.

Harry was shown round the bungalow by an African accountant in her forties. Pinkie, an albino, would use a double bedroom as her office. Jack had commandeered the biggest one. The single bedroom, the secretary's office, was opposite the bathroom and kitchen. In an L-shaped room, the dining area overlooked an uncultivated back patch.

'We assumed you would prefer your desk facing the dining area's window. Tsabo will sit here.' Pinkie pointed to a large wooden

---

* Page 56. See sketch-map of Kolokuana.

conference table encircled by assorted plastic chairs in the lounge area – its two windows facing an equally uncultivated front patch and the road. 'Come and meet the staff. They're outside, unpacking stationery.'

'This is Muella, our secretary.' A stunner in her late teens or early twenties, and quick to tell Harry that her boyfriend came from London and managed a department in the main street's British bank. Lucky chap, in more ways than one!

'This is Matagassa, our cleaner, her friends call her Fuzzy.' In her late thirties and also attractive, though her hair let her down, she said she lived in a village on the way to the central highlands and had three daughters. 'Two are twins,' she added proudly.

The security guard shook both of Harry's hands, much as a long-lost friend would do. While estimating the man's age Harry was distracted by a bald pate protruding through a trilby's missing crown. He habitually estimated a person's age on first meeting, but local people over forty too often had him stumped. He couldn't believe that Jack was only nine years older than him. He also had difficulty pronouncing long African names. His version of Jack's surname sounded like some peculiar sort of chimney, according to Tsabo, and he'd made Harry keep repeating after him: 'Tsah-mana-chee-moan-eh.'

'What should I call the security guard?' he furtively asked.

'Call my father Fred,' Tsabo replied, keeping it simple.

Harry was speechless! The females whooped with laughter, ululated, pranced around, and Tsabo said something in Gwato to his father who shook both of Harry's hands again.

Fred – forever Fred – led him into a shed on the back patch and showed him some rusty tools, before hobbling round a scruffy compound and describing in understandable English, with copious gesticulations, how he would make a good garden. When the rains came! Impressed by his father's renewed vigour and amused by Harry's unusual interest in horticulture, Tsabo had just joined them when a vehicle careered into the bungalow's compound, smothering them in dust. 'Morebo is the relief team's driver,' Tsabo said.

Speedy Gonzales would be an apt means of recognition, Harry reckoned. Though once bitten, twice shy, he decided to bide his time – the driver was probably Jack's grandson. Although he turned out be unrelated, Harry nevertheless re-christened him Speedy.

No lover of gossip, yet when a grapevine happened to drop a juicy fruit right in his lap, Tsabo was duly grateful. He checked and, sure enough, a drought workshop was about to be held in Mavimbi. He told Jack and Harry that his middle sister was on a public health course there and he needed to visit her. He reminded them while Harry awaited Madam Thelma's permission to knock on her chief of mission's office door.

'The UN's drought sensitising workshop in Mavimbi starts next Monday and ends on Friday,' Suleiman explained. 'The finance minister has directed that nine delegates from this country are to participate and my development budget will pay for their flights, meals and hotel room. I shall attend the keynote speech on the final day.'

'I'll go,' said Jack, known to be dead keen on freebies. 'I'll take several chief planners and somebody from the local Red Cross.' No mention of Tsabo or Harry.

'We must select individuals who will gain the most from this important workshop and whose participation will benefit drought relief, otherwise all the money and effort will be wasted,' Suleiman cautioned. 'Your six months here, Harry, was made possible only by milking my budgets to cover your internal costs, not external expenses, though I'm close to finding a solution. Meanwhile, you and Tsabo should both plan on flying to Mavimbi on Sunday. Now the appeal. We'll go through this latest draft. The final one, I trust.'

Jack looked decidedly edgy. His familiarity with any draft, let alone the latest one, was, at the very most, sketchy. Suleiman distributed copies, reviewed the appeal page-by-page, offering advice here and there, before addressing an uncommonly silent Jack.

'I suggest you send the document to the finance minister, mentioning in the covering letter all those who have helped with its preparation and urging its prompt approval. After it has been distributed within government, I shall circulate copies to all non-governmental relief agencies and UN agencies working in this country. You should also take a copy to Mavimbi, in case you need to refer to it. The approved document must be faxed to UN headquarters well before the international donors' conference in London in a fortnight's time. I shall accompany the minister and I understand that you will formally present the government's aid requests. He has asked me to vet your script and calculations. I'd also like to see your explanatory map and vufoils.'

Horror-struck, perspiration steamed up Jack's spectacles and ran down his cheeks. 'No one's told me about the conference in London,' he fibbed. 'Your UN relief co-ordinator's the appeal expert. He must go. I'll say this in my covering letter.'

'With greatest respect, Mr Tsamanachimone, *your* finance minister insists that *you* are to present *your* country's appeal for donor assistance.'

Jack wanted to be dropped off at the finance ministry and still hadn't returned to their bungalow office when, next morning, a UN driver delivered an envelope addressed to Harry. The hand-written note inside read: 'Your telephone appears not to be functioning. You may fly to Mavimbi on Sunday, courtesy of the British high commissioner's petty cash. A person-to-person expression of your gratitude would be appropriate, for there will likely be further calls upon Richard Riddington's beneficence. All the best, Suleiman.'

Richard had also paid for the army helicopter, enabling Jack, Tsabo and Harry to visit six southern districts and a northern province's safari-lodge in only three days. It would have taken the best part of three weeks by road, along the south's tracks Harry had heard so much about and through all the dustbowls they'd observed whilst airborne. However, he must very soon sample those tracks and dustbowls at ground level, and whatever other hazards the south had in store. This morning he was driving Tsabo to Richard's office.

Upwards of twenty Commonwealth high commissions and foreign embassies, each in a neatly kept, barbed-wire-enclosed compound on both sides of a pothole-less street, were modern, two-storey buildings. They had been purposely designed and constructed to look alike – so that one country's diplomats would feel in no way inferior to another country's diplomats. Only the national flags fluttering at the same height and the ornate national crests embossed on identical iron double gates distinguished them apart. A discerning eye would have noticed, however, that the Union Jack's domain had recently grown a trifle bigger. Patriotic sentiments, such as the kudos derived from Great Britain's leading role on the UN security council, within the international donor community, on peace-making and peace-keeping operations in sundry hazardous places, were titivating Harry's pride-buds when Tsabo drew his attention to the much larger extension, opposite, taking shape beneath two proudly fluttering flags that resembled the Stars and Stripes.

This latest game of beat-your-neighbour was but a modest contribution to the globally relentless pursuit within diplomatic circles to keep pace with, and preferably ahead of, the Jones's or their multi-ethnic equivalents.

Richard Riddington waved aside Harry's thanks. 'Do you like my new toy?' he asked, his attention focused on a gleaming, jet-black, aerial-bedecked, Range Rover into which he was easing himself. 'Far superior to those shoddy Yankee jeeps and cheap Asian jobs,' he scoffed, glancing disdainfully at the dust-covered, battered, off-white Japanese land cruiser from which Tsabo and Harry had alighted. Trading rueful smiles, they slunk back inside their cheap Asian job confident that one-upmanship, as ever, reigned supreme. The land-cruiser then hid the expensive British job in a mini-cloud of black oily smoke, as it loyally chugged off towards the main tarred road – conveniently close enough to afford diplomats a hasty getaway should necessity demand.

Suleiman had finally convinced his superiors of the urgency to bolster the country's relief capacity. Through his doggéd persistence, a welcome if belated reinforcement was arriving that day. 'Now it's over to you and Tsabo,' he'd told Harry.

Leaving the main tarred road ten miles south of Kolokuana, the land-cruiser skirted the baggage-handler's and ground staffs' slums. Customs and immigration officials drove to the airport in the cars they'd bought with their ill-gotten gains. Prostitutes bussed there, hoping to snare an arriving sugar daddy. The airport's managing director and his several deputies held daily court at the back of terminal building in the cocktail bar, a singularly unwholesome grotto owned by a retired senior policeman, rumoured to be a drug baron. Tsabo had taken Harry in there once to view the set-up. Once was enough!

Bisecting a barren plateau, the gravel runway which the single-prop aircraft, linking Kolokuana with Mavimbi, negotiated twice daily on its inward and outward flights. At the far end of the runway a tattered, horizontal windsock; at the other end a wooden hutch stood on stilts, the control tower; on one side of the modern spacious terminal building a car park part-filled by noon, deserted soon after; on the other side, a tarmac apron where the daily aircraft refuelled, near a rusting Soviet jet-fighter donated long ago to a putative ally whose latter-day governments rapidly found far too expensive to service and arm, let alone fly anywhere. The present-day finance minister kept it there to deter dissidents.

Glinting in the midday sun the plane banked to line up with the runway, glided silently from windsock to control tower, revved to a saunter, turned and then halted on the apron. The pilot opened its door, lowered its steps and onlookers tried to spot through the terminal's grimy windows the person or persons they'd come to meet amongst the handful of passengers, though most Africans had come for a rare, exciting outing. Much like 1920s' Londoners who'd taken a tram to Croydon to see a tethered airship that might catch fire.

Tsabo and Harry were expecting a young white American, the flight's only white, as it transpired. Once the new arrival had bribed his way through the snail-paced customs and immigration procedures, he found himself being greeted as "our urgently needed drought relief press and information officer" which he quietly asked Harry to repeat.

A UN probationer, Glen glumly confessed to having no knowledge of drought relief or the press. By professing to have none either, Tsabo's off-the-cuff icebreaker, rather than comfort the shy young newcomer, had the very opposite affect. So Harry drove them both to the UN clubroom to do a spot of team building.

The Hovel

Behind the Catholic Cathedral – a red brick, black-tiled edifice, dominating the crossroads at one end of the main street – the library where Tsabo had catalogued books, before going up to Oxford. Beyond that, the seminary's thatched huts where he'd eaten, read late every night and eventually fallen asleep in the room he'd been grateful to reoccupy on returning to Kolokuana. His recently ordained classmate regularly patrolled the town centre urging street-boys to stop stealing, glue sniffing, fighting or whatever. He had also pledged that Harry's always beaming shopping bag carrier was in all respects trustworthy.

'Befriend him and take an interest in his welfare,' the young priest had urged. 'I wish many more, well-meaning people would help the far too numerous orphans and outcasts.'

Apart from his weekly shopping rendezvous with Happy Sam, Harry had set aside that Saturday to visit Tsabo's mother and his youngest sister Palima. They lived with his aunt, his father's sister, whose husband had divorced her soon after their wedding.

Having driven south along the main tarred road to a squalid suburb, Tsabo then had to negotiate an appalling track, stinking sludge obscuring its potholes. Their expected arrival had been seen – two middle-aged women and a frail old lady, aided by a stick, emerged from the shack, each wrapped in a grey blanket, followed by a teenaged girl in a brown gymslip, three boys in assorted garb and a barefooted toddler in a pink frilly dress.

Tsabo's short, stout, sad-looking mother conversed through her son. His smiling sister was taller, slimmer and eager to demonstrate her command of English. Palima had passed her school-leaving exam and would help her mother clean offices, until she found a job. She wanted to be a teacher, but the training courses cost too much money. The aunt said her mother-in-law spoke no English – so, thanks to Tsabo's tutoring, Harry demonstrated an elementary grasp of Gwato.

'Peace be with you, madam. You stay well? I bring you and the family a present.' He offered the frail old woman the largest box of chocolates on sale in Berney's Bazaar.

'Peace be with you, sir. I stay well, thank you.' When her wizened hands had broken open the box's slippery cellophane wrapping, she cautiously sniffed its contents.

Lining up, all wide-eyed and hopeful, their eager palms raised above their foreheads, when every child had received one of the white man's sweets the three boys skidaddled, shouting 'good morning' in mid-afternoon, with the toddler squealing in hot pursuit.

The aunt invited Harry into her home – clumsily laid cinder-block walls and a tarpaulin roof. The unseen bedroom the aunt shared with her four children and mother-in-law. The living room sparsely and shabbily furnished, with newspapers strewn over a dirt floor. A sack hung in the pane-less window. No electricity just a candle waxed into a jar. Rats had left liberally scattered visiting cards and the smell wasn't from a bed of roses.

Outside the back door a flimsy lean-to housed a pygmy cell where Tsabo's mother and Palima slept. In another cubicle, a single-ring paraffin stove stood beside a bag of maize-meal, half a cabbage, rotting garbage and unflushable toilet, its convenience Harry felt no urge to sample.

In answer to his questions, the aunt explained that they had to queue for water from a hand-pump, half an hour's walk away. They washed themselves and their clothes in a tin bath in the kitchen. Parafin for her stove was too much money and she burned cardboard or sometimes bits of wooden boxes her children found to heat water and cook food. They slept on mats under blankets and also in their day clothes on many very cold nights.

The frail old lady and Palima had left the living room, Tsabo's mother was sobbing and he made his feelings known to Harry in no uncertain terms. 'What did I tell you after you flew here? No mains water or sewerage in slums like this and it was shit in those potholes we drove through. This slum's shit, next door's shit, dog, cat and rat shit, and God knows what else! Yet even if this place had a sewer, neighbours would wreck it, because they'd hate others to have more than them. I believe thou shalt not covet thy neighbour's possessions, only cranks believe the lowest common denominator prevails and all that crap.'

Tsabo shielded his eyes with one hand and wiped them with the other. His anger and bitterness, so untypical of him, had startled Harry – and what had his mother thought of her son's tirade of unknown words? His aunt was clearly shaken.

'Will you help us Mr Harry?' the aunt pleaded.

'It's not his responsibility to help. It's *mine!*' Tsabo yelled back. 'And God knows I'm trying very, very hard.'

There were heated arguments between him and his aunt, then between his mother and her sister-in-law; unintelligible but audible to Harry who'd fled outside. Tsabo certainly had a predicament – whether to leave his loved ones again and complete his legal studies or, by working, to free them from rank medieval living conditions. Visiting just those few parts of the south had exposed Harry to some of the suffering and privation endured by the rural destitute. Now he'd witnessed a portion of the hardship and misery besetting the urban deprived.

Tsabo flung himself back into the land-cruiser, slammed the door and stared through the windscreen, too angry to speak.

'You're doing all you can, Tsabo, to help your parents and Palima,' Harry ventured. 'By qualifying as a barrister overseas, as soon as you can, you will also help yourself.'

Mentioning overseas at such a sensitive moment was tactless, but essential. Tsabo had achieved a great deal, but still had a great deal more to achieve. He had to be reminded that he must be called to the bar. Not only was Harry determined to make this happen as soon as practicable, Belinda's letters never failed to remind him to remind Tsabo.

'I've said what I had to say,' Tsabo re-erupted, 'and said it right in front of my aunt. We had a hard time in Katama. Yet my mother always kept our rondavel and our few bits and pieces clean and tidy.

Now I have to compare my cherished home with that disgusting hovel. My aunt's responsible for what you saw, but she won't let my mother or sister do anything. She's not poor. She's a job-for-life, civil servant and her mother-in-law looks after her kids. She knows I'm earning a reasonable salary, loathes me giving my parents money and by keeping things in that disgraceful state, she hopes I will give her money, too. I have to tell you, Harry, the vast majority of locals, even my tribes-people, are consumed by jealousy. They will do their utmost to prevent others succeeding. And if an enterprising person succeeds, they will do their utmost to ruin that person's livelihood. It doesn't stop there! When they meet a white man, particularly a white man who smiles, they sidle up to him and beg for help. Just as my aunt did this afternoon! Then they hold their hand out to him forever more.'

'Thou shalt not be enterprising, right? . . . At least your aunt tried to be.'

No reply. On the way back to the town centre, they passed many litter-strewn decrepit huts, fomenting another outburst.

'Look at all that squalor, on both sides of the road. When the government set up this resettlement area they called it *Ocean View!* What a fantastically ludicrous name! We'll walk round that disgraceful shambles soon and you'll see what real filth and poverty can do to people. It's infested with vermin and most probably with tokolosi as well.'

'Tokolosi. What the dickens are they?'

'Mythical, dwarf-like creatures, part of tribal folklore. Some Obangwatos believe that, if you get a tokolosi on your back, it will never stop thwarting your best endeavours.'

'Are you sure they're mythical? I think we may have one in our office.'

The allusion to diminutive Jack tickled Tsabo who even managed to smile. Harry could recall a few tokolosi imitators who'd plagued him in the past – one devious back-stabber had thwarted his best endeavours repeatedly and gleefully.

'Please understand, Harry, I took you to meet my mother and sister, not to involve you in all that. My mother hardly got a look in and Palima took off. They're really ashamed of that dump and only remain there to be near my father.'

'Look on the bright side. Your aunt now knows you're on to her game. Let's hope she mends her ways, though mending that hovel will take an awful lot of cash and work.'

With a shrug of his shoulders, Tsabo led the way from the rushing din of the capital into the calm hush of the Catholic Cathedral. Its rows of lofty columns and a distant altar would have graced quite a few British post-industrial revolution cities but for the sudden contrast of temperature on entering and the fact that every pew was full.

Harry, a lapsed Presbyterian turned rebellious Anglican, had toyed with converting to Catholicism. When he'd mentioned this to his American wife, Belinda, a devout Southern Baptist, her grimace presaged a re-think. Now he was queuing to be blessed by a priest – Tsabo to receive the holy sacraments. He respected the ritual, adored the whole-hearted singing, found kneeling amidst such a large, devoted congregation fortifying. He prayed that he might be given the guidance and strength to play a meaningful part in delivering rapid relief to maybe a million or more drought victims, who were out there, somewhere!

Yet More DiaryFodder

Being a Sunday, the airport's baggage-handlers were absent, Jack was crabby, so Harry and Tsabo carried his cases, as well as their own, across the tarmac and the pilot loaded them into the back of the aircraft. Four of their country-team – from water, food, nutrition and the Red Cross had already emplaned – the two from health and agriculture failed to show up. Nor, as it would depressingly turn out, did they catch a subsequent flight.

Their depleted delegation arrived at one of Mavimbi's five-star hotels when cocktails and canapés were being served, among heavily scented tropical flowers and blossoming shrubs. After a four-course dinner, eased down with a choice of excellent wines, Harry treated Jack and Tsabo to a night-cap in the plush, air-conditioned bar – yet so much flagrant opulence played on his conscience. By courtesy of Richard Riddington, British taxpayers had unwittingly stumped up the money for his travel, accommodation and meals.

'Not the most frugal venue for a drought sensitising workshop,' Harry commented.

'You can say that again,' chuckled Tsabo, sipping an iced crème de menthe frappé.

'The UN's keeping up appearances,' mumbled Jack. He gulped down his third whisky and tottered off to bed hugging the almost empty Haig Black Label bottle the barman had bequeathed him, re-confirming that Jack and alcohol blended none too well.

'I wonder how Glen, our American recruit, views the prospect of being left in charge while we're on holiday?' mused Tsabo.

'Glumly,' Harry surmised, draining a cut-glass goblet of its three-star brandy.

Next day, all seven country-teams were required to draw up a chart, listing drought relief agencies across the top, drought relief tasks down one side indicating the agency undertaking each task by placing a cross in the appropriate column and then adding a footnote stating who supervised whom. The result? Seven psuedo-football-pool-coupons littered with crosses, plus a profusion of footnotes. The workshop director's verdict? Re-structure relief and improve control, as quickly as practicable. Jack rolled up his team's chart and handed it to Tsabo who passed it on to Harry.

There would be other low points: foremost amongst them, a pathetic explanation as to why the UN's famine early warning system had failed to alert not just itself, but also its own agencies based in the seven drought-hit countries, the NGOs there, now gearing up to relieve drought, and the countries' governments. Among fewer high-points, resources were pledged for relief training and arrangements for transporting donor aid from African entry ports to drought victims were finalised. The show-stopper was a New Zealander's amusing professorial exposition on how the "El Nino Effect" periodically warmed ocean currents to cause both droughts and floods, often concurrently and in close geographical proximity to each other. He dismissed reducing carbon emissions as pie-in-the-sky.

True to its title, the workshop did sensitise country-teams to the broader implications of the regional emergency; also providing a congenial opportunity to meet old friends or make new ones in opulent surroundings where the UN, as Jack had hinted, would be seen to be flying its flag. The hotel had been festooned with pale blue reminders.

On the last morning delegates, directing staff and honoured guests assembled for the VIP's keynote address and a final discussion. Jack placed himself in the front row and Harry and Tsabo joined him – but with the reluctance frequently shown by non-African churchgoers who filled the back pews first. Arrayed across the stage, flanking the VIP, a UN dignitary, were six of his illustrious colleagues all offering themselves for admiration rather than scrutiny. The three white males, in unsuitable suits, competed to commandeer their superior's elusive ears. The three black females, in flowing pastel-coloured gowns and matching gargantuan head-dresses, exposed delegates they knew to expansive waves. The less worthy residue were granted a radiant dental advertisement.

Noticeably restive throughout the VIP's speech, only when it ended did Jack's seating strategy become clear. He'd already demonstrated to Tsabo and Harry an ability to rudely ask awkward questions, a reputation that must have spread far beyond them. Had he stood on his chair, he would have been an even bigger hit with his fans.

'Does the panel think, that the UN's ethereal modalities for obtaining prompt and favourable responses to our urgent requests for donor assistance will work?'

'Ethereal modalities' echoed round the hall. Airy ways of doing what you promised to do. Harry was impressed. Tsabo looked astonished.

The placatory answers received from the stage in no way allayed Jack's misgivings. Moreover, the heated exchanges between an irrepressible Jack Russell Terrier panting in the front row and the seven majestic Great Danes occupying the stage certainly enlivened their receptive audience. Decorum was restored only when the VIP had raised both hands to silence this unknown, insolent, unyielding intruder – the VIP's face spoke volumes.

With the final discussion dawdling to an uncontroversial close, all of a sudden, Tsabo re-stimulated proceedings.

'Sir. The UN maintains five separate and spacious offices in Kolokuana, the capital of a drought-ravaged African country. Might not a single, combined, office suffice?'

A deathly hush preceded muted comments on the stage and loud chortles in the hall. The VIP hastily asserted that the subject had already been agendered as a priority issue for active consideration within the top echelons of the United Nations – whereupon, the male rising star seated next to him grabbed at the chance to earn a stack brownie points.

'We must assume, Mr Chairman, that the questioner actually understands the UN system and has not overlooked the fact that each of the five agencies, he referred to, functions under its own mandate, with its own budget, and according to its own procedures. It would be self-defeating, therefore, to integrate our separate offices in his country's capital or in any other country's capital. Furthermore, it would constitute change for change sake.'

'So you want to preserve an *un*-improved status quo?' Tsabo queried with the polished acridity of an Oxford debater. Still standing, his verbal attention returned to the VIP.

'Mr Chairman. All five UN agencies share the same mission . . . the timely provision of effective humanitarian relief. Why cannot they also share a common relief mandate and a unified relief budget? If there are sound reasons for permitting exceptions to that rule, the UN should permit them. But it should not be ruled by exceptions, surely. A sensible form of integration would trim cumbersome, wasteful bureaucracies and help to introduce an efficient, economical structure with flexible, responsive procedures. This should achieve, with fewer staff, far better value-for-money. Money and effort thus saved would provide additional money and effort for relieving great suffering. It is encouraging, sir, to hear of this top-level, impending review and I trust fellow delegates will join me in hoping that your overdue initiative will enjoy the prompt success it undoubtedly deserves.'

A standing ovation within the hall, no more comments from the stage, a few words of appreciation from the workshop's director for the panel's "invaluable" contributions, then Jack and most of his African fan club eagerly made haste to the drinks-on-the-house bar.

Tsabo and Harry were about to leave in a taxi – one to visit his sister, the other to buy gifts to take back for the rest of the relief team, when Suleiman who'd been present at the final session, forestalled them in the hotel foyer. He was *livid!* Both the questions which had caused the most difficulty, indeed umbrage, had been asked by delegates from what he called his representative domain.

His day was really made, however, when Jack didn't show up at Mavimbi airport that evening. The finance minister had flown from Kolokuana, but he and Suleiman had to fly to London without Jack, who was supposed to present his government's appeal for donor assistance at the international donor community's meeting.

A British Airways receptionist rang Harry at the hotel. She said that a Mr Suleiman al Rashid had asked her to explain what had happened, which she duly did, and to relay the message that he had a copy of the script, but no vufoils. If they were brought to the airport, she would send them on the next flight to Heathrow and have them delivered to Mr Rashid's London hotel. Harry thanked her, replaced the receiver and resoundingly cursed Jack. When told, Tsabo could barely contain himself. The lives of countless members of his tribe and their remaining livestock depended on the approval of his country's appeal for donor assistance. Yet their fate now hung on rushing a dozen vufoils, displaying key data justifying the government's requests for emergency aid, to an airport receptionist!

Harry had checked before they left Kolokuana airport that Jack had his script and the vufoils, but he couldn't be found that evening, nor next morning before Tsabo and Harry left for the airport. The receptionist who'd phoned Harry was on duty all weekend. Harry said he would put the duplicate vufoils in a sealed envelope addressed to Mr Rashid, take it to Kolokuana Airport and give it to the pilot of tomorrow's flight to Mavimbi. She said she would tell the pilot. Harry thanked her and told her manager how helpful she'd been.

While waiting for their flight to Kolokuana, he and Tsabo scanned a local newspaper and a headline caught their eye. It summed up Jack's precarious predicament pertinently: "New Model Coffin Going Down Well."

That cheap joke Tsabo instantly binned when he heard the disturbing news awaiting his return to his seminary digs. His former headmaster had had a stroke! He phoned St John's Mission first thing next morning, arranged to visit Father Patrick that evening, hot-footed it to Harry's cottage and asked if he might use the land-cruiser.

With Tsabo driving and the vufoils delivered to the pilot, Harry wondered where Jack was – probably still drunk in a Mavimbi police-cell. Perhaps he'd never intended to read out the script, Tsabo and Harry had drafted, at such a high-powered meeting, let alone try to answer questions about data he didn't understand on a dozen vufoils on a screen. With so much at stake, Suleiman ought to have insisted that he give the presentation. A lesson learnt for the future, if Jack had one.

Harry made up for missing his Saturday Gwato class by trying to master its amusing word order, grating repetition and many comma-emphases. He began with: 'I went there, every day, and I did this, before, and I did that, after, and I will do both again, now, also!'

To the east jagged high peaks, to the west the central and southern highlands were barely visible through a dust-layered heat haze. Traffic on the main tarred road had been much lighter than expected and it was too early to call on Father Patrick, he'd still be resting, so Tsabo suggested they visit an old haunt of his. Not waiting for a reply, he turned off the road just short of Mabela and headed east up a deeply rutted track strewn with rocks. The chassis bounced and shuddered, the engine surged powerfully, as the land-cruiser climbed ever higher and nearer a dome-shaped pinnacle. After two hour's hard going, the narrow track petered out and an even steeper path zigzagged its way upwards. Tsabo executed a heart-stopping multi-point turn, parked by a sharp bend in the track and went to add some stones to a large pile of stones supporting several small crosses. When back in the land-cruiser, he said: 'That's a shrine to lost riders. My father told me always to put stones on that pile, to bring me good luck, when I rode home or to Mabela . . . This is the nearest we can get to my village on four wheels.'

'We're well over eight thousand feet.' Harry indicated their exact position on his map.

Tsabo nodded, politely. 'I rode many times down that bridle path and down this track, then up them at the end of each term. It took me a day to reach Katama. The pass, just to the left of that pinnacle, is almost half way . . . . I'm afraid I've never been home since returning from Oxford . . . ' He lapsed into semi-hibernation.

Two thousand feet below Mabela nestled soundlessly at the bottom of a sheer cliff, the smoke from its cooking fires vertical in the fast-cooling air. All was so still, so odourless. Harry might have felt sanitised, but for the dust. It was everywhere, in his beard and hair, covering his shirt, shorts, socks and boots, on every exposed part of his body, irritating his eyes, nose and throat. Throughout the land-cruiser's laborious ascent it had thrown up clouds of the suffocating stuff. At least there were no flies this far up.

Facing the sinking sun, they overlooked a vast plain stretching far into the distance, with a wide meandering riverbed and the main tarred road they'd left behind. From such a superb vantage point they could trace upwards of thirty miles of shiny metalled twisting ribbon spanning deep ravines, dodging jutting escarpments, crossing barren land ravaged by drought, skirting communities threatened by famine.

'That main tarred road was built after I left school,' Tsabo explained. 'You may have seen bits of the old track on our way south. The journey from the capital to Mabela used to take ten hours, now it takes only three, but the number of accidents and fatalities have shot up alarmingly. Most people drive too fast and overtake dangerously in vehicles very often in bad shape.'

'I noticed.'

'Maize rarely flourishes out there on the Mabela plain and in the highlands. Yet my tribes-people keep trying to grow it, even though their crops too often fail. The last two failed disastrously. They ought to change to sorghum, it's more drought-resistant.'

'Springs and rivers dry, water levels getting lower in wells, boreholes and reservoirs.' Harry sounded like a desert nomad rehearsing a funereal dirge.

'You're right. For eighteen months women have trudged mile after mile, day after day out there, with empty containers on their heads, searching for water. If they find some, it most probably shouldn't be drunk. Every time I read or hear that word *typhoid*, I think of my loved ones and friends over those high peaks in Katama . . . What an unholy plight!'

While Harry tried to take it all in, his mind strayed from those current realities back to happier times when this spectacular panorama was various shades of green. It must have changed dramatically since Tsabo's school days. Now there were no trees or bushes, all burned as cooking fuel. Just unfenced, once arable, strip-fields in an untilled, unplanted wilderness. An ever decreasing number of scrawny animals roved waterless over-grazed rangelands, guarded by herd boys urged on by their elders to search for non-existent pasture. Hungry families prayed for rain, further punished by soaring inflation and by plunging livestock prices; unable to sell their surviving livestock or to buy unaffordable imported food. The situation was desperate throughout the south, the prospects bleak, extremely bleak to the cruellest power of "n" and precisely as Tsabo had said. An unholy plight!

Like the previous year and probably the next, that landscape was far too arid for any semblance of comfort or hope. Shimmering under a relentless sun by day. Frost-bitten by night. Harry knew that thunderstorms rarely occurred in winter. But why hadn't it rained last summer and the summer before? Was El Nino to blame or was the climate changing? Dusk, a full moon, stars close enough to touch and his turn to drive.

The diversion had made them late. After a hurried tour of St John's Mission, Tsabo and Harry were ushered by a nun along a stone-paved passage to an iron-hinged door with "Headmaster" neatly carved into the wood and "Do Not Disturb" in bold lettering on a used envelope hung on a nail.

'By the way, Father Patrick calls me Patrick, too, which can be confusing,' Tsabo warned.

The nun led them into a dimly lit room. Tsabo introduced Harry to an elderly giant in a faded brown cassock who struggled in vain to rise from his chair. The nun scolded him, wrapped a fallen blanket round his legs and took his temperature. It was normal. She told the visitors they must not tire her priest, and when she came back, they would have to go.

'The Sister told me you were coming Patrick. How are you my son?'

'How are you, Father? That's far more important.'

'Nothing a dose now and again of the old Jameson's won't put right, don't you know. But she found the bottle, luckily with most of the whisky unsampled which, very sadly, failed to survive. Now, tell me what you've been up to.'

Tsabo described his UN job, reminisced about his school days and the priest dug up a host of amusing anecdotes. His Irish way of telling them made them even more amusing. And he was, indeed, the white man who smiles.

In a break in their dialogue, Harry asked: 'What brought you to Africa, Father?'

'Many aspire to help the oppressed, the needy, the suffering, though so few get up and go. The Lord chose to send me here, to help teach His children.' He pressed his fingertips together and gazed into space. 'Sometimes, I ask myself what keeps me here? After close on forty years, endeavouring to fulfil the task He entrusted me with, I have only to look as far as Patrick there, then recall with equal pride and affection a host of young faces, full of hope and expectancy. I'll remain for as long as He and they want me to.'

The nun brought her priest his pills, double-checked them, filled his glass with water and hung around. It was time for the visitors to take their leave.

'I'll find another bottle, so drop by again,' Father Patrick whispered. 'Bottoms up,' his jovial voice rang out and raised his glass as if proposing a toast at a water-tasting beano.

'See you soon,' Harry promised.

'Best wishes Mr Harry and to your family Patrick. Go well my son.'

'Stay well Father.' Tsabo's voice betrayed his unrelieved anxiety.

He drove to the Mabela Hotel in silence and shut himself in his room, until Harry told him, through the keyhole, he must eat to live.

A silent supper companion, Tsabo did eventually speak. 'Father Patrick was always so robust and lively. Not frail and chair-bound! I hadn't the heart to tell him to retire and to enjoy a well earned rest. He might have thought I didn't appreciate all he'd done for me.'

'He most probably read your thoughts and explained why he's remaining in the job to ward off any suggestion of that kind. I understand your concern, though, but it be may be best to consult some of your nun friends before confronting the lion in his den. Anyway, how are you going to tackle your aunt?'

'I'll pay for the repairs, provided she lets my mother and Palima keep the place clean.'

'How about us organising a barbecue for the relief team and also inviting your mother and Palima? Harry suggested.

'Every one ot them deserves that . . . incidentally, a barbecue's called a braai here.'

Reckoning he ought to have known that, Harry asked: 'How's your father's leg?'

'Well on the mend and he's very happy to have a job.' With that, Tsabo retreated into his shell again.

They were lucky, Harry often said, to have Tsabo's father working with them. Fred, a respected, conscientious, good-natured man, only entered their bungalow to tend the coal fire in the L-shaped room. Every morning, he sat on the back door step sipping a mug of Fuzzy's steaming tea, then removed his crownless trilby and made up the fire, cooked mealie-meal and snatched some sleep in his shed. Every afternoon, he stoked the fire and inspected the office compound's fence. He could do no gardening during the winter, yet kept himself busy hoarding every scrap of waste paper, cardboard or wood he could find to burn on the fire, picking up litter, sweeping up dust, greeting people when they arrived, passing the time of day with them, waving farewell when they left. Every evening, he wrapped his blanket about him and patrolled the compound throughout the freezing night. Not much of a life for an erstwhile police sergeant and a gold mine's shift-foreman.

'Listen to this!' Tsabo blurted out. 'A girl attends an interview at the UN health office in Kolokuana. The African doctor will approve her application to attend a public health course, but only if she has sex with him. When he's told she's pregnant, he tries to cancel her course, does a flit, and his former secretary will sell the girl his new address for bags of money. When the girl's brother meets her in Mavimbi, he's shocked to discover she's a mother and she pleads with him not to tell her parents about her baby. Who is this girl? She's Dinea, my middle sister! . . . I'll find that sod, have no fear.'

Just once had Harry seen how angry Tsabo could get when he bawled out his aunt, but had never heard him swear. Tsabo's tone of voice had reflected his concern, respect and affection for Father Patrick. Now his eyes revealed such hatred and resentment that when he found that sod, it was unlikely he'd stop at giving him a piece of his mind.

Harry wanted to say, don't get involved, let the UN deal with the swine, but he knew what Tsabo's reaction would be. His would have been the same had his daughter been put in the family way by a rapist. Doctors were too few and far between in Africa, yet there was no room for that sordid blackmailer's ilk.

'Perhaps a quiet word with Suleiman is called for,' Harry suggested.

'I'll check Dinea's story first.'

Tsabo pushed his food away. 'Goodness knows how my eldest sister and her family are coping with this terrible drought. I've not heard from her and nor have our parents. After we'd flown over my village, I said how guilty I felt for not visiting her. Up in those mountains this afternoon, with Katama a day's walk away, my conscience kept urging me to go home. A day's walk away, that's all it was, though it seemed as far as Mars, just as Oxford had seemed light years from my village. I want to go there, and do everything in my power to help my relatives and friends, but never have time.'

'Make time Tsabo. Ride there tomorrow. I'll cover for you.'

Matashaba

When she was young, she washed Palima, her baby sister, and rocked the cot. Her father said God made her a mother. She slept on the family's mat next to Tsabo, before he went to the mission school. She hurried from the school across the gorge and worked with her mother in her field or in their rondavel. She helped her grandmother, every evening, to cook their family's mealie-meal. Dinea never walked with her, or helped their mother or their grandmother. She remembers her mother saying: 'Dinea thinks you try to be best, always. I will speak to your jealous sister, again.'

All her school reports said: 'Matashaba is a friendly and helpful girl who tries hard to learn.' One of her sister's reports said: 'Dinea is a pretty and clever girl who will go far.'

When their father came home from the mine, he read his children's reports and never said one was best, not even Tsabo's very good reports. Their father is a kind man.

Dinea is a nurse in Kolokuana. The only town she has seen is Mabela. She took Sekiso there and her kind husband bought her a blue blouse and skirt to wear at Tsabo's speech day. Dinea came by the bus and their father was angry to see Dinea's short white frock. Her shoes had high heels, her hair had long braids, her lips and nails were red. Dinea was angry, also, when their mother told her to wear Palima's blanket to hide the frock and her big breasts. Dinea wants to be a film star.

'What is a film star?' she asked. 'They are American words,' Dinea said.

She is one year older than Dinea and seven years older than Palima. They are tall with good small waists. She and her mother are short and fat, like many Obangwato women.

Palima came to her home after school to talk to her and laugh, always. She slept there, at weekends, when her husband was in the mountains, making and mending paths. She loves Palima, very much. She loves her husband very much, also, and hopes Sekiso will grow strong like his father. He has his uncle's fair skin. Maybe he will be tall and clever, also. Maybe Tsabo studies in England, still. He was nineteen, when he left home, and she was twenty-one. The good Lord gave Sekiso, one year after, a brother and sister. Tsabo and her parents have not seen the twins. Maybe Dinea will not be happy to see them.

Her husband was born in the village across the gorge and they lived there. No man in that village must marry a Kataman woman. Their marriage made much trouble. But when the twins came, most people in her husband's village made peace and spoke to her. They said twins were a good omen and made the evil tokolosi go away.

She cleaned the police-post, to earn a little money, to help feed her family. Her mother rode Pat, Tsabo's pony, from Katama, early every morning, and filled two gourds in the stream and looked after the children. When she fed her children, every evening, she saw her mother ride up from the gorge, back to Katama, and the smoke from her grandmother's fire, also.

Her husband's mother brought her and Sekiso mealie-meal, every evening. His mother rocked the twins in their cot and told her never to speak to their chief or his bad men.

The drought killed her husband's sheep, last year. Wild animals are late, also, or have gone north. But not the baboons. They steal food and water, and steal babies, sometimes. She is not scared of them, but she fears for her children. Her husband has four goats only, now. She ties them close by her door, at sunset, and she gives them some animal food her husband bought. Her dogs eat rats or other bad things, and they guard the goats, also.

She was happy before the two very dry summers came. Now, every morning, she looks for a cloud, but she never finds one. Maybe God will send clouds, very soon. This she hopes.

She has many happy memories, but some are not happy. She will never forget the fires burning the rondavels in Katama and the village across the gorge and the families with no homes, or the night a policeman came to her home in the village across the gorge.

'You are a Mashedi woman from Katama. Your father was in the police, before, and works in a mine, after. A message comes from Mabela, by the radio. Your father was hurt in the mine, one day before. I am sorry. He is in the hospital close by the mine, now.'

She wept, very long. The policeman found her husband, he was working close by. Her husband rode to Katama to tell her mother the black news and he rode to Mabela, after, to speak to the hospital, by the telephone. They said her father's leg was hurt, bad! They said, also, he would not walk for many weeks. Her husband told Dinea in Kolokuana, by the telephone. He said Dinea promised to tell Tsabo in England by the telephone, after.

She sat with her mother and Palima outside her hut, praying for help and asking God why this came to the very kind man. They looked for dust from a horse's hooves. Maybe it was her husband's horse. She will never forget how thankful they were to hear the news that took two days and so many miles of hard riding to get. The news was not good, but better than they thought. She will never forget her husband's great kindness and courage. Riding in the night is very hard and if people fall from a horse on the steep narrow path in the high peaks and are found, they are buried under stones and their name is written on a cross, there. She saw two big piles of stones with many crosses when she rode to Mabela.

The policeman came to her hut, again. He brought good news, now. He said her father will go to the hospital in Kolokuana by the bus, soon.

When the stream in the gorge had no more water, she stopped working at the police post and her husband's mother looked after her children. She climbed, then, to the high waterfall with her mother and other women, every day. When the spring dried up, there, they walked down the gorge and found water. People must never go near the border with the next country. Soldiers shouted at them, but they let them carry home water.

'This bad water will not brew beer, now," a man said, 'and beer will keep us well, all the days. This water will bring Ksolli, after, and if Ksolli and hunger come, together, they may kill us, after, and we must drink boiled water, only.' But the dung cooked their food! She and other women walked far, every day, and they found no dung, many days. Most animals were late, now.

She sees the kind men, still, with five sick women and a herd-boy tied to their backs riding to Mabela, and they rode back with six coffins, soon after. She hears her children, still, crying for food, and remembers thinking, if my breast milk stops, how will her twins stay strong, after? She remembers asking Jesus, every night, to wake her children, every morning, and to tell her husband where to buy seed to plant, if the rains come. The rains will come, one day. This she hopes. No, this she knows.

Her grandparents said their water and food must be given to her children, now, and they gave their rondavel to her and told her huband to save the money he paid for the hut across the gorge. Her grandparents lived with her mother and Palima, after.

Sitting in her grandparent's rondavel her eyes fill with tears. Her grandparents are late, now. Her father and Dinea came from Kolokuana. Their family and friends wore black neck-bands. The priest took them to the burial ground and they all prayed by the grave. They had nothing to thank God for the old people's great love, long life and peaceful rest.

Their father's leg hurt bad, still, and she told him he must stay in Katama.

'You have no doctor or nurse, close by,' Dinea said. 'Our father must stay, close by a doctor. Our mother and Palima must go to Kolokuana, also, and take him to the hospital, every week. Our mother will find work to pay for food and two rooms, and for Palima's school. If Tsabo comes from England he must help them, also. This drought is very bad, here, and it will stay very bad, many months. This I know.'

'Why are you right, always?' she asked Dinea. 'Maybe other people are right, also.'

She will never forget the morning her parents and Palima rode down into the gorge. She and Sekiso pray for them, every night, and hope they all stay well, now. Maybe they will come home, soon. Their rondavel waits. Her husband will post her letter in Mabela, but her hand shakes, now, and she will not ask him to write to her parents.

No maize plants grew in her family's field, last year, and this year, also. The gorge has no water, now, and more people of both clans have gone to Kolokuana. The last time her husband rode home he said chiefs ask too much money for clean water, even from people dying of thirst. He said some chiefs sell dirty water!

Men came to build a big tank close by the police post in the village across the gorge and many donkeys carry water from Mabela every week to fill the tank, again. She rides Pat there, every morning at sunrise, and is so happy to bring back a gourd of clean water.

A Red Cross woman came to ask the women of both clans questions about their fields and crops, livestock and pasture, their husbands' work and money. Katama's headman told his clan to give true answers. He said if they help the Red Cross, hungry people will get food. Jesus heard two of her prayers, and he will hear more, soon. This she hopes.

The calendar her kind husband bought in Mabela tells her he comes back from his new job, at the week's end. He has more money to buy water and food and medicines, now. Sekiso loves to have his father at home and loves Tsabo's pony, also. They ride together. Her husband said his food-for-work gang is making a track across the Mabela plain and she asked him why no track comes to Katama.

'You rode by the path over the high peaks, one time. No track will come that way. You walked down the gorge, many times, to get water. That way leads to the soldiers, guarding the border. If they make a track to Katama, maybe it will meet the road in the next country. If I am right, I will buy an old truck and you, my wife, will learn to drive.'

'You are very clever my husband and you will be the boss of all the tracks, soon. You will buy a *new* truck and I will drive our family to Kolokuana. Yes?'

He puts a hand on her big belly and feels the baby kicking. 'You will give me another strong son. This I know.'

'I will give you another pretty daughter. This I think.' They laugh and cuddle.

He rides down into the gorge, at sunrise, and up the other side. She waves many times.

When the priest rings his bell, the sun is high. With her twin son on her back and her twin daughter in her arms, she and Sekiso go to the café. Kneeling in the dust, close by, the priest blesses her and her children. He asks, always, if her family in Kolokuana and her brother in England stay well, but she never has answers.

Her children are sleeping, at sunset, when she sees a man try to open the door of her parent's rondavel. It is *Tsabo!* She runs to him. 'Tsabo I pray, every day, you will come. But I dream, now. This I think.'

With her head on his chest, he kisses her hair and he feels like the brother she cuddled when they were young. Holding hands, they walk down to their grandparent's rondavel where she and her family live, now. Maybe he knows their grandparents are late. He asks no questions. She blows on the fire and cooks mealie-meal and brews tea. She touches him, also. Yes, he is here, she is not dreaming. But how long will he stay? She brings him food in their grandmother's cooking pot and he drinks tea from their family's mug, after.

'You went from this place how many years, before, Tsabo?'

'Four years and one half, before. You have very much to tell me Matashaba. This I know.'

His sister obliges in full measure. Her's is a woeful story, his far briefer. He describes England and Oxford, his job and their parent's situation, careful not to cause her distress.

'Dinea stays well, also?' she asks.

'She is at a nurse's school in the next country, now.' Tsabo keeps her baby a secret.

'Her school report was true. Dinea is clever and will go far.'

'Our parents sent you many letters, and I sent many, also. They came to you, after?'

'The postman left the village across the gorge when this bad drought came. No letters come, after. Letters are not good. Speaking is much better. Tell our parents and Palima I love them, very much. Say my husband and our children love them, very much, also.'

'You are happy to stay in this place Matashaba?'

'My family is happy, still, but living is very hard, here. Many villagers are late. Many are hungry and thirsty, and many are sick, also. Many donkeys bring water from Mabela, every week, now. Maybe the Red Cross will bring food for people with no money, very soon. This all Katamans hope.'

'The system's starting to work,' Tsabo mutters to himself and then seeks the answer to a question he has dreaded asking. 'Is my pony late?'

'Pat is not late, Tsabo. He and the herd-boys will bring grass, tomorrow. This I think.'

'I must take water for the horse I ride from Mabela. It eats food from a nose-bag, now, and is tied to a rock close by our parent's rondavel. Will it stay safe this night, there?'

'Tie the horse to the post close by this rondavel Tsabo. My goats are tied there, also. I will give the horse water and my dogs will guard all of them.'

After fetching the horse, he unties two sacks from its saddle. 'I bring you maize-grain and dried beans Matashaba.'

'Thank you, thank you, Tsabo. I will give some to the hungry Kataman children, after.

Tsabo kisses three sleeping children lightly on their foreheads – then in the moonlight strolls past the corral where only familiar smells linger. His father's cows used to be kept there, he'd often milked them. Had they survived this ravenous drought, they'd now think him a stranger, ignore him and continue chewing the cud, if they had any to chew.

'Is this the place I vowed never to leave?' he asks the same tall aloe plants, the same huge boulders poised as if to roll and crush all within their path. Before moving on, his thoughts fly back to Oxford, so full of jollity and gravity, though sometimes too full of its own importance. He digs deep in his memory bank for the opening lines of a poem which spelt out so poignantly how he felt, far away from all he held dear. "Breathes there a man, with soul so dead, who never to himself hath said, this is my own, my native land. Whose heart hath ne'er within him burned, as home his footsteps he hath turned, from wandering on a foreign soil."

Tsabo's footsteps now turn towards the rondavel he knows so well. Stretched out on the mat he'd slept on countless times, his body unused to a hard day's ride and an unyielding floor, the wooden rafters supporting ageing thatch haven't changed. Nor has Matashaba, but his village certainly has.

He hears the rondavel door unlocked and shielding his eyes from the blinding sunlight flooding in through the opened door, he greets his sister and a young boy shyly peeps at him round his mother's long skirt.

'Peace be with you Sekiso. How many years come to you?'

'Five years come to me, close by Christmas, uncle.'

'You are rested, now, Tsabo?' his sister asks.

'I said last night, Matashaba, I will ride to the village across the gorge and bring you water. But the ride from Mabela makes me sleep long and makes my body stiff, also.'

That makes her laugh.'The sleeping mat makes your body stiff, not the horse. A herd boy brought me water, at sunrise. You will eat mealie-meal and drink tea, now?'

'We will all eat and drink, now. And Sekiso will take me to my pony, after. Yes?'

'Wait uncle.' Sekiso scurries out and in a flash Pat is standing in the doorway, tossing a tousled head and snuffling an excited greeting.

'Oh my God!' Tsabo leaps up, flings his arms around Pat's neck, and an unforgettable muzzle rummages under a memorable armpit.

Sekiso claps his hands. His mother's hands try to hide her tears when she gives Pat the remnants of the previous evening's mealie-meal, just like her grandmother used to do.

Sekiso leads his uncle to the burial ground with Pat ambling beside them. Standing by his grandparent's grave, Tsabo notices six wooden crosses with "*Ksolli Inga-ku*"* written below the names, amongst them Mueketso's! Tsabo's body freezes, transfixed with shock and grief. As boys, they had played together most days, as teenagers had ridden together. He remembers Mueketso's pride at being a skilful herd-boy, his desire to become a man, his taunts because Tsabo had never been to initiation school or circumcised. Remembers their undying friendship. He kneels in prayer. 'Rest in peace beneath these parched rocks, Mueketso, and stay close to my dear grandparents, forever.' He crosses himself.

Cheered up by Sekiso's constant chirping and Pat's faithful company, Tsabo tours the village, chats with the headman and other friends. He spends the rest of the day with his sister and her children. She tells him she will have a new baby, soon. He'd noticed.

Before sleeping, he writes a note, offering to pay for Sekiso's schooling at St John's and enclosing money for her, the children

---

*   Died of Tyhoid.

and some for his precious pony. Pat's mane is no longer black and silky, just grey and spiky. Ribs show through his brown skin, once so smooth and shiny, now dull and withered. Grievously, his days are numbered.

At dawn he kisses the twins, still asleep in their cot, summons the strength to bid his dejected pony farewell, gives Sekiso's hand a manly shake and hugs Matashaba.

'When will you come home, again, Tsabo?' His sister clings to him.

'Stay well' is all he can muster, then mounts the horse and rides away, waving but not daring to look back. So powerful is the tug of loved ones, especially those in adversity.

'Go well Tsabo,' he hears his sister repeating until her voice fades.

She had insisted that two herd-boys ride with him. While following them down the twisting path, climbing to the far rim, and passing by the village across the gorge, he has much to ponder over: Matashaba's moving account of their father's homecoming; their grandparent's last days and funeral; their parent's and Palima's sad departure from their treasured home. The villagers' mass exodus. Mueketso's typhoid! Donkeys that keep the water tank full. The Red Cross food survey. His brother-in-law's food-for-work job. His brave sister's and her husband's determination to see out such a deadly, crippling drought and to keep their fast-growing family's home in Katama. That was what she had told him, but what else could she have said. She looked well, had lost a lot of weight, but her hands shook, most probably caused by worrying about no end of things. Even so, she and her family, as well as most of his friends had survived. His grandparents had died through old age, but Mueketso would have enjoyed so many years as the local farrier.

At the top of the pass over the high peaks they water and feed the horse and the herd-boy's ponies before they drink water from the gourd. They put stones on the shrine to lost riders and do likewise on the shrine near the sharp bend in the track, far above Mabela.

He and his family had prayed here, after that life-changing Speech Day. Three days ago, he and Harry had sat in the land-cruiser here. Its tyre-marks are still in the dust.

Father Patrick had retired for the night. The nuns are only too willing to cook Tsabo supper and provide a bed. Most of them he has known for years. When he takes them into his confidence – they adore secrets – countenancing their much-loved priest retiring is way beyond their contemplation and acceptance. Sister Marie Louise, his very first teacher at the mission school, takes him aside and says permanent retreat is what their priest needs, deserves and must have. In a packed minibus taxi, carreering north along the main tarred road, he decides to speak to the archbishop who more than four years ago had kindly lent him his raincoat, in case it rained in England! When returned to its benevolent owner, his eminence had hung it on the same holy hook – until it rains in Kolokuana. The raincoat is still there, pleading to be worn.

'We are all very concerned,' the archbishop assures Tsabo. 'But Father Patrick will know when it is time to hand over the reins at St John's. To do otherwise is bound to cause such a dedicated priest and diligent headmaster undue offence.'

Tsabo returns to the office feeling more at ease with himself, even though Katama's problems and those of his sister, her family and their friends are only partially solved. He has to accept that the dire conditions in which they are struggling to survive are no more punishing than those experienced by far too many Obangwatos. Finally coming to terms with this strengthens his resolve to help put an end to the drought catastrophe as soon as practicable, and also to help insure against a recurrence. Being called to the bar can wait.

Matashaba had so much to tell her husband about Tsabo and all the money he gives to their family and Pat. She will ask her husband to buy two bags of horse meal for Pat. When he rides home, at the next month end, Sekiso sees him, first, and he runs to greet him.

'Yes, Father. Uncle Tsabo stays well and he is very tall,' she hears their firstborn say. 'Maybe I will go to a big school in Mabela when seven years come to me. This my uncle hopes. This I hope, also.'

Tackling Apathy

Just two solitary hilltops pierced the dense, refrigerated fog blanketing Kolokuana.* On one, the police radio pylon resembled the mast of a vessel lying at anchor; the flat roof of Suleiman's office, a lighter moored alongside. On the other, a mile or so to the west, the president's palace perched, majestically; the army barracks and public cemetery sprawled across its nearest slope. Below them, the drought relief team's bungalow glistening white in the early morning sun. The first frost of winter greeted Harry's fourth Monday in a part of Africa he'd been daft to assume, before leaving home, would be semi-tropical.

Gathered round the land-cruiser the women welcomed him back from Mavimbi, their faces betraying the question on the tips of their tongues – what did he buy us there? So, conforming to local custom he dispensed presents. A hand-bag-calculator for Pinkie, the meticulous accountant. A perfume miniature for Muella, the curvaceous young secretary. A colourful headscarf for Fuzzy, the cleaner with unruly hair. A book on journalism for Glen, the budding press and information officer. A brand new trilby for Fred, the security guard, to replace his crown-less antique. A flashy tie for Speedy, the driver, who said he couldn't wear it with his T-shirt, but he and all the others thanked Harry for their present. Before long, though, Fred asked him: 'Where is Tsabo?' When told he rode to Katama, Fred's smile rapidly faded. 'Why he not take me, also, Mr Harry?'

Not until his son had assured him later that week that Matashaba and her family were well and happy to stay in Katama, would Fred's smile return. The grim details Tsabo kept for Harry and Glen. Although donkeys delivering water once every week and villagers registered for food were heartening signs that two relief measures were having the desired effect, many more were urgently required.

---

*   Page 56. The sketch-map of Kolokuana.

Harry alerted the Red Cross and all five UN agencies based in the capital, but no senior government officials who'd let him enter their palatial offices, agreed to discuss the emergency without Jack being there.

A fortnight later, his whereabouts were still unknown and to have contacted his wife would have blown the gaffe. If asked where he was, Tsabo and Harry said all the country-team leaders had remained in Mavimbi for further briefings. But Harry must have trotted out what seemed an authentic alibi once too often and Glen rumbled him.

'Didn't Jack present the appeal for donor assistance in London, then.'

'Change of plan,' grunted Harry, sifting through the previous week's mail.

Friends had kept him in the hotel bar after the workshop and they forgot to remind him to go to Mavimbi Airport. But Jack didn't say where he'd been since. He probably couldn't remember. That he'd reappeared the very morning Mr Mboko returned from London was no fluke. The local police had found Jack, taken him to the finance ministry and Mboko had given him one hour to prepare a progress report on every aspect of drought relief.

Being asked about what he had or hadn't done, invariably threw Jack into a tantrum. Was it because he objected to the effrontery, the exposure, or the inconvenience? Or had getting pissed out of his pesky little mind, missing the flight to Heathrow and nearly scuttling the country's aid requests become second nature? Shoving all that in his mental pending tray, Harry set about typing the "speaking notes" Jack had demanded.

Mr Mboko began by asserting, a touch pompously, that it was his presentation, in a drunkard's absence, which had secured the international donor community's pledges of food aid in exactly the quantities he'd requested.' Suleiman had given the presentation!

'What about all the other things you asked for?' was Jack's deflating riposte.

Suleiman replied. 'Donors already assisting your country minister, will adjust their aid programmes and will give precedence to drought relief. The majority of water, health and agriculture bids will be met in this way. Your government may also wish to contribute,' he suggested, endeavouring not to sound too over-optimistic.

The time had arrived for the progress report. Jack removed his spectacles and read out the speaking notes, which explained how the workshops in Kolokuana, then in Mavimbi, also the district visits by helicopter, would assist drought relief. Food registration should be completed by the end of this month. Looking up from his crib, Jack said: 'If you don't pay the Red Cross for registering all those starving Obangwatos, they won't need food.'

Mr Mboko accused the Red Cross of blackmail, sabotage, and much else. Before Jack could dig himself an even deeper grave, Harry read out the rest of the speaking notes.

'We have four recommendations minister. First, assess drought victims' needs in order to prioritise relief. Second, release government food reserves and offer a realistic price for the northern province's surplus food, so that distribution can start as soon as registration is completed. It will take time for donations to arrive from overseas. Third, transport water from the north to bolster reservoir holdings in the south. And fourth, set up small working groups in the capital to assist with planning, co-ordinating and improving relief. A timely, successful humanitarian search and rescue operation will only be achievable, however, if sufficient government money is on the table.'

The table was flooded with ministerial coffee, conveniently drowning Harry's proviso. Two non-ministerial handkerchiefs swiftly became mops. Jack just sat there and smirked.

'Once relief requirements have been assessed,' Harry resumed, 'a national plan will be drafted. When you have approved the plan and also allocated the resources to implement it, minister, relief operations will start and continue for as long as necessary.'

'I like *national plans*,' Mr Mboko enthused, though the water, agriculture and health ministries know what's required. They've already got all the information.'

'No they haven't! Need assessment surveys are essential!' spluttered Jack, having told Harry during the relief team's first meeting that the surveys were time-wasting rigmarole.

The minister either hadn't heard what Jack said, or had ignored it. 'Doing surveys in the southern province would be very difficult. There are so many cut-off people up there.'

'The Red Cross is coping,' Jack mumbled, too audibly.

The minister eased his bulk from his long-suffering chair, ponderously manoeuvred it to the front of his desk and proceeded to address Jack with disdainful acerbity.

'Who do you work for? Me? Somebody else? Or nobody?' He paused for effect. 'I have established a new cabinet committee, the drought relief ministerial task force. You, Mr Tsamanachimone, are to brief it on progress every month and you are to brief me, in my capacity as its chairman, more frequently.'

In the far cooler temperature outside, Harry asked if key civil servants involved with relief would be present at the task force meetings. No reaction from Suleiman, apart from a polite form of Arab wait-and-see gesture. None from Jack, either, but when back behind his desk, his mood abruptly swung from seething anger to scalding retaliation.

'That finance minister is only interested in our many problems because he wants to get re-elected and get even with my youngest brother. They've fought ever since they were at Kolokuana University. Now he's dreamt up that task force, to get at me.'

'The task force must be regularly updated,' Harry replied, 'to enable its members to oversee relief, as well as to exercise their right to make or change policy. We must also report to a top-level official. Access to the finance minister may be handy for us, but it's bound to antagonise the government's chief secretary and the permanent secretaries of ministries. They must attend task force meetings. To marginalise them would be fatal.'

'We haven't got time to keep on going to meetings which achieve nothing and writing minutes nobody reads. I've heard that the chief secretary and permanent secretaries have decided to ignore the emergency unless we're transferred to a ministry.'

'Which one?' Harry asked. 'We'll have to work with most of them.'

'We don't fit into any ministry and I won't report to the chief secretary. He used to be my deputy and we never got on.'

'This is *crazy!* The task force will be a waste of time, the finance minister and your brother fight, and you and the chief secretary never got on. Who should we report to?'

'To that minister, like he said.'

'I'm not disputing what he said. But we must also report to a senior official, who is readily available to direct and supervise two equal counterparts, and to support us when we need supporting. The minister in charge of finance, who also runs the country, might not have enough time to support us.'

'I know the Mboko man,' Jack smirked. 'He agrees something and then says he didn't. Write the minutes of that shambles we've just been to.'

'Instead of minutes, which you think nobody reads, I'll type a summary of decisions. You may even have time to read it yourself.' They grimly shook hands.

'What makes Mr Mboko tick?' Harry's diary queried. 'Tsabo believes he's nothing more than a puffed-up tyrant, who tramples on anyone in his way, who enjoys being seen as the all-powerful saviour of a nation in dire adversity, and a peddler of half-baked ideas. In a guarded moment, Suleiman had said Mboko's the best of a non-descript bunch of cabinet ministers. A local newspaper had alleged that 'Gang-Bang Mboko' is a womaniser who boasts about his conquests; an accompanying shot of him with his office cleaner's two teenage daughters proved that all the rumours were true. It was also claimed that men who have sex with his girlfriends are tortured and then disappear. The other local paper accused its competitor of lying. Their bicker is now sub-judice. Despite media gossip and all the character-assassination that goes with high office, Emmanuel Mboko is arrogant, abrasive and possibly over-sexed; he's also combative, spooky and could be interesting to work with. Only time will tell!' Harry closed his laptop, locked it in his desk drawer and always kept it in his cottage after work.

A visitor inquired if it were possible to speak to the boss. Assuming she meant him, Jack hid in the toilet, probably to rue his run of bad luck, contemplate his tiny navel and re-gird his little loins. The BBC correspondent – the spitting image of a frightfully charming Margaret Rutherford in her heyday, all tweeds and straw hat – strode in and proceeded to ooze eccentric bluster, feigned confusion and chortling humour. Her exclamations "Oh, how bloodsome!" Glen found especially puzzling. Having mastered the facts surrounding the emergency, she leant out of a window, coo-eed to her driver and asked him to bring in "the gear." Harry said his government counterpart must feature in an interview that may subsequently be broadcast, before ushering her and the gear along the passage and into Jack's room. Horrified to be confronted by an intimidating female, he became seriously twitchy when realising she was recording his guessed answers to her difficult questions.

That evening's World Service news, beamed to every corner of the globe, featured a communiqué from Kolokuana, which began with the lady hooting at the hash she'd made of pronouncing his "terribly tricky name" rapidly followed by "call me Jack." His inputs were more than slightly confusing – hers a professional appraisal of how things were, or how they appeared to be. She concluded the interview by saying: 'In the south of this country, far too many people are dying for want of clean water, decent sanitation, enough food, medicines, proper nursing care and hospital treatment. It is now a race against time to keep them and their livestock alive. Donor aid is on the way, and much more is due to follow, yet innumerable problems still need solving. I shall report, again, once I've seen how the rest of this drought-assaulted region of Africa is faring.'

The national media had shown scant interest in relief plans and proposed measures. Yet that wasn't the only reason why Glen's first press conference had failed to attract customers. Intense media interest now focused on the Japanese businessmen who wanted to know how they might assist the country. Jack refused to talk to 'chinks' – then, just as Tsabo and Harry were leaving to meet the visitors, they were called to Suleiman's office. So, Glen glumly drew the short straw, the sole remaining straw, and slunk back several hours later looking even glummer.

'Do you want the bad news first?' he lamented.

'Fire away.' Harry was prepared for the worst, after that session with Suleiman.

'The chief secretary said, because Japanese people are very keen on African holidays, their businessmen's money must be spent on promoting tourism and building nice hotels. Our proposal to build small dams throughout the southern province would take years to achieve. I said work must start now, in case it rains, but he disagreed.'

'That's shameful. Why the hell didn't Jack go?'

Harry knew the answer as soon as he asked the question. Jack hadn't gone because his arch-enemy, the chief secretary, would be there. Yet Glen might well have been offended by the insinuation that had Jack gone, the outcome would have been different.

'I wasn't criticising you, Glen. You did your best. What's the good news?'

'At last, our telephones and fax machine work.'

It was Suleiman's first visit to the drought relief office. Fuzzy made him a mug of tea and after Pinkie had shown him round the bungalow, he asked to speak with Jack and Harry in private. Tsabo grimaced at Harry – both had prophesied fireworks.

'At our meeting with the finance minister,' Suleiman began in his gravest tone, 'you claimed, Mr Tsamanachimone, that the Red Cross had threatened not to start distributing food until reimbursed for registering drought victims.'

'It was a warning. Not a threat.'

'Whatever it was has regrettably resulted, to cut a lengthy and very painful story short, in the Red Cross operations officer resigning. Mr Mboko said Harry should stand in, but I managed to convince him that Harry is responsible, with yourself, for planning and co-ordinating *all* relief activities. In the end, I was pressurised into agreeing with the local Red Cross director that Tsabo should be appointed.'

'So you're paying me back for asking that question at the Mavimbi workshop,' Jack bawled, quivering with anger. 'You give me Glen and you take away Tsabo. Dirty tricks, that's what you're up to. Tsabo's *not going!*'

'It will be greatly to our mutual advantage to have Tsabo managing Red Cross relief operations.'

Before leaving Suleiman thanked everybody in the relief team for helping to save the lives of many thousands of drought-stricken people and their remaining livestock.

He told Harry afterwards: 'Blame me for agreeing to Tsamana-chimone becoming your counterpart. Don't let him loose with a microphone, again, nor be interviewed for world-wide consumption. I could have also done without having to placate my local senior UN food, childcare, health and agricultural colleagues. They objected to that excellent BBC correspondent's failure to mention their, dare I say meagre, relief contributions.'

Although reluctant to change employment, Tsabo's new contract matched his plan to postpone qualifying as a barrister. He would also be working with the local Red Cross society's director, whom he admired, while keeping in close touch with his father, Harry and Glen. Jack's obstructive attitude and truculent manner would *not* be missed!

Red Cross headquarters, housed in a dingy attic above a main street shop, was now Tsabo's base; emergency food distribution throughout the south his responsibility; water supply and sanitation his mounting concern. But the chance to acquire Japanese money to build dams had been recklessly squandered! Where would the money come from, now? This question he asked Harry at their first Friday afternoon get-together.

'Suleiman's taken up the cudgels,' Harry optimistically replied. 'By the way, when we flew over the northern province there were dams everywhere, yet we saw precious few in the south. Is it because your tribe has lacked the resources and skills to build them?'

'Able-bodied men have always had to find employment elsewhere. Another reason is, Obangwatos tell their children dam-water may give them Ksolli, that's Gwato for chronic diarrhoea and typhoid. This worst of all droughts proves the urgency to teach everybody how to check that dam-water is safe to drink, or if it isn't, how to make it safe.'

'The trainers being trained to work simple test kits, will then train community water-minders. We must hope it works.' Harry hesitated. 'It's impossible to make anything work properly here. Jack and I, for instance, are caught up in a farcical wrangle between the finance minister and senior civil servants over who controls relief. Why all this acrimony and petty rivalry when there's so much to be done and scarcely time in which to do it?'

'I'm not surprised. Certain powers-that-be would prefer you to fail. They would *hate* Jack to succeed.'

That shook Harry and it also rang a loud bell. When they'd visited Tsabo's aunt, he'd condemned the vast majority of his tribes-people for doing their utmost to ruin those who were or tried to be enterprising. Harry now realised he was being cautioned.

'You mentioned on the way back from your aunt's place the poisoned dwarfs that get on people's backs and thwart their best intentions. What did you call them?'

'Tokolosi. Why the sudden interest?'

'I've got one on my flaming back. Take me to Happy Hour.'

No good moping, Harry reckoned, climbing into Tsabo's Red Cross truck. Nor could he pack up and go home. The British weather, skirt lengths and share prices fluctuated, though so did morale. When his spirits sank, he had to remind himself that he was embarked, of his own free will, on a frustrating crusade. Yet, only by striving to integrate all relief agencies within a single, responsive structure with clear, agreed channels of control and reporting, plus the rest, would timely aid stand a chance of reaching its destination, all the drought victims. But how many are there, where are they, and what do they need most?

By the time he and Tsabo reached *their* destination, the UN club, that familiar voice inside his head was listing his weekend tasks: type background notes, propose guidelines aimed at achieving immediate objectives, and then discuss them with Suleiman. Leave preparing a national relief plan until your guidelines have been thoroughly tried and tested. Harry nodded, vigorously, prompting

Tsabo to cast a quizzical eye over his passenger. The pressure was starting to tell on Harry, as well as on himself. Also, the gulf between what had to be done and how to make it all happen, rapidly and effectively, threatened to widen still farther. Now he was nodding, though Harry was too deep in thought to notice.

The pool table's cloth was tricky. Its holes were repaired with sticky-tape. Professional players would have aimed-off when making shots. Imagine the outcome lesser exponents achieved, when most of the Friday night pool gang were novices – only the Russian air traffic controller, in self-estimation, came near to achieving perfection. Now and again, Tsabo pulled off an astonishing shot that onlookers dismissed as beginner's luck. Being a Virgoan, Harry sought perfection, unpretentiously he thought, and liked others to think. His desire, always to win, demonstrated how his strong competitive streak could produce classy results. He was working on his consistency! Fozz, the Foster's sinker from down-under, relied on the F-word to divert attention from his constant howlers. He and Harry were locked in combat when two African strangers sloped in. Mkwere, stocky and in his thirties, introduced himself, but not the sullen young giant with him. Mkwere said they'd recently joined the club and had driven all day to play pool. Other than that, they drank only lemonade and left immediately after taking on each other, twice running.

Fozz had seen them up in the mountains near Mabela. He'd been told that Mkwere might be a prospector and the youngster his bodyguard. But, to Harry's disappointment, Fozz knew nothing about a mining concession.

Tsabo kept his mouth firmly shut. The name, Mkwere, had been underlined in a recent fax from his former Oxford tutor. Having decoded the fax, before burning it, Tsabo had memorised its contents: "My cousin Harry remains hell bent on finding our grandfather's grave which is near some old mine workings in the southern province. A London firm has tasked an East African, known as Mkwere, to find out who has re-opened the mine. Tell Harry only a convincing minimum, you are aware of the dangers. Vigilante, gardo, ordo."

Tsabo complied later that evening, in the privacy of Harry's cottage.

'When diamonds were discovered about ninety years ago, a cartel closed the mine and fairly recently it was re-opened. Before you arrived, the UN objected to helping a country with untapped wealth which cabinet ministers, here, dismissed out of hand. It's all kept securely under wraps. However, if my reliable sources are anything to go by, people we'd never suspect are up to their necks in a diamond scam, or can't wait to get in on the act.'

'My grandfather may have died while prospecting in Africa, hopefully in this country, and I'd like to find out whether there's a grave. Whereabouts is the mine?'

'I don't know. But what I do know is that, if you go snooping around, things could get rough . . . very rough!'

Harry's diaries, faxed weekly to Dermot in Oxford, never mentioned the mine again, but he remained determined to find it and also their grandfather's grave, if there was one.

He then asked if I minded receiving the diaries monthly, due to pressure of work, and whether they contained too much detail. 'No to both questions!' I faxed back. 'Monthly is fine and "details" are what prospective disaster managers *need!* Belinda's in good shape, whoops, in good form and misses you in spades. Must rush, all the best, Dermot.'

I was about to drive to Heathrow, then fly to West Africa where rebels continued to trade diamonds, other minerals and timber to buy weapons. Efforts to stop this had so far been stymied by the United Nations' inability to agree sanctions, even though proven evidence existed of terrorism and murder sprees. Governments and NGOs had launched campaigns protesting against 'blood' diamonds that reputable traders said tarnished their image and reduced sales. They and the World Diamond Council hoped to introduce a system of certificates that is supposed to create a paper-trail from mine to retailer but may well encourage forgery and bribery. Meanwhile, a powerful diamond cartel has placed an embargo on all new and re-opened diamond mines to protect its profits and shareholders' investments, even though seven drought-stricken African countries, some with untapped riches, desperately needed money for drought relief. While conflicting vested interests played a selfish form of tug o'war, the embargo continued to be circumvented by various means. I aimed to leave West Africa with signed government pledges to enforce existing legislation fairly yet firmly in every case, including the prosecution and imprisonment of criminals found to be implicated in far too many blood diamond scams.

Onward then to Mavimbi, where the British ambassador had laid on a security-cleared helicopter pilot to fly me to the re-opened mine near Katama and I spent the day with the manager, Mkwere. Back in April, after white mercenaries attacked the mine, I had a hair-raising ride over the high peaks to Mabela's hospital, hoping to arrive there before the captured mercenary died – I failed! Two days later, none of four more captives spilled the beans. Soldiers still guarded the mine and patrolled the area. Mkwere's concerns, which I shared were: 'Who in Kolokuana controls the mine he manages? Who is financially benefitting from the mine's increasing diamond production? Are more white mercenary attacks expected? Are attacks likely by Afrikaner extremists seeking funds to help thwart Nelson Mandela's approaching election as South Africa's first black president?'

That evening the British police adviser in Kolokuana unconvincingly assured me that he shared these concerns. They were also shared by the British high commissioner there, the British ambassador in Mavimbi and my undisclosibly located handlers.

Grandpa Africa

Once a handful of intrepid explorers had enlightened darkest Africa, speculators by the hundreds flocked to illuminate its untold treasures. The Nile's elusive sources had been discovered, precious stones were being uncovered, and there was even talk of building a Cape-to-Cairo railway. Somewhere, maybe over the next horizon, shone El Dorado.

So it was that a discharged cavalry subaltern had ridden from embattled Mafeking, in search of a fortune – unaware that the butler's daughter who lived near his father's Ulster estate had borne his son, that grieving relatives and friends mourned his death.

Donal Henry Burke became a name on a cenotaph when he had, in fact, joined another lice-infested ruffian, hacking at rocks and sifting grit from dawn until dusk. Then, like so many of his kind, disease took its toll and he never found El Dorado.

Shortly before the outbreak of war, in 1914, his father received a redirected envelope containing an unsigned note written in pencil, obviously with a shaking hand, that briefly described Donal's sojourn in life's departure lounge ending with the words: 'I buried him in the grave beside my own, two weeks ride west of Mavimbi, near our mine workings in a gorge with high mountains and wide plain beyond.'

During World War II Donal's son happened to dock his flying boat at Mavimbi, and while repairs were carried out, he hitched a lift in an aircraft, hired a horse and searched for the graves. When he and his crew were lost at sea, his infant son inherited the family mystery. Henry, named after his grandfather, on going down from Oxford became Harry. It sounded more manly.

Soon after retiring, Harry had come across the note amongst his late mother's papers and spent several months combing mining company records, studying geological reports, poring over maps; all to no avail. He may now be one step nearer solving the mystery and once again read the directions that would hopefully lead to his grandfather's grave. The wide plain, possibly the Mabela plain, would have been be about two week's ride west of Mavimbi and was encircled by high mountains and gorges, but combing them would take a lifetime. Still, it was a start . . .

He switched on the gas cylinder outside the cottage's back door, ignited the single-ring stove and inadequate heater, extracted the last portion of that week's all-in stew from the fridge's icebox and rejuvenated supper. While forcing it down, clad in his fleece-lined parka with several layers beneath, he mulled over a grave-locating strategy, then opened his lap-top and typed the heading of some background notes.

Drought Relief Requirements in the Southern Province

'Near to a million people may be drought-afflicted, with one person in three vulnerable to starvation in worst-hit areas. Apart from the majority of younger men employed outside this country, it is estimated that more than half the remaining work force has no paid job.'

'Most households grew their own food until the current crisis made subsistence farming untenable. A second consecutive maize crop failure, the inability of better-off families to help their needy neighbours, steepling inflation and a collapsed livestock market all exacerbate the plight of resource-less Obangwatos. They can neither afford to buy food nor sell their animals to get money to feed themselves. A vicious, countervailing circle! Any crops that have withstood such severe, prolonged drought may still be destroyed by winter frost and hail. Moreover, the rapid storm-water run-off at high altitudes can savage steep fields, intensify erosion and further degrade soil quality. Since arable land and pasture are very scarce in the south, without donor aid the local food problems will most likely escalate.'

'Water sources barely meet the needs of an ever increasing population even at the best of times. After sixteen months of the lowest rainfall in seventy years, supplies have failed or may soon do so. During this winter, occasional storm could bring brief bursts of rain, possibly snow in the highlands. Sub-zero nights will make those weakened by sickness, hunger and thirst susceptible to hypothermia. Throughout next summer, the wet season from October to April, international weather centres forecast unchanged cloudless skies and abnormally high temperatures.'

'The emergency is scheduled to end after next May's maize harvest. If, as predicted, crop yields are minimal and/or drought-induced water and health problems are not solved by then, relief operations will have to be extended and more donor aid may be required. We should accept the likelihood of this happening and plan accordingly.'

'The drought's adverse affects are being compounded month-on-month, year-on-year, yet the government may excessively rely on the Red Cross, other NGOs and local voluntary bodies to supervise, as well as dispense, relief which could compromise accountability should the system break down or prove inadequate. The government must take the lead, must bear the largest share of the relief load, and must actively monitor and improve internal emergency activities. Combating a catastrophe of such weighty, though as yet un-assessed, proportions will also need substantial UN and donor assistance. It will test everyone's resolve and demands collective, both internal and external, remedies.'

'Delivering remedies could be far from easy, however, since many Obangwatos live in isolated settlements where bridle paths, but few motorable tracks and hardly any radios or telephones, make tenuous communications slow and arduous. Logistics are also certain to pose formidable challenges, particularly transporting and portering water – assuming that enough four-wheel-drive bowsers and donkeys are available. Nonetheless, donors expect their aid to reach every entitled person, as soon after it arrives in the country as feasible. Moreover, donors insist on their aid being used solely to alleviate drought, even though it may well be impracticable to differentiate between the temporary (sic) affects of drought and the permanent impact of widespread, endemic malnutrition and poverty. Most people living in the southern province evidently fall into both categories.'

Closing his lap-top, he considered the notes an essential starting point, but they conveyed not an ounce of succour to the multitude of defenceless beings most probably shivering in their huts. His two healthy grandchildren, tucked up in warm beds had never been thirsty, hungry or seriously ill, nor were their wardrobes ever empty.

Circumstances were very different for the majority of people living in the mountains, valleys, gorges and plains of the drought-molested south. Fiercely proud, though always appreciative of help, they were part of a tribal society of diminishing resolution, clinging desperately to the slippery slope of over-dependence on external aid. Yet, when donors responded, academics bereft of practical experience accused them of aid paternalism. Our drought victims were mercifully oblivious to such patronising jargon and to its professed merit. In their case outside aid was a legitimate necessity and aid was a right all genuinely needy people deserved – a right also requiring them to help themselves – unachievable when thousands clung to their tortured lives by a thread, while their waterless means of existence disappeared, while their loved ones and irreplaceable livestock perished.

Dependence on external assistance deprived people of their self-reliance and dignity, too many pundits said, yet the suffering and bereaved were hardly likely to worry about losing their self-reliance and dignity, when disaster resulted in tragedy, or crippling loss of livelihood, or both. Their primary concern would be how to survive and recover – not to question where their means of survival and recovery had come from!

But what was this nation doing to help itself? Why wasn't the drought-less, relatively wealthy, northern Kasodi tribe helping so many drought and poverty stricken, southern Obangwatos? Army and police manpower, transport, equipment and radios must also be utilised. Moreover, if Kolokuana's too few reservoirs were not upgraded now, its ever-increasing population's water supplies might fail – not might, *would* fail! And what was the government doing about that?

Struggling free of all his layers of clothing, he remembered Belinda asking in a letter: 'Why don't people living in the south grow suitable crops, sell them and thus earn money to tide them over such a terrible calamity? Trade is always better than aid.'

He'd replied: 'They exported wool and mohair before drought struck. Now, ironically, umbrellas are their sole exports and even in the good years they have to import food.'

Lying in bed, he read: "Africa is as unique as its culture, both too easily misconstrued. Only by living hugger-mugger with its people, and sharing their tribulations, can visitors begin to understand them." What had he learned about the locals? Most existed from day to day. Even Jack, with a degree in communist economics saw no farther than his pebble-lenses. He and many others were loath to look ahead and prepare for the worst that all too often happened. And when disaster struck yet again, they would request the Almighty, in whom they had undying faith, instilled long ago by old-fashioned donors, to send help from new-fashioned donors, the wealthy foreigners who had so much, when most of them had next to nothing. It all became a nightmare . . . .

The clock/radio blared the six o'clock BBC World Service News. His nether region demanded quick release from the blankets, his frozen extremities desired a lie-in, his head printed its customary list – ignite heater, visit bathroom, dress, make tea, cook porridge, have breakfast, finish notes. Finish notes! The nightmare returned and his body remained snugly prone for just five extra minutes. He dressed, before visiting the bathroom, shot through the rest of the list and then got down to typing some more background notes.

'Once the results of need assessment surveys are known, a national relief plan will be prepared. Meanwhile, the guidelines already agreed*, together with those now proposed, will hopefully accelerate effective search and rescue operations . . .'

The telephone was ringing! Ever since he'd moved into the cottage the blasted thing had stood on the bedside table, stubbornly inert. Unusual for his daughter, nothing had gone wrong! She asked how he was and why he hadn't answered her previous calls, but before he could explain, she was off again.

'I think somebody wants to say a few words. A *few* words,' she added, optimistically.

---

*   Listed on pages 66-67.

'Hallo Grandpa Africa. My daddy told me you've got lots of lions and el'phants and g'raffes and naughty monkeys near you. Can you see them all the time Grandpa? Or only sometimes?'

His five-year old grand-daughter had poleaxed her Grandpa Africa!

'I can see them only sometimes darling. How are you? And how's your little brother?'

'I'm fine and so is my brother. But he's a silly-billy and can't say words.'

His end of the line laughed; hers giggled delectably.

'Have you got something to eat and drink Grandpa? 'Cos my mummy said you are hungry and haven't got any water. Grandpa, do you know Grandma came to our house? And we dressed up and we played lots of games and we had tea upstairs in my new, very big, bedroom . . .'

'Emmy,' he heard his daughter shout, 'your breakfast's getting cold.'

'I want to tell Grandpa about my new, very big bedroom.'

Her mother cruelly separated them, promising she'd phone after lunch and let Emmy say what she wanted to tell him. Bewitched and buoyed up, he ran across the Akroyd's garden, leapt into the land-cruiser and sang all the way to Berney's Bazaar. But when he got back with the weekly shopping, his grand-daughter's lingering voice prevented him re-activating the lap-top. Where was her new, very big, bedroom? Perhaps her parents had the attic converted, with roof-lights so that she could see across London. He couldn't see through his windows, every pane was frosted over – but why with *fern*-shaped ice? And why might her roof-lights be obscured by similar fern-replicas during winter? Come to think of it, he'd seen windows covered with frozen ferns all over the place. Was there an explanation for this global phenomenum, which had escaped his notice and why ferns? He'd always liked deep snow and high mountains still fascinated him. Ever since gazing at a prep school atlas his eyes had been drawn to the highest altitudes, coloured white – Himalayas, Hindu Kush, Rockies, Andes, Drakensburg – most of it in former Basutoland. The Basotho King, Moshoeshoe, pronounced Moeshwayway, had ridden all the way from his highland redoubt, south to a railway station at the end of the line from Cape Town, to ask the British provincial governor for Queen Victoria's protection against marauding, murdering Zulus. He also remembered reading Rider Haggard's *King Solomon's Mines.* Had it not been for the riveting exploits of Allan Quatermain, Sir Henry Curtis, Captain Good, and a wizened witch, Gagool, whose bald yellowish skull expanded and contracted like a cobra's hood, his wanderlust might never have brought him to Africa. Only to be told, soon after arriving here, that evil tokolosi got on people's backs and thwarted their best endeavours. He'd come across none yet, though imagined they'd emulate Gagool's appearance and wizardry. When he last read the book, most of Quartemain's and Curtis's endeavours seemed far-fetched, but had proved far more successful than his feeble efforts to help overcome so many vicious affects of this seemingly endless drought.

The phone was ringing! He sped into his bedroom and seized the receiver: 'Thank you for ringing back so soon Emmy. Tell me about your new, very big, bedroom darling.'

'Sorry. Wrong number,' another familiar voice quickly said.

'Wait! Apologies to *you*, Suleiman. I'm expecting a call from my grand-daughter.'

'I must admit to being a trifle concerned. Anyway, phone me when you've completed the background notes and we'll discuss them.'

Technolgical wonders never ceased! Harry's laptop had somehow re-activated itself.

The UN car sent to collect him that evening climbed the hill to his office, passed the litter-strewn army barracks with rows of shoddy wooden huts, then the Kolokuana Club, now the officers' mess, opposite the public cemetery – "The Place of Rabbits" in Gwato. Outside a lofty fence reinforced with barbed wire, an armed soldier inspected his and the driver's ID cards, and checked with his superior before admitting them to the Diplomatic Compound. Large, modern houses lined both sides of a pothole-free road. The car's head-lights exposed lawns, flower beds, names on gates, national flags, but no Union Jack. The British high commissioner's three-storey residence, built over a century ago, stood on the bluff above the river where, pre-drought, the ferry boat plied back and forth. The driver pointed to the president's palace on the hill's summit, beyond a row of cabinet ministers' mansions. Another armed soldier checked their ID cards, before letting them proceed, and at a sizeable two-storey villa's front door, Suleiman, in a sweat shirt and jeans, welcomed Harry, in a grey suit and faded college tie, to his humble abode.

His Australian wife, Diane, was visiting their son and daughter at school in England, so it was baked beans on toast for supper. Suleiman scanned the background notes on Harry's laptop, added a couple of guidelines and returned to the introduction.

'This paper,' it began, 'recommends the rationalisation of the current hotchpotch of ad hoc emergency relief measures and also proposes guidelines for endorsement by resident donors, approval by government and implementation by relief agencies.'

Suleiman keyed in an extra sentence: 'The guidelines equally apply to the emergency relief activities of all five UN agencies based in this country.'

'You'll recall me saying that my four senior UN colleagues' had objected to that BBC corespondent's failure to mention their relief contributions. I must warn you, Harry, three of them who head the UN's food, health and agricultural agencies invariably *go it alone!*'

That trio with their precious mandates, budgets and procedures – shades of the Mavimbi workshop – refused to be co-ordinated by a redundant, management consultant bent on imposing his own rules. All ambassadors and high commissioners resident in Kolokuana endorsed the guidelines. How would polititians, civil servants, the army and police react?

Of the non-governmental organisations (NGOs) that had agreed to help with relieving drought, the four international charities operating within the country were already active. The few national charities, mostly church-sponsored, had pledged unspecified support so far. The local business sector, of limited potential, had yet to spark.

Murphy's Law

Tall, well-built and in his forties, Jenkins Makimbo, the country's Red Cross director and the elected spokesman of the NGOs that would or that might be assisting drought relief, advertised energy, veracity and networking skills. Time spent humouring a disparate and partisan bunch of expatriate and local charity workers, priests, representatives of women organisations and other volunteers had taught him to wield his talents cannily. As a rule, individuals were significant because of the post they held. Jenkins proved the exception. His post had gained in significance because *he* held it.

Apparently he'd inherited the name Jenkins from a Welshman, who'd retired – it was assumed he'd retired – from the Brtish Army after both Boer Wars, and had re-built the Obangwato paramount chief's kraal in the mountains above Mabela. Harry visualised a suntanned Taffy repeatedly reaping his just rewards by breeding lots of little namesakes who bred lots more until Jenkins eventually emerged looking even more suntanned.

'NGOs have endorsed the guidelines. Will ministers approve them?' he asked Jack.

'They won't read them. I get things done by talking. Not writing! I'll tell every senior civil servant what to do. If they don't, I'll tell them again.'

'You can tell them only when everyone's present, so that everyone knows what has to be done and who's doing what. This guidelines-paper calls for concerted action, with all relief agencies playing their part. It also proposes that five working groups are set up in the capital and six district relief teams in the southern province. The Red Cross wishes to be represented on all six district relief teams and on the food and health working groups, Save the Children Fund and Caritas on all working groups, Oxfam on the . . .'

Jack exploded: 'I'll decide who does what!'

'What's wrong?' Harry asked him.

'What's right? You circulated all this rigmarole without consulting me.'

'I gave you the draft. Didn't you read it?'

'You read things, I fix things. That's what we agreed.'

'We also agreed that I'm the one who *writes* things.'

'It's playtime boys, let's get some fresh air,' Jenkins suggested.

Jack preferred to go to the Horseman's Rest. The fresh air must have whetted his thirst buds. But they stayed un-whetted, temporarily no doubt, for his and Harry's next meeting was in Suleiman's office and they were running late.

Jack had scarcely set foot inside the door when Sulieman, well briefed and limbered up, sallied forth to inflict a swift clinical kill.

'Do you accept the guidelines, Mr Tsamanachimone, or do you have other suggestions?'

'No,' said Jack.

'You don't accept them? Or you don't have other suggestions?'

'The relief co-ordinator will answer your questions.'

Harry was stymied with no choice but to decline to comment on guidelines he drafted, and having achieved that, machinating Jack disappeared like a pea from a shooter.

Baring his palms, Sulieman pulled an ugly face. 'He's his own worst enemy.'

'No he's not. *I am!*' Harry slammed his briefcase shut and tore after Jack.

Perhaps it wasn't a tokolosi on his back, Harry thought, stumbling down the stairs, but that chap Murphy who'd infamously decreed that, if things could go wrong, they would. And they damned well had!

Stung by Jenkins Makimbo's criticism, Jack now started weekly conferences, though invited only civil servants. Unable to make the first, Harry attended the second, brimfull of expectation. Jack asked if there were any matters arising from the previous minutes. Blank faces! No one had received the minutes or if they had, they hadn't read them, or hadn't brought them to the meeting. So Jack wasted half an hour laboriously reading the minutes aloud. Since the action already agreed had inevitably not been taken, the ground had to be re-trodden and the delay accepted. This meeting's agenda and also the legality of Jack's drought relief role became excuses for a verbal punch-up.

'Today's four-hour charade created chaos! When it should have had the very opposite effect,' Harry typed in his diary that evening. 'Tetchily deploying his pet stock phrases –"You're getting on my nerve (never plural) – We don't want a lot of rigmarole – Just give me the gist, you're the expert" – he kept adjourning proceedings (smoke-breaks) and also condemned the government for failing to take the lead in a national emergency. Yet Jack is no model. Leadership is a journey to an agreed destination, at times a sprint, more often a marathon. Leaders attract and inspire followers – encourage them to pull together and support each other as members of a team which may well remain intact, even beyond its declared destination. Leaders thank team members, when thanks are due, guide or bring them back into line if they stray. One of a leader's worst experiences is to look behind him and no one is there! But Jack never sought a single input from those able to help him. Instead, he alienated them by denouncing their reluctance or their "assumed" reluctance to help relieve such bad drought. His few allies dwindle – his many enemies multiply and become inceasingly critical. Me? No choice! An ally, an uneasy ally.'

Hardly a soul attended the next conference, and those who did, probably had nothing else to do. By abandoning his innovation Jack forfeited a potentially valuable opportunity to review progress, discuss problems and plot the way ahead – collectively. Had he begun afresh and invited representatives from all relief agencies, as well as key civil servants, it was odds on nobody would have turned up. Drought victims deserved far, far better.

'Not the best of weeks,' Harry's diary moaned. 'Yet one must plough on, bolstered by the hope that suddenly all systems will be working, all targets met, every relief worker on the ball, swarms of civil servants constantly toiling and competent. All surviving drought victims and livestock fed, watered, healthy, and itching to emigrate, most wild animals had already done so.' After cleaning his teeth, he told the bathroom's mirror: 'Churchill's secret of success was to go from one failure to another with no loss of enthusiasm.' Harry decided not to mention that in his diary before faxing it to Dermot, because his cleverer cousin would have back-quoted a rousing Churchillian exhortation.

Mr Mboko agreed the drought relief guidelines. The water, food and training working groups were set up straightaway. The health and agriculture ministries took a rain-check!!

Alistair Croft, the ever-pessimistic Scot, was inveigled in to chairing the water group of eight members, charged with rapidly expanding and enhancing emergency measures of their concern. Challenges abounded. Four-wheel-drive bowsers were available only in Mavimbi: their hire expensive, their allocation to districts and their routing contentious. If villages were un-reachable by bowser, water would have to be transferred to containers and carried by donkeys. Though assembling enough donkeys and containers at numerous, often remote, transfer points, then recovering them, would require constant monitoring. Inflatable tanks would have to be bought and mounted on flat-bed vehicles, static tanks built, all water sources and supplies in the south classified as satisfactory, inadequate or failed. Sanitation and hygiene would have to be revolutionised. Even so, without a great deal more money, far too little could be achieved. Obtaining enough money, an outcome fraught with uncertainty, hinged upon the accuracy of rapidly produced cost-estimates, an exercise fraught with difficulties. Yet another vicious circle needed squaring.

The transport ministry's adviser – a living caricature of the archetypal English gent, whose sartorial elegance matched his lucrative mastery of theoretical logistics in calmer African backwaters, offered to chair the food group. Though the practical complexities of food aid very quickly precipitated his graceful withdrawal and Tsabo ably filled the breach.

A Red Cross food aid co-ordinator had been assigned to all six southern districts and plans were made to site and to staff two hundred distribution points. The food group's twelve members were confident that entitled households would receive their first month's emergency rations on target, the end of this month, but rejected the acclaimed merits of "cash-for-work" instead of issuing "free" food. Dispensing cash was far too risky, so they decided to place their faith in "food-for-work" and would await the results of the track-building project under trial on the Mabela plain.

Motivated by a misguided determination to promote self-reliance, the UN's local food chief replaced a charity's long-standing school-meals service with a gardening scheme, whereby all schools were to grow food in gardens that had been waterless many months, and would likely remain so for many more! Ignoring all the protests, led by Suleiman, and repeated threats of violence, the food minister weakly agreed with the UN's local food chief. A decision the food minister and every cabinet colleague would regret – to say nothing of its scandalous impact on countless Obangwato schoolchildren.

The training group started life as a two-man-band. Uncle Bill's invaluable expertise greatly helped Harry plan courses at their Friday afternoon meetings in Kolokuana. Uncle Bill, whom Harry first met during the helicopter tour, could also spend more time with his fifteen grandchildren and, as an extra bonus, his wife would do his weekly laundry.

All forms of healthcare were criminally neglected. The hospitals in Kolokuana and Mabela were inadequate, hygiene education non-existent, sanitation a lurking killer. Drought had again high-lighted these shameful deficiencies. Though, rather than conform to the guidelines Mr Mboko had approved and help to create a health working group, the health minister tried to create his own version. Jenkins Makimbo suggested he hire miracle-men.

Protecting the dwindling number of livestock and whatever pasture had survived was no less important. But why weren't southern families being encouraged to grow, when it rained, sorghum – more drought-resistant than maize – or grow cash crops, such as fruit and nuts, sell them and with the proceeds buy maize staple? But there was no escaping the fact that a society founded on conservative traditions and powerful superstitions was by no means receptive to change, despite the necessity to try anything that might alleviate suffering and prevent death. Yet the government officials who were expected to bring about reform were themselves Obangwatos and among the people the reformers must convince were their families, friends and fellow tribes-people.

If most of the southern province were in Europe or America it would not be farmed, Harry reckoned, and it was unlikely that a foreign commercial foodstuffs company would provide the seed, fertiliser and irrigation equipment required to make southerners food-self-sufficient. Nevertheless, it was worth trying to get some foreign companies involved. Improving household and national food security were realistic targets, provided generous donations continued to arrive from overseas and were delivered as directly as practicable to drought victims or sold in local markets with a small part of the profits helping to fund drought relief and the largest part going to the producer. Alternatively, if that small part of the profits or additional funds were used to buy locally produced food, markets might begin to recover, to attract more trade and might even reduce inflation. However, market-recovery depended on southern subsistence farmers having surplus food to sell, *after* they had fed their dependents, and whether the northern province's surplus food came south. It also depended on water levels in aquifers, reservoirs, springs, the availability and depth of boreholes, all other water sources and supplies – above all rain!

In the finance ministry's lift next morning, Jack struck a deal – if Harry answered the questions, he would read out the speaking notes. Mr Mboko filled the chairman's throne at the head of the table, four cabinet ministers were seated on each flank, Jack and Harry faced the chairman who eloquently declared open the inaugural meeting of the ministerial drought relief task force and then with no pause gruffly demanded Jack's progress report.

He read out the speaking notes: 'The Red Cross has completed registration surveys in the south, minister, and is distributing the government's food reserves. Caritas, a Catholic NGO, will survey the two northern districts nearest the central highlands and is not likely to find drought problems. Compared with our first estimate, more than twice the number of persons in households vulnerable to starvation have been registered, so we will require more than double the amount of food aid requested in our appeal for donor assistance.'

'Unless registration is done properly, of course you'll need more food. I've been told that people have been registered without an interview. How can you be certain that donor aid is being correctly targeted?' the chairman smugly inquired.

A dig in his ribs reminded Harry of their deal. His response was uncompromising.

'*We've* been told that quite a few politicians and chiefs obstruct the Red Cross registration teams and amend their findings. By repeating registration surveys, quarterly, we intend to eliminate errors and omissions, accidental or otherwise. We would have also publicised the correct registration procedures, in a monthly press-release, had representatives of the information ministry and the local media attended our weekly briefings.'

'From now on, their attendance is obligatory,' the chairman growled, glaring at the information minister, a singularly secretive young lady who'd earned the nickname "The Shredder" during her apprenticeship in the justice ministry.

'May I pass round this list of proposals for task force consideration,' Harry asked.

The chairman nodded. He already had a copy, smuggled past his bossy secretary by his office cleaner who granted him a variety of favours a local newspaper had alleged.

'There are eight proposals listed,' Harry explained. 'Firstly, we propose that the task force announces, in a press release, that the state of emergency, due to last until the next maize harvest, will be extended if the drought hasn't broken or drought-induced water, food, health and agricultural problems aren't solved by then. Secondly, we propose that the press release also outlines current and planned relief measures, as well as stressing the requirement for all government employees to assist with implementing them. Third, we insist that the Red Cross is immediately reimbursed for undertaking registration and for distributing food aid throughout the south. We have other proposals, chairman.'

'Proceed,' the chairman intoned with judge-like solemnity.

'Item four requests permission to hire more four-wheel-drive water bowsers from the company in Mavimbi. Item five recommends that the training of civil servants in their electoral duties is postponed until much nearer the event, thus enabling water engineers and other key officials to play a full part in relief operations. Item six, seeks a waiver of sales tax on crop seed and fertiliser. Item seven, draws attention to the scarcity and ever diminishing number of draught animals in southern districts and urges the government to overhaul its tractors, so that ploughing can begin when rain permits planting. Item eight, requests authority to use army and police manpower, transport and equipment if civilian and donor resources no longer suffice. Two proposals have been excluded, in case the list falls into the wrong hands. The guidelines you've approved, chairman, require health and agriculture working groups to help plan and co-ordinate relief. Regrettably, these groups haven't been set up. Even more regrettable, the under-5s' growth-monitoring and feeding programme hasn't started. It appears that those responsible for introducing this crucially important programme are falling behind.'

The health minister angrily sounded off in Gwato – "bringer of rain" and "rude white man" being the only rebukes Harry could interpret.

'Yes, the bringer of rain said *falling behind* which means *catching up* in English,' was the chairman's stinging rebuff.

To have asked why the agriculture group had failed to materialise would have been fruitless, for the gravity of the occasion had overcome the relevant minister. He was fast asleep – gaping mouth, snorts, the lot! The last of the Obangwato paramount chiefs, he'd been gifted the agriculture portfolio as a sweetener when this impoverished Third-World Republic had set forth on its transformation from a thriving Crown Colony.

'Mr Tsamanachimone!' the chairman shouted, but nevertheless the agriculture minister slumbered on. 'Mr Tsamanachimone!!' he shouted, this time loudly enough to wake the dead – still no success. Reverting to normal volume, which was still too loud, he told Jack: 'Draft a press release and include every proposal on this sheet of paper, stating that the ministerial task force has agreed them all. And your minutes must be detailed,' he said, glaring at the comatose head slumped on the nearest ministerial colleague's shoulder.

'Shall I circulate the agenda before your next meeting?' Jack asked, having somehow mislaid his self-confessed contempt for such bureaucratic trappings. He'd told Harry that writing minutes and attending meetings were a waste of time.

'All agendas must be approved by me before circulation,' the chairman bellowed and signalled to Harry to remain. Having brought in two mugs of coffee and a large plate of biscuits, the secretary helped an august sleepwalker find the door.

When they'd gone, Mboko said: 'I got my office cleaner to obtain an advanced copy of your list. Disobeying me, my secretary gives cabinet ministers that sort of thing before meetings and they pay her to warn them of all unpleasant surprises.'

And you splurge your ministry's petty cash on your amenable cleaner, Harry wanted to say. Mboko passed him the plate with the few biscuits he'd managed to resist eating.

'Thank you for preparing those guidelines,' he said. 'I've set all the wheels in motion to transfer water, food and animal fodder from the northern province to the south, though I couldn't agree to the government's chief secretary supervising relief. He and Tsamana-chimone have never hit it off.'

'It seemed more sensible than tacking the relief team on to the health ministry's social welfare department.'

Mboko laughed. 'So you have heard about all that skulduggery! I don't think comrade Jack would have appreciated being called a social worker. No. Both of you will continue to report to me and if appropriate to the task force.' He paused and looked Harry straight in the eye. 'I'd like you to do something for me, Mr Burke. Update our appeal for donor assistance and show me your draft? Provided our requests are accepted, and there is no reason why they shouldn't be, the arrival of a lot more food aid will hit the local media's headlines well ahead of September's general election.'

Harry needed no reminding that 300,000 more drought victims than estimated were entitled to the monthly ration and that an alarming quantity of additional food would be required to see them through the next three months, without taking into account goodness knows how many under-nourished and acutely malnourished children under-5. However, he was in the humanitarian relief business, not some brown-nosed spin-doctor peddling political propaganda. Wait a minute, he thought. Why not try a little leverage?

'I'd like you to do something for *me*, minister. Leaving aside the sensitive issue of that diamond cartel's embargo repeatedly compelling your government to request donor aid, I have a pressing interest in locating my grandfather's grave.'

Harry took a photocopied note out of his wallet and handed it to Mboko. 'I'm showing you this, which I'd like back please, because it indicates where the grave and the century-old mine workings may approximately be and also because I leave here in mid-October, *after* we've got the extra food aid and *before* your re-election.'

With elbows propped on his desk, chins resting on clenched fists and lips moving as if in silent prayer, Mboko studied the tragic account of the two prospectors' last days, their burial pact and the scant directions to their final resting place.

'Interesting,' was all he said.

The photocopy slid across the minister's highly polished desk towards Harry, much to his relief. But as the lift returned him to ground-level, Tsabo's warning deafened his ears: 'If you snoop around for the grave, things could get tough, very tough!' Harry cursed his stupidity. Why had he shown Mboko, of all people, that note?

Back in the land cruiser, Harry couldn't believe his ears – Jack was *humming!* While driving along the main street the humming intensified and while waiting for the robots to turn green, Harry thought the tune resembled a sort of Russian dance often accompanied by soothing mandolins and daring acrobatics. Outside their office, the humming stopped. Jack would have far rather been in one of his pet bars, than faced by a piled-high in-tray, always full of problems. Without receiving even a moment of his cursory attention, he'd chuck the lot in his rubbish bin, then sit and gloat while Harry retrieved everything.

Reluctant to leave the land-cruiser, Jack said: 'If I'd known you were going to hand out all those bits of paper at that meeting, I'd have burned them before we went.' He lit a fag, produced a couple of beer cans out of thin air and gave one to Harry. 'If you stay until it rains, I'll buy you a six-pack.'

Harry felt the tokolosi release its grip on his back. It was last seen scaling their office compound's barbed-wire fence and scampering off towards the town-centre, in search of its next victim.

There were masses available! He kept wriggling against the driver's seat to make sure the poisonous dwarf really had decamped. And all that wriggling, as well as his miserable failure to drink any beer, flummoxed his incorrigible counterpart.

Furling the Flag

Harry's landlord, Dennis Akroyd, invariably drove his vintage Jaguar fearing the worst; a fear volubly shared by his wife, Angela, and also on this year's Queen's Birthday silently shared by Harry. The engine kept spluttering, there was an oily smell and smoke billowed from beneath the bonnet. Pleasantly surprised to have reached the high commissioner's residence without having to push Dennis's pride and joy, or resort to shanks's pony, they queued to sign the visitors' book, and after more queuing, to be officially welcomed by Richard Riddington. He very kindly invited them to stay on for a post-reception supper, before introducing his newly arrived wife, Petrona, whose countenance was anything but celebratory or welcoming.

The Akroyds went their separate ways: Dennis probably to try and seal an engineering contract; Angela to consume the latest expatriate gossip and add just a few tasty morsels of her own. Harry latched onto Berney, of Bazaar fame, but then had to scan the mass of heads, searching for Dennis's – intoxicated Jack wanted to meet him! Dennis was easily spotted. He wore a flat-cap at all functions, great and small, indoors and outdoors, to stop the sun bleaching his hair, he claimed, even though it would be merely a matter of months before his forehead reached the nape of his neck. Six-feet-three Dennis appeared totally non-plussed when six-feet-two Harry introduced a wobbly five-footer as his *counterpart!*

There were other distractions. The cluster of media smarties, out to trap and trick well-oiled targets into disclosing some juicy indiscretions, contributed zilch to the formality or festiveness of the occasion – nor did the army's brass band confined beneath the veranda and striving to concoct an excruciating cacophony of discordant noises.

Richard Riddington took centre-stage and reeled off a detailed list of all the aid Great Britain had donated to the country, augmented by a microphone with recurring feed-back and only mildly put out by a TV camera that kept panning elsewhere.

He concluded with a magnanimous toast to the president, the government and nation. In response, Mr Mboko apologised for the president's indisposition, praised British generosity during this grave crisis and reciprocated with a rousing toast to: 'Queen Elizabeth, her nice family and all her lovely people.' Neither of them was put off by the sideshow being enacted nearby. Harry had to remind Dennis to remove his flat-cap before the first toast and then both of them had to restrain their inebriated little friend after the second. Now locked between two bearded janitors, Jack waved an empty glass in the air and shouted his slurred tribute to 'Her Majeshy'. Instantly relieved of the potentially lethal weapon to avoid him losing his name – had he not lost it already – he remained manacled, as it were, while the army band violated one national anthem more brutally than the other. When freed, he wobbled towards the nearest bar, barging into people's knees, with Dennis and Harry hard on his heels, alert to woebegone incidents on the way.

An African grasped Harry's arm. 'We meet at last. How are you coping with Jack?' he asked, with a wry smile, but before Harry could answer he talked to someone else.

'Bloody rude bloke, the chief secretary,' Dennis uttered and they resumed the chase.

Jack, a re-charged glass clamped in his chubby little fist, was entertaining Angela and a bevy of her female accomplices by performing a sort of war-dance, with hostile grunts and gestures. Goodness knows how long that lasted . . . or what happened next!

It was early evening when Richard led Harry out to the deserted veranda for a relief update – only to be distracted by a media smarty rushing out of the bar and throwing up over the verandah's balustrade, causing Richard to explain, in his matter-of-fact way, that the vomit had fractionally missed the big-drum, but might well have hit the big-drummer.

The update was postponed, the staff began clearing up the reception's more acceptable vestiges and Her Majesty's flag was furled for an umpteenth year.

In a study, the Akroyds and Harry met Petrona Riddington's mother and also Sasha, an enormous Alsatian presented to the

British high commissioner on the sudden departure of the Russian ambassador. Yeltsin, now the post-Soviet president, had begun stamping his new-found authority by sacking all communist ambassadors, but with Moscow still in turmoil, Kolokuana's replacement was not expected soon.

While Suleiman and Diane caught up with the latest newspapers, Richard showed one of his treasured videos of prime minister's questions at Westminster, and Angela Akroyd described the riding club's myriad attractions to both of the new arrivals. Petrona said she loathed horses! Her mother said she did, too, then tearfully recalled a beautiful budgerigar who had died a long time ago. Since nobody appeared to be watching his excellent video, Richard took the dog for its evening walk and Harry tagged along.

Leaping into the garden, the Alsation immediately located the pile of chunder, exactly where Richard had said it would be. He was even more chuffed when barking a command in Russian, Sasha – obviously a KGB sniffer-dog – forsook the chunder and obediently sprang to heel. Another command and the mastiff led the way across a rock-strewn levee to a wide river bed laced with several stinking, stagnant pools . . . Not the most congenial of viewing points from which to admire an umpteenth imperial sunset.

After supper, what started as just a marital tiff soon became a vitriolic slanging match, with Petrona calling all the shots and Richard very much on the receiving end. She cut short or poured scorn on his dithering responses, accused him of being a workaholic, said his speech had been very boring and much too long. And when her mother wanted to talk about the beautiful budgerigar she'd loved so much, he'd taken that bloody awful dog for a walk. Thereupon, Petrona and her mother executed an offended, arm-in-arm exit.

Richard looked utterly drained. He paced about the room before glancing at Suleiman, raising his hands in desperation and muttering pathetically: 'Sasha will have to go.'

'That's worse than a stack-a-kangaroo-shit, Pommie!' Diane exclaimed, piling on the 'Strine. 'Sasha and you are good mates.'

'Maybe I should have the dog,' Suleiman helpfully suggested. 'You told me, Richard, that your wife intends to spend most of her time in London. No dog, so no excuse for her lengthy absences.' But Diane wasn't too chipper, her doting goddess was a lilac, tail-less Persian cat.

Petrona, her mother and lots of luggage left on next day's flight to Mavimbi, Suleiman withdrew his dog-care offer, and Richard and Sasha remained good mates.

None of his associates really knew Richard, though the few who thought they knew him reasonably well, rallied around. With his marriage on the rocks, he became obsessed with telling or reminding everybody that virtually nothing remained of the rich colonial heritage that had once promised so much, yet had been profligately squandered away. A devastating fact he would never be able to live with. Now the last in a very long line of British chief justices had gone, to be replaced by the justice minister's brother!

Harry eavesdropped while Richard took on the drought relief ministerial task force. 'My earliest predecessor created a crown colony, here, one of Queen Victoria's growing number of African dependencies, by drawing lines on a map, and then drawing another line to keep two warring tribes apart. The southern Obangwatos and their inveterate foes, the northern Kasodi tribe. The Queen's representative presided over an advisory council comprising the paramount chiefs of both tribes, the British governors of both provinces, and several nominated members who were later replaced by elected members. Successive advisory councils oversaw the gradual introduction of case law, alongside existing tribal laws, and much improved governance, water supply, health care and education. More and far better bridle paths enabled mounted police to patrol outlying areas. Motorable tracks came later. The few tarred roads, telephones and busses linked new, rapidly expanding, townships. The modernised agriculture quickly led to the lucrative export of maize-grain, mohair and wool. Between both world wars, trade developed to such an extent that this country could proudly boast of an economy among sub-Saharan Africa's most promising. This would bring the unified nation great benefits, even though, as is sometimes claimed, indigenous industries and trade could have been more energetically promoted. There is criticism of the lack of freedom and democracy under colonial rule, yet regular elections have been held here for nearly a century. For the vast majority of Africans today elections remain way beyond their reach, and their wildest dreams. On gaining independence in 1968 this nation saw the appointment of its first black president and the Africanisation of central and local government. Kolokuana Grammar School founded in 1878 and renamed the International High School in 1972, retained its British headmaster, as well as most of its Commonwealth teachers. Mission and other schools continued to flourish. But soon school-leavers far outnumbered available jobs, thus many sought employment overseas, with the talented seldom, if ever, returning home. I have to admit that my predecessors failed to train enough water conservation, irrigation and sanitation engineers, nutritionists and public health nurses, agriculturalists and veterinary staff. Nor, since independence, have this country's governments trained enough of them and other specialists. Hence the sorry state of the southern province, the suffering, hardship, loss of life and livelihood far too many Obangwatos have to endure. Now we face a much stiffer challenge, with AIDS threatening to supplant poverty and recurring drought as the principal means of reducing your ever-increasing population, but Catholics must never use contraceptives! Even so, due largely to the widespread practice of unprotected sex, your predominantly Anglican northern province is fast becoming a veritable AIDS hotbed and the rest of your country is now seriously vulnerable.' A morbidly accurate finale to Richard's soliloquy.

Harry happened to overhear Mr Mboko privately thank the high commissioner for not mentioning the mining embargo or the corruption within the country. Richard usually did.

His self-awarded licence to spread "the word" detonated the cabinet's fury and Mboko weakly agreed to request Britain's prime minister to replace the high commissioner with somebody who would respect diplomatic protocol. Only after London cropped Richard's horns was the request withdrawn. The local pro-government daily carried an information ministry statement proclaiming "victory!" Its anti-government competitor ran an editorial condemning the cabinet and siding with the British high commissioner. It also published Jenkins Makimbo's letter praising Mr Riddington's contributions to drought relief and for encouraging so many volunteers 'to help with solving our nation's increasing problems.'

Before going up to Oxford, Tsabo had been a fan of the British Council's library, which had provided the bulk of his late-night reading. The books had proved more useful than most of those he'd been cataloguing in the Cathedral library at that time. Since returning to Kolokuana and when his work allowed he arrived early enough to be first through the British Council's door, since within minutes, the reading-rooms were crowded with local people devouring British newspapers, secured to sloping desks, with at least four readers huddled round each desk. In separate rooms, many others listened to BBC World Service radio programmes and a crowd watched BBC News real-time, now beamed from London by satellite, instead of all the out-of-date recordings which had *accidently* missed several daily flights from Mavimbi – or so the information minister, alias the Shredder, alleged.

Tsabo rarely scanned the "Court" columns in British broadsheets, though one morning he spotted an item worthy of photocopying and passing on to Harry.

'Montseigneur Le Comte des Vavasseurs wishes it to be known that his eldest stepson, The Honourable Richard Caitland Mont-Prellet Riddington, an esteemed member of Her Britannic Majesty's Diplomatic Service, is no longer married to Petrona (née Tracey), an offspring of Dulcie Daze, a retired dancer.'

Along the Way

It would be Tsabo's first tour of the southern province since joining the Red Cross. The bold side of his persona urged him to stamp his authority on the widely dispersed staff's drought relief activities. The prudent side advised respect for their greater experience. He invited Harry to accompany him, to add some patriarchal expertise and asked Speedy, the drought relief team's re-christened driver, to share the driving. Speedy needed no persuading. He'd go anywhere, as long as there'd be plenty of skirt available.

Heading south along the main tarred road he whiled away the miles by relating his life story. He grew up in Mabela and went to school on the opposite side of the town from St John's. Although the same age as Tsabo, they never met as youngsters, but their fathers were good friends. Several years after Tsabo's father left the police to work in the mines, the Mashedi family stayed at Speedy's home and attended a speech day at the Mission. Then his father resigned from the police, also, and was now a bank's security guard in the capital. After leaving school at sixteen, Speedy hawked T-shirts and jeans, until a gang of thugs demanded protection money. Now, at last, he had a steady job with a weekly wage.

Big, strong and handsome, he handled English with flair, and had the broadest smile and loudest laugh in Kolokuana. He was also inclined to boast of manly attributes, which females apparently flocked to worship. But he was *not* happy about driving Tsabo's white truck with red crosses all over it, because the many sick people lining the road, hoping the ambulance would stop, belonged to his tribe. With no room in the truck, all he could do was wave! Two wheels, four tyres, six full water containers, spare parts, tools and four jerrycans of diesel fuel filled the loadspace, covered with a tarpaulin tied down by ropes. Three rucksacks, Harry and a pile of his large-scale maps took up most of the back seat.

Having attended a district meeting, they stayed overnight at the Mabela Hotel and first thing next morning called at the government fuel pump. They adopted a slick routine – Speedy pumped vigorously for all of ten minutes, Harry inspected the truck, and Tsabo signed the attendant's chit. Keeping the truck and the four jerrycans topped up with diesel needed to be carefully planned, due to the long distances between re-fuelling points and the truck's heavier consumption on the mammoth, roller-coaster, rides awaiting it. Even though none of them had driven beyond Mabela before, they were more than conscious of the fact that no longer would tarmac smooth their way.*

Now rocks, ruts and potholes jolted every body-part. Now Speedy's endless bleating about his priceless manhood never recovering – or words to that effect – grated tediously. Now glare, heat, sweat, dust, fatigue, thirst, would test their endurance and driving skills. Water breaks, vehicle checks and limb-stretching would challenge their time-keeping.

Within three hours, they were admiring Uncle Bill's new "operations room" where his drought relief team met and the Red Cross food aid co-ordinator was based, as would a public health sister, if the under-5's programme ever got off the ground. Displayed on the walls were easy-ref data, maps, named mug shots of local members of parliament, chiefs, village headmen, relief supervisors and key volunteers. Uncle Bill, a retired miner, could certainly teach the other five district administrators a thing or two and he'd agreed to play a leading role on the drought relief courses Harry would start, soonest.

Yet more hairpin bends, steep gradients and views of the snow-capped southern highlands lay round every corner as they drove from one distribution point to another; spurred on by the supervisors' assurances that every household entitled to the prescribed ration had received maize, dried pulses and cooking oil. Most distribution points comprised a secure storage facility, with enough space for lorries to unload food and people to queue.

It took them, in round figures, five hours and a hundred shade-less miles to reach the township where the helicopter had landed in a blizzard, and they slept at the same lorry driver's hostel. This time they shared the freezing hut with only one snorer – who would

---

*   Page 68. The sketch-map also traces this journey

wake them at an ungodly hour by revving his engine right outside the pane-less window.

The district administrator's welcome that morning, although courteous, conveyed an innate suspicion of prying strangers. His report dwelt upon the urgency to allay hunger, thirst and disease, but little else. The district engineer told of repeated attempts to alert his parent ministry to a rapidly worsening water crisis. The district medical officer requested details of the under-5s' growth monitoring and feeding programme, she'd heard about on her radio. The rural development officer asked for money for livestock husbandry, but the agriculture officer said all the money would end up in the chiefs' pockets. The Red Cross food aid co-ordinator complained of a lack of teamwork, which his colleagues ridiculed. A newspaper reporter scribbled avidly and Harry set about solving the team's problems.

Then the district administrator announced in Gwato: 'The chiefs speak, all of our clans have bad drought and all of them must have food. The palaver comes, before. The big riot comes, after. This I know.' More reporter-scribbling – even more while Tsabo explained the emergency relief procedures.

There would, indeed, be a riot but the rioters would turn turtle, blaming the chiefs for their plight. Elsewhere chiefs and their henchmen were beaten, some were maimed, while policemen stood and watched. Radio Kolokuana's newscasters spared no details and now, at last, described relief activities at six o'clock every morning and evening.

At a distribution point overlooking a gorge – aspiring to Grand Canyon proportions – frail figures wrapped in raggéd blankets waited in a line for maize-meal and dried beans, but none had a bottle for cooking oil dispensed from a drum. An old man, so weak and exhausted he had to be carried, never made the front of the line. His corpse was dragged away in an emptied maize bag. Then up from the gorge came a group of gaunt, beaming, young women, each with a baby strapped to her back, having traipsed twenty miles from their village and slept in the open. Overjoyed and clearly extremely grateful to be given food for their families, they sipped water from a can, gingerly passed from hand to hand. They would rest a while before retracing their steps, now with a month's rations balanced on their heads. A shallow grave had been hacked in the concrete ground – the old man's stick marked the spot. His blanket had vanished.

At the next distribution point, a hut surrounded by barbed wire, the supervisor showed them a sheaf of registration lists with the names of people in his area entitled to the food stacked in the hut which he would start issuing tomorow. His visitors were about to leave, when they noticed a small boy crouching outside the barbed wire. Desperately thin and scantily clothed, he said he was six and his sick mother sent him three days, before, to get food. Choking back tears and clutching a ration card tightly to his chest, he was given water and a month's worth of rations for his family. The supervisor took pains to describe the way back. Though whether that brave child – the same age as Happy Sam – found the paths that would lead him home, with his sack of precious contents still secure, sadly had to remain open to dismal conjecture. Thieves were on the lookout for sack-carriers.

Those two heart-rending incidents and the expectation that so many others were surely happening throughout the south agonised Tsabo, subdued Speedy, and distressed Harry. Yet, by witnessing such misery in all its stark reality, at least they could appreciate more readily and clearly, the extent of the privation besetting so many Obangwato households.

The quest to dispense salvation, though gaining pace, would neither catch up nor keep up with the problems unless more attention was paid to detail – problems like no bottles for cooking oil were too easily overlooked, back at the blunt-end. "Top-down direction and co-ordination are indispensable management tasks. Bottom-up evaluation is just as essential." That slogan, however hackneyed, had urged Harry to propose in the guidelines the earliest provision of one mobile monitoring team per district, dedicated to fine-tuning relief wherever aid deliverers and aid consumers met. Case proven. But the six teams had yet to be funded and recruited, before being trained and deployed. Case pending!

Within an hour they approached a stores shed, one of several simple metal structures the public works department had recently constructed in the southern province's remotest fastnesses. Since all of its stock had been delivered to distribution points, the storekeeper conducted them round an empty space.

Speedy explained, far too loudly, to Harry: 'He's showing us this, because he's scared of getting the sack for running out of what he ought to have.'

Harry nodded sagely. 'I'd have done the same,' he told Speedy, back outside the shed.

'Is the track over those mountains okay?' Tsabo asked, impatient to move on.

'No vehicles use it now,' the storekeeper replied gloomily.

Perhaps he knew of some fatal accidents that were best kept to himself. Harry looked askance at the solid row of pinnacles towering above them, unrolled one his smaller-scale maps on the truck's bonnet and suggested to Tsabo that they plot an alternative route.

'The only alternative would take at least two days! Speedy, you kip in the back, Harry will drive and I'll navigate. Let's give it a go.' Tsabo was adamant, arguing pointless.

Spring-busting ruts and sump-splitting rocks made the going slow in the extreme, and even in the lowest gear, difficult. Then the track disappeared! Undeterred, Tsabo thought he could see where it might resume, but that meant negotiating a precipitous slope. With its engine roaring and its steering wheel spinning, the truck slewed on the loose scree, as it crept ever nearer the gap between two massive crags, in which Tsabo placed so much faith. Having achieved that without mishap, Harry steered an equally hazardous course to their second objective, the summit of a pass exceeding 11,000 feet.

The view was worth all the sweat and adrenaline. While they surveyed peaks bathed in sun and valleys cast in shadow, a man and his teenaged son and daughter greeted them.

The man said they had been to see his parents who lived close by the stores-shed, now 3,000 feet below them, and were walking home. Home happened to be in the direction in which Tsabo was determined to go and guides who knew the track would come in handy. When offered a lift, their faces lit up. With the rucksacks and Harry's maps crammed into the truck's already over-full rear loadspace, Speedy said he could get them all in, but only if the girl sat on his lap. Tsabo advised the girl to sit on her father's lap.

A near-vertical descent made driving no easier and his glance in the rear-view mirror reminded Harry that he now had three extra bodies and souls to keep intact. At the foot of a boulder-strewn riverbed, the remnants of the track clung to a narrow ledge, high above and alongside a cavernous, meandering canyon. Manoeuvring the truck round the sharp corners in re-entrant after re-entrant, down which water would have formerly cascaded, called for teamwork. By leaning out a rear window, Speedy checked the gap between every successive rock overhang and the truck's roof. Tsabo checked its nearside wheels, forced perilously close to the edge of one sheer precipice after another, and Harry tried to keep his palms dry. This was definitely no joyride!

And so it persisted for ruddy hours until the teenaged son pointed to a cave apparently with bushman paintings somewhere within its depths.

Tsabo decided to investigate and Harry dried his palms again. They clambered up the rock-face, eased their way into the cave, and as their eyes adjusted to the gloom, several grey images began to take shape on a smooth stone wall. And the longer they peered at them, the more colourful and life-like the images became. Lions, elephants and giraffes dominated the centre. Wildebeest galloped and antelope leaped on either flank. A serpent entwined itself across the foreground. A rainbow spanned the background – enthrallingly skilful artwork, captured on Harry's flash-lit film.

'Bushmen still roam the Kalahari Desert hunting and gathering whatever they can find to eat,' Tsabo explained. 'That's their god, Mantis, up there. Long ago, they would chant to encourage the animals they and other bushmen had painted to pass through that wall to the Otherworld. Then, Mantis willing, they would follow the animals. Kalahari bushmen, the little people we call them, speak like this.'

His palate and supple tongue manufactured a string of peculiar clicks which, try as he might, Harry found impossible to imitate. Frustrated, he returned to the paintings. Mantis had escaped his camera's notice, so he too was snapped for posterity's sake . . .

Or was Mantis female? Tsabo's girlfriend, Jill, with her Oxford doctorate in anthropology would have known.

At last their next objective came into view – just a desolate village, on a barren plateau. The grateful passengers were home! There an assembly of donkeys waited by a bowser to have their water containers re-filled, before carrying them to communities unexplored by the most tenacious of vehicles. It was there that Tsabo was refused permission to report his whereabouts on a police short-wave radio. It was also there that the track forked – one branch spiralling down into the canyon – theirs spiralling up towards more peaks, past a spongy morass fed by an unseen, heroic spring – a verdant sanctuary for two herd-boys and their remaining goats. The wetland, among the precious few that could have survived such an all-consuming drought, would stay neither damp nor green for much longer, were grazing livestock to continue depleting what little was left of its pasture.

'If there are other wetlands, where the hell are they?' Harry's outburst echoed back at him from across a valley and his notebook's list of lessons learnt lengthened still farther.

From the summit of a second pass, almost as high but much easier to conquer than the first, Harry could see the sparse lights of their final objective twinkling in the darkness – the army helicopter pilot's birthplace, where the village headmen had handed back the pens and blank scraps of paper.

The hotel had only two beds available, so they spun a coin to decide who would sleep in the truck and with two contenders left Speedy called tails instead of heads. Undaunted, indeed overjoyed, he set off intent on finding warmer, far more exciting accommodation.

Harry exercised legs, weak at the knees, arms that felt detached from shoulders, hands that were still shaking, more than ready for a couple of beers, a hot meal and a good sleep after more than seven hours of strenuous, adventurous helmsmanship.

Quite by chance, he pulled back the blanket on his bed. A trail of rat-droppings ran the length of the mattress and across the floor to a semi-circular hole, neatly gnawed through the bottom of the door. Tsabo fetched the manageress, who said she didn't let this room often, because it was next to the kitchen! They turned down free board and lodgings. Her offer of a spotless replacement mattress and two clean blankets Harry accepted. With the soiled blanket blocking the rat-hole, he had a fairly peaceful if watchful night's rest.

Next morning's discussion with district officials and local volunteers inspired hope for a brighter future, though Tsabo had to educate the township's solitary nursing assistant in the basic elements of emergency health measures. Her treatment hut was clean and tidy, quite well-equipped, and because she lived there, opening-hours were when people came.

Next morning they back-tracked to the nearest of the two highest passes and forked down into the deep canyon skirted the previous day. At the bottom of the canyon – a geological phenomenon an early pioneering cartographer with commendable imagination had named the "Main Gorge" – they crossed a wide, very dry river bed and zigzagged their way north, up into the central highlands.

Dave, the Yorkshireman Tsabo and Harry had briefly met during their helicopter trip, made them a welcome mug of tea. 'Yon district administrator got pissed off with waitin,' he said, 'an booggered off 'ome.' His progress report was equally blunt – in short, just he and the Red Cross food aid co-ordinator were active on that district's drought relief front. They made an odd pair: Mrs Totsi, an immense local woman of few words; Dave, as spry and skinny as a jockey, also a hilarious raconteur. Nor could he be accused of stinting on swearwords or lacking the Yorkshireman's native wit. A comic, who looked comical, in a beret worn like a tin-lid, unlit roll-your-own behind one ear, pencil-stub behind the other, hands in pockets to help his braces keep his shorts up, legs that would never win a beauty contest but would captivate the crowd.

In the hut where he taught herd-boys, whose animals were dead, carpentry and metal-work, three mattresses each with a pillow and two blankets soon filled the space between both rows of work benches . . . As it turned out, Speedy "slept" elsewhere that weekend.

It would be all go for Tsabo whose daylight hours Mrs Totsi made sure were gainfully employed by visiting all fourteen food distribution points that she oversaw, meeting their supervisors and talking to customers: 'entitled food aid beneficiaries' in relief jargon. Mrs Totsi had also ensured that Tsabo would find no problems to solve or take back with him.

Meanwhile, Dave and Harry were riding to a far-flung cattle-post and would find its arid rangelands littered with carcasses, surrounded by squabbling hyenas and by vultures impatiently awaiting their turn to pick the bones clean, but with no human in sight.

Once a fortnight Dave had taken the elderly white owner his mail and slept in the log shed – nailed to its door 'Taking what's left to market!' scrawled on cardboard. Dave fed and watered the horses he and Harry had ridden, made a fire with just one log, heated a wodge of mealie-meal and handed Harry half. After they'd eaten that, Dave took a water bottle and mug out of his saddle bag and brewed tea in the mug which they shared.

'How come you're running a skills centre in the back of beyond?' Harry asked him.

'I were a central 'eating fitter in't Leeds till a piss-arse roon over me missis. Never felt nowt, bless 'er. Couldn't settle, kids were married an woonna them charities took me on.'

Harry didn't know what to say. Sorry would have been hopelessly inadequate.

'You must have been through the mangle,' was all he could summon.

'Belly-aching's never got nobody nowhere. We moos 'ave a drink or two, in't UN bar down Kolokuana. Get there on't soddin mountain road. A *road* they call it! It'd tear goots outa me pushbike, let alone a boos with squawking bloooody chickens on't next bleedin seat. When it's doon with stoppin an startin, an creepin oop fookin back alleys, it's cost three quid in our dosh, took as long as flyin from Loondon to Mavimbi, an boogar drivin knows nuthin if engine or summat packs oop.'

'Won't the charity lend you a vehicle?'

Dave shook his head and his beret fell off. With it back in place, he wriggled into his sleeping bag. The beret was still on his head when he woke Harry at sunrise next morning and somehow stayed there while blowing on the log's embers to brew a mug of tea.

Harry wondered how Dave would react if asked to do some snooping – riding back to the district office, Harry decided to take the plunge.

'Know of any mine workings?' he casually inquired.

'What sorta mine workins?'

'Not really sure,' Harry fibbed. To have said 'diamonds' would have contravened the country's official secrets act, if there were one, and he'd end up festering verminously in one of Kolkuana's gruesomely primitive jails, eating God knows what!

'My grandfather did some prospecting in this part of Africa and I'm very keen to find out what became of him.'

'Poor beggar copped it, did 'ee?'

'Lots of them did in those days. Anyway, if you see or hear anything, Dave, tell me on the quiet. It seems that mining's a government hot spud.'

'Can't be too careful rown 'ere. Afore tha can say Jack-blooody-Robinson, tha'll be oop soddin creek with no fookin paddle. Mooms the word, lad, an that's a promise.'

It had taken a week to tour the six southern districts and, despite Dave's vivid description of what lay ahead, they had no choice but to set off along his belovéd mountain road, the only motorable route across the central highlands. Having conquered more than several high passes, they eventually arrived at the fork where Dave's bus would have turned east to Kolokuana. They continued north. Another two hundred miles farther on, they began a long tortuous descent to an endless green plain. They reached the capital of the northern province at sundown and booked into a smart hotel on a broad avenue, flanked by blue jacaranda blossom. After a long luxurious bath and filling hot dinner they had eight hours sound sleep under mosquito nets and between pristine white sheets with matching pillow cases. All Harry's thorough searches had exposed not a single rat dropping.

Their arrival at the provincial governor's office next morning was greeted by shouts of "Go back to Kolokuana!!" Brushing aside newspaper reporters and a television crew, the governor said the protesters were Anglicans – opposed to the Catholic NGO teams about to start food registration surveys in two of his districts. They took their places at one end of the town hall, relief workers and members of the public packed the middle, protesters wearing the opposition party's baseball cap and hoisting placards bearing stop-at-nothing exhortations were infiltrating across the opposite end of the hall and along both sides.

A ringleader shouted: 'Our party demands free food for everybody. No Catholics will decide who gets food in *this* province. We'll do that!'

Then the chanting and dancing began. To visitors trying to help, the performance was bizarre – to the locals, presumably very much business as usual.

'I think we should adjourn to my office?' the governor burbled nervously.

'No we won't,' Tsabo replied. 'Imagine all the cheering when we leave, to say nothing of the bad press. Come on Harry, rustle up a few shaming words for these wreckers.'

Standing shoulder-to-shoulder in the centre of the hall, Tsabo waited until the hissing and booing stopped before describing Harry's job as the drought relief co-ordinator.

'Peace be with you, ladies and gentlemen,' Harry started in Gwato, then continued in English. 'Last week, Mr Mashedi and I visited the south of your country where we found great hardship and distress. Caritas, a Catholic charity, will check if any families of your tribe living in the two districts nearest to the central highlands need help. By co-operating with this charity's registration teams, you can make sure that all genuine drought victims receive food quickly, fairly and compassionately.'

An elderly priest's prayer broke the silence. His denomination mattered not – it was his perfect timing and the loud amen his intervention evoked that saved the day.

The governor suggested their visitors describe the situation in the south. With the TV camera and reporters' notebooks at the ready, Tsabo grabbed at the chance to address a far larger audience than the hundred or more pairs of cocked ears in that crowded hall.

'Red Cross teams make lists of all the people badly affected by drought who have no crops, no animals to sell and no money to buy food. District administrators send the lists to Kolokuana, and when Mr Tsamanachimone has approved them, everybody entitled to food aid is given a named and a numbered ration card. The Red Cross transports maize-grain, dried beans or peas, and cooking oil from stores sheds to distribution points set up throughout the south.'

'Why doesn't the Red Cross do that for our tribes-people?' a protester asked politely.

'I work for the Red Cross and know that we haven't got enough staff to send to your two districts, but we have trained the Caritas teams to carry out registration surveys there. If you have complaints, your governor should refer them to Mr Makimbo, the Red Cross director, and he will decide what to do.'

Unsurprisingly everyone cheered. Although an Obangwato Catholic, Jenkins Makimbo was popular countrywide and frequently hailed by the national media as Jesus Makimbo.

'Most of the food,' Tsabo continued, 'is coming from overseas and is being given only to people facing starvation, because of bad drought. The many children under five who are seriously underweight must be given extra rations. Regrettably thousands of them are being neglected because they haven't been given extra rations in the south.'

'What about the north?' a belligerent voice called out.

'There is no drought in the north, except perhaps near to the central highlands. Everybody living in drought-affected areas, who needs help, will receive help. I was about to explain that children under-five must be weighed and measured every month. Under-5s who are under-nourished will be registered, their carers will cook the extra rations and a nurse will make sure that the children eat the extra rations. Acutely malnourished under-5s will be fed a special diet in the nearest hospital. That's what is supposed to happen, but it is *not* happening. Now water. Many communities have none, others are suffering severe shortages. Drought has caused pit-latrines to leak and sewage is polluting water supplies. Water-minders are being trained to test and treat supplies, yet typhoid and other diseases may still kill far too many people. Drought has also killed many animals and is likely to kill many more. Ministers and civil servants are either unaware of these problems or not trying to solve them.'

When the applause had died down, a media-man said the speech would be broadcast on that evening's radio and television news. If this actually happened, Tsabo would score a public relations triumph! Though rather than gloat, which would have been entirely out of character, he told Harry that he intended to sue the puny finance minister for devoting grossly insufficient resources to the ever-worsening disaster – a drastic act of last resort, probably, but he was fired up and his eyes had that steely glint of determination. By the time they reached Kolokuana, his mood had mellowed. He rang Suleiman and Jenkins Makimbo to warn them of a possible broadcast. Speedy said he'd go to all the bars where Jack cadged the odd drink or three and tell him to go home and switch on his television.

Just as Harry opened his back door, two rats, both monsters, darted past him into the garden. He'd never noticed any droppings and the only evidence he could find were teeth marks on the soap his maid had left in the sink. He showed the Egberts the gnawed soap and asked how the inevitable onset of bubonic plague might best be neutralised.

'We've got rats, too.' Dennis unsuccessfully reassured Harry.

After the seven o'clock news headlines, Tsabo's speech appeared on the Akroyd's TV screen, transmitted in full with Gwato sub-titles. Tsabo had surpassed even himself! And so, at last, had Kolokuana's television station, even though it served only those living in the capital and both provinces who could afford a television set, pay the licence fee, and in the mountainous south, receive programmes relayed by sparsely located pylons.

No amount of searching the cottage and every square inch of his bedding would yield further evidence, but Harry could hear the pestilential creatures scuttling and squealing above the bedroom ceiling. Having itched and scratched for too much of that night, even in the daylight he could find no bites or fleas.

Later that morning he and Jack found themselves in the finance ministry. Before they could ask why they were there, the minister's bossy secretary had propelled them into the inner sanctum. All members of the ministerial drought relief task force, their top officials and several others were present, but only Jenkins Makimbo made an effort to greet them.

'What's your problem this time?' Mr Mboko demanded, glaring at the health minister.

'Which one of my problems?' Jack's knee-jerk reaction was *not* appreciated.

'I've seen a video of last evening's seven o'clock news,' the health minister whinged. 'That arrogant Red Cross worker, Mashedi, must be sacked for his unwarranted criticism of my plans to implement my under-5s' growth monitoring and feeding programme.'

'Consider this proposal,' Mr Mboko replied caustically. 'Sack the useless members of your staff, show the rest the video and quickly convert your so-called plans into effective action. Then come back here for another chat.'

'Your new rules delayed my under-5's programme.'

'New rules were essential because you directed hospitals to charge for treating acutely malnourished babies and young children. Why did you do that?'

'Waiving charges would create a dangerous precedent.'

'Do you honestly believe that mothers, without money to buy food, will take their sick children to be weighed and measured with your threat of a hospital bill they cannot pay hanging over their heads? Red Cross volunteers get an allowance to cover their expenses while registering households facing starvation or issuing food. Yet you have taken it upon yourself to deny voluntary health workers their appropriate incentive. Pay them the same allowance and waive the hospital charges! . . . Mr Makimbo, please convey our thanks to young Mr Mashedi and tell him that we have *all* benefited from his excellent lecture. Things can only get better. They must not get worse.'

The health minister stalked out, angrily pursued by Mr Mboko. It was no secret that both were vying to succeed the indisposed president, who'd played no part in governing the country since his election four years ago. But neither these undisputed facts nor their fractionalising impact on or within all levels of government received any local television or radio coverage. The information minister's censorship talents had guaranteed that, but even she couldn't stop this latest confrontation being leaked. Who was the culprit?

The secret service hounds were loose, their noses sniffing for scent, and the local press had a field day!

Harry now had a tape recorder, making it possible to produce verbatim minutes of that mega-fractious session and its expected repercussions, enabling him to get to bed earlier. Yet he was still wide awake when the clock/radio on his bedside table blasted out the five o'clock World Service News. Having seen men in black shades and suits patrolling the town, he'd assumed they were secret service agents. But who controlled them and would they descend upon him and demand to read his diaries? He got out of bed, wiped the tape recorder clean and, sparsely clothed, temporarity hid his laptop in the Akroyd's garden.

Wherever Speedy went in Kolokuana, everybody knew him – in shops, offices, on pavements, whilst driving, admirers shouted and waved – and he responded with verve. The same happened that evening at his first Happy Hour, though he was very soon distracted by the amount of skirt around, of all cuts and colours. The hunter began his prowl, to pick and trap his prey. Yet, judging from the reaction of the many unattached females in that jam-packed bar, it was they who were doing the hunting and their quarry was this cool, muscular hombre with the upstanding reputation and John Travolta swagger.

'You drove extremely well down south.'

Harry's compliment failed to capture Speedy's attention, so Dave had a go.

'What did tha think'a central 'ighlands lad?' Dave had to repeat his question.

'Okay. But I didn't sleep much,' Speedy replied, naïvely, his eyes still roving.

'Course tha didn't blooody sleep. Tha were too busy screwin fookin croompet.'

'Aw, come on, give us a break. A school teacher invited me to her birthday party.'

'So tha took all bleedin weekend to blow 'er fookin candle out.'

Speedy may have elaborated had not a remarkably top-heavy brown maiden in a frock with an outrageously plunging neckline indelicately seized one of his arms. Dave nudged Harry, but before he could utter one of his choicest remarks, they were made privy to the tail end of the briefest of chats not meant for their ears.

'So you want a bit of fun,' said Speedy.

'Plenty fun,' said she.

And they disappeared, just like that, without as much as a wave.

'That was slick,' Harry chuckled. 'Another beer, Dave?'

'Nigh time I pushed off. I'm bloody knackered. Near on didn't make it 'ere. Accident blocked soddin mountain road.'

'By the way, did your cattle-post owner friend get his cattle that survived the drought to market?'

It was a sad story. In brief, the owner got them there, but couldn't sell them and let them run loose. When Dave next took him his mail, he was confused, unsteady on his feet, worried about money and insisted on riding a couple of days to his sister's place and ask her to pay his bills. Dave hadn't seen him since.'

Outside the bar Harry cautiously asked: 'Heard of any mine workings yet?'

'Not a dickey bird, but got me feelers out.'

Dave refused a lift. Apparently, when visiting Kolokuana, the scrimping charity which paid him a "tenner a week" to pass on his skills to the locals, insisted he bunk down in the cellar under its office, near the UN club, arousing some extra-special profanities.

Just as Harry was about to leave his cottage and stroll over to the Akroyd's for supper Angela swept in, effusing conviviality, parading her clean Barbour jacket and mud-green Hunter wellies, her silver cigarette-holder erect and jubilantly dangling a plastic bottle of washing-up liquid, to replace the soap Harry's rats gnawed. Dennis padded along behind in a scruffy anorak, his flat-cap erect and solemnly dangling a brace of fearsome-looking contraptions he vowed would exterminate all invading vermin.

Send in the Clowns

At the first meeting of the ministerial task force Jack had been told to draft a press release which he'd asked Harry to type in university English and this Mr Mboko had transformed into a script worthy of his much-heralded, televised and radioed "Address to the Nation."

He began by explaining why the state of emergency, declared four months ago, might have to be extended and then highlighted his numerous achievements. After a surfeit of – I have done that, I am doing this, I shall do even more when re-elected – he courageously announced: 'From tomorrow, water is to be used only for essential purposes in both the northern and the southern provinces. As chairman of the ministerial drought relief task force, I shall personally decide when, where, and for how long public water supplies will unavoidably be discontinued, the media will publicise the restrictions and the police will enforce them. Every person who disobeys these restrictions will be fined or imprisoned. Because of the increasing danger of water-borne diseases, you must take much greater care with sanitation and hygiene. You must all boil water for ten minutes before drinking, cleaning teeth, washing hands and food, cleansing wounds and so forth. I will also ensure that water testing and treatment, sanitation and sewage disposal are improved, now. Food distribution to entitled people is working satisfactorily, but demand has exceeded supply. So, in addition to requesting larger food donations from overseas, I shall transfer water, food and fodder from the northern province to all drought victims in the south. I shall also ensure that every acutely malnourished baby and child under five years of age receives free hospital treatment and specially blended, highly fortified food. I expect every citizen and expatriate to assist relief agencies to introduce, improve and sustain all emergency measures.' The Gwato version followed.

Harry switched off his portable clock/radio, which he'd brought from his cottage, so that the office staff could hear the minister's speech. Jack, however, was holding his head in his hands. 'I spent hours writing that press release,' he groaned, 'but it had no election gimmicks in it when it left me.'

'How can I boil water for ten minutes?' Fuzzy, their office cleaner, pleaded. 'I burn all the cardboard my daughters find to keep us clean and cook food.'

'Infectious bugs hide in empty pipes, and when water flows again, the bugs are swept along the pipes,' Harry warned. 'That is why water must be boiled for ten minutes. Please also remember that some electric kettles switch off without boiling water long enough.'

'My mother hasn't got an electric kettle,' said Speedy, flashing impeccable teeth.

'There's one here,' snapped Pinkie, the accountant, 'washing vehicles is banned, also.'

I'll get some firewood and water containers,' Jack promised.

'And after work Glen will load a full water container into the boot of my car,' chipped in Muella, the young secretary who teased Glen, the shy American press and information officer, incessantly.

'I think you meant to say your fiancée's car,' Glen thought aloud.

While Fred, patrolled the office compound the rest of the team went to the UN club to help Muella celebrate her engagement. Jack even bought a round! Her fiancée, the lucky Londoner who managed a department in Kolokuana's British bank unfortunately couldn't make the party – correction, *fortunately* couldn't make the party, because Muella was an absolute cracker! It was her first appearance in the UN's clubroom and its male members hoped it wouldn't be her last. But Speedy hadn't noticed the stir she'd caused. He and his busty dolly bird must have been too busy recalling the previous Friday night and planning loads more frolics.

Next morning Happy Sam was standing near a check-out counter at Berney's Bazaar, beaming from ear to ear, but while they were carrying the shopping across the street, he started shivering. His vest had many more holes than the manufacturer had inserted, his shorts were torn and when Harry asked him where his blanket was, the expression on his grubby face replied. It had been stolen! He scampered off with a note, instead of the usual coins, to buy a hunk of bread before haggling with a blanket seller.

The transaction had been seen. In a flash, the beggars who frequented the Horseman's Rest car park, known to change into their stinking working garb in a taxi on the way to town each day, clustered around the land-cruiser, jostling for position, their gungey palms outstretched. Harry pressed the door-lock switch and drove off, angrily disgusted.

While driving back to the Horseman's Rest for lunch, he spotted Happy Sam parading a bright blue jumper, which would also protect his chapped knees.

'How long can he hang on to that?' Harry muttered. 'The boy's goal is to survive from day-to-day with his body intact, finding enough food and clothing a bonus.'

Suleiman had asked Harry to entertain an official from UN headquarters and Tsabo had offered to help. But neither had expected to meet a shapely American in her forties, aspiring to the name of Jinky! Even though her make-up was immaculate, she extracted a mirror from her handbag, touched up her lips, patted her ash-blonde hair, dabbed powder here and there – perfectly aware that the female ritual would stifle all male conversation.

'Do carry on daarlings,' she drawled. 'I'm listening.'

Fluttering jet-black eyelashes and thrusting forward twin plumpies, Jinky focused her not inconsiderable charms unerringly on Harry. Her perfume made him want to cough.

'What's brought you to Kolokuana?' Harry thought he should ask.

'To do my performance reviews, including yours honey.'

Jinky certainly provided refreshingly, different, company. When briefed on the emergency her attention never strayed, her questions always pertinent. And once the drought relief project's performance review had been arranged, she drooled over the cute trace of Irish brogue in Harry's lovely English accent. Considerably taken aback by this assertion, Harry had never been told, not even by his wife, that he'd retained an Irish brogue. Jinky must have got hold of his CV. The Afro-lilt, still faintly discernible in Tsabo's otherwise flawless Oxford accent, elicited no Jinky comment.

After her lunch thank-yous, she hip-swayed towards the door, which had Harry wondering how she managed to get around the world on those skyscraper heels. How the devil did she get around the world, period? He was in two minds and only one entailed leaving.

Quick to pick up the vibes, Tsabo suggested they play pool. So Harry sought refuge in the faithful old land-cruiser and all three of them made haste to the UN club.

'You missed out there,' said Tsabo, re-racking the balls.

'What do you mean?' Harry asked, indignantly. 'I won that game.'

'Jinky was obviously hooked on you. I bet she wouldn't mind a bit of performance review later on today.'

'She didn't whisper her rondavel number for nothing.'

'You must be joking!'

Visibly uncertain whether Harry was having him on, Tsabo eventually asked: 'What's happened to your Mr Tokolosi then? Organising a braai at the office. On a Sunday, too. It's not like comrade Jack to be around at weekends.'

'I think a witchdoctor must have exorcised him. He's even started calling me Harry.'

'He was charm personified when he asked me to invite my mother and sister. By the way, will you be taking anyone?' There was more than a hint of censure in Tsabo's voice.

'Depends on tonight's performance review,' chuckled Harry, chalking his cue.

Harry had invited the Akroyds to the braai, but Dennis had forgotten and taken the dogs on a trek. When Harry arrived with a blonde in the land-cruiser, Tsabo's eye-balls flew into orbit and returned to ground-zero only when realising that the passenger was not the glamorous globe-trotter but Harry's equally glamorous landlady, fetchingly sporting skin-tight jodhpurs, riding jacket and boots. Jack introduced Harry and his partner to his wife and had to be reminded that Angela was married to Dennis, the couple he had met at the Queen's Birthday reception. Jack's brow furrowed, most probably he couldn't remember the reception, let alone who were there. To avoid any more embarrassment, his much younger and taller wife, a primary school teacher, glanced at Angela's jodhpurs and said their four daughters, aged from seven to twelve, loved riding ponies. Angela beamed and lapsed into horse-and-stable-talk, prompting Harry to circulate.

All the team were present. Fuzzy was wearing the headscarf Harry had her bought in Mavimbi. Muella's fiancée turned out to be a reasonable bloke – not the cradle-snatching seducer Harry had envisaged. Pinkie was dispensing cans of coke from a tin bath full of ice. Speedy made his rowdy presence heard behind a smoky braai-stand. Glen guarded a table on which were displayed the least over-ripe of Berney's Bazaar's imported bananas.

While Tsabo showed his mother and Palima around the bungalow's offices, his father relaxed on the back door step, warming his gammy leg in the sun, proudly doffing the brown trilby Harry had given him to passers-by and merrily exchanging thumbs-up signs.

'Grub's ready,' Speedy shouted. Jack made sure his family and Angela were first in the queue. When it came to Harry's turn, Speedy unceremoniously deposited the last lump of charred mutton and a hefty heap of baked beans on Harry's flimsy papier-mâché plate. It buckled and the mutton nearly slid off, evoking its server's uncalled-for ruderies.

'I thought you would have brought your hot cookie. Getting a good work out?' Harry inquired, with a nod and a wink.

'Very!' Speedy held up a monster sausage on a fork, gazed admiringly at the monster and dumped it on Harry's plate. 'I'll try one of Glen's bananas next. That should be very good, too. I'll let you know.' He grinned without unclenching those unsurpassable teeth.

Speedy not only collected the mail, he possessed a rapacious desire to explore its inner-most contents. Envelopes addressed to Harry, except those with his wife's hand-writing, he placed directly under Harry's nose, nonchalantly inspected whatever else happened to be on the desk, and if Harry still ignored him, he gently eased the envelope even closer. Then they both fell about laughing.

A copy of a fax, addressed to Suleiman, regurgitated Speedy's curiosity. 'Rather than having to keep transferring money from your other budgets,' it read, 'I'll send you funds specifically allocated to drought relief, together with my proposal for a follow-up disaster management project, which Harry may wish to vet – and improve! Regards to all, Jinky.'

Peering over Harry's shoulder, Speedy asked: 'What's disaster management?'

'All you need to know, your lordship, is that you've probably got a job for life.'

During his performance review, Harry had emphasised that relief efforts must not stop at saving lives and livelihoods, but also strive to eliminate the root causes of disasters by effectively preventing, preparing for and responding to their in too many cases inevitable recurrence. Jinky had contended that all UN and most NGO relief agencies had proven to be well prepared to respond to crises. Athough for most African governments, mitigating against disaster was a whole new ball-game. Turning the tables on Harry, she'd suggested he prolong his stay and prepare the country's disaster management plan, strengthened by enforceable legislation, only to sit back, admire his gulp and smile.

After re-reading her fax he drove to the cottage to assess all of the implications, both positive and negative, without interruptions. Foremost among the negative implications, Belinda's reaction, or rather her objection, for he assumed she'd have serious objections to her husband's prolonged absence. How much longer, though? He'd have to get down to making a time appreciation, though his brain wasn't in the mood for all that right now. If he sat in the Ackroyd's garden, might he be able to concentrate better in the fresh air? No! He could see Angela talking to some of her female friends out there. He'd go and sit on the toilet, his favourite place for solving difficult problems, but he could only grapple with his wife's inevitable . . . The phone was ringing in the bedroom. Having hoisted up his trousers, he got there in time to hear Speedy say: 'The post office is waiting for me to collect your parcel. I'll need your passport and some money to pay the custom's charge.'

'Who's the parcel from?'

'I'll tell you after I've been to get it.'

'Oh, yes, of course. Thank you very much Speedy.'

He returned from the post office next morning with the parcel, addressed in Belinda's handwriting. Anything with her handwriting on it always barred his snooping, but by now his inquisitiveness had overwhelmed him.

'Your wife has written on this label, old socks of no re-sale value. Does she want us to wash them or something?' He slit open the parcel's wrapping-paper with his jack-knife.

Out from a pair of Harry's rugby relics tumbled dozens of water purification tablets, six packets of Bisto gravy powder, three jars of Marmite and some sheet music. The sheet music attracted Speedy's extra-special scrutiny, inducing Harry to explain that he'd been invited to sing at an important social function and must practise beforehand.

'Did you hear that Glen? Harry's a *singer!*'

'I sang bass back in the States. What are you Harry?'

Pitching his normal speaking voice an octave higher, he replied: 'I'm a tenor.'

'What? Little Glen's a bass and big Harry's a tenor? I don't believe it!'

Speedy shot off to spread the word. Nothing was sacrosanct.

Harry's singing career – if one might refer to it in those glowing terms – had started way back when he'd warbled, just by himself, the first verse of *Once in Royal David's City* with shorts under his cassock. After gravitating to the eminent alma mater of hordes of Oxford scholars and Whitehall mandarins, also a sprinkling of dodgy cabinet ministers, opportunities occasionally came his way to re-demonstrate his prowess. To mention just two: he'd serenaded several of his house-matron's many hen parties with the falsetto aria *Fine Knacks for Ladies*; then performed *Jerusalem* in a far more comfortable tenor key – the high-point of a former pupils' reunion dinner which, without doubt, had clinched his subsequent appointment to the school's revered board of governors. When the pressures of globalisation had compelled him to hang up his management consultancy boots all too prematurely he'd considered assisting one of two world-famous Welsh male voice choirs.

But Belinda had preferred a Cotswold lodge to a Morriston semi or a Treorchy terraced dwelling. So, he'd had to make do with the back row of the local choral society. His only solo, before being snatched away to Africa, had occurred, momentarily, at the Kennet and Avon Canal Users' Easter Jamboree, when his rousing final "Alleluia" at the thundering climax of Handel's chorus of that name, rang out across the boatshed a whole beat sooner than the society's overwrought conductor had expected.

Now he must recruit a competent accompanist and rehearse *Ave Maria* and *Send in the Clowns*. The organist of one of the capital's two cathedrals would have obliged, had he not been caught abusing a choirboy. So Harry borrowed the choirmaster's tuning-fork.

The highly respected American ambassador, an ancestral product of the slave-trade, looked forward to his next appointment on several of the Pacific Ocean's islands. Richard Riddington, more than anxious to promote his candidature as the replacement doyen of Kolokuana's diplomatic community, volunteered to stage the ambassador's farewell on the "Glorious Fourth of July" and then devoted a great deal of his redoubtable energy and precious time to ensuring that the army's brass band was otherwise engaged. But finding an alternative form of acceptable entertainment remained a problem, until recalling that after the ladies had withdrawn and the port had been passed round the table at one of his more frequent, but very expensive, black-tie dinners, Harry had sung something called *The Foggy Foggy Dew* and quite a few gentlemen guests even knew the risqué words and had joined in!

Harry managed to persuade Glen to come with him to the first rehearsal. Staggered by Glen's richly powerful bass voice, he invited Richard Riddington to the second rehearsal.

That was how Glen and Harry came to present themselves to the galaxy of dignitaries, seated in the reception chamber at Richard's residence. Harry's two tenor numbers went all right on the night – Glen's *Deep River* and *Just A'Wearying for You* went much better and deserved the louder applause. Richard thanked them both, but huffily informed Harry that several high-ranking guests had taken his singing of *Send in the Clowns* as a personal affront. 'No comment,' Harry huffily replied. Having overheard that exchange, Suleiman not only congratulated Glen and Harry, he suggested they sing at one of the UN club's Happy Hours, which he would arrange and have publicised.

In the floodlit yard outside the club's bar, the duo gave a repeat performance, but this time with Speedy crouched behind them, just itching to bang his bongos. Unable to resist joining in, regrettably he spoilt Glen's *Just A'Wearying for You* by hotting up the rythmn.

Glen had every right to be furious, yet all he said was: 'If Speedy brings the bongos, I won't do concerts again . . . if there are any.'

'I'll ban the bongos,' Harry reassured him, though Speedy wasn't too happy.

Before leaving in the government truck to go to a wedding, Jack had told Speedy to take his daughters home from school in the UN land-cruiser. On the way back, while hanging upside down in his seat belt, he'd realised that the wheel rolling down the hill in front of him must have been one of his. A lorry driver had got him out of the seat-belt, towed the land cruiser to a garage and taken him to the hospital for a check-up.

Next morning Speedy, slumped in a chair beside Harry's desk, described his perilous adventure and ended with a disconsolate: 'Sorry Harry.'

'Thank God you weren't near the edge of one of those highland tracks. Any injuries?'

'A few bruises, but the land-cruiser's got more than bruises.'

Harry went and confronted Jack. 'I believe you told our driver to take your daughters home from school in the land-cruiser yesterday. Is that true?' No reply. 'Is it true?' Still no reply. 'What if the wheel had come off with the four girls on board. How would you have explained that to your wife? And where would I have stood, if Speedy and the UN vehicle had been written off?' This also drew a blank. 'Look, Jack, what you do with the government truck is your business. Just leave the tasking of the UN land-cruiser to me.'

Jack stubbed out his fag, lit another and inhaled deeply. His eyes looked repentant, but his mouth stayed shut, though his brain had plenty to think about.

Harry made a couple of mugs of tea and gave one to Speedy. 'If you're fit enough, ask Mr Tsamanachimone's permission to drive the government truck and take this envelope to Madam Thelma.'

'Will I get the sack?' Speedy mumbled, staring down at his designer desert boots.

'In the envelope are an accident report stating that you were delivering documents and a note reminding Mr Rashid that he promised me a replacement four-by-four. Several are parked in his office compound. Get one of those and your job's safe.'

Beeping his triumphal arrival, a signal for the office staff to come out and admire his prized acquisition, Speedy proudly drove it around the back patch. Resisting the urge to wash the brand new land-cruiser – drought restrictions – he dusted and polished its cream bodywork and upholstery before taking it to a garage to have the anti-theft devices fitted.

Later that day, having sped along a straight stretch of the main tarred road, Speedy announced his satisfaction with this latest model's performance and comfort. Then, on a winding stretch, he kindly allowed Harry to have a much slower, accompanied test drive. Equally impressed with the new land cruiser, on returning to his office Harry insisted that he take charge of the vehicle's log book in one of his aiming-too-high attempts to prevent every future unauthorised journey Speedy might be tempted or asked to undertake.

Once the old and battered, off-white model had been repaired and thoroughly checked, Glen was loaned his own four wheels – well, hopefully four – though hardly a week had passed when he phoned the office from the Horseman's Rest. He was stuck in traffic near the hotel, the truck's battery was flat and he needed jump leads.

When Speedy swept onto the scene, drivers were leaning on their hooters, the habitual crowd of onlookers had assembled and a policeman was taking particulars.

'What's your problem young man?' Speedy inquired, every inch the professional.

'I want a jump.'

'What? Here? In the main street?'

Glen never understood Speedy's jokes, but the copper laughed.

Unhappy Hour

There couldn't be too many nicer places in New England than Vermont. Glen was doubly fortunate. He grew up there and his home fronted a picturesque lake. But during his final two years at high school, disaster struck twice. His father died and the family's boat-hire business folded. Virtually penniless, he and his mother went to live with his sister down in Boston, Massachusetts. Having applied for various jobs, he was told at a UN interview that, provided he successfully completed a year's probation, he would be rewarded with a university place to study international aid. A degree had always been his target.

So, Glen found himself pitch-forked into a drought-torn region of Africa, posing as a press and information officer, living and working with strangers, and doing his utmost to relieve other people's suffering.

Confused by Jack and wary of Harry, it had taken a while to settle down. He'd quickly discovered that Jack hated paperwork, whereas Harry was a stickler for precise wording, forever asking for information, always checking details, typing briefs and gazing at maps. Yet Glen rated Harry's training skills highly and welcomed his friendly encouragement. Tsabo, Fred and Pinkie were great. So were Muella and Fuzzy – even though they both constantly teased him. Jack seldom spoke. Fathoming Speedy was beyond him.

Almost five years apart in age, in most respects Glen and Speedy were as dissimilar as chalk and cheese. Short, slightly built, solemn, polite, shy, unassuming, unworldly, Glen, the younger of the pair was, by his own admission, the kinda guy who takes confetti to funerals and a wreath to weddings.

Brash and mega-confident, Speedy regarded himself as one of the boys and a bit of a wag. But, like most boyish wags, his gags were not always funny and could be tiresome. Accepting most things at face value, thriving in tight corners, living by his wits, he got by nice and adequately, thank you, and was very handy to have around. He'd stretch out his leather jacket on any convenient surface for any female, as long as she had big tits, jutting buttocks, and legs right up to her armpits. Facial beauty seemed not to concern him over-much – hence one of his many borrowed, much too often repeated, snappy catch-phrases: 'Why look at the mantelpiece when you're stoking the fire?'

Humour of that type didn't click with Glen. He just continued with what he was doing, while Speedy fired for effect – again and again. Yet they were the best of pals and great lads, differently intelligent, and fun in their individual ways. That was how Harry would have wanted them to be, had he recruited them. They were counterparts: complementing each other and performing their contrasting duties commendably. Glen collated, recorded and made every effort to master all the information and also drafted press releases. Speedy, on the other hand, considered he had the more colourful job. He wasn't an office boy. He was a driver and drivers drove. He was extremely keen on driving, as it gave him a reason for being absent from the office for as long as possible, whilst keeping females variously amused. When Harry shouted for him, Glen was quick to explain that Speedy had taken a document to a cabinet minister's secretary or Madam Thelma, had gone to the post office, the Red Cross office, or some other official-sounding outfit around town. He also warned Speedy of likely reprimands.

On one of Jack's rare non-hangover mornings, he'd probably thought he ought to speak to Harry. 'The best thing about Glen and Speedy is that they've nearly replaced Tsabo.'

The L-shaped room now became the drought relief operations centre and Glen was re-designated its controller. With a new appointment card pinned to his shirt, he briefed Jack and Harry on the week's programme, fastidiously written in felt pen on one of his many wall charts – large and low enough for Jack to read without having to stand on a chair.

'All working group meetings will start at nine and finish by eleven whenever possible. Today, the training group. Tuesday, the water group. Wednesday, the food group. Friday, the group chairmen's co-ordinating meeting.'

'What about Thursday?' asked Jack, clearly bucked by his error-spotting ability.

'Thursday's a public holiday sir. I believe it's your country's Independence Day.'

'Have you circulated all the minutes and agendas?' Jack barked, running for cover.

The ticks on Glen's chart showed he'd already done so.

'Other skeduled commitments this week. Today, a briefing on the emergency at the English prep school at noon-time and at the international high school an hour later. That's me and Harry. The finance ministry's budgetary review starts at eleven and could last all afternoon.' Jack scowled. 'Mr Croft wants to talk with Harry at two o'clock, a Professor Archer's coming at three, a meeting with the UN local bosses at four.' Harry frowned.

'Tomorrow, nothing additional noted. Wednesday afternoon, Harry has to discuss the vulnerability study in Mr Rashid's office. Thursday's the public holiday. So that takes us through Friday. If Speedy's done with delivering our first monthly drought relief situation report, maybe we'll all go see what's doing at Happy Hour.'

Jack's shoulders were twitching. 'What's this vulnerability study?' he asked Harry.

'Because the government needs assessment surveys never happened the UN is funding a rapid vulnerability study. I'll tell you more after the meeting.'

'I nearly said we don't want a lot of rigmarole.' Jack laughed. He actually laughed!

The talks at both schools paid off. Not only were pupils told about drought relief, they took home a copy of the situation report for their parents to read. Prep school youngsters were invited to write to Uncle Harry, saying how they were helping. One sent a drawing of himself in a bath, above the caption: 'This water washes my family, then it flushes our toilet.' Many teenagers at the international high school were keen to devote their holidays to weighing, measuring and feeding under-nourished children. They became disillusioned when told they'd have to wait until the health ministry's under-5s' programme started.

The British public could have a donation added to all their water bills which a charity used to improve basic amenities in least-developed countries, such as teaching villagers how to maintain hand-pumps and do simple water quality tests. When Alistair Croft came for his weekly grouse, not the Scottish variety, Harry showed him the charity's leaflet.

'I've seen this advertisement before. All the examples are in India. I'll think about it.'

As ever over-burdened with pessimism, Alistair was nevertheless proving an effective if melancholic chairman of the water group. Swings and roundabouts!

Professor Archer arrived next. 'The British high commissioner mentioned you. So I thought I'd call by. After retiring, I was looking for something really worthwhile to do and offered to act as the link between our diocese in England and the Anglican diocese in this country. We're strongest in the northern province, but recently we've concentrated on building clinics and growing wood-lots in the south, to attract more followers. We're about to open another clinic, if we can find a competent doctor and a well-trained nurse.'

He pointed to a village in the central highlands on the wall map and looked as if he expected Harry to wave a magic wand and shout Hey Presto, here's a doctor and a nurse!

'I'll see what can be done,' Harry said. 'How are your trees coping with this drought?'

'Disastrously, I'm afraid. Our voluntary workers try to stop people cutting them down, but now not even stumps remain. It's disheartening to say the least.'

'I passed a wood-lot recently. Half the trees had died and the rest were dying. Surely it's fair game for dead wood to be burnt on cooking fires. There's precious little else.'

'We've told our staff to give dead firewood to the poor. But you will know that chiefs tend to requisition anything of value or in short supply for themselves and their cronies.'

'Would your link be interested in sponsoring a new process I've read about recently, which converts suitable rubbish into fuel pellets for fires, and also shipping us unwanted clothing? Both would be tremendously useful.'

'Fund-raising is hard enough already, without taking on more commitments. The only way we could help is by sacrificing our two existing projects. Even so, I think most of the local priests would regard garbage re-cycling and the rag trade as rather demeaning and thus detrimental to Anglican prestige. If their reaction's more positive, I'll phone you.'

'Thanks for coming. Hope to hear from you soon. All offerings gratefully received.'

While driving to the UN meeting Harry felt like a misery who's only happy when he's unhappy. It was still so difficult to get anything constructive done. Was it his fault or was he trying to achieve the impossible? Perhaps he'd fly home for a week away from it all, then return refreshed. That wouldn't work. When he got there, he'd want to stay there.

There was no room in Suleiman's office compound and he had to park the new land-cruiser by the roadside, hoping none of the far too numerous vehicle thieves were around.

It was the first time Harry had met all five senior resident UN representatives in one room. The trio were there who'd taken exception to being co-ordinated, all sweetness and light to his face but he'd never expose his back to any of them. When Suleiman requested a progress report, Harry named the countries that were donating emergency food aid and the smug boss of the UN's local food office insisted that all donations be attributed to his agency because they arrived under his auspices. Harry's criticism of the lack of an under-5s' growth monitoring and feeding programme, the health chief took as a personal slight and proceeded to extol his many personal virtues, as if embarked on a ego-trip rather than a humanitarian search and rescue operation. The UN agriculture supremo highlighted the failure of household food-security and livestock husbandry in the south, though had done nothing to remedy these and too many other deficiencies. The UN childcare director had good news! His agency had procured the specially blended/highly fortified diet, urgently required for treating acutely malnourished under-fives. Harry then asked why drought victims migrating from the southern province to another country were re-settled by the UN, while those moving to Kolokuana received no help at all, even though they had left their homes in the southern province for precisely the same reason – unremitting drought! A visiting expert ruled: 'Every person migrating from one country to another country is classified as a refugee and falls within the UN's assistance remit. Every person migrating within his or her country is classified as a displaced person and is therefore the responsibility of his or her government.'

'What happens if their government cannot or will not help them?' Suleiman demanded, but his question remained unanswered and the meeting broke up in stroppy stalemate.

Harry returned to his office mightily disgruntled, to find Fuzzy sprawled on the floor near his desk, sobbing her heart out. Piece-by-piece, her pitiable story unfolded and Harry was shocked by how little she earned. Having totted up her living expenses, her bus fares to and from work, her three daughters' school fees, her weekly food and water bills, he stared at the result as much in desperation as disbelief. Her expenditure was around twice her income! He showed her the sums and asked how she coped.

'My husband has no work. My father and brothers give me money.'

Confirming that Fuzzy's wage was correct for a cleaner, Pinkie said she would try to get her upgraded to office assistant. But now came a far more despairing plea for help.

'My husband *steals* my money. I must leave him and bring my kids to Kolokuana. Let me be your maid and let us stay at your place. *Please*, Mr Harry.'

'Sorry Fuzzy. I have a maid and no spare room, but I'll help you find one.'

Crestfallen, she stumbled off to brew the day's last three mugs of tea.

Always cooped up in the office, Glen had visited none of the surrounding countryside, so on Thursday's public holiday he'd be introduced to the central highlands. Harry hadn't driven along that part of the mountain road before, but if Dave's fookin boos could make it, his new land-cruiser certainly would. He collected Glen from the UN hostel and three hours of arid mountainous terrain later, parked at the summit of the highest pass. Quietly circumspect till then, yet clearly impressed by the scenery, Glen felt compelled to remark that he'd never imagined how such a bad drought could cause so much devastation. They stopped for a second break on the way back, at a small traveller's lodge overlooking the capital. Just the spot to try out the radio that Richard Riddington, after hearing of Harry's romp over peaks and beside canyons with no means of communication, had insisted must be installed in the new land-cruiser and dished out more of his petty cash. Harry switched on the radio, tuned out all the crackling and slickly enunciated his opening transmission.

'Hello zero. This is seven. Message, over.'

'Sunray speaking. Go ahead, over.'

Harry had expected a clerk to be monitoring the British high commission's radio net, not Richard himself! His second transmission went even slicker.

'Seven. Am at a travellers' lodge overlooking the capital. Where are you? over.'

'By myself at the office on a public holiday. Out!'

Harry switched off the radio and sheepishly glanced at Glen who looked embarrassed.

Near to the foot of the mountain road, Harry diverted to the village where Fuzzy lived and asked a woman where her home was. The tearful woman told him: 'Fuzzy's husband wanted more money to buy more beer. She said she had no money and he stabbed her in the chest! Our village headman drove Fuzzy and her father to the hospital in Kolokuana. He drove very fast. This I hope! One of her brothers tied her husband's legs to his horse and rode to the police-post.'

Harry's legs buckled at the knees! He mumbled his sympathy, clambered back into the land-cruiser and that voice inside his head chastised him: 'Why didn't you listen to Fuzzy and rescue her before it was too late? Tell Glen how bloody stupid you've been, then get yourselves to that death house of a hospital in double-quick time.'

The Asian doctor's prognosis: 'Stable, comfortable and very lucky to be alive. But I'm afraid your friend will be left with an ugly scar from below her throat to above her heart.'

Fuzzy's father and Harry shared a night-long anxious bedside vigil. Pinkie and Muella took over in the morning. Earlier that afternoon, Harry slowly drove her father and Fuzzy – sedated, bandaged, and lying under two blankets across the land-cruiser's rear seat – back up the mountain road to their village midwife's hut. She promised to take very good care of Fuzzy and change her dressings twice a day. Her father and mother wept while shaking Harry's hands and her two brothers thanked him for all he had done to help their family. While driving to Kolokuana, he thanked God over and over again for Fuzzy's survival, but remained greatly concerned about how her three young daughters would react when they came home from school and were taken to see what their father had done to their mother. An uncaring drunkard, he deserved to be dragged by a horse to the police-post.

Sitting alone outside the Happy Hour bar, preferring the evening chill to the crush and racket inside, Harry pondered over the week's ups and downs. Peaks? Both school visits. The launch of a rapid vulnerability study, and if its report recommended stricter, easier to apply food aid entitlement criteria this might reduce aid requirements, stem the mounting deficit and help him with updating the appeal for donor assistance. Troughs? Mavimbi's juggernauts loaded with donated food aid, impounded at the border, until import tax was paid. Aid wasn't subject to tax! The genuine issues were the hefty demurrage bill that the drought relief team would somehow have to pay and the transport ministry's objection to foreign vehicles entering the country, thus denying local hauliers the opportunity to make money and corrupt ministry officials to take their cut. A deeper trough – that UN meeting he'd left in a huff. There were some cantankerous people within the UN's local set-up, prejudiced people, promoting their own prejudices. Like himself, too often! He blamed himself for criticising the UN's wasteful, cumbersome procedures, also for showing its onerous, wide-ranging responsibilities scant regard. Yet some very untoward things went on within the UN's bureaucracy. Multi-ethnic representation among its staff appeared to count much more than merit and experience. Mr Ping, Suleiman's deputy, hadn't returned from home leave in South Korea and a francophone African man, who spoke no

English, now sat in Mr Ping's high-backed leather armchair behind the expansive mahogany desk, trying to make sense of transport requests, stationery requirements and menial such likes. The five local UN agencies, including Suleiman's development staff, competed instead of co-operating. The deepest trough – Fuzzy's horrific stabbing, the pain and torment she'd suffered and would still be suffering. Having found her sobbing on the office floor, he'd unforgivably failed to heed her desperate pleas for help and then respond to them. He had failed Fuzzy in a big, big way!

Fear of failure had haunted him since childhood. None more so than right now, for not only the lives and the livelihoods of drought victims by the hundreds of thousands were at stake, but now also Fuzzy's life, as well as her own and her young daughters' livelihoods.

Altogether an Unhappy Hour!

Trounced at pool and not in the frame of mind to risk another, Harry eased his way into the bar, needing a beer with his pals. Jack's Russian, picked up in the 1960s at some Soviet university, was being tested by that vodka-swilling air traffic controller; Speedy canoodling with his busty dolly-bird; Tsabo and Glen too engrossed in their game of darts to notice his rotten intrusion, lousy presence or pathetic retreat.

Back at the cottage, he phoned Angela Akroyd and asked if she minded him showing up early for supper. 'Of course not, silly!' Mooching across the shrivelled-up garden, he prepared himself as best he could to withstand her boisterous company. His morale would receive a welcome fillip, however, when Dennis uncorked a bottle of South Africa's best Pinotage, then another. After several glasses of that, plus two of the Akroyd's deceased chicken's cooked, sliced legs between four slices of bread, Harry felt almost near-normal. After a couple of large brandies, he didn't care how he felt.

Staggering home, with his feet trying to keep up with paving stones that kept going all over the place, and with each of his eyes scanning the stars in a disjointed attempt to find the Southern Cross, he ended up embracing an exceedingly thorny rose bush. He lay there for quite a while, painfully clinging to it, but the stupid thing still refused to bloom.

A New Stamping Ground

Emblazoned across the front of both national dailies, the headline 'Health Minister Forgot to Feed Them' could not be missed. Nor, immediately below, could the lurid photograph of dead babies, their naked corpses laid out in rows on some unidentified arid acre.

That day, in a capital where rumour flourished, Kolokuana was a gossiper's paradise, abuzz with all kinds of tales. The health minister had sacked his secretary, because she'd betrayed him. The health minister wanted to give up his difficult job and had forged the photograh. Mboko had forged the photograph, because he hated the health minister. The entire machinery of government, such as it was, seized up. Most senators and members of parliament, every civil servant, whatever their status, swapped guesses. Lesser fry fretted over all those dead babies! How many more Obangwato babies and children had suffered the same fate they asked each other?

The local radio station's seven o'clock news provided several intriguing answers. The health minister had resigned. Mr Mboko's sister would replace him. The Red Cross, not the health ministry, was now responsible for starting and managing the under-5's growth monitoring and feeding programme. Because of Mr Mboko's very heavy workload, as the country's conscientious finance minister, the government's chief secretary would control all drought relief activities. The governor of the southern province had retired.

What listeners had *not* been told, but would soon leak out, was that the photo of dead babies had caused cabinet ministers so much consternation that, unless the drought relief buck was immediately passed to a civil servant, the chief secretary no less, they would be chucked out at the general election, as well as lose their mansions and their many perks!

Next morning, the pro-government paper applauded the changes, backed Uncle Bill as the southern province's next governor and thanked Mr Mboko for everything he had done and was still doing to make the nation a shining example of what Africans could achieve, if given the opportunities Americans, Europeans and most other foreigners already had.

The opposition party's mouthpiece carried the bold headline 'Nepotism', then accused Mr Mboko and his sister, as well as Uncle Bill and his nephew, of 'incestuous trickery.'

'Who is Uncle Bill's nephew?' Harry asked, handing the newspapers back to Jack.

'That crook of a government chief secretary, of course.'

This *floored* Harry! He'd had absolutely no idea that Uncle Bill and the chief secretary were related. How would this affect the way he and Jack went about their business?

Mr Ngoshi Junior, the chief secretary and Jack's arch-enemy, had plotted to transfer the drought relief team to the health ministry's social welfare department, heaven forbid! What did this man have in store for them, now? And what did Suleiman think of the chief secretary controlling relief? Even Madam Thelma didn't know where her chief of mission had gone to and as ever, was disinclined to assist Harry, one of her innumerable pet hates.

Suleiman phoned around midnight, nonetheless his answers to Harry's questions were wide awake: 'Under no circumstances will Mboko's sister be entrusted with this nation's bad health,' he said. 'Mboko will stand in, until a much respected doctor has been elevated to the senate. All that bullshit on the local News about the finance minister's very heavy workload was codswallop! As for your understandable concern about the chief secretary controlling relief, we shall have to wait and see. Sleep well.'

Two letters signed by the finance minister arrived on Uncle Bill's desk. One, addressed to all district administrators, ordering them to discharge their drought responsibilities better. The other, addressed solely to him and obviously written by someone else, contradicted the first one. 'In view of your exemplary performance as a district administrator, you are hereby appointed to a much more important post: the governor of the southern province.' Mboko had added in his ministerial purple ink: 'I hope to be the first to congratulate you, unless my secretary disobeyed my order not to tell anybody.'

Although Mabela was half the distance to drive to and from
Kolokuana where his wife lived, Uncle Bill wanted to stay put
where his knowledge of the areas and their numerous drought-
related problems would be of most use. Having politely turned down
promotion by letter, he found himself treading the finance minister's
well-trodden carpet.

'By accepting this key position, you will be able to keep a
fatherly eye on your old stamping ground, while starting from
scratch in five others,' the minister said.

But that tactic didn't fool Uncle Bill. He'd made good use of
carrots and sticks all his working life. 'By not accepting that key
position,' he said. 'I will remain with my people. If I leave them,
minister, you will appoint some un-elected politician who knows
nothing and who cares nothing about them, their needs, the
emergency, or the job! I will move to Mabela only if my rural
development officer takes over from me and only if I'm allowed to
replace local government officials working in the southern province,
who I don't trust or are no good.'

'This national emergency demands stability, not upheaval and
confusion!' the minister indignantly replied, having just sacked the
health minister and a provincial governor. 'In any case, your rural
development officer is totally unacceptable. He's a civil servant.'

'A civil servant would be replacing a retired miner,' advised
the chief secretary, a civil servant himself. 'By approving the
appointment no precedent would be set, since it would still be
the only district administrator's post not filled by your political
nominee.'

'I'm going back to my old stamping ground,' Uncle Bill said,
shifting his feet.

Mr Mboko extricated his bulk from his creaking ministerial
chair to shake Uncle Bill's hand. 'You will move to Mabela. The
civil servant will succeed you, but you will dismiss no local
government official without my say-so. Go well, Mr Ngoshi Senior.'

On reaching the far end of the ministerial carpet, Uncle Bill
muttered to his nephew: 'Get the election delayed. That minister
demands stability, not upheaval and confusion.'

'I'll see to it,' the chief secretary muttered back, shutting the ministerial door behind them. Mr Ngoshi Junior did most of his muttering behind shut doors.

In his second broadcast to the nation within a fortnight Mr Mboko cited the president's indisposition as justification for the cabinet's *collective* decision to postpone the general election – no mention of the need for stability, the nature of the president's indisposition, or a revised election date.

With his immediate future decided, Virgoan Harry perfected his regular domestic routine. On Saturdays, after his weekly shop, he worked at the cottage, sometimes with Tsabo. On Sundays, having washed his smalls, he cooked all-in stew – chopped mutton and onions, defrosted or tinned peas or beans, Bisto gravy, plus seasoning. When the conglomeration was cold, he filled eight empty margarine tubs and crammed them into his fridge's far too small ice-compartment. On weekdays, he left the cottage at seven o'clock most mornings and returned at the same time most evenings. After work every Monday, he rejuvenated three portions of his *specialité unique*, which the Egberts helped him eat. After Happy Hour on Fridays, he shared whatever they were having for supper and so far, by the grace of God, they hadn't inflicted on him their version of his *récipé extraordinaire*.

Suleiman's and Harry's relationship had always been amicably productive. They now met at the UN club after work every Tuesday, while Suleiman's wife attended her Gwato class. On Tuesday evenings there was rarely a customer to witness a Muslim lacing his fruit juice with brandy or to overhear conversations not meant for eavesdroppers' ears.

Suleiman waited till they'd settled at the table farthest from the barman before asking Harry: 'How did your wife take your decision to stay on for another year or thereabouts?'

'Quite well, really.'

After much soul-searching, Harry had phoned his wife and explained why he wanted to see the job through. Neither sounding surprised, nor particularly happy, Belinda had said she would not be joining him because she was too busy designing dresses. It was no use arguing. She was as obstinate as he was. After his sleepless night, spent in a divorce court, he'd phoned again and a drowsy voice had invited the caller to phone back later. He'd forgotten the time difference! Having listened to several instalments of the World Service News, rather than prolong his agony, at eight o'clock he'd driven to Suleiman's office, had signed to complete two years and, at the stroke of a pen, acquiesced to all the promptings to stay on to which he'd been subjected – from Suleiman himself, from Jinky, Jenkins Makimbo, Tsabo and even from Jack. He'd also have loads more time to find his grandfather's grave. Belinda's written response would doubtlessly be arriving shortly!!

He was propelled back to the present by Suleiman saying: 'Flying to New York, one night, I happened to be seated next to a young Australian fashion model and found her tales of life on the cat-walks . . . unusual! Although we had very different personalities, we holidayed together, eventually married and were blessed with a son and a daughter whom we had to send to boarding schools in England. We are paying the penalty of having to move house all too frequently. Kolokuana's diplomatic compound wasn't exactly Diane's scene, yet she soon became a sought-after guest at social functions – often boring for her and at times a touch unnerving for me.'

Harry had heard the tittle-tattle – Diane's stylish elegance and witty candour were *not* popular with certain longer-in-the-tooth, sharp-clawed ladies of so-called lofty status.

'On taking up my first post in Africa, also my first as a chief of mission,' Suleiman continued, 'I had to place most inherited development projects on hold and concentrate on relieving drought. Yet there were no reports of previous drought crises for guidance, nor drought relief plans. You know the rest.'

'What was the local hierarchy up to?'

'Not much. Unless it sparked the Red Cross would step in, Jenkins Makimbo warned me. We'd both realised that an effective and timely response would be achievable only if the government and nation were placed on an emergency footing. When I suggested this to ministers, they blamed the president for indecision. A president I've still not met! The cabinet prevaricated, hoping that rain would come to its rescue. Rain that never came! After several fruitless attempts, I persuaded Mboko to declare a national emergency, but he insisted on managing government relief, with me managing non-government relief. He eventually agreed that a UN official and a local counterpart would jointly plan and co-ordinate *all* relief activities. UN headquarters authorised me to recruit an appropriate individual on a six-month assignment, but I would have to fund the post. Having raided my budgets, I asked Richard Riddington to contact his people in London and within days, two names with career details arrived by fax and I rang both contenders. One changed his mind on hearing what the job entailed. The other, whom Tsabo happened to have already recommended, was a chap called Harry Burke.'

'And he was dumb enough not to change his mind.'

'At least you weren't deaf.'

Suleiman called the barman and ordered refills – then asked a question, so strikingly obvious, that it was ludicrous that neither he nor Harry had thought of asking it before.

'Have you noticed that people in local high places keep banging on about a disastrous drought when most of us haven't a clue what conditions are actually like in the south?'

'Why not borrow the army's three larger helicopters.'

The three Huey helicopters, American relics from the Vietnam war, each seated nine passengers. The overwhelming number of applications to go sightseeing compelled Suleiman to allocate seats – nine cabinet ministers; seven senior civil servants; seven foreign diplomats; three guides and himself. When Mboko held a ballot his name didn't come out of the bag, so he cancelled the trip because no soldiers would protect the passengers. Most of them were VIPs, very important passengers, but nobody laughed at his joke. Anticipating the protection problem, Suleiman had a trick up one of his sleeves.

Parading in camouflaged fatigues in the army barracks at sunrise, nine cabinet ministers, the chief secretary and six less senior civil servants, Richard Riddington, two other high commissioners and four ambassadors responded to Suleiman's roll-call. Then three carefully selected groups and Suleiman ran across the parade ground, ducked under whirling rotor blades, their jungle hats held on their heads with both hands, and scrambled aboard their assigned Hueys. Their three guides brought up the rear. Tsabo and Harry had stuffed their jungle hats in a pocket. Jack's blew off and was chased by the emplaning officer.

Down in the southern highlands, the Hueys hovered above a remote stores shed where 4 x 4 trucks were being loaded with food, to deliver to distribution points. On the Mabela plain, they landed at a distribution point where food aid was being issued to ration-card carriers, where children were being weighed and measured, and where extra rations were being cooked for more than a hundred under-nourished under-5s. At an isolated hamlet in the central highlands, the visitors watched a bowser pumping water into a static tank and chatted to women, queuing to fill two gourds per household. The visitors gaped when the three Hueys took off and flew away – the signal for Suleiman to expose his next trick.

'Since we are all dressed as soldiers,' he announced, 'we shall complete our outing in an army vehicle's loadspace, without a canopy, to make it far easier see how drought has destroyed the surrounding countryside.'

Bouncing along the notoriously bumpy mountain road, Richard Riddington must have thought that singing *The Eton Boating Song* – particulary the 'we all pull together' bits, with actions, would cheer everybody up, as well as warm them. Alas, only Richard knew the words. But, although his fellow dignitaries tried hard to copy the pulling together bits, they found keeping their balance alarmingly hazardous in the back of a bucking lorry.

At the travellers' lodge, where Harry and Glen had broken their journey on the day of Fuzzy's stabbing, twenty-seven grounded-flyers rowdily gathered round a braai, scoffing the lodge's fried sausages and swigging its cold lager which they had to buy. It was well past midnight when every weary and better educated dignitary was safely in bed or wherever.

During the trip Harry and the chief secretary had been in the same group. Now that the government's senior civil servant had a "pivotal" emergency role, he was keen to change everything – even insisting that relief activities be run from Mabela, nearer the problems. Harry highlighted the snags. The drought might spread farther north. Ministers might take a back seat. All the UN and NGO relief agencies were based in Kolokuana. Moving the drought relief team to Mabela would hamper planning and co-ordination. To have drawn attention to the personally disturbing fact that Mabela was almost water-less would have proved self-defeating. Thrown on the defensive, Harry had invited the chief secretary to join him and Suleiman in the UN club's bar on the following Tuesday evening.

Suleiman had repeatedly tried to get the diamond mining embargo lifted and each time the chief secretary had sabotaged the negotiations. Since then, Suleiman had never trusted the man. He and Harry now intended to discover what made this Mr Ngoshi Junior tick. An intention thwarted right from the start by their guest claiming to be a teetotaller, when they'd both seen him sinking gin at the Queen's Birthday reception and knocking back lager at the helicopter trip braai. With their puny attempt at playing detectives thwarted, their cunning guest departed with a bladder part-full of brandy-doctored-coca-cola, never to reappear on Tuesday evenings or any easier to handle whenever their paths crossed.

The Red Cross had found establishing, supervising and running over two hundred food distribution points a monumental challenge. Now Uncle Bill set about forming the same number of community relief teams, each led by a head teacher, so that pupils could take home and bring back messages about needs, problems and solutions. Each team would include a volunteer trained to test and treat water supplies, another to maintain and repair hand-pumps, and two retired miners qualified in fire-fighting and first aid. The Red Cross nursing assistant, who weighed and measured the community's young children, also saw that those who were under-nourished got extra rations and that the acutely malnourished were sent to hospital. Building teams was one thing, keeping them together quite another.

Uncle Bill's project soon became a major headache for his helpers and even for hands-on Uncle Bill himself – team members' frequent attendance at family funerals, weddings, and such like, being the most popular excuse for over-long absences, thus causing relief activities to creak or fail. Even so an encouraging, if sorely belated, start had been made.

There were other reasons for believing that the chaos phase could now be on the wane. International donors had come up trumps with food aid, but Mboko insisted that 10,000 tonnes of yellow maize must be exchanged for white maize, his Obangwato tribe's staple diet. Red Cross relief staff flourished under Tsabo's stewardship, and the members of the six teams that Harry had selected and trained, were all set to monitor and where necessary improve relief activities in each of the six southern districts. He and Speedy toured three districts every month, sharing the driving if no army helicopter was available.

Yet, even if the chaos would give way to consolidation, drought recovery could still fail. Water supply, food security, healthcare remained precarious – sanitation, hygiene, livestock husbandry, rampant soil erosion badly neglected.

Then there was HIV/AIDS – a terrifying scourge, as prevalent in the northern province as renewed tuberculosis and malaria. This crisis had become so critical that the UN chief of mission in Mavimbi, with no drought problems, had been given extra resources to treat the mystifying disease wherever it erupted in that African region and to stop it spreading.

The first known HIV-positive case in the southern province was a miner on leave from South Africa and had been detected almost a year ago. Now, AIDS sufferers threatened to outnumber acutely malnourished under-5s in Mabela's inadequately small and equipped hospital, with overstretched staff mostly untrained or barely semi-qualified to treat AIDS.

In the southern province HIV-testing and drought relief competed for scant resources. In Kolokuana, where prostitution was Big Business, testing had been delayed by "lack of staff" while government offices overflowed with idle or under-employed civil servants. It was common knowledge that leading politicians, among other notables, had cornered the capital's sex industry and HIV-positive test results would punish profits. So, no testing!

'This killer-disease could soon reach epidemic, even pandemic, proportions!' Harry's diary recorded. 'Forever preoccupied with funding-problems, Suleiman has asked me to highlight the absence of HIV-testing in high-risk Kolokuana and to mention well proven remedies at tommorrow's ministerial task force meeting. A Mboko rebuke's expected!'

In the event, all of Harry's tinkering with delicate phrasing was made redundant by the far cleverer question posed by the newly appointed health minister, Dr Solomon Khami, a local general practitioner and widely acclaimed paediatrician.

'Should drought or AIDS top our list of priorities?' he asked the task force chairman.

'Equal top,' Mboko invented.

'Paying the mounting interest on your government's colossal foreign debt should also be top,' Suleiman bluntly suggested. 'Furthermore, getting the diamond mining embargo lifted would greatly assist with achieving solvency and assuring the southern province's earliest possible post-drought recovery, as well as funding HIV-testing in Kolokuana.'

'Minister,' butted in the chief secretary. 'Mr Rashid has offended diplomatic protocol. Our foreign debt, the mining embargo and HIV-testing are none of his business.'

'They are of legitimate concern to the UN,' Suleiman politely reminded him.

Minister Mboko glared at the chief secretary. '*You* have offended diplomatic protocol. Get out!' he bellowed, his copious perspiration flying in all directions.

An unbowed chief secretary announced his casual departure by slamming the door.

The Mboko glare now alighted upon Harry. 'And you are going to tell me the weather forecast hasn't changed.'

Gloomy nods from the phoney Bringer of Rain.

Africa-Transforming Technology

Progress on the technology front in August proved promising. Professor Archer's fax had raised hopes that a cheap method of re-cycling suitable garbage, to produce fuel pellets, would likely materialise early next year. With brushwood a past luxury, no cardboard or firewood to burn and so many cattle dying, the dwindling amount of dung made cooking a nightmare for rural Obangwato women. For urban families, the daily hunt for packaging, discarded by shops or markets, had become as frantic as fruitless. Cardboard and wooden boxes were being hoarded by trades-people and everyone else fortunate to have any. But without fuel, the food aid drought victims received might just as well have remained in stores sheds. Fuel pellets would be manna from heaven, provided they could be produced locally and sold cheaply – so how would the hungry multitude cook in the meantime?

Wind-up radios should arrive sooner. Of the tiny minority of rural people who owned a radio, most could no longer afford batteries. Glen's weekly drought relief bulletins were heard by inadequately few Obangwatos. For the vast majority, a wind-up version would be a miraculous blessing unless they had to buy it. For relief supervisors and workers, its value could not be overstated.

Whilst "mobile" phones were conquering the developed world, an Indian millionaire's son in Mavimbi bought his brothers, one of them Berney of Bazaar fame, a "cell" phone to boost profits. With a satellite dish now fixed to the police pylons above Kolokuana and Mabela, and in the northern province's capital, Berney invited Mr Mboko to declare the links open, though the army's brass band unmelodically molested the crowd's acoustics.

The national media hailed cell phones as 'Saviours of the Drought-Afflicted' and that was no empty claim, for landline telephones were like gold dust in the southern province. Outside Mabela only district offices, police-posts, army camps, very few doctors and fewer nurses, plus wealthy and privileged people, had a landline telephone – whether it worked was a different matter. High and low frequency radios predominantly used by the army and police were also unreliable, particularly in the south's mountainous terrain.

A local cell phone revolution seemed likely to achieve so much. The spread of better governance at all levels, the dissemination of market information, greater efficiency and stricter economy, were but four advantages. Yet there were very serious problems, among them: popular demand; the exchequer nearing empty; Mabela and some other townships, but hardly any villages had electricity in drought affected areas and cellphones had to be re-charged.

An unexpected development would test Suleiman's temper and shrewdness.

The information minister very soon realising that cell phones would spike her censorship ardour, intended to ram her proposal to ban them through parliament, until persuaded by most cabinet colleagues that cell phones were an invaluable means of monopolising and exercising power. By imposing a punitive purchase tax, the government would not only restrict ownership, but also reduce its deficit and promote censorship. Cell phones would help the secret service to increase its strike-rate, too, and the money required to build and run more prisons would be raised by stepping up blackmail. Their conversation went un-minuted, though Mr Mboko secretly assured Suleiman that the cabinet now had a plan to convert the government's big deficit into a big surplus and to reduce donor aid. Suleiman asked what the plan was. When Mr Mboko mentioned, confidentially, the cabinet's cell-phone tax, censorship and blackmail proposals, Suleiman said he would spread the word far and wide, unless the cabinet reconvened immediately with him and the chief justice in attendance. He also insisted that ministers must swear on oath to reject the cell phone tax proposal, because restricting ownership would nullify the tremendous improvement in communications urgently needed, and would penalise not only drought victims and relief agencies, but also the government and the entire nation. As for the censorship and black-mail proposals, the publication of his UN-approved statement would most likely result in the withdrawal of donor aid and any other external assistance the country was receiving.

The cabinet backed down . . . and then titbit by titbit it all leaked out.

Needless to say, everybody who was anybody hankered after possessing one of these wonderful inventions. Mr Mboko struck a deal with Berney who promised the delivery of enough cell phones to satisfy the needs of cabinet ministers, top civil servants and senior army and police officers. Suleiman discovered that a hefty bribe had featured in the shady transaction. So, key relief workers and district officials were given priority. One hundred cell-phones were ordered, the government and UN would share the cost, but were warned that delivery could take several months.

As luck would have it, Suleiman knew a Polish engineer who had left the UN to lead a private enterprise project involved with low-cost solar panels generating electricity. Jurek invited Suleiman and anyone else who would like to come to his wife's village where he now lived and see how the system worked.*

Suleiman had hired a civilian helicopter. 'The army's are either broken or bespoken,' he said, with that detectable hint of enforced dishonesty that Harry had to emulate when, for example, the truth might be too punishing for an elderly drought victim to withstand.

The civilian pilot flew them to Mabela, to pick up Uncle Bill. Heading west to the far side of the Mabela plain, the pilot followed the gorge separating the central and southern highlands, hovered just beyond the gorge's southern rim and Jurek guided him down.

Three solar panels assembled from kits and laid out on a north-facing slope provided a cooking stove, light bulbs and a borehole's water pump with electricity and could provide all the village's domestic requirements. Water pumped from the recently sunk borehole, down in the gorge, irrigated fields there, so that villagers could grow fruit to exchange for maize. Before more kits arrived from the project's sponsor, Jurek would train and employ solar-panel-assemblers where there were jobless people, empty buildings and good roads.

---

* Page 68. Sketch-map shows the village's location.

'They're all waiting for you Jurek.' Suleiman said. 'Many thanks for showing us solar power in action and congratulations for what you've achieved so far.'

Walking to the helicopter they met Jurek's wife, the district's public health manager. 'Tsabo Mashedi came to see the solar panels last week,' she said. 'His sister was one of my bridesmaids, while we were on our course in Mavimbi and we were both blessed with firstborn sons, there. Obangwato people think coincidences bring good luck. This I hope.'

When airborne Suleiman asked on the intercom: 'Any solar power comments?'

'From what we've been told,' Harry replied, 'Jurek's backers seem prepared to take a gamble, but very few drought victims can afford to buy a solar panel.' Macro-pessimistic Alistair Croft, the water working group's otherwise excellent chairman, would have said that so Harry quickly added: 'Jurek could be on to a winner.'

'Every community headman and all key relief workers with no electricity must have a solar panel and a cell phone as quickly as possible,' Uncle Bill insisted.

They circled above a tented camp, way out on the Mabela plain, and landed near a track which women were extending. Some hewed the baked earth with hoes or flattened it with rakes, others broke up rocks with spades or spread rubble, without a man, draught animal or mechanical implement in sight. The province's few remaining oxen were too weak to work and the far fewer tractors, bought on the cheap from a recently bankrupted vendor, were unavailingly awaiting spare parts or simply beyond repair.

A sturdy young man rode in and Uncle Bill introduced the site foreman to the visitors. 'He said he's been trying to find a mechanic who will come and repair his water bowser. He's as tireless as his brother-in-law, Tsabo.'

Harry had read before leaving England that coincidences were powerful in Africa and never to be taken lightly. They're also ten for a penny, he decided.

'This food-for-work gang has a woman from sixty households registered as vulnerable to starvation,' Uncle Bill explained. 'At every month end, each woman is given food for everybody in her household and the next gang takes over. In future, if fit men and women refuse to work for food, because other people get free food, they will be told they will get no food. I could employ many more gangs, given enough of the right equipment.'

'I'll scrounge it, if your best gang assembles Jurek's panels,' was Suleiman's remedy.

'That's a bargain.' Uncle Bill shook both of Suleiman's hands so vigorously, his arms risked dislocation. Recovered, he glanced at his watch and suggested they move on.

About to tour the southern province together, Uncle Bill and Harry were dropped off at Mabela. But instead of heading north, back to Kolokuana, the civilian helicopter flew east, towards the neighbouring country. Where's that off to? Harry wondered. And were all the army's helicopters really broken or bespoken?

Those questions would remain unanswered for the best part of a year.

The helicopter landed just across the border. Reg Trimble, the British police adviser, was waiting there. A policeman, also in civilian clothes, told Suleiman to lie on the car's back seat with a blanket covering him and drove to the nearby town. Reg led Suleiman through a café into a storeroom and a bearded giant greeted them in Afrikaans accented English. Reg said: 'Exchange envelopes,' and as pre-agreed Suleiman handed his to the Afrikaner, who reciprocated. Then, with nothing else spoken, the disguised policeman drove to the helicopter with Reg again seated beside him watching for hostile vehicles and Suleiman as before lying on the car's back seat under the blanket.

In his Kolokuana office, Reg removed a minute camera from his watch-strap and went to develop the negative. The result: a full-face shot of the Afrikaner handing Suleiman the envelope. Reg smiled, a rare trait, and told Suleiman: 'This felon's the leader of a gang wanting to re-open the old mine workings near our border with a neighbouring country to help fund Afrikaner opposition to Mandela's election.'

The Afrikaner's envelope contained a large amount of local currency and a typed note. It read: 'We paid well. Now deliver!' Reg locked the cash, photo and note in his safe and said he would inform the South African police.

Suleiman's envelope had enclosed a copy of the diamond cartel's latest letter to him, again refusing to lift the mining embargo. He could have saved himself a lot of angst, had he known the secret Reg knew – the old mine workings had re-opened eight months ago.

That evening, Uncle Bill confirmed that food-for-work was much the best way to reduce the growing amount of free food being distributed. Cash-for-work would be too difficult to administer, risked increasing corruption, and the cash might not be spent as intended. The trickiest issue he and Harry had to discuss was the chief secretary's idea of managing relief from Mabela, which they held in abeyance, though it sparked a surprising reaction from Uncle Bill.

'Beware of my nephew, he's got many irons in the fire. He wants to move you here to get you out of his way and he'll definitely try to get rid of Jack, they're old enemies. But Jack's an old stager like me, we know how to handle Mr Ngoshi Junior.'

If one of the irons in the fire involved a diamond scam, that could explain why he'd sabotaged Suleiman's efforts to get the mining embargo lifted and why he'd accused him of offending diplomatic protocol.

It also explained why Tsabo had warned me, Harry reckoned, that 'people you'd never suspect are getting in on the act.' Harry was now pretty sure that one was the chief secretary, but who were the others? The information minister, alias the Shredder, definitely. At least two more cabinet ministers, probably. The perpetually indisposed president, if one existed, possibly. Jack, unlikely. Jenkins Makimbo, no way. There was no shortage of potential culprits.

'Was your mine in this country?' Harry asked, hoping to eliminate Uncle Bill.

'No, down in South Africa. I went there from Kolokuana University and didn't see my parents for fifteen years. When I became the mine's first black safety officer, I married a Kolokuana girl, came home more often, always sent her money and never played around. Most migrant workers spent their wages on prostitutes, full of disease, looking twice their age, boys as well as girls, a few so young they should have been at primary school. All of them trying to earn food, clothing and a roof over their heads. There were always crowds of them outside the mine's gates, along the road to our Obangwato hostel and when some were found in bed with men, I banned them from our hostel. The grateful residents who took turns to guard the building called me Uncle Bill . . . my middle name is William, but many Afrikaners called me Kaffir. I'd rather not say what the others called me.'

'How did you become a district administrator then?'

'Shortly after retiring, I met my nephew and found myself in a job and in a district that were strange to me, yet I got by. Then, more recently, the local member of parliament told me to concentrate on getting him re-elected and not to bother with the drought. So my secretary dealt with the election preparations and I formed my district's drought relief team. You met the members soon after you arrived. Remember?'

'Tsabo and I were very impressed, but I forgot to ask if you set your team targets?'

'Always know what our people need. Get it quickly from within our district. If you can't do that, get it from somewhere else, quicker.'

'Bottom-up!' Harry exclaimed and Uncle Bill eyed the white man suspiciously.

Harry's first visit to southern districts with Uncle Bill and his third with Tsabo, who went with them, confirmed their worst fears. Chronic diarrhoea and typhoid were more widespread, water scarcer and, despite strict control, food demand still exceeded supply. If no extra food arrived from donors and the northern province rationing was inevitable. Stock-theft of drought victim's few remaining animals had escalated and several cases of the dreaded cholera had been reported, yet no reports had reached Uncle Bill, Tsabo, the drought relief team or central government! The main reason was that local government officials were scared of losing their jobs. The chaos phase was not waning, as Harry had hoped, but still in full swing!

An isolation ward must be equipped in Mabela's hospital to treat cholera. Those of its overstretched staff who could be spared from treating AIDS patients and malnourished under-5s, must be taught how to identify and treat cholera, as must nurses working in the cholera-detected and nearby areas.

Most chiefs regarded food control as an encroachment on their right, long established by tribal custom, to decide who should receive rations. That cut no ice with Uncle Bill, as a district administrator he'd never made decisions of that nature without first consulting local chiefs, nor must other district administrators. Monitoring teams still found chiefs forging registration lists, thereby delaying food distribution whilst inquiries were made and adding to the logistic pressures of distributing rations to so many locations monthly. Uncle Bill's answer was to distribute them – bi-monthly. When it was claimed that food requisitions were going astray, they were delivered to him and his driver took them to Kolokuana. Not only were there protests, even riots. One chief had told men to ransack a lorry load of maize and children were trampled to death in the scramble. Two soldiers now rode shot gun with every load, a precaution the cabinet had hitherto shunned. Rifles might be stolen or some soldiers might sell them. Harry's permitted means of protection against snipers' bullets was a stun-grenade, or he could summon reinforcements, if there were any nearby, on the land-cruiser's radio. He'd shout for help if the radio didn't work! Although carrying a firearm ran the risk of inviting lethal retaliation, Suleiman had asked the cabinet to review its personal security policy urgently.

While a district administrator, had Uncle Bill's frequent visits to communities and his extensive intelligence network exposed flaws in the relief system or in those responsible for making the system work, he had corrected them and reprimanded offenders. To those deserving thanks or praise, he had responded unequivocally and gave credit where credit was due. More potent weapons in his armoury were rockets, the verbal variety.

Both incentives featured prominently whilst touring his new-found districts, though he hadn't bargained on finding blatant corruption on his "old stamping ground." Instead of giving drought victims emptied maize bags to carry their rations home in, as Tsabo had stipulated, several distribution point supervisors were selling the emptied bags. The Red Cross food aid co-ordinator attached to Uncle Bill's former district had approved their sale! Now pinioned to a wall and threatened with live burial, Uncle Bill released him only if both he and Tsabo swore on oath: 'We will repay every person by yesterday.'

'Or as soon as humanly practicable,' Tsabo stoically added, when it came to his turn.

Uncle Bill's squat shape, his big round spectacles, his head jerking from side to side in case he missed anything, reminded Harry of the rhyme that had always made his grand-daughter giggle: "A wise old owl lived in an oak. The more he saw the less he spoke. The less he spoke the more he heard. Why aren't we all like that wise old bird?"

At the district office with the leatherbound books on a shelf, Harry again took down the 1886 edition of *The Regulations for District Commissioners* and Uncle Bill borrowed it. On the way to Kolokuana, the final leg of a fortnight's slog, he and Tsabo shared the back seat and leafed through its pages, handsomely printed by Her Imperial Majesty's Stationery Office.

'Sometimes I wish we'd never chucked out the British,' Uncle Bill confided.

'I think they left of their own accord,' Tsabo soothed him.

What is left of what they had left? pondered Harry, a lone eavesdropper driving north on a deserted main tarred road. Long gone were the clear cut legal codes and the delegated powers which had enabled dedicated colonial men-on-the-spot to settle disputes, dispense justice, solve problems and ensure fair play. In their place, a confusing tangle of tribal laws and unenforced government legislation, an obligation to refer even the most footling of issues to higher authority and, as witnessed during that tour, the readiness to ignore or the failure to report calamities, suffering and privation, lest today's politically appointed encumbents lost the many perks that went with their jobs. And who were the real losers? The poor, the sick, the cadaverous, whose lives and livelihoods depended on the ability of merciful donors and relief workers, but also on sundry indigenous bosses, to protect them from disasters, both natural and man-made. Most of the ruling elite offered no help, no sympathy, no fair play, no simplification or enforcement of legislation – Uncle Bill would move mountains for everyone in genuine need of his compassionate and tenacious help.

Two district administrators and eighteen of their principal henchmen failed to measure up to his punctilious scrutiny and he politely informed Mr Mboko that he was replacing them. Once their successors were settled, every local government official in the southern province attended a drought management workshop and would return to Mabela for six-monthly refreshers. A similar training-cycle would, as soon as practicable, cater for non-government paid or voluntary relief supervisors working in the southern province and in Kolokuana's shanty suburbs.

Not all of Harry's training endeavours prospered. His attempt to hold combined army-police relief courses within the capital's military barracks that had reasonable facilities was aborted when the police commissioner forbade members of his force to enter army property. Mr Mboko countermanded the order, but such was the long-standing enmity between the two uniformed services, the chief justice was required to pronounce upon the matter. He ruled in favour of combined courses – provided they were held on neutral territory – and further ruled that when civil servants were selected for similar instruction, their departments must release them. Yet, despite this, rarely were civil servants' courses well attended and the police continued to ignore the call to take part in combined training.

No sooner are plans made than they need revising, Harry reminded himself, before re-amending his training programme, then typing: 'In future most courses and workshops will be held at St John's Mission during school holidays, by courtesy of Father Patrick.'

Harry had rung him before leaving Mabela with Uncle Bill and Tsabo to tour districts, and had apologised for not having time to visit him. The priest was back to his jovial self.

'I've found another bottle of Jameson's,' he chuckled. 'Pop in when you can and we'll enjoy a tot or two. Young Tsabo drops in most weeks to tell the nuns and this old priest what the Red Cross is doing to help all those hundreds of thousands of poor, suffering drought victims and also how the whole outside world is faring for that matter. The nuns have always so enjoyed listening to Tsabo in full flow. The archbishop's given me his old wireless set and I get all the News every early morning from the BBC. I'm sure you're a World Service fan, too, don't you know.'

The much loved and respected priest whom innumerable Obangwatos had long called "The White Man Who Smiles" certainly lived up to his praise name. The impostor whom fewer and fewer colleagues nicknamed "The Bringer of Rain" had yet to earn his spurs.

Uncle Bill had said during their tour of districts: 'Get that government chief secretary off your back and spend half of every month working in the south.' And now the phoney rain-bringer decided to agree.

The Landlords

The wilting black Homburg – a shade too large. The slightly tatty dark blue overcoat – a trifle on the tight side. The droll tone of voice, pouting mouth, sad demeanour and well-timed innuendo. They'd all enhanced the police adviser's brilliant performance. Although obviously hailing from East London, not East Cheam, he'd made a thoroughly convincing Anthony Aloysius Hancock, much to Harry's surprise. The supporting cast was great, too, notably Sid James, mimicked by the British Council's versatile librarian.

The Akroyds and Harry had strolled up to the Horseman's Rest to sample the amateur dramatic society's latest production, and also whatever the much-publicised international menu would offer. The Homage to Hancock Night had kicked off with *The Blood Donor* followed by an apology for French onion soup. *The Radio Ham* and the stodgy spaghetti bolognaise had preceded *The Cold* and the solid bread-and-butter pudding and luke-warm custard. Although the meal wasn't so hot, the evening's entertainment had surpassed their wildest expectations. Decked out in her Saturday best, Angela had hooted with laughter throughout, frequently prodding Dennis to ensure that he stayed awake and occasionally checking that Harry's hearing aids were still working.

Always in the mood for a party, she invited several "special" friends back for drinkies. Dennis uncorked bottles of Pinotage and the nectar began to flow. Most guests stayed for just a quickie, but Kieran O'Kelly, the Irish consul, and Pippa, his Swedish wife, lingered on – to soak up Angela's version of the current expatriate gossip. Prattling away between sips of red wine and blowing smoke-rings at the kitchen's rafters, when her inexhaustible repertoire became exhausted, she asked Harry to play one of his many Welsh male voice choir tapes and had a little weep each time he obediently retrieved the ballad *Myfanwy*.

Another bastion of local white society, Kolokuana's Equitation Club, founded in 1863, had over the years metamorphosed into a predominantly female outfit, affording women and teenage girls regular opportunities to ride long, hard and skilfully on weekend timed-endurance contests. Angela, the endurance champion and the club's long-serving chair-person, gave riding lessons, drilled the more experienced riders, managed the stables and ensured the grooms stayed up to scratch. An exceptionally knowledgeable and energetic equestrian, her steely determination to keep the club going was exemplary.

The male members tended to render encouragement from the sidelines, though Dennis was forever on the go, fetching and carrying. Now an established cottage dweller, Harry very soon found himself masquerading as a gymkhana ringmaster and next day manning a remote endurance contest check point, then driving to the finishing post, filling a water trough and pitching a tent. Thereafter, he ensured that the drought crisis took precedence at weekends and helped host the club's parties, endeavouring not to hear the ceaseless female chatter about inseminating and vaccinating horses, harnessing and exercising horses, and mucking the darlings out. Angela also dished it out in big dollops when they ate, drank or travelled together, but Dennis just let it all wash over him like most of life's complexities, and Harry asked how he managed to do it.

'I often ask myself that. Yet, when my wife wakes me, yelling for a groom, I generally manage to do it, somehow.'

The club's males were compelled to attend its every function, thus earning their wives, partners, girlfriends or illicit lovers bonus points. The females earned many more if they attended club social events in dung-blemished Barbours and mud-covered Hunter wellies, thereby advertising their readiness to help the club in every practical way. They also liked congregating round the fire in their chairperson's lounge and the aroma was so noticeable that Dennis eventually took it upon himself to ban stable gear within his home.

The standard feminine livery became a navy blue sweater, a pleated grey flannel mini-skirt, black stockings and stiletto heels. They kept the club's silk headscarf, a rich cream with red polka dots, worn conventionally, if heads hadn't had time to fix their hair. More often it beautified the neck, fastened with a showy brooch – its centrepiece normally a riding crop, abnormally a whip.

The premier social event on the club's calendar was Epsom Night, held at the Horseman's Rest. And then the females really went to the races, made-up to the nines, adorned in next to nothing, jiving with each other, though some *did* let the males, by tradition in fancy-dress, take the odd, hampered turn on the floor. Harry wore the groom's outfit he'd bought at Berney's Bazaar and Dennis posed as a bookie, enabling him to wear his flat-cap. The British police adviser, alias Tony Hancock, caused female brows to lift when he arrived not in fancy dress and with a black girl whom he claimed was his secretary. They smooched for an hour or so and left early! At midnight the disc jockey and several male club members appeared to become stallions, hastening their departure, each escorted by a female. Harry's groom's outfit had attracted no such attention – luckily? Lying in his own bed, that routinely unforgiving voice inside his head primly commended his self-control.

Dennis supplemented the fast-dwindling income from his engineering firm by selling his paintings as well as South African wine. Harry bought a monthly crate of red Pinotage and also shared the churn of springwater, which every week Dennis drove the round-trip of fifty miles to re-fill at Monica's stud-farm. 'Angela has many best or special friends,' Dennis had told Harry. 'Monica is her *very* best friend, though she usually remembers to say, apart from my husband of course.'

Having invited Jack and his wife to supper, Harry re-heated five portions of his all-in stew: the concoction Dennis and Angela braved every Monday evening. During the meal one of the Dobermann twins strode into the cottage. Jack clambered onto a chair and his wife fled into the bathroom. Most local Africans were terrified of the Akroyd's dogs.

To restore calm, Angela described just one of her innumerable adventures. 'I drove across the border recently to do some shopping and went to a café at lunchtime. I managed to resist all the fattening things on the menu and ordered a bowl of vegetable soup. A man asked if I minded him sharing my table. He drank his coffee, ate his sandwich and sauntered off. I couldn't resist the gooey cake he'd left on his plate and was gobbling it up when he came back with a second mug of coffee!' Angela shrieked with laughter, Jack looked puzzled, and his wife politely said it was funny.

On Fridays, when Harry had supper with the Akroyds, who did the cooking could be a lottery. Their kitchen was the sort of facility found in a commune, he imagined, where every one present mucked in, except Angela who always had other priorities. It took an age to recount her day's experiences in a degree of frivolity proportionate to her intake of Pinotage, until Dennis asked if they were going to eat that evening. It was often well past nine o'clock by the time he and Harry stood on arms reversed and got things going on the stove, with Angela still very much in full flow. She detested cooking and housework, though simply adored lengthy chats on the telephone, if it worked.

Whether they dined in the bungalow or the cottage, their fare was frugally nourishing. During that winter, Angela's ceaseless repartee and endearing antics helped to keep them warm and if Dennis felt like talking he was amusing, as well as wise. Harry enjoyed and much appreciated their company, for without them and their circle of friends, he would have made few contacts outside work. Though Angela wasn't always boisterous or horsy, and one Friday evening she described her childhood.

'Life was very hard as a missionary's daughter. We had barely enough money to live on, and after we'd moved from a black township in Zululand to a jungle clearing in New Guinea life was no easier. When my father died, my mother took me home to England and I qualified as a nursing sister. After university, I taught psychology at a swanky London hospital, but jolly soon got itchy feet. While on holiday in Zululand, almost twenty years ago, I bumped into Dennis down in Durban. On retring from the Indian Army in 1947 his father had become a missionary within Durban's large Indian community.'

'If you taught psychology, why do you keep saying, I'm too thick to understand that, when all the time you're psychoanalysing me?' Harry said, hoping it sounded like a joke.

'I always found male patients much more difficult than females,' Angela retaliated, having not appreciated the joke.

Dennis diplomatically changed the subject. 'It was really quite a *coincidence!*' Harry's ears pricked up. 'Whilst attending a post-graduate course at London University, I lodged in the same street as Angela's hospital.'

'Long before I worked there, though. Why don't you tell Harry where we first met?'

'Would you believe in the back of a police van?'

'In a police van with blood pumping from his leg to be precise.' Angela had fire in her eyes. 'The South African police shot him just for attending a peaceful anti-apartheid rally, literally threw him into the back of that van and I just happened to be there.'

'If you hadn't been there, I wouldn't be here. But they never stopped hounding us, like most of our persuasion. That's why we moved north to Kolokuana.'

Walking the dogs next day, he told Harry a great deal more – between long drawn out silences. They got to know far more about each other and after returning to the bungalow, Dennis revealed his latest watercolours, all skilfully composed landscapes portraying ruggéd, hostile mountains set against cloudless skies, with match-stick figures, human and animal, searching a barren, arid plain. Will it ever rain? Harry muttered to himself and, as if reading his thoughts, Dennis grimly shook his head.

The Akroyd's kitchen also resembled an animal farm. Two of the four dogs and one of the two cats were much in evidence. The wretched rooster that woke Harry at an ungodly hour most mornings sometimes stayed with the hens in the garden. The Dobermann twins competed for attention, with Trilby preferring to rest his head in Dennis's lap, Bonnet's in Angela's. Treated as pets, they were also guard dogs, howling when Dennis or Angela left their bungalow's compound. They howled longer when both left. The twin's mother guarded the main gate near the security man's hut and the space where Angela parked her pick-up truck and Harry parked the land-cruiser – not far from the lean-to where Dennis garaged his belovéd Jaguar. The young Labrador, Biddy, reared by the cottage's previous tenant, spent most evenings there and the tabby cat slept there to scare off the rats. Harry only ever saw four, all of them monsters, before perishing in Dennis's traps. The greedy ginger tom remained for the most part on top of the Akroyd's fridge, with his green eyes alert to extra scoffing opportunities.

Their maid, the security man's wife, looked after the bungalow, did their shopping and washed and ironed the laundry, Harry's included. His maid, Dennis's secretary's mother, cleaned their offices during weekday mornings and the cottage in the afternoons, leaving before Harry returned. Angela asked him why he never sent his maid to Berney's Bazaar. He said he rarely saw her and suggested that, because his and Dennis's shirts, slacks and socks kept getting muddled up, the dhobi arrangements needed rationalising.

Therafter, Angela ensured that Harry met his maid *before* he went to work and that his maid did *all* his chores, *before* cleaning the offices. Unfortunately, his maid had filled the clothes line first, leaving no room for the other maid's washing. The provision of another length of wire stretched between two extra poles in the Akroyd's garden, with white pegs for one maid and green for the other, the national flag's twin colours, put an end to that particular episode of their daily ructions.

No sooner had that been sorted out, than there was more turmoil. At five o'clock on a Sunday morning, Dennis hammered on the cottage's back door and shouted: 'Get dressed quickly, in old clothes!' Harry had nothing *old*. He slung on his body-warmer and anorak over a T-shirt and shorts. There was room for only two in the front of Angela's pick-up, so he climbed into the load-space and in next to no time his every extremity was *frozen!* Angela drove south on the main tarred road as fast as her pick-up could go and not much slower along a bone-shaking track. In half an hour they arrived at what turned out to be a stud farm. Just behind and above its buildings flames were leaping and smoke billowing. The steep clamber up a rocky escarpment thawed Harry's extremities.

Blackened from head to toe Monica – Angela's very best friend – thrust spades and sacks at them, hastily explaining that she and helpers had spent the night preventing the fire from reaching the pipe that carried water from the precious spring over the ridge and down the escarpment. She must also have feared for her horses and property, though they failed to warrant a mention. The four of them went to the farmhouse around noon looking like coal miners, washed only their bare extremities, enjoyed a fried-egg sandwich and a mug of tea each, while brooding over the woeful fact that fires could start any time at any place. Everything, everywhere, was still bone dry!

Now it was Harry's turn to knock on a door – a rondavel door at the Horseman's Rest, to collect a visiting doctor, a fellow guest at the British high commissioner's dinner. Though he hadn't expected to be greeted by a female doctor, certainly not an attractive brunette, draped in a slinky black gown, accentuating an amply stacked figure, yet concealing very little else. Having said he'd wait outside, she invited him inside, and asked what he'd like to drink. He dithered, so producing a duty-free whisky bottle, she poured him a blinder.

She had recently joined the UN, in some sort of senior capacity, was now familiarising herself with Africa and would be staying two nights in Kolokuana, prior to moving on. Her name, Arrabella James, had a nice ring and some unidentifiable, American musical coursed through Harry's brain. She'd been born and educated in two of the best London suburbs and was married to an anaesthetist. Extremely risky being married to an anaesthetist, Harry reckoned. She had no children. He wasn't surprised. She didn't look the type.

En route to the high commissioner's residence, Arrabella hinted at several more of her credentials. While queuing to be received by Richard Riddington, she pressed her torso against Harry's, giving him maximum benefit of her perfume and requiring him to brush face powder from his dinner jacket. On entering the reception chamber, she sneaked an arm through his and gripped it tightly. The women cast frosty glances in their direction, most men grinned inanely and Harry rued his tiresome role – a convenient spare file that made up the numbers at highfaluting functions.

A petite, chic blonde confronted the tall, raven intruder. 'I'm Angela Akroyd. Dennis is my husband. Harry lodges with us,' she added, protectively. Dennis received a dig and removed his flat-cap. 'Oh, yes. Sorry! I'm Dennis Akroyd. Have you met the Irish consul, Kieran O'Kelly, and his Swedish wife, Pippa?' 'Hi. I'm

Diane Rashid. This is Suleiman, my old man.' And so it continued all round the reception room. Arrabella had aroused an almighty stir. It reverberated from wall-to-wall.

A stubby and oily-looking chap bowed deeply. 'Gooda evening madarm. I ama Doctor Paulo Domaggio. I hopa you 'ada a gooda flighta. I will 'ava the greata pleasure to meeta you again tomorrow. This isa my wifa, Natalia. Natalia, this isa Doctor Arrabella Jamesa, my bigga bossa. She 'as justa took over the worlda family planning programma.'

Natalia's *décolletage*, just as revealing as Arrabella's, caused them visibly not to take to each other. How this voluptuous siren could manage any family planning programme, let alone a worldwide one, defeated Harry. The Indian butler's gong then urged them to reinforce the crush already consulting and most probably criticising the seating plan.

Mr Mboko, flanked by Richard and Suleiman, sat facing Arrabella. She was placed between Harry and the Italian doctor. Diane Rashid on Harry's other side, he found comforting; Angela's screeching laughter at one end of the dinner table, discomforting. At the opposite end, Dennis did a double thumbs up.

Richard, as usual, talked shop and after saying that the drought relief co-ordinator was doing a first rate job, an Arrabella hand crept under the table and squeezed the top of one of Harry's legs, substantially adding to his discomfort.

As dinner progressed, so the bolder the exchanges became betwixt a brazen Arrabella and a scintillating Diane, right across Harry's chest, as it were. Around the dinner table, hilarity flowed as freely as the wine, and long before the speeches, everyone appeared to be merrily pickled – the deadpan high commissioner an abstemious exception.

Having welcomed his guests and paid tribute to Mr Mboko's outstanding service to his country by magnificently motivating emergency operations, Richard then eulogised, much longer than he should have done, on the merits and sensitivities of family planning, both on the local scene and in the global context. 'I'm sure there is no abler person than Doctor James, to direct the application of such a personal precaution as contraceptives.'

He'd surely meant to say *contraception*. This slip of the diplomatic tongue but more so the image it conjured up of a rampant Arrabella frenetically applying a slippery condom, brought forth a ripple of titters – aptly in her case. Richard concluded with his copybook magnanimous toast to the country's president, government and nation.

Mr Mboko thanked the high commissioner for his kind compliments, apologised for the president's absence, due to a very serious illness, and raised his glass: 'To my Host and Hostess.' This was a shame, because Richard no longer had a hostess.

The ladies withdrew, the gentlemen passed the port, Emmanuel Mboko laughed at his own expense and everyone else laughed accordingly. But not Richard! He was more than probably still brooding over his family planning faux pas.

When assisted from the land-cruiser, outside the Horseman's Rest, Arrabella shivered and drew Harry's dinner jacket closer around her scantily clad torso.

'Night cap?' The question was casual, though her eyes gave her game away.

'Terribly kind of you, but I seem to have contracted a headache.'

'That's easily cured. I'll fetch the night porter and you can park inside the compound.'

She strutted off and the porter in the outsize army greatcoat and Russian tank driver's leather helmet, who'd manhandled the monster case when Harry first arrived, opened the compound's gate. Harry gave him a moderate tip, parked the land-cruiser and reluctantly proceeded to Arrabella's rondavel. She'd switched on an electric fire and was hanging his dinner jacket in the wardrobe.

'What's your preference?' she asked, clearing the settee of various knick-knacks.

'Definitely not another of your whiskies, not after all that wine.'

She gestured to him to sit down, perched herself on the bed and phoned reception.

'Hello, there. Send across two bottles of your best red wine, with two *decent* glasses, straightaway please. Yes, on my bill. Byee.'

She joined Harry on the settee and was gushing about the heavenly evening when the porter delivered her order, precariously balanced on a tray, and shuffled off with a measly tip. Harry uncorked a bottle and checked its label – pinotage!

'Why did you smile?' Arrabella asked, prissily, her eyes still mischievous.

'I buy this brand of wine from the owner of my cottage.' He quarter-filled both glasses.

'Tell me about your cottage Harry,' she purred, stroking his beard. 'A virile growth means a *virile man!*' She nibbled his ear and its hearing-aid fell out. 'What was that?'

'Cotton wool. I produce loads of wax.' That'll cool her ardour, he reckoned, plucking out his other hearing-aid and hiding them both in his trouser pocket farthest from her.

'A first dose of my special headache cure will purge every bit of wax you've ever had. A second dose and you'll be over the moon.' She giggled and moved even closer.

'My headache's gone, thanks.' Trying to keep his distance, with no success, he decided to try a bit of harmless conversation. 'How many years did you say you've been with the UN?'

'I didn't. Soon after I became a public health consultant my husband got a job in some shitty kind of joke place, so we parted company. Since then my career's taken off in leaps and bounds. Your little Arrabella's working her way up very nicely!' The top of his leg was squeezed again, but this time her busy hand lingered.

He used to be decisive. Now he wasn't sure what he was. 'I'd better go,' he croaked, struggling to release himself. 'You must be exhausted after your endless overnight flight, and tomorrow's your big family planning day. Remember what his excellency said in his speech about contraceptives?'

'I stayed in Mavimbi last night and I'm most definitely not exhausted. His excellency can keep his revolting condoms. I like it for real!'

Now he *did* break free. She picked up the unopened wine bottle, but before throwing it at him, subsided in a sulking heap.

'Have a super trip Arrabella,' he managed to mumble, hot-footing it towards the door.

The engine roared into life, the porter opened the compound gate and the land-cruiser manoeuvred its agile way between the hotel car park's gaping craters.

Within ten minutes Harry was laying in bed, half-listening to the midnight news from London, half-regretting his over-hasty departure. Then that voice inside his head started nagging: 'Belinda never strays from the straight and narrow. She follows the cat's-eyes in the middle of the road, while you keep thumping the kerb. She thinks you court disasters, when you're supposed to prevent them! It's resolution time again, Harry. Don't drink too much, and steer well clear of wanton females who entice and beckon. There are always plenty at Happy Hour, ready to pounce on a white man who smiles, so don't smile, either! If it comes to the pushing and shoving stuff, use one of his excellency's contraceptives, but not when you're with Arrabella, she likes it for real! Do you remember that?'

'Of course I remember it,' Harry protested. 'That's why I fled! Why the hell don't you let me get some sleep.'

When the clock/radio woke him, just the trousers of his dinner suit were slung over his bedside chair. How could he have driven back without a jacket, on such a freezing night? His hearing-aids were still in the trouser pocket. He crammed them into his ears, threw on some clothes, tore out of the cottage and scurried across the Akroyd's garden towards his land-cruiser, not knowing where to go or what to do – only to be confronted by Angela.

'How did you get on last night? . . . Or should I say, how did you *fare* last night? We all thought your doting escort's an over-sexed man eater.'

'I escaped unscathed, I'm very pleased to say, and was tucked up in bed, my own bed, by midnight.'

'How long's she staying?'

'A couple of nights.'

'If you need to be *un*-available, I'm meeting Monica later. We'll be your alibi.'

Balanced on the outsides of both shoes, Harry's feet rocked back and forth, a life-long mannerism when he felt gormless or embarrassed which quite often made people curious, even worried. Angela blinked a bit and asked: 'What's wrong with your feet?'

215

'It's my dinner jacket. She wore it when I drove her back to the Horseman's Rest and walked off with it.'

'Leave it to me. I'll fix that vixen.

Angela collected the dinner jacket from Berney's Bazaar. She had taken it there to get the stains removed, stains caused by Arrabella spilling wine on the garment. Pleased with the cleaning, Angela hung it on a hangar on Harry's back door knob, and after he'd thanked her later, she said: 'Arrabella must have flown to her next family planning session rather impeded, not physically, only facially. A lens of her sunglasses had probably tried its best to hide one of her darker than usual roving eyes.'

Private Enterprise

Both in their late-thirties, Angela short and slim, her complexion peaches-and-cream, her blonde hair gathered in a pony-tail. Monica dumpy, freckled and suntanned, her bobbed hair auburn: a microbiologist in Angela's London hospital, she came to Africa on holiday and stayed to teach African women weaving. She bought and renovated a disused school, employed more women and used the rest of her savings to rescue a run-down stud farm. The school comprised a largish sandstone building and several small out-houses. Maybe a hundred girls and women sang as they wove in the former classroom. Beautifully crafted tapestries hung on the walls, two awaiting shipment to England, their labels addressed to Professor Archer, who'd recently found a process that converted garbage into fuel pellets. Monica designed tapestry patterns in one out-house and the others were used for washing raw materials, combing, spinning, dyeing or storage.

'Obangwato families supplied our mohair and wool, until drought compelled us to buy from the northern tribe,' Monica explained dejectedly.

'You've just ruined your success story,' Angela chided.

Monica headed south along the main tarred road to visit Arthur, a white man born and bred locally. 'About your age,' she told Harry and parked beside what appeared to be a derelict bungalow. She knocked several times before a black girl, with only a see-through nightie on, came to the door. Not another Arrabella, Harry muttered under his breath. She invited them into a squalid kitchen, littered with scraps of food covered in flies and then disappeared, presumably back to bed. When Arthur eventually showed up, in a dressing gown, he made them coffee in mugs that looked as though they hadn't been washed for years. They accepted the coffee, but didn't add milk. Monica checked Arthur's few sales-receipts, paid him his cut, and said Angela and Harry were British.

'I flew to London twenty years ago and met a lovely young lady there. She came back with me and gave me a fine son, but soon got fed up with this place and took my son to Johannesburg.' Arthur proudly showed them a photo of a teenager in his school blazer.

Monica related the sad story on the way to her farm. 'Arthur was left a great deal of money and the bitch bled him dry. His parent's thriving trading post went bust, so she left. She pays their son's school fees with her dubious profession's earnings and Arthur hawks tapestries without much success. He's now besotted with that maid and her mother grabs his meagre income.'

Dennis Akroyd and a young Indian couple joined them at the stud farm. The husband and his wife offered to tour the world's markets selling Monica's tapestries, if they were adequately compensated. Monica said she would ask the British high commissioner for an enterprise grant. She had a "soft spot" for Richard Riddington! Dennis and Harry got the braai going and other guests arrived, including a hero of Harry's. Having exposed an East African tyrant's killing-sprees, Lawrence Kwawenda was cruelly subjected to years of crippling torture and foul incarceration. A distinguished intellectual and a champion of lost causes, after settling in Kolokuana, he had created and now managed the consultancy firm which had successfully completed the UN-sponsored rapid vulnerability study.

Lawrence briefed September's task force meeting. 'My experienced staff assessed the state of people's health and well-being in a representative sample of communities in all six southern districts. A summary of their principal findings is on the screen and also on the first page of the report which is on the table in front of you. I'll begin with the video my assessors made during their travels throughout the south of your country.'

For the next half an hour, the task force had to sit through a sequence of scenes that no single word could possibly describe – disturbing, desultory, repugnant, distressing were simply inadequate. Weeping mothers lovingly laid their babies, many no longer infants, to rest or kept knocking on a health post's door because the notice "Gone to Kolokuana" in English meant nothing to them. Filthy, rat-infested, pit-latrines leaking faeces and the corpses of animals floating or partly-submerged in pools of the gunge. Litter everywhere, much to the rats' delight. Toddlers scurrying after the rats, holding them up to their fly-infested eyes to take a closer look, before dropping them into their carer's cooking pot, to supplement that day's solitary meal, as well as tomorrow's, probably. And so the torment continued. There were gasps of horror, expressions of disbelief, the odd remark mocking the photographers, some accusations of criminal deception, plenty of furrowed brows and trembling hands, even some tears and nose-blowing. After a coffee-break, Mr Mboko had to order his cabinet colleagues to watch a second video.

Beaming faces now filled the screen, the faces of deliverers and consumers of relief in all its sorts, shapes and sizes. The video was followed by a puerile ministerial debate that would bring out the poet in Lawrence. He muttered to Harry: 'The over-heated versus the under-heated, the blind leading the bland, but let's be kind to those who know no better.'

Lawrence resumed his teach-in: 'In view of the worrying food deficit, let us focus on food availability, then on national and household food security. As you will know, all households vulnerable to starvation had to convince a registration team, that they were resourceless due to drought and not some other adversity. The questions may have been difficult to answer or they may not have been answered truthfully because of a tendency to conceal money remitted by people working away from home. The assessors identified several reasons, summarised in my firm's report, why food requirements have increased, legally or illegally. If the corruption blighting food registration is eliminated, the easier to apply and stricter eligibility criteria, now proposed, should reduce requirements without penalising genuine drought victims. The report also recommends *quarterly* registration surveys of every community in the southern province, which include the availability not only of food, but also water, sanitation facilities and primary health care. Tsabo Mashedi has offered to draft legislation which, when approved, should be immediately enacted and stringently enforced. Sound laws, stringently enforced, will help district relief monitoring teams to investigate registration irregularities, empower courts to dispense justice, firmly yet fairly, and compel judges to pass sentences that deter corruption.'

'We further recommend food-for-work, rather than cash-for-work, as the alternative to issuing free food, since too many carers may use the cash to get drunk on home-brewed beer, when the children in their care are undernourished, or worse, acutely malnourished. I'm afraid the assessors came across far too many instances of alcohol-influenced, child-neglect. The report also contains vulnerability data on which to base a renewed appeal for donor assistance, if additional aid requests are justified, and draws government attention to the need for adequate food reserves. Should the mounting food deficit require rationing to be imposed, food reserves will enable the task force to increase the rations of those in danger of dying of starvation. These reserves need inspecting and turning over regularly, as do all household reserves. Both national and household food-security should therefore feature in the post-drought recovery plan. Effective food security will help insure against future disasters. I'm aware,' Lawrence added, glancing at Harry, 'that Mr Burke has been requested to draft the drought recovery plan and an updated appeal for donor assistance.'

'May I conclude by commending the achievements of everyone closely involved with relieving untold drought-inflicted suffering, saving lives and livelihoods, and striving to create a more contented aftermath. This emergency has also severely tested the generosity of aid donors and has reminded us that we Africans keep on shooting ourselves in the feet and that far too many Africans take sexual promiscuity as granted, as well as *for* granted. Yet there are African politicians who conceal, minimise, or even ignore, the grievous fact that HIV/AIDS is threatening, right now, to decimate their electorates. Indeed, it has been a threat for some while. An unpalatable, unrecognised, unaccepted threat that must . . .'

'Are you blaming me and my government for not stopping this illness ignorant people have caused?' Mboko asked.

'AIDS is a rapidly spreading, life-threatening disease that needs priority detection and treatment,' the new health minister asserted. 'It is not a routine illness that can be swept under the carpet and forgotten. HIV-testing is underway in the northern province, where AIDS is already a very serious problem, testing has begun in the south where the problem is worsening, but testing is yet to start here, in Kolokuana. Have HIV-tests been cancelled or postponed?'

'Postponed until after the general election when more civil servants will be available,' Mboko replied dismissively and then resumed his attack. 'You also said, Mr Kwawenda, that another request for donor assistance is unnecessary. Why did you say that?'

'The consultancy report ought to be read before the task force decides whether to submit a second appeal,' Harry advised. 'I must also warn you that donor-fatigue caused by the increasing amount of external aid countries in this Afrcan region are demanding is being criticised more frequently in the international media.'

Rather than care what the international media published, some ministers said foreign newspapers should be banned from entering their country. The agriculture minister, who slept a lot at meetings, asked what donor fatigue was and Harry promised to tell him later.

'You failed to mention, Mr Kwawenda, the urgent necessity of managing relief operations from Mabela,' the chief secretary said, in a demeaning tone of voice.

'The report recommends that relief should be managed at district level, supervised at provincial level and directed at central level.'

'I supervise all aspects of drought relief,' was the chief secretary's churlish riposte.

'No longer,' Mboko snapped. 'From today, district administrators are to manage relief activities, the governor of the southern province is to supervise them, the bringer-of-rain will continue to co-ordinate them and I shall direct them.'

Jack's head and shoulders were twitching. 'What about me?'

'I'll let you know . . . What's that noise?'

Something was ringing in one of Lawrence Kwawenda's pockets. He silenced the din, extended what appeared to be an aerial and spoke into an oblong contraption held tightly to one of his ears. 'Yes, I can hear you perfectly. How's the weather in Mavimbi today?'

'How did you get that before me?' Mboko fumed.

'Private enterprise, minister.'

Harry was about to drive south when his landline phone rang. 'The family in the government flat next to mine has moved,' Uncle Bill said. 'I'll take you to see it this afternoon.'

The flat wasn't much to write home about, just a windowless cell in a row of cells with a bedstead, chair and cupboard. A grim communal privy and a water pump stood outside in the yard. The flat would satisfy Harry's transient needs after it had been cleaned, so under Uncle Bill's supervision, his neighbours started cheerfully scrubbing. The women and all the children seemed surprised to have a white man in their midst, especially a white man who smiled and greeted them in Gwato. Eyeing Harry up and down, one woman passed a comment that had the others splitting their sides. And when African women laughed, they *really* laughed! Though the coin Harry had given each child, landed up in their mothers' palms, when he'd wanted them to buy something for themselves. Perhaps he should find some other place to rent during his fortnight every month based in Mabela.

'You looked annoyed just now,' Uncle Bill said, driving to his office. 'Those children always try to help their hard-up mothers in every way they can. I'm very proud of them.'

Crushed silence! Harry felt like a toad the size of an elephant. Perhaps a bit of a leg-pull would relieve the tension and he experimented with: 'I'd imagined the Mabela Hotel would have offered you, the new provincial governor, its best luxury suite free of charge.'

'You can stay there if you like, though you'll never catch me living it up in that den of debauchery. It's full of married men in bed with their floosies, married women having it off with herd boys, the younger boys and also girls get paid for doing favours in toilets.'

'I've heard that the many Africans, who enjoy a bit on the side, call their exertions bed rest. Why?' Harry heroically queried.

'Our imperial masters called hotels, rest houses.'

The track joined the main tarred road, which would soon become a bumpy, unpaved street with barely enough room to squeeze Uncle Bill's pick-up truck between the many groups of women trying to sell whatever remaining possessions were of any worth. Most others were doing what came naturally, just hanging about chatting outside empty shops.

'Where can I buy a small fridge, a primus stove and some paraffin?' Harry asked.

'Whites don't come here anymore. I'll get what you want.'

'Come to think of it, I haven't seen any of my sort whenever I've been here.'

'There's only Father Patrick and he's having a well-earned holiday. You'll be okay, as long as you stay near me.'

Uncle Bill parked beside the police station, crossed the street, disappeared and soon reappeared with two packets and a bottle containing maize-meal, dried beans and cooking oil. 'The chap down that alley gets food on the black market. But that's racist, I'm told. If you give me cash, I'll buy yours when I buy mine. We'll leave the food aid for those who need it most. You can use my kerosene stove. No refrigerators, we Obangwatos haven't invented them yet.'

The women had cleaned Harry's flat. He preferred "bedsit" – it sounded better. Uncle Bill thought bedsit would get confused with bed rest.

'The women also use my stove,' he said. 'Their men never send them money, so I give them food, paraffin and a friendly shoulder to cry on.'

Harry now felt like an elephant the size of a toad.

Tsabo kept in touch by ringing him from district offices; their land-line phones usually worked. Roll on cell phones! While Tsabo toured his vast bailiwick – a demanding and mandatory routine, Harry jacked up the drought management course he'd run during his next fortnight here. He also drove out to the track-building/food-for-work site where the helicopter had landed and again met its foreman, Tsabo's brother-in-law. An energetic, tough, level-headed young man already earmarked as the manager of many more of this province's food-for-work projects. Over a thousand women and half that number of men now worked for their households' rations who would otherwise have received free-food – largely down to Suleiman scrounging hand tools and arranging the contracted provision of earth-moving equipment – though not forgetting Uncle Bill's food-for-work recruiting drives. He'd also given Suleiman a list of equipment requirements to enable many more food-for-work sites to function. At last, 'progress' became a more frequently used word in drought relief jargon.

But that was not all. Once Jurek's solar power apparatus had been tried and tested, he had deepened the borehole in the gorge, irrigated more fields and his wife's clan looked forward to picking fruit and harvesting sorghum to barter for maize. Uncle Bill had found a building in Mabela suitable for use as a solar-panel factory when refurbished. However, there were still problems! Although Jurek's private sector backers provided the cheapest kits on the international market, the cost of the silicon cells that converted the sun's rays into electricity would likely increase. No shortage of sun, but far fewer customers and a lot less money to fund the initial production target. As always, one step forward, several back! Yet this crisis could persuade Jurek to take his wife and son to Poland, and the first fifty cell phones earmarked for key relief workers and community headmen in the south's worst drought-affected areas might be diverted to the northern province to help combat AIDS and the renewed malaria and tuberclosis epidemics. Gridded electricity was more widely available in the north and re-charging cell phones much easier than in the south.

It was Speedy's turn to drive. He and Harry were both feeling down in the dumps, and with Kolokuana in sight, they still hadn't worked out what was bugging them. Perhaps it was because nobody had warned them of all the problems awaiting them there.

Among Harry's mail awaiting attention on his desk, Speedy found an envelope with a Boston USA postmark – inside the envelope a note in familiar felt-pen handwriting which he read and quickly gave to Harry.

'Hi Harry. After a long illness, my Mam's mercifully passed away. Cancer! Made it in time. Mr Rashid got me home real fast. Couldn't call you. It all stacked up mighty quick. Thanks for your help and friendship. Hope to meet with you some place. Start studying for the UN-sponsored degree this fall. Say Hi to the team. In haste, Glen.'

Harry stared at the words in utter disbelief. Glen had never said his mother was ill, let alone terminally ill. When sorrow gave way to bitterness, he phoned Suleiman only to be gleefully told by Madam Thelma: 'Mr Rashid flew to a conference in Geneva more than a week ago and won't be back for another week.' Speedy and Harry tore off in search of Jack, and eventually found him behind a stack in the capital's grinding mill's warehouse, counting sacks of maize-grain.

'Why didn't you phone and tell us Glen was leaving?' Harry asked. 'We'd have driven back, to sympathise, say farewell, to thank him for God's sake.'

Speedy said 'yeah' and wandered off gutted.

'If Mboko hadn't ordered me to check all this stuff donors and the northern tribe keep sending us every day,' Jack moaned, 'I might have remembered to phone you.'

The three of them consoled each other over a couple of beers in Jack's bungalow. He sent his eldest daughter to a café to buy three more six-packs with the cash Harry had to lend him. With Glen gone, neither Speedy nor Harry wanted any more beer and they both returned to the office to finish reading Harry's mail.

Glen's successor, hailing from the southern highlands, had never seen money before he boarded at a mission school. All the families in his village had bartered wool and mohair for food and medicine. On leaving Kolokuana University with a degree in English and his middle name Simon-Peter shortened to Pete, he grabbed the chance to become the UN's drought relief press officer with both hands. All too familiar with drought, he proved his ability to learn quickly about the many relief activities while on tour with Tsabo.

After Pete got back, he read all Glen's press releases. Below the last paragraph of his final one, somebody had written: 'A selfless young American's legacy to every drought-tortured Obangwato.'

Hobbling Harry

When motor vehicles replaced horse-drawn carts a colonial governor had a fine highway laid down from Kolokuana's maize-grinding mill, through the neighbouring country and into Mavimbi's docks, to accelerate maize-meal exports. Now juggernauts towing trailers were accelerating donated aid *imports*, including maize-grain, in the reverse direction.

Harry had never visited the town just across the border and hitched a lift in Angela's pick-up. She headed north on the main tarred road and forked right. For the first eighty or so miles the terrain was dusty and treeless, for the next forty eucalypts abounded, for the final ten the tarred road, fairly straight until then, meandered beside a wide slow-moving river with dense vegetation on both sides. Before the drought, that river had risen in the central highlands, cascaded down the gorge, just below Jurek's wife's village, meandered across the Mabela plain, bent north, skirted Kolokuana and then turned east towards the coast. Just over two hours after leaving Kolokuana Angela parked her pick-up, they both joined a long queue to bribe a border guard to check their passports and who should by-pass the queue? Mkwere, the phantom prospector, and the young black giant, his assumed bodyguard who'd occasionally played pool against each other, but never against anybody else, at Kolokuana's UN club.

Mkwere invited Harry and his lady friend to a bar he owned and served them ice-cold white wine, not to be sniffed at on a hot and humid afternoon, but refused payment. He'd just refilled their glasses a second time, when a fierce argument broke out between him and several Afrikaners. Angela's Afrikaans didn't stretch to understanding what it was about, but thought Mkwere was being told to do something. His assumed bodyguard then punched a white man and, in next to no time, chairs were being used as battering rams, bottles as coshes and broken glass flew everywhere. Suddenly, a dog seized Harry's right leg, he fell sideways and his left wrist buckled under his weight. The dog's teeth gripped so powerfully a policeman had to kneel on its head and prise its jaws open.

Harry's heart beat unevenly, his trousers soaked with blood. Angela used his shoelaces as a tourniquet, Mkwere brought towels, she wrapped his mauled leg in one, Harry held the other to his cut chin.

He remembered nothing more till the back of his leg was prodded and heard someone say: 'Stabilise the heart first!' He was laying face down with his head in Angela's arms.

'The bleeding's stopped,' she told him. 'You'll be given a transfusion, rabies injection and general anaesthetic. All the wounds must be thoroughly cleansed before stitching.'

He signed a consent form where she indicated, a needle pricked his arm . . . .

Above a mosquito net a fan making a light bulb swing, room small, walls white, one window, curtains closed, Angela by the bed, his watch missing, he asked her the time.

'Nearly seven o'clock. I drove you here just after three this afternoon and you went to theatre at four. I rescued these.' She helped insert both hearing aids and put his watch on his right wrist, the other bound tightly with padded bandage.

A nurse came to check his temperature, blood pressure and pulse rate. She showed the results to a bearded, turbaned doctor who nodded sagely and said to Harry: 'The front and back of your right leg is nicely stitched up. The loss of tissue, at the back, made suturing difficult. Because of muscle damage and bruising, it will be several weeks before you can walk freely. The nerves could take longer to recover. There is also a risk of thrombosis. You will have another blood, heart and urine test and your wrist X-rayed in the morning. You will continue to receive plasma and antibiotics intravenously. I have prescribed pills to ease or kill pain, reduce swelling and help you sleep.'

'I'm most grateful for all the care . . . and that you didn't have to do any amputating.'

'But for Mrs Akroyd's first aid and her speed in getting you here, it could have been a whole lot worse. The night sister will come to check you and the drip every hour.'

Harry was thanking Angela when Monica arrived. They would both stay at a hotel and beat a hasty retreat when the sister brought Harry a bedpan, the pills and a glass of water. She hoped he would sleep all night.

Drenched in sweat and petrified by the HIV-infected blood circulating within him, he was dragged back to semi-consciousness by a nurse offering him tea – but the torment didn't stop! How long until the symptoms show? And when they do, what will Belinda, our family, relatives and friends think? And what about the stigma? All those who knew me at school, at Oxford, in my firm, in the Cotswolds, chums down the pub, what will they say? They'll say, there's no way I'm going to the funeral of a bloody idiot who had unprotected sex with only he knows who. How had he got himself into such a frantic mess? Nobody deserved to feel *this* devastated! An outcast in the hard school of chance mishap, overburdened with fear and desolation, dreading premature death. He could have done without so much misery, particularly with the battle against drought-destruction fast gaining ground, but not being there to see everything he and many others had been doing through to finality. This hurt, really hurt, right down to his numb leg . . . Stop all that morbid stuff, get a grip, take control, but he couldn't. His frustration made everything far, far worse.

'Your tea's cold. Did you sleep?' Monica breezily asked, opening the window.

'Wouldn't call it *sleep!* They gave me a blood transfusion. You're a microbiologist, so please test me for AIDS.'

'Bulk blood's always HIV-tested in Mavimbi before it's sent to hospitals.'

Harry had his doubts. Serious doubts! Things didn't happen like that in Africa – then just as the whole damned torment was starting all over again, two hefty nurses came and lifted him off the bed onto a commode-chair. Monica wisely found something else to do.

With the drip contraption still held in his right hand and his left arm now in a sling – fortunately his wrist wasn't broken – Monica was wheeling him back from X-ray when she asked whether he parked his vehicle in the Akroyd's compound and walked across their garden to his cottage, alone. Harry nodded, wondering what was coming next.

'You'll have to watch your step. Dennis and Angela may not have mentioned this, but both the Dobermann twins have a very nasty habit of attacking people. I've never trusted either of them. Last weekend they savaged a vegetable seller who had opened the Akroyd's unlocked gate and was about to knock on their front door. The locals are on the warpath!'

That adds up, Harry thought. Trilby and Bonnet often growled and bared their teeth at him when . . . There were raised voices out in the corridor. Richard Riddington stormed in, hurriedly pursued by the ward sister and, at a more gentlemanly pace, by Suleiman.

'How are you?' What happened? Who did it? Do I know him?' Richard often sounded like a machine-gun.

Harry related what had occurred, or what he'd been told had occurred, and unusually for Richard, he listened before storming off, exclaiming: 'I'm going get to the bottom of this scandalous brutality!'

'Oh, isn't he wonderful?' gasped Monica, all of a flutter.

Suleiman winced. He assured Harry that the UN's insurance policy covered hospital care and would contact Tsabo who was touring in the south, alert Tsamanachimone, then remembered he was sharing Richard's Range Rover and took off at a far sprightlier pace.

One of the hefty nurses withdrew the drip from Harry's arm and supported him while he hobbled back and forth along the corridor. He was in bed when a sombrely apologetic Mkwere arrived, handcuffed to a bumptious young police inspector who informed Harry that he wouldn't have to make a statement because nobody died!

On his midday round, the doctor said an HIV-test was not necessary. Angela, back on duty, undertook to change the patient's dressings and apply the ointments, every morning and evening. She would also drive him to the hospital in a week's time for more tests and check-ups. Harry was discharged that afternoon, still with an abundance to worry about.

Angela hadn't contacted his wife. He'd preferred to break the news himself. Shocked, Belinda wanted to fly out immediately, though calmed down when reminded that Angela had been a highly qualified nursing sister in a posh London hospital. Belinda questioned his sanity, however, after he'd said he expected to be back at work in a couple of days.

Harry had an unexpected visitor that evening, the British police adviser who had aped Peter Sellers very convincingly at the amateur theatrical group's "Hancock Night."

'Acting on Mr Riddington's official request,' he began, 'I have taken statements from various witnesses in the town across the border, and would now like to hear the victim's *story!*' he emphasised sarcastically. 'Before that, however, I must ask whether you have shown the note, which is kept in your wallet, to any person or persons in Kolokuana, or elsewhere in this country, or in neighbouring countries.' His pen and pad were poised.

Thunderstruck by the question, yet more so by the revelation that this man knew, not just of the note's existence but where it was kept, Harry had to admit he'd shown the note to Mr Mboko. And only to him. As for the victim's story, Harry said his memory of the dog-mauling was hazy and suggested a chat with Mrs Akroyd would be a safer bet. The shifty ferret echoed Tsabo's earlier warning not to snoop around for graves – or anything else – and snooped off, leaving Harry in no doubt that he distrusted the sleuth. A retired chief constable to wit.

'Things could get tough, very tough,' Tsabo had warned. For Harry they already had and could well get tougher, a whole lot tougher. He had no choice but to lie low.

Within twenty-four hours a bruise stretched from his groin to his toes and he stayed in bed, his raised right leg resting on some of Angela's pillows. Belinda, Suleiman and Jack rang to ask how he was. Tsabo and Uncle Bill rang from Mabela . . . then Speedy rang.

'I'll bring your mail, and when we've both read it, you can tell me what to do.'

'No thanks, Speedy, maybe next week.' Soon the phone was ringing again.

'Hallo Grandpa Africa.'

Harry pretended not to recognise his grand-daughter's instantly healing voice.

'Who's speaking please?'

'Me! . . . Grandma told my mummy you've got a poorly leg and I want your poorly leg to get better quickly, Grandpa, and everybody wants your poorly leg get better quickly.'

'Hearing you is making my leg better darling.' Her birthday had been and gone during his purdah of harrowing torment and bitter remorse. 'What's it feel like to be six?'

'Fine. But I can't wait till I'm seven! Thank you for the African necklace Grandpa. All the beads are very pretty. I had lots of presents and lots of friends came to my party and they gave me lots more presents and I pulled out my wobbly front teeth.'

'Do you look funny without them?'

'Only when I look in a mirror . . . Grandpa, my mummy wants to speak to you.'

'Aren't there dogs where you're living?' his daughter asked.

'Everything's under control. Besides, I like this cottage and my landlords.'

'You must move. Think about it. I'll call you tomorrow.'

With his head slumped on a pillow, he cursed himself over and over again. How could he have let Mboko read that note? The AIDS torment returned with renewed vengeance! He wanted to phone Belinda, yet couldn't face telling her about all this endless torture, how stupid he'd been to show Mboko the note, nor about the police enquiry. He was 'oop soddin creek with no fookin paddle' as Yorkshireman Dave would've aptly described it.

While Angela washed the wounds, applied the ointments and re-bandaged his leg, he calmed himself down enough to say: 'I really appreciate all your tender care but wouldn't it be best if the Dobermann twins were kept chained up when I'm around?'

'Leave it to me,' she insisted. And when Angela insisted, she always meant business.

Back from the hospital check-up, now with only half of his stitches, Harry stayed put in Angela's pick-up truck until she'd made sure the Dobermanns weren't loose. He had to unbolt a metal gate, as high

231

as a stake-and-wire fence, to reach his cottage and screwed to the inside of his back door was an intercom . . . . Angela answered his test call.

'While we were at the hospital, poisoned meat was thrown into our garden. Dennis has taken Trilby and Bonnet to have them put down. Sorry, must go. I'm going to cry again.'

'Wait! Do you want me to do anything?' But Harry was talking to himself.

Dennis solemnly buried the twins amidst his rose bushes which still refused to bloom and Angela tearfully marked the double-grave with two crosses, with hobbling Harry a supportive mourner – yet also, it must be said, a relieved one. Angela would cry all night, while Dennis painted a watercolour of the Dobbermann twins. He brought it to the cottage to show Harry and would wait a while before giving it to Angela.

The twins' mother, tied to the security man's hut, endlessly barked at all the Africans peering through the compound's double gates. Biddy, the young black Labrador, who relished not being bullied by the twins, spent even more of her time lovingly curled up with the tabby cat in Harry's armchair. The greedy ginger tom would not have been missed, nor the pre-dawn crowing rooster and all his clucking hen-friends – but every one of those critters had survived.

The UN doctor removed the rest of the stitches, declared Harry's leg free of infection and took a blood sample, which Harry posted to Mavimbi for HIV-testing. Back at the office, he was fussed over: Speedy continued helping him with the mail, of course. Fuzzy made him extra mugs of tea. He and Fred sat in the sun admiring each other's gammy leg, deciding what vegetables to grow in the compound's garden that Fred had commendably made and enjoying the sandwiches Pinkie brought to work for them, as well as herself.

Being crippled, Harry could dispose of a mounting typing backlog. With food supply steadily improving and his proposal to restrict aid requests to water supply, health care and other urgent requirements now approved, the abridged-cum-updated appeal for donor assistance winged its way, with Suleiman's blessing, to Jinky at UN headquarters.

Next in line, the solar-panel distribution list, giving priority to fifty key relief workers and village headmen in districts worst hit by drought – soon to be ticked in the finance minister's purple ink. But Alistair Croft hadn't had time to contact the charity that taught drought victims how to ensure water was safe to drink and how to mend hand-pumps.

'The can do and can't do of humanitarian aid endeavours,' Harry's diary commented.

Later that week the UN doctor gave Harry the letter confirming that his second HIV-test was negative. While still worrying about the questionable reliability of all HIV-testing, Harry went on his Virgoan way trying hard not to rejoice . . . Then, while Speedy drove him back to the office, he couldn't stop himself yelling Yippee! Gad Zoons! Wunderbar! He expected to be asked what he'd yelled, but Speedy just gave him a bewildered look.

Harry's post-drought recovery plan's framework, with sections dealing with water and sanitation, health and nutrition, food and agriculture, training and logistics, budget and co-ordination was approved by ministers at their October meeting. They also agreed that his drought relief guidelines and Lawrence Kwawenda's vulnerability study report should serve as starting points and that Harry and Jenkins Makimbo should finalise the plan. Yet it would not be worth the paper it was typed on without legislation to enforce it and this was where Tsabo came in. Before parliament debated his draft emergency powers bill, he faxed a copy to his former law tutor, Dr Dermot Macausland, inviting his infamous red-ink corrections.

I faxed his draft back with minimal amendment and my best regards, together with a note thanking Harry for his latest diary and wishing him well, but when I came across his account of the police-dog encounter, I phoned Belinda straightway. Although she did her level best to sound light-hearted, I could tell she still felt mortified.

Half-expecting some calamity to occur ever since I'd read in one of Harry's previous diaries that he'd shown the note about our grandfather's grave to that finance minister, Mboko, whom, among several other Kolokuana prominents, members of my 'Circle' had kept and still kept under constant surveillance. Yet, to be honest, I was as keen as Harry to solve the century-old mystery surrounding our grandfather's fate. However, there was no escaping the fact that I'd been instrumental in sending Harry to that country to help alleviate a humanitarian catastrophe in unstable, potentially perilous circumstances. Guilt weighed heavily on my conscience. I had to get him out of there, now! I faxed the part of the diary describing the dog-mauling incident and Harry's hospitalisation to my 'Base' with an encoded recommenddation. An encoded clearance to extract him was faxed back later that evening and I dialled his cottage phone number.

'That can't be my clever cousin Dermot. Has the College burnt down?'

'No such luck. You're not fit enough to remain there. That's why I'm phoning you.'

'Read my next diary. What's the news from Oxford?'

With the leg wounds now scabs, the UN doctor sanctioned an end to Angela's tender care and a resumption of Harry's fortnightly stints in Mabela. He delayed going until after the Remembrance Sunday service held in the British high commissioner's garden, which was also attended by scores of pensioners from near and far proudly displaying their medals and uniform remnants. After Richard Riddington had done justice to a second world war citation and presented a replica gallantry medal to a long-retired former private who'd mislaid the original, another old soldier with a regimental sergeant-major's insignia on a wrist stepped forward, saluted and proclaimed: "God Save The King!" Had Her Majesty been able to grace such a gallant congregation with her presence, she would have surely excused the sergeant-major's oversight. For Harry, it had been a limp-curing experience.

While driving south, Speedy said he'd enjoyed the service, but believed the bongos would have helped the hymns. Harry suggested that he should have said: 'You can't beat the bongos for hotting-up hymns.' Speedy capped it with: 'That's not holy!'

The disaster management courses went well and they arrived back from Mabela just in time for the UN Christmas bring-your-nosh-along braai, though there would be a mutton burger for those who'd forgotten to bring their nosh and for offspring who couldn't stomach home-cooking. Madam Thelma, Suleiman's secretary with the gravelly contralto voice, eventually agreed to let Harry help her lead this year's carol singing, and in keeping with the festive spirit, Speedy could bring his bongos, if he only *tapped* them.

Under the stars in the UN club's yard upwards of two hundred people of sundry creeds and pigments joined in the carols, their words projected on a screen. The smoke from the burger-stand didn't make all that many cough too much. Most had just attempted to get their tongues round the host-country's national anthem in Gwato when *Auld Lang Syne* appeared on the screen three hours early. Yet everyone linked arms and played follow the leader to the beat of Speedy's bongos. As the bongo-beating grew ever louder and faster, so the bigger and happier the heap of togetherness grew.

'Okay, Harry?' 'Five out of ten, Speedy.' A hearty handshake was Suleiman's verdict, which prompted Harry to say: 'I meant, *nine* out of ten, Speedy.' After all, banging those bongos had been an inspired way to round off a party. The togetherness heap, particularly those on its top, and most others must have thought so, too. Bumper bar takings!

The sun's first rays enhanced the UN chief of mission's gleaming limousine. In front, Suleiman beside his chauffeur, whose light-blue livery matched the UN flag fluttering on the bonnet. Soon Speedy, clutching the bongos to his bosom, then later Harry, stumbled out of the back, unsteadily disorientated even when reunited with their respective havens of rest and recuperation.

Diane Rashid required Harry's bearded, tottering presence later that day – for a *fitting!* With that over and done with, four fathers, masquerading as reindeers, practised towing him until the barrow's wheel fell off. Still adorned in the clinging red plastic Santa Claus outfit, stuffed with three pillows, in the largest-size gumboots Suleiman could buy, a sack slung over a shoulder and sweating buckets, Harry squelched ever nearer the hubbub.

'Where's your snow Santa?' a boy pleasantly called out.

'It was on my hat, but it melted. Can you see it running down my face?'

'No!' the petulant little monster had the audacity to shout back.

235

'Have you been to Scotland yet?' a mother asked.

'My next stop.'

'When you're in Glasgow, give my kid-sister a big kiss.'

'If she's as bonny as you, I most definitely will.' That earned Harry an eye-watering whopper, landing mainly on his chin, which did nothing to staunch his perspiration.

Now penned in by giggling kids, and those closest mistaking his beard for a glued-on fake trying to pull it off, blonde Diane in her coolest outfit passed the parcels which he passed on. Whoever had nicked his sack couldn't have noticed it was empty.

With his duty done he squelched back to Suleiman's bathroom, struggled free of the clinging costume, showered, then, for the first time since leaving home, weighed himself. He'd lost twenty-one pounds, the majority that afternoon; though his AIDS-scare and that snaky police adviser's questioning had also done over-much to create the new-look, slim-line figure grinning at him in a full-length mirror.

'Government offices will close for two days only,' Mr Mboko had decreed and "Have a Happy Hard Working New Year" posters were distributed, to be stuck on every office door. Most ended up elsewhere. However, on discovering that Jack and all other government employees intended taking a week's leave, Harry had a quick word with Suleiman and managed to secure the last cheap seat on an extra Christmas Eve flight from Mavimbi to Heathrow. Terminal 3 was emptier than usual and he sped through the green channel, within his cabin-bag lurked the Santa Claus outfit, less the fattening pillows, and a sack of goodies. Still rushing he took the tube to London, enrobed in a public toilet and then jogged along frosty pavements in the full regalia, now appreciating the plastic costume's snugness and unsparingly returning the salutations, seasonal or otherwise, of passers-by.

Belinda would phone him in Kolokuana at nine o'clock – her time. Breathless, because of his valiant, sustained, physical exertions rather than excitement – he imagined, and triumphantly rang his daughter's door bell with merely minutes to spare!

"My wife staggered as if about to faint, but my swift embrace parried her fall." This all too brief description of a never to be forgotten moment he would frequently recount, with Belinda well out of earshot, to handy listeners, too often not for the first time.

Laughing through tears and hand-in-hand, they joined their family in slow-time. Their grandson was too busy with his new toys to notice the apparition. Their grand-daughter showed off her new front teeth. Their daughter and son-in-law were abnormally speech-less. After all the hugging and kissing, a less excited Santa dipped into his sack and gave them each a little gift from sunniest Africa. Then a cork popped, glasses were charged, rousing adult toasts exchanged and the infamous scars exposed. It went without saying that, despite all the hurry and flurry, a Christmas with his loved ones around him was not only fun, but delightfully enjoyable and infinitely un-missable.

In far away Katama, Matashaba soothed their children's cracked lips, nostrils and fingers with the grease their kind father brought home.

'The bad drought will stop, very soon,' he said. 'This I pray.'

'Amen,' she whispered and holding hands, they bent to kiss their children's foreheads.

Changes Afoot

With perfect timing, just as they arrived home, it started pouring. The first rain Harry had felt for months. He unzipped his cabin bag, unearthed Belinda's New Year present from under the Santa Claus outfit and unrolled a Monica masterpiece tapestry of packable size.

'This is an Obangwato village,' he explained. 'These huts are called rondavels and they are herd boys, wrapped in blankets, leading livestock to graze up in the mountains. Those are their herd dogs. Do you like it?'

'I love it!' Her comment after inspecting the back: 'Admirably professional.'

His anniversary gift would be a night in their honeymoon hotel. With their garden now weeded and their bedroom redecorated, he could take on anything – even the congested motorway. Striding arm-in-arm along a deserted wind-swept beach, clambering up a cliff path, they hoped for a glimpse through the swirling mist of the lighthouse he'd rowed to, a quarter of a century ago. Belinda loved rain, and with his umbrella blown out to sea, he quite enjoyed getting soaked to the skin. During dinner he acquainted the hotel guests he'd gathered together with Africa's numerous challenges. Belinda had read it all in his letters and had imagined a romantic candle-lit table-for-two, yet had long come to accept that Harry always must have people around him and tell them how to solve the problems he held dear. Had he been a better listener, he would likely have become as successful a university tutor as his cousin Dermot – both fervent Ulstermen, quintessentially English, proud to be British, though with never an insular thought in their heads. Dermot more serious – Harry made her laugh, even when they were spitting fire at each other, generous to a fault and a proven success at most everything he took on.

He'd shared his African worries with her. He blamed himself for being overly critical of many with whom he worked, at times not without justification. He'd found the litany of careless lapses very frustrating. The lack of, and too often the absence of, urgency

238

and compassion totally inexcusable in life-threatening situations; the habit of "pushing" doors marked "pull" utterly bemusing. He also regretted criticising Jack, an awkward character, now reformed apparently, who'd frequented Harry's letters.

Harry spent the return motorway journey dodging juggernaut spray, and next morning, approaching Heathrow the deluge showed signs of abating. It had stopped when Belinda forlornly watched an Africa-bound jumbo jet climb steeply and disappear in dense cloud.

Why did I finally weaken and agree to visit Harry at Whitsun, she kept asking herself while miserably driving home – a home with no very suntanned, much slimmer, fitter and more vigorous Harry – a home with none of his obsessive, now lovable, fads and foibles.

The sky was clear above Paris, aglow to port, a meal served above Marseilles, the blinds closed over Algiers, the blinds opened after breakfast above the northern province's lush pasture, the humidity high when a flimsy single-prop, eighteen-seater, left leafy Mavlmbi in its labouring wake and banked west. Somewhere en route, Harry had swapped his cosy Cotswold life-style for a land of harsh African-reality, now his second home, but without his precious Belinda and with Whitsun four long months distant.

Kolokuana airport was sunny, its temperature a mere forty degrees and Speedy was waving hallo at the window where he'd waved cheerio eight days before

'How was it?' Speedy asked, his eyes a-twinkle, his impeccable front teeth exposed.

'Great. Wife, family, being with them for Christmas, all great. Had any rain?'

'Rain! What's that?'

There were now four armchairs in the cottage's living room, a larger wardrobe in the bedroom and Angela's note on a new kitchen table: 'Welcome Home, essentials in fridge. supper's at seven.' The anti-Doberman palisade outside the back door had gone. Having shut himself in the bedroom, Harry phoned Belinda, then returned to the kitchen table and read the letters placed under his eyes. Speedy had already read them. Harry felt as though he'd never been away. It felt no different when helping Dennis peel the spuds and cook the meal while Angela updated them on the latest expatriate gossip – she a bright spark, Dennis a canny extinguisher, Harry a reluctant walker back to an empty cottage. His early night ended when the six o'clock World Service News blared out yet more brutal tyranny, ethnic cleansing, disease pandemics, health care failures, donor pledges. Too soon, Speedy kept honking the land-cruiser's horn in the street very near his bedroom window.

Nothing had changed at the office: Jack conspicuous by his absence; Glen's successor, Pete, drafting another press-release; Fred sweeping up dust; the rest eagerly awaited their presents – four leather jackets bought in a Cotswold market at a fraction of Kolokuana's going-price: Pinkie's maroon, Muella's white, Fuzzy's beige, Speedy's black, the colour he'd requested. Harry's popularity soared! Blue gardening overalls for Fred who'd never request anything from anyone, and also a black leather jacket for Pete, who said he hadn't worked there long enough to deserve such an expensive present. The contents of a duty-free Rothman's carton awaited Jack's solitary live match hiding among all the spent ones.

There would, however, very soon be changes. Muella married her fiancée in London and they settled there. As damaging products of the cabinet's centralisation paranoia, Pete was withdrawn to the information ministry, probably because his press-releases were too damned good – Pinkie sucked into the finance ministry's bureaucracy, yet still trying her utmost to protect and project the interests of drought relief, though through no fault of her own, too often failing. Civil service obstructionism as ever hampered relief. The biggest change was Jack's sudden dismissal by his arch-enemy, the chief secretary, and despite the strongest of protests, there was no turning back. Jack needed a job – to keep his two eldest daughters at the international high school and the two youngest at the English prep school. One of Suleiman's budgets enabled Jack to continue checking the maize-grain, arriving most weeks at Kolokuana's grinding mill from overseas, as well as the northern province's fast-dwindling food and fodder contributions. Fuzzy had gone to help Jack.

Harry was ordered to close down the drought relief office by the government's chief secretary and to share his personal assistant-cum-sleuth's office. Fred and his wife moved to Mabela, he to work as a foreman, she as a cleaner, in Jurek's solar-panel factory. Their youngest daughter, Palima, remained in Kolokuana to complete her teacher training course.

'Here endeth a doomed attempt to build a team in Africa!' Harry's diary lamented.

He and Speedy now prolonged their absences in the south from two to three weeks per month. Harry stayed in the Mabela "bedsit" and Speedy lodged with his grandparents – when not being worn out by a magnificent lady about twice his age known as "Princess!"

Mr Mboko's early return from an extended Christmas break encouraged the slippery chief secretary and his smooth aide-cum-sleuth to slide into dangerous obscurity which was not good news! Then they were spotted in the UN club's bar where, to Suleiman's mounting alarm, the presence of crookéd senior policemen, corrupt officials, out-and-out thugs and sundry shady characters had multiplied of late. When government secret service agents, the African men wearing black suits and black shades, started using the bar as a regular rendezvous with the local under-world, Suleiman closed the club and had the pool table moved to a room on the ground floor of his office block.

The country's ambassador to India replaced the chief secretary. Mr Floors made an impressively swift, behind-the-scenes, impact. Lawrence Kwawenda would overhaul the macro-bloated civil service. Tsabo's emergency powers bill was despatched to parliament for prompt enactment. Harry's draft post-drought recovery plan would be reviewed.

With his new office now all to himself, and a pleasantly helpful female secretary next door, Harry reverted to halving his months between Kolokuana and the south.

He and Suleiman had frequently discussed the disaster management project, proposed by Jinky almost a year ago. Mr Floors asked who would lead the project and Suleiman said Harry Burke would be happy to take it on – when his drought relief and post-drought recovery commitments permitted. Next on the redoubtable Mr Floors' packed agenda was persuading the powers-that-be to call an early general election.

'You'll be lucky,' Suleiman commented, needlessly as it transpired.

He told Harry what he and Mr Floors had said. 'I also suggested that you both finalise the recovery plan as soon as possible. The cabinet's been haggling over it far too long.'

Having seen a suprisingly young Mr Floors leaving his office, true to form, Harry had estimated his age – mid-thirties – also a head shorter than himself and not nearly as slim.

In Mboko's weekly broadcast to his people, he outlined: 'My Blueprint for a Glorious Future.' Having claimed the credit for Mr Floors' initial achievements, and added several of his own, he exultantly announced: 'Our general election will be held on Easter Sunday when most of your menfolk are likely to be home from their work elsewhere. I have even more, very welcome news for you. On Good Friday, just seven weeks from today, I shall declare the national drought emergency over and done with forever. Yes, my dear friends, over and done with forever and ever.'

Suleiman switched off his office television and asked Harry: 'Isn't the emergency due to end a month *after* Easter?'

'That's why Belinda's arriving in May.'

'You're aware, of course, that Diane and I will be delighted to put you both up.'

'Once my wife has said she wants to stay in the cottage, there'll be no shifting her. But thanks all the same. Belinda will be delighted to find that she shares a common interest with Diane. My wife wears the expensive dresses she'd designed and I foot the bill. Your wife gets sent fashion-row freebies and your bank account continues to prosper.'

Suleiman laughed. 'That's not entirely true. I often buy Diane delightful lingerie.'

'You dirty old man!'

Mr Floors, the very novel chief secretary, was born into a hard-up, Cape-coloured family of anti-apartheid activists. Denied a university education, he and his doting parents were evicted from their Cape Town shack and exiled in Wales. Whilst earning an economics degree, Kabinda Niceboy Floors got through a variety of nicknames – Boyo, Lovely Boy and Planks the most respectable. He had married Honey, a media studies undergraduate from the Welsh Valleys, who suffered a similar fate. Honey Floors became Sticky Floors, though the Afrikaans pronunciation of their surname, Flers, never stuck. She had wanted to rename him Sunny Boy. He had opted for, Sonny, and returned to Africa with Sticky clinging to his hand. Mr Floors chuckled. 'I ought to have said, my *adhesive* Sticky. After eleven years in the foreign ministry, here, to be trusted with a prestigious ambassadorship was an utter, undeserved surprise. India's scenery and potentially thriving economy were enviable. There were far too many *un*-enviable aspects, though. Blatant poverty the most obvious. I expect you were shocked to find so much poverty in the south of this country.'

Harry nodded. 'Obangwatos were already selling their livestock to fend off starvation. Though water was and remains the major problem, with poor governance a close second. Without the internal provision of essential resources and know-how to allay health care, nutritional, sanitation, hygiene and agricultural deficiencies, donors have been generously striving to fill a gaping void with substantial external aid.'

'My Indian friends would have replied to that: 'Oh, my goodness, what I am hearing I am believing. They got their lilting accent from we Welsh, you know.'

Harry liked the humour, liked the man, relaxed in an armchair with a mug of coffee, and now suggesting they use first names. Harry also admired the unassuming way Sonny had recounted a clamber from hounded penury to where he was now, without mentioning his widely known university stardom. His forthright, positive approach to myriad new-found and vitally significant responsibilities, some highly sensitive, Harry much admired.

'Quality of life and social justice never come cheaply or easily,' Sonny continued. 'All the same, it's reassuring to hear from you that too little outside assistance is not a local deficiency. It is, in numerous other disaster-stricken nations. But we're both aware of the pitfalls that go with accepting donor aid. Degrading suffering people's self-reliance and causing them to rely too much on handouts, to name just two, but that's typical of today's least

243

developed countries. What were the biggest challenges awaiting your arrival here?'

'Excessive top-down direction, little bottom-up participation, and some relief agencies unwilling to accept that concerted planning and swift action were essential. This resulted in widespread fragmentation and too much time wasted trying to co-ordinate them, when so much had to be done to alleviate suffering and to save lives and livelihoods. Bluntly, the situation was as bad as it could get. Yet the genuine needs of thousands of drought victims were ignored by battalions of idle bureaucrats here, in the capital. There were too few competent officials in southern districts, too many corrupt chiefs and their henchmen, and most community headmen had no means of rapidly communicating their problems to districts, bottom-up.'

'Bottom-up participation can also increase fragmentation and hamper effectiveness,' Sonny said. 'Too many countries have to deal with too many donors and relief agencies, each with their pet projects, budgets and operating methods. I'd hate to guess how many you've had to deal with. No, don't tell me! Regrettably, drought is a weapon of mass destruction and we must be thankful for every scrap of help we can get. Maybe soon, we shall cast aside our drought-mapping tools, oil our poverty-mapping machinery and buy stacks of HIV anti-retroviral drugs and syringes. It defeats me how black politicians can hoodwink millions of black people, people of my colour, in to believing that the whites invented AIDS to kill us off. Inadequate politicians with inadequate epidemic-treatment regimes tend to act inadequately . . . anyway, enough of that for the time being. In future, every policy we and trusted colleagues propose will begin with a concept, reflecting this country's actual situation and capabilities, its proneness to god- and man-made disasters, as well as its limited means to prevent, respond or combat such crises. My preface to your recovery plan will stress this. And although your short, sharp guidelines balance necessity and reality, none guarantee obedient, efficient or peaceful compliance, as you will know only too well. Go ahead with having the recovery plan distributed to all who must comply with it. I've highlighted on this copy the guidelines which in my opinion and it's only one opinion are vital to improving the lot of all distressed southerners as rapidly and effectively as feasible.'

Among the guidelines Sonny had highlighted were the far fewer published soon after the drought relief team had stumbled into existence.* Others included:

- Safeguard wetlands and water sources/supplies more efficiently.
- Build small rural dams, enlarge urban reservoirs, buy and deploy much more irrigation equipment.
- Trap and conserve rainwater by every practicable means (it will eventually rain).
- Enact and enforce laws regulating land allocation, land-use, crop-enclosure, pasture-protection and livestock husbandry.
- Set up district seed/fertiliser banks, grow drought-resistant and cash crops.
- Sell produce locally to strengthen market trading, prolong the freeze on sales tax.
- Tackle Obangwato endemic malnutrition and poverty – in tandem.
- Incorporate more nutrients in the south's food chain.
- Accelerate widespread hygiene education and sanitation improvements.
- Provide an effective health care facility within a day's walk/ ride of communities.
- Upgrade health-posts, clinics and hospitals; increase their number and capacity.
- Provide care in enough orphanages; house and help destitute adults find work.
- Restart school meals, stopped last year.**
- Step up drought recovery/disaster management training.
- Eliminate corruption while introducing fair, devolved and transparent governance.

---

* Pages 66-67.
** Page 136.

'With Tsabo's Mashedi's Emergency Powers Bill enacted and Lawrence Kwawenda's overhaul of the civil service completed, the drought recovery plan stands a better-than-average chance of getting off the ground, but wlll the general election result nullify these efforts?' Harry asked Sonny. 'The northern province is the opposition party's power base. If it gains most votes, will Anglican northerners continue to send water, food and fodder to Catholic drought victims in the south?'

'The Emergency Powers Act may have to be enforced,' Sonny replied. 'By the way, I've booked a Huey helicopter to take both provincial governors and both of us on a tour of all northern and southern districts. There'll be ample time for all of us to discuss with district officials and local representatives whatever potential problems crop up. Before we go, I need a desk and chair on your next drought management course.'

Sonny proved a model course pupil, absorbing other pupils' views before injecting his plain common-sense and enlivening humour; reserving the trickier questions until he and Harry were alone; his suggestions constructive, his compliments encouraging. In short, he exemplified what this country and its government so urgently needed.

Uncle Bill chaired the meetings and summarised discussions in all six of his southern districts – as did the northern province's governor when they toured his eleven districts. Sitting at the back of each meeting, armed with Harry's tape-recorder, Sonny ventured forward only to settle disputes, to close each session in uplifting fashion, and to thank everybody for their valuable contributions. They now knew who the new chief secretary was and his priorities, whereas his predecessor had remained a remote non-entity to the vast majority of them and their compatriots. Fortunately, he had remained a remote non-entity, Harry reckoned, for that conniving man had caused problems instead of helping to solve them and we haven't heard the last of him, most probably.

Back at his office desk Sonny transposed the tape-recordings into a succinct two-page report, mostly good news, but not shying away from warranted criticism. Out of courtesy, he showed a copy to Mr Mboko who praised it and refused to return it to its author!

Mboko began his next televised/radioed address by reading out only the good news in Sonny's report, claiming that he had written the report. He concluded what amounted to a blatant electoral stunt with these rousing words: 'Everything I have always done for all of you, my dear friends, and for our wonderful country, is being done in the way I've always wanted it done and the way I will always do it in future. God bless you, everybody!'

That Darling Little Boy

After months of politicians politicking the registered electorate, minus the many men and women working in other countries unable to get time off from their jobs, exercised the democratic right to choose a new government, keep the old one, or have another try later. Thousands of highlanders, hundreds aided by a walking stick, happily trudged by path or track for miles, even days, to the nearest polling station; the drought had left far too many with nothing to ride. Most northerners went by car, taxi or bus to cast their vote.

When the Commonwealth monitoring team declared the election free of corruption the results were published – foremost among them: Emmanuel Mboko's paper-thin majority in the capital's wealthiest constituency and Jenkins Makimbo's unopposed victory in its poorest. Which ministry would Jenkins get, and who would replace him as the country's Red Cross director? He swapped posts with the health minister. The anti-cell-phone, anti-everything-and-everyone, censorship driven, information minister, alias "The Shredder", lost her seat to a civil rights campaigner. It was reliably rumoured that she'd pursued her sacked chief secretary ally into dangerous obscurity.

Jurek's wife now represented her own and many more Obangwato clans in parliament, thereby tying Jurek more securely to his solar panel factory. More candidates than ever before had stood as Independents, including Jenkins Makimbo. Would they tip the scales in favour of the former governing party? They pledged, in the interest of continuity, their *qualified* support. With the election satisfactorily over and Whitsun just round the corner, Harry could prepare for his wife's visit.

Belinda hated flying overnight without Harry beside her, yet everything worked out fine. On arrival in a country where the dry midday heat made her gasp for air, she also found the landscape unimaginably arid, the mountains barren, all the poverty alarming.

But now she more clearly understood why she'd been be a husband-less wife and soon would be again.

Harry's cottage was much better than she'd expected, the Akroyds a charming couple, Berney's Bazaar quite impressive, and she adored Happy Sam. While carrying her two full plastic bags of groceries, the beaming little street urchin proudly showed her some of the places where he'd slept and hidden food. Back at the cottage, she washed his grubby face and hands and they chatted in pigeon English with lots of signs, which made them giggle. When she gave him a parcel and he discovered within it a *new* T-shirt with *a big horse's head* on its front; he jumped up and down with joy and clapped his hands. Having seen-off two extra-large servings of sausages and fried bread, he seemed anxious to keep the T-shirt in the cottage.

Tsabo, looking just as handsome, came for a hugging reunion. Harry took them to the Horseman's Rest for supper and managed to get the table nearest the electric fire. She'd been surprised how cold it was, until reminded that mid-winter was only a month away. The roasted maize cobs, corn-on-the-cob in her cookbook, and a red wine called Pinotage were delicious. The boiled mutton and peas, edible. The jam tart, declined. The frequent to-ing and fro-ing of males and females betwixt the bar and what she took to be the way to the bedrooms brought on a bout of intrigued fascination. She did her Southern Baptist best to look disgusted, but Tsabo had noticed her curiosity and put her in "The African Promiscuity Picture" before telling her everything under the local moon. Harry drove her back to the cottage, they washed and cleaned their teeth in boiled water, before he hurried her off to bed. Sleep was what she longed for, but her husband had other ideas.

Next morning *organised* activity took the Akroyd's kitchen by surprise! Dennis was submerging bottles and cans under blocks of ice in the sink, Angela defrosting trifle and Monica preparing salad. Outside in the withered-up garden, Speedy had lit the braai and was chatting up Belinda while Harry busily arranged, then re-arranged, all the tables and chairs, necessitating the re-designing and copper-plated re-scribing of three replacement seating plans nailed, then re-nailed, to the hen house roof – whence that goddam rooster performed and kept on re-performing the neigbourhood's daily pre-dawn wake up call.

At noon, precisely, Richard Riddington stepped down from his aerial-bedecked, flag-flying Range Rover. Suleiman and Diane arrived in her pick-up. Sonny and Sticky Floors in a battered jalopy, rapidly followed by a dusty old minibus driven by Tsabo with Uncle Bill, Jenkins Makimbo, Lawrence Kwawenda and their wives aboard. While Belinda and Harry circulated, Dennis dispensed Pinotage and Tsabo served beer and soft drinks to the guests: sun-shaded by Mabella-manufactured, Angela-decorated, umbrellas. Speedy then performed an unscheduled slapstick comedy act, with his blasted bongos, when he should have been grilling Berney Bazaar's de-tinned marinated herrings, baking jacket-potatoes and stopping the baked beans boiling over. Harry abstained from the too lengthy applause that Jack found useful for camouflaging his uneasy, tardy appearance.

'Sorry. My wife forgot to remind me and she didn't have time to get ready.'

An inventive way of apologising, Harry reckoned, dipping a hand into the sink's ice and quickly handing Jack a freezing can of lemonade. Then thinking Harry was otherwise engaged, Jack's cold dip soon came up with two cans of beer which he drained behind the hen house, the nearest he could hide to the sink. His fag smoke gave his game away.

With the late afternoon's temperature plummeting every one gathered in the Akroyd's lounge to listen, at Angela's insistence, to Harry's Welsh male voice choir tapes. Having fetched them from the cottage, he had to play *Myfanwy* first – Angela's favourite. It also happened to be one of Sticky Floor's many favourites and, hailing from the Valleys, her soprano voice and Welsh words drowned the tape-recording. So Angela asked Harry to play it again, but this time it was drowned by Speedy's bongo-beating and Jack's loud, discordant humming, reminding Richard Riddington to thank his hosts, on behalf of their guests, for holding the party on a Saturday which had made it all the more enjoyable for him because he worked every weekend, as well as weekdays. 'No wonder Richard's then-wife had accused him of being a workaholic,' Harry reminded his diary that evening.

Belinda's first week had flown by! Sunday with Suleiman and Diane Rashid. Monday and Tuesday out and about with Diane. Wednesday a dress design teach-in. Thursday the dinner at the British high commissioner's residence where she sat next to Mr Mboko, the hugely obese finance minister who ran the country – and too much else, apparently. The touchy-feely type, who'd have the clothes off a female in ten seconds flat, given half a chance. With a supercilious smile, he asked if she'd found her grandfather's grave. Harry, looking sheepish, even panicky, leaned across the table and said: 'It's *my* grandfather's grave and the answer's *no!*' Mboko's entire body shook with laughter and Harry had a lot of explaining to do in bed that night. On Friday he drove her to the summit of a mountain road. He'd said the panoramic view from ten thousand feet would be magnificent. But the mountain road was a steep, narrow, tortuous track that scared her, the altitude made her dizzy and an incident on the way down *petrified* her! After several attempts to overtake, a wildly hooting driver squeezed his bus-full of passengers past Harry's vehicle, forcing it perilously near to the edge of a precipice. No more rural escapades, she insisted, though relented when Monica invited her and Harry to spend the weekend in her stud-farm's granny annexe. Her free and easy company Belinda found relaxing after the previous week's rather contrived social whirl. They discussed tapestry design all day while Harry rode Monica's horses. At least he had supper with them, and this time, Belinda took *him* to bed. She was frozen, but so was he!

Having tucked into a full-English breakfast every weekday morning, Happy Sam took her shopping and showed her *more* places where he'd slept and hidden food, but wore his horse's head T-shirt only in the cottage. They spent her second week's afternoons at the equitation club's stables where Angela began teaching Happy Sam to ride, while Harry attended meetings he couldn't afford to miss and spent most evenings typing his diary.

Belinda had always wanted a son. Harry had wanted three, of course. He had to have three of everything! She phoned Richard Riddington and asked if it were permissible to adopt an African boy. 'Apply for a visa covering the total period of the boy's primary and secondary education. Before he's finished school, ask an immigration official what to do next. Let me know how you get on and if you need my help.' After reading her scribbled notes back to Richard, she said: 'Huge thanks! Your advice is greatly appreciated.'

Belinda also wanted to meet Fuzzy, the woman who had been stabbed. During her final evening in the cottage she had to answer a barrage of questions about herself, her house and her family before Fuzzy would describe her way of life which she probably had made sound better than it really was. She had never been to the airport and asked if she could go with them. Harry suggested she stand outside the Catholic Cathedral at eleven o'clock next morning, wearing the headscarf he'd bought her in Mavimbi, to make it easier to see her in the Saturday crowds. Painfully aware of Belinda's disquiet, he quickly told her that local people expected a present each time foreigners returned from overseas or wherever.

Belinda's final few hours in the cottage were desperately forlorn despite Happy Sam's beaming presence. Given a big bag of sweets and an even bigger hug, he realised "Ma Lady" was going when Harry carried her cases out through the front door to his vehicle. Happy Sam stood by the roadside in his belovéd T-shirt, waving despondently, and she bravely returned all his waves until traffic separated them.

As her flight became ever more imminent Fuzzy's chatter helped to lessen the tension, then admiring Belinda's four lovely rings, she asked if she could have one. Harry gulped!

'Two are my engagement and the wedding rings,' Belinda said, 'the others were my mother-in-law's and my grandmother's. I can't give one away.' The loudspeaker's call to emplane and Fuzzy's tearful farewells saved more embarrassment.

'Sorry about that. It's all part of the local culture,' Harry said while leading Belinda to the departures entrance. They clung to each other, until an African man shouted at her: 'If you don't hurry up I'll shut this gate and you won't fly.' Harry shouted back: 'If you shut that gate you won't get a tip.' The man carried her cases out to the aircraft and made sure Harry could see him loading them through the rear door so that the pilot could stow them.

While crossing the tarmac Belinda glanced back nervously. Harry waved both arms and she waved back. The aircraft taxied to one end of the runway and roared past him, with his wife somewhere inside its flimsy fuselage. After taking off and banking east, it was very soon lost in the brilliant midday sky. Within two hours she would be waiting another four hours in Mavimbi airport, with renewed trepidation, to board her overnight flight to Heathrow. Disconsolately ambling back to the land-cruiser, Harry kicked himself for not spending all of every day with his cherished Belinda . . . Just the two of them, alone!

Driving back to Kolokuana, he asked Fuzzy why she'd left the relief team and gone to help Jack at the maize-grinding mill.

'We are cousins. He gave me the office cleaner's job at the relief team's office, also.'

Then why hadn't Jack helped Fuzzy before and after she'd been so cruelly stabbed? No uncharitable thoughts! Harry reflected, instead, on the local people's frequent claims to be related to each other, genuinely or if it suited them.

Since being mutilated by her drunken, imprisoned, now divorced husband, Fuzzy had lived at Ocean View, the capital's most squalid suburb, infested with rats no doubt. Also infested with tokolosi – according to Tsabo. But Harry had never ventured nearer than the main tarred road which bisected the sprawling, fetid slums. He asked a wall-lolling youth to guard the land-cruiser, tipped him, then followed Fuzzy to a row of windowless cells. He'd met her ten-year-old daughter and twin girls of nine once before, at the office braai. Each wrapped in a blanket, they greeted him shyly. Behind them, he could see a sleeping-mat laid out on a dirt floor. Fuzzy went to check if the land-cruiser was still there and he asked the eldest girl if there was a shop close by. She led him along a stinking alley, an open sewer alive with rats, to a bread-stall. He bought the last three loaves, which she carried home as gingerly as if they were the crown jewels. He gave the girls some pocket-money and hurried back to the land-cruiser. Shiftless neighbours stared at him, most of them mildly curious, some clearly hostile. The youth guarding the land-cruiser had flitted and his seven deputies refused to budge unless they too were given a tip. He acquiesced! Beating a hasty, mobile retreat Harry felt more than relieved to still be in one piece . . . though he'd seen none of the tokolosi that might share Ocean View with other residents.

Fuzzy and her daughters must be found somewhere clean and safer to live. Yet, however hard Harry wracked his brains, he came up with no workable solution. Her former parents-in-law blamed her for their son's gaoling and had called in a witchdoctor. If Fuzzy took her daughters back to their village, the spell cast upon her could well prove fatal. There was no alternative, she must move. He'd buy her decent furniture and pay her rent. After all, he'd been paying her daughters' school fees for nearly a year, and by not heeding her pleas for help he was partly responsible for that appalling scar. But if she and the girls were to move to better, far healthier accommodation, it would rapidly become known who was footing the bill. Fuzzy could never keep anything to herself. It would be much wiser to let matters take their natural course – local people overcame problems in their own way. Besides, Fuzzy was Jack's cousin. This time he must help! I've got more than enough to worry about, Harry reckoned. My wife, for instance. Belinda hated flying. She hadn't wanted to come here and wasn't too thrilled with what awaited her, apart from all the friends she'd made. No more Belinda visits! Of this he was certain, and by going off to meetings, typing his diary, always doing his own things, he'd badly neglected her. That's why she'd spent so much time with other people. He must get back to the cottage. Belinda had a mobile-phone and might ring him from Mavimbi's airport.

After his sleepless night of bitter grief, re-churning over in his mind how to break the news, hyper-anxious to know that his wife had arrived home safely, yet willing the phone not to ring. Then, when Belinda did ring, she sounded so relaxed and happy.

'Everything's great! Except the garden's a jungle and there's loads of mail. I'll let you know if your help's needed. Anyway, what have you been doing with yourself?'

'I dropped Fuzzy home, bought her bread, but driving to the cottage, a crowd blocked the main street and policemen were searching people and vehicles. At first, I thought a shop had been burgled, then I saw . . .'

'Stop! You're going to say something dreadful's happened to that darling little boy.'

Tsabo's truck, white with lots of red crosses, was the hearse. His ordained classmate, the solemn priest in black. Tsabo and Harry, the only mourners, in grey suits and dark blue College ties, Tsabo's new, Harry's faded, their bare heads bowed under the relentless sun while the priest read out the 23rd Psalm, a thanksgiving prayer for a brief life, another of forgiveness for the unknown culprit or culprits. And then that oh so final 'ashes to ashes' prayer, committing an innocent child's remains to the welcoming embrace of a Lord in a Heaven that had always been beyond his reach and also his imagination. Tsabo and Harry slowly lowered the short wooden coffin into its ultimate resting place, followed by some handfuls of dust. When the gravedigger's shovel had done its work, Harry laid a bunch of wild anenomies on the grave. Tied to it, a farewell card with this message: 'To Belinda's darling little boy and Harry's best plastics-carrier in the world.'

On a wooden cross soon to be erected at the farthest end of the public cemetery – "The Place of Rabbits" in Gwato – the inscription in bold, gold-painted lettering read:

HAPPY SAM

Seven Years Young
He Died on his Pavement Home
Clinging to a T-Shirt

Within a week the wooden cross had gone, probably burned on a cooking fire, and a concrete cross stood in its place. Harry brought wild flowers, when he could find any, and often met the young priest who had conducted the funeral service and was visiting every street-boy's grave. But some day, they would all become just unmarked mounds of hard-baked clay, which a sudden downpour would turn in to sunken, unvisited quagmires.

More Ups and Downs

Sonny and Sticky Floors, a delightful couple, were charming in their different ways: both genuine, down to earth and more. Friends they chose carefully, though once made, their loyalty was unfaltering. In short, they were a lovable pair who adored each other! Sticky welcomed her mates as she called them, literally with open arms – Sonny more guarded. His friends were those he respected and who respected him. Mutual trust and talent also scored high.

They had returned to the bungalow they'd enjoyed living in before going to India. The capital's middle-class Residential Area was closer to the town centre and far homelier than that snooty Diplomatic Compound, where the chief secretary's mansion they'd been told to occupy stayed empty.

That evening was their house-warming party. While Sonny saw to the drinks, Sticky left the Vindaloo curry to simmer, baked Welsh cakes and set about buttering slices of another of her native delicacies, bara brith – a fruit loaf which, after Sticky, was Sonny's tastiest nibble. The clinging red sari brought out the best in her slender figure and made her jet-black hair shine all the more. Sticky had wanted him to wear his white maharajah outfit, but without the big turban which hid his curly hair. Still re-acclimatising, Sonny had opted for thick corduroys and his baggy pullover that hid a moderate paunch. She inspected him before they welcomed their guests.

Sitting or squatting as near as possible to the inadequate electric fire, replete with food and home-made shandy, their guests were entertained by Sticky: no meagre raconteur of witty frivolity. Her endearing Welsh accent rolled off an actice tongue, with 'by yer', 'by there' and 'you know' aplenty.

Now she handed round copies of what appeared to be the lyrics of a ballad and invited the guests to help her perform it. 'Just for a bit of fun, you know.' But warned that Sonny would award marks for everyone's voice quality and dancing ability. Sticky la-lalled the simplest of tunes through, only once, then nine braves had to have two goes in attempted unison and inventing some sort of dance.

"Kabinda Lovely Boy Floors had lots of names, Sonny the last.
Honey, Sonny's missus, became Sticky and this one stuck fast.
On a choppy passage to India, Sticky clung to a slippery deck.
Heavily pregnant, Sticky got the ship's nurse to quickly check.
Then Sticky had Smelly in a clammy monsoon near New Delhi.
Smelly's stinky nappy gave Sonny and Sticky nasty delly-belly."
laughter and unseemly remarks sacrificed the rest!

Sonny announced that all nine braves deserved top marks. His comments, however, would go down better with some than with others.

'Emmanuel Mboko too much jigging, but no singing. Richard Riddington, retired hurt. Suleiman Rashid and Dennis Akroyd, tried hard. Their wives neck-and-neck winners, until one of Diane Rashid's high heels broke and Angela Akroyd's undergarment broke loose from its moorings. Jenkins Makimbo and Harry Burke sang far too loudly. Punter Bryant strutted around like a cockerel stalking a hen. Although its beak kept moving, no sound came out.'

'I was clucking quietly,' objected Punter, a drought-recovery newcomer.

'Of course you were, luv. Don't worry about it,' said Sticky. 'Sonny! Get that wine you hid out the back. Any more of your shandy and I'll be clucking. The hard stuff's by yer, folks, on the Welsh dresser my poor little gran left me.' Now the party really took off!

Speedy arrived, three hours early, to collect drunk drivers. Not liking what he saw, the quickening beat of his bongos soon hotted up the old timer's jiving. And that Mr Mboko! Shaking his rolls of fat all over the place, tripping up the others and himself, trying to flirt with Mrs Floors. A smashing bit of totty! Wouldn't mind doing a turn or two with her.

He mentioned this to Harry out in the garden, during a breather, and was told not to be so rude or something a lot ruder . . . His ears didn't work, sometimes.

It was gone midnight when he drove the Akroyds and Harry home, then went back to collect old Fatso Mboko, who wanted to go to the Horseman's Rest to pick up a younger totty. Oh yeah, thought Speedy. In your pissed state, you won't find it. Getting a hard on?

No chance! Instead, he dropped his passenger near the Diplomatic Compound gate, out of range of the sentry's rifle, but near enough to watch a drunkard searching for his ID card. Speedy returned to the Horseman's Rest where his middle-aged Mabela beauty, Princess, who'd come in a taxi two weeks ago, would be waiting for a "kiss" – Harry's preferred alternative in his diary record of next morning's probing chat with a knackered Speedy.

Sonny had talent-spotted Punter Bryant at the Calcutta Derby or perhaps at some other horse-racing venue. His memory, always sharply reliable, had been blunted by whisky – the one and only time he had let Sticky and himself down. Still, he didn't back a winner every day of the week. In fact, he'd never bet on anything, until Punter had assured him that his tip in the four-thirty was a certainty. Punter was not just a serious punter, but also a seriously proficient operator in the Save the Children Fund's Indian set-up. When that contract expired, he had followed Sonny to Kolokuana to become the British charity's country-director. After all, horse-racing was a very popular pastime in South Africa. Yet driving two days and a night to get there, then two days and a night to get back, would take up far too much of his annual leave and he had a frail mother to visit in a Somerset nursing home. Apart from his responsibilities as a caring son, and the lucrative hobby he now conducted by phone, his commitment to post-drought recovery would prove total!

Of the five working groups, which had helped plan and co-ordinate relief, most had performed commendably well. Some had mushroomed in size and needed a shake-down. The agriculture group, a late starter, still searched in vain for adequacy. Harry believed a revised structure would, not only assist post-drought recovery, but also hasten effective disaster management in the longer term. Sonny agreed his proposals, Suleiman endorsed them and the cabinet eventually approved them.

Sonny would chair the water and sanitation group. Uncle Bill wanted to lead the food group, leaving Tsabo to concentrate on his Red Cross duties. Jenkins Makimbo, now the health minister, continued chairing the health group that would also take on nutrition, as well as reforming community and hospital care. Punter

Bryant would head the agriculture and food security group. Harry would remain the co-ordinating group's chairman. Each group would have ten members, all of permanent secretary or equivalent status, plus two highly rated district officials and two co-operative chiefs. All post-drought activities were to be funded from a delegated budget and given maximum publicty.

So Pinkie and Pete joyously returned to the fold. Pinkie papered Harry's office walls with budget data and offered to allocate places on the courses he ran in Mabela. As well as drafting situation reports and press releases, Pete volunteered to be secretary of the restructured working groups. They both shared Harry's office. Speedy now strove to read all *their* mail, in addition to Harry's and the clerk's next door.

That evening's diary ended with this faint-hearted exhortation: 'Here beginneth the final attempt to build a team in Africa.'

Harry smelt a rat when Mboko's bossy secretary armed with a plateful of chocolate cakes and a jugful of coffee quickly ushered him into her minister's inner sanctum.

Mboko handed Harry two cakes and licked off the chocolate left on his fingers! 'Remember those disaster management proposals you sent to the cabinet for approval,' he said. 'Would you remind me what disaster management means and what a delegated budget is.' Mboko had been finance minister for goodness knows how long!

Harry drew a clock face on a ministerial notepad and wrote: 'Disaster Impact' at noon. 'Response' five minutes later. 'Recovery' at four. 'Mitigation' at six. 'Preparedness' at eight o'clock. 'Disaster Warning' at five minutes to midnight.

The podgy pupil still looked puzzled. 'What is mitigeration and prep . . . prepardless?'

'Once you know the threat, in your case mainly drought and man-made disasters, you decide the urgent measures required to mitigate, prevent or reduce the disaster's impact. If they are unsuccessful, or if you haven't been warned of an approaching disaster, you try again. For preparedness, read *readiness*. The process is on-going, except disaster impact, hopefully, and requires frequent review and updating. Delegated budgets are the financial resources given you or by you to your staff or other people's staff for managing functions like those round my clock. Disaster management involves effective planning, mounting, sustaining, checking, improving and co-ordinating every function round the circle, and also involves training people to carry out their assigned roles effectively. Okay so far?'

'Have another cake,' chuffed Mboko, forgetting he'd already scoffed the rest.

Harry poured himself a coffee. 'Effectively responding to a serious disaster crucially depends on efficient early warning, on enforcing relief measures and on indivual people's skill. In the case of drought, as well as rare tornadoes, flash floods and heavy snowfalls, weather forecasts are *vital!* The Emergency Powers Act now empowers the president, the cabinet, parliament, civil service, army, police, non-governmental organisations, etcetera, to enforce relief and recovery measures. Also, the performance of everybody responsible for implementing the measures swiftly and effectively, must be honestly, accurately and regularly assessed.'

Mboko eased his bulk from his heroic armchair, rubbed his chubby palms together and thumped Harry's back. 'As clear as *diamonds!*' he bellowed, quivering with laughter and thumping Harry again. 'Before you go, bringer of rain, what's the weather forecast?'

Having lost his praise-name and name-card long ago, Harry found Mboko's well-worn joke more than boring. But the British weather centre's latest fax had hoisted his flagging spirits from their perpetual drought doldrums. He happened to have the fax with him and read out: 'A build-up of intense low pressure over the southern and central highlands next month is expected to produce heavy rain and possibly floods in lower-lying areas.'

A beaming Mboko phoned his secretary. 'Buy plenty more chocolate cakes' . . . She says there's no more of my petty cash. Can you lend me some?' Fatso Mboko didn't get any.

In that evening's broadcast to the nation he got the weather forecast almost right, there was no mention of floods, but he made a pig's ear of explaining the disaster management circle and clock timings. He went on to describe "his" new working groups and how he'd told them to work very hard every day to stop disasters happening and to work very hard every night, also, when disasters happened . . . Harry couldn't listen to anymore.

Then the fun started! Which senior civil servants, district officials and chiefs would represent their peers in these new groups? Parliamentarians demanded a voice, too. The opposition party's paper accused "Young Mr Floors" of monopolising power – its editor organised protest marches and dished out placards and baseball caps. When the police put up road blocks, the protesters, mostly Anglicans, invaded the Catholic Cathedral and the army turfed them out. Shots were heard in the main street and then outside the finance ministry. High above the rabble, in his barricaded penthouse suite, Emmanuel Mboko remained rooted to his king-size throne, unmoveable and unmoved. Even when loudhailers shouted – "Resign, Resign" – he stayed permanently put. Even when told that one of his top officials had disappeared, and others were being held hostage, he never flinched. But he did weaken sufficiently to reach for his pink telephone and ask Suleiman if he should declare a state of emergency. 'Advised to impose a curfew,' he wrote in purple ink on a crested notepad. 'Advice rejected – policemen will loot shops.' He rang his wife to say he would be sleeping in the office, then slept with his office cleaner on the mattress she kept in a cupboard. Next morning, with the mattress stowed away and the windows wide open, he briefed his cabinet colleagues on the situation as he saw it and also told them how they could solve all the problems. Jenkins Makimbo accused him of failing in his duties to the nation, of sacrificing the many people badly injured and those who'd disappeared without trace. Next day, the opposition party's newspaper displayed on its front page an enlarged snapshot of Mboko and both of his cleaner's teenage daughters boarding a cruise-ship in Mavimbi. The protesters dispersed, with most of them returning to the northern province, yet the atmosphere in Kolokuana remained ominously tense.

Men in black suits and black shades now patrolled its streets in expensive Mercedes off-roaders – their nickname 'The Benzi Tribe' – their nightly rendezvous the former UN club bar to meet up with corrupt civil servants and policemen, shady traders, gangsters, drug-pushers and such like.

Suleiman fast-forwarded the plan to co-locate all five of the UN agencies with offices in the capital. He would integrate their staffs, budgets and administration, as well as provide in the same building a strictly "members only" club with a smaller bar, larger television set, new pool table, bigger pool room and other harmless attractions.

Why Sonny found himself anchored in a wheelchair had never leaked out, not even to the local press. 'The hooded goon, a secret service agent most probably, said he'd kill me if I didn't confess to treason,' he told Harry. They were in Sonny's garden – the bungalow might be bugged. 'I emphatically denied the accusation! Stretched on a rack, a revolver held to my forehead, I also denied being in the pay of white men in my birthplace, South Africa. I woke up two days ago, in a bed in the hospital you were in after a dog mauled your leg. I couldn't even lift a finger.' Sonny grimaced. 'Whether I'll walk again . . .'

'It'll be soon. Meanwhile, I stand ready to push you and this contraption whenever, wherever.' Harry called everything technical a contraption.

With the garden Sonny's office and Sticky his stand-in secretary and principal pusher, Sonny functioned as normal, and those who came to meetings, to brief him or to seek a decision also got a Welsh cake, a buttered slice of bara brith and a nice cup of tea – or as many as they wanted. Harry called in on the way to and from work most days. In fact, he saw a lot more of Sonny than Suleiman. Jack came to Harry's cottage for a regular natter, twenty fags and a box of live matches. Government food and fodder reserves were still mounting, seed and fertiliser banks up and running – mainly down to Jack, Fuzzy and scores of others. But, unless the rain came soon, the low levels in Kolokuana's too few reservoirs and its ever-increasing population, even severer water restrictions would need to be enforced, hitherto by untrustworthy policemen, in future by dependable soldiers.

Within a month, Sonny was on crutches or seated behind the chief secretary's desk. A fortnight later, Sticky's party was a best ever! Uncle Bill and Tsabo endeavoured to sing the radio station's signature ditty *Hop on a Horse* resonately assisted by those few who knew the Gwato words. Speedy and his bongos were otherwise engaged.

Harry placed fresh wild flowers on Happy Sam's grave in "The Place of Rabbits." Then, beyond the cemetery, a security guard admitted him to a Red Cross compound. Inside the gate, vehicles were parked under a corrugated-tin roof beneath a static water tank on high wooden stilts, encircled by eight thatched rondavels covered in ivy and surrounded by dead shrubs and live weeds. Shadows cast by the security lights obscured all the door-numbers. Counting the rondavels, clockwise, he unlocked the third. The furniture, gas stove and small fridge were less presentable than those at the cottage, but the sink was clean, so were the basin, toilet and shower behind an internal wall. If the Akroyds moved to South Africa and a rondavel happened to be available he would snap it up, he decided, while driving to the Horseman's Rest. Harry was about to have supper with Dr Solomon Khami, a softly spoken and highly respected paediatrician – the health minister Jenkins Makimbo had succeeded after the general election.

Solomon, now the director of the country's Red Cross Society, said he'd qualified at Bristol University, as had all three of his sons: one a neuro-surgeon in London; another a general practitioner in America; the youngest in New Zealand, yet to choose between a hospital or community career.

'With our family so widely spread, my wife and I share the dream of becoming world travellers, when we finally retire. Meanwhile, my wife devotedly labours night and day as my surgery's midwife and looks after her ailing parents.' Solomon omitted to mention his doubling-up as a dedicated and ever-ready rescuer of drought and AIDS orphans.

'Do you also practise in Kolokuana's hospital?' Harry asked.

'I used to . . . until I became exasperated! The equipment was always unserviceable or missing believed stolen, administration non-existent, the less said about hygiene and care standards the better. None of my sons will work here. It's not the draw of decent

263

facilities and pay abroad, it's the attitudes here. If doctors try to improve things they're undermined and tend to give up. It's as if Newton had propounded a fourth law. To every attempted action, there is an opposite and bloody-minded reaction.' He bowed his head and muttered: 'Please, Lord, forgive the swearword . . . Were my wife and I able to leave, we would go, though we'd hate to abandon our patients, who fear that, one day, we'll no longer be around, mainly because our care is free. However, I shall never work in that death house of a hospital again, not for all the cattle in the northern province, and most of my colleagues have similar feelings. It's a crying shame for everybody, especially the far too numerous departed.'

'Why doesn't the hospital have an accident and emergency unit? What would happen, for instance, if a plane crashed when landing at the airport and caught fire?'

'The passengers and crew would most likely die while the ground staff, police and any onlookers stood by, helplessly. Someone might remember to phone for an ambulance, but even if the hospital's switchboard operator answered the call and an ambulance went to the airport, no paramedics or life-saving equipment would be on board. Nor are doctors and nurses trained to deal with serious accidents. In Kolokuana, with its half a million or more starving, diseased and accident-prone people, there are only four ambulances. They are old and too often off-the-road. Each southern district has one. A pick-up truck with no first aid kit or a stretcher! The northern province has sufficient ambulances, paramedics and equipment, including defibrillators and an emergency blood bank. Before you came here, the flying doctor service had to move its Cessnas from Kolokuana's airport to the airstrip near the town just across the border. The servicing's efficient and it's safer there. With the necessary government funding, the army could base and service them within its secure barracks, with its helicopters, providing more readily available aircraft for casualty evacuation. My predecessor as the local Red Cross Society's director, Jenkins Makimbo, now our health minister, suggested this and we can count on his strong support.'

'What about fire engines?'

'You may well ask. The Red Cross is preparing a report on them, or should I say *the* fire engine. The police have one that ought to be at the airport when planes land, but too often the driver parks it outside his home or takes his wife shopping. The police also have no fire-fighting equipment. And the ladder that will reach a building's third floor window is mounted on a lorry which is shared with the electricity and telephone companies. There are no fire engines in the south. I despair at the seriousness and extent of these problems and by the absence of resources to solve them. Although very few problems are entirely insurmountable, I'm afraid that's too rarely the case in ever-expanding Kolokuana and the long-suffering southern province.'

'If the army ran the ambulance and fire services, and made them work effectively, it would give soldiers a productive role, instead of shooting at policemen putting up road blocks, and dispersing the rioters, last month. Yet it has now been proved that policemen were shooting at soldiers! It's no secret that the police force is unreliable. How would the army acquit itself, if it had to defend this country's interests and maintain security?'

'Even during those worst apartheid times, South Africans used to train and equip our army. Now soldiers must guard food aid lorries, stores sheds and such like. South Africa helped because this country often harboured anti-apartheid terrorists and helicopters flew in troops to flush them out. Our soldiers used to man fuel pumps, now party workers man them. The ruling party fills every key job. And who did Mr Mboko nominate to succeed that scoundrel he sacked, my predecessor as health minister? His loud mouthed arrogant sister! We must thank God it didn't happen.'

'It's difficult for an outsider. Everyone seems to be related to everyone else.'

'You'd be surprised if I told you who I'm related to. However, that's best left unsaid.'

'I'm well used to African surprises. Your briefing's greatly appreciated, let's meet again to discuss the donor-approved plans for combatting likely flash-floods, heavy snowfall and tornado disasters. Canada will provide some heavy-lift helicopters and logistic support.'

The waitress, another of Fuzzy's many cousins, cleared the table and crabbily asked if they were leaving soon. Solomon's offer of a lift home was uncrabbily accepted.

'Many thanks for the meal Harry. Will that rondavel meet your requirements if you need it?'

'Very comfortably. The phone works and the water tank's full.'

'I shall look forward to calling in, once you're settled. I'll tell my secretary you'll be coming to pay the rent and tie up loose ends.' Their handshake sealed the deal.

That discussion enabled Harry to complete the draft disaster management plan, though Suleiman's superiors, the plan's sponsors, would approve the draft, only if he withdrew his proposal to co-locate the offices of Kolokuana's five autonomous UN agencies.

Dennis and Angela sold their bungalow, Harry's cottage and the large compound, found a house near Durban and moved there – so sure were they of Mandela's election as South Africa's president and thus a major sea-change in South African politics.

With his belongings and Saturday shopping in the land-cruiser, Harry trailed a long queue of crawling vehicles bound for Happy Sam's cemetery. After tidying the grave, he drove to the adjacent Red Cross compound and happily took possession of an internally re-decorated rondavel. His domestic routine now changed. With no Akroyds to keep him company and to share his all-in stew, his maid, Dennis's former secretary's mother, still did his chores and his neighbours were already firm friends. A young couple on one side: a Slovenian Lutheran and his West African Muslim wife taught at the recently established agricultural college built within Kolokuana University's campus. On Harry's other side – a social services director loaned by a British county council to instal a probationery service, the first in this country, while also striving to overhaul and reform its under-funded, over-bureaucratised social welfare system.

After work, around seven most evenings, Harry climbed the water tank's ladder, filled two kettles, boiled their contents and when cold, filled four large plastic bottles and stood them in the fridge. He used one bottleful to heat his all-in stew, wash himself and clean his teeth last thing at night and first thing next morning, with enough left over to cook his breakfast porridge and brew tea. He drank the other three at the office or during his many travels. To save water, the Red Cross compound's residents used a pit-latrine, which their men took turns to disinfect. Solomon had assured Harry before he'd agreed to take over a rondavel that men from the town's transformed water and sanitation service would come once a week to empty the latrine, dispose of its contents, and fit a tap to the compound's water tank to reduce the risk of ladder-climbing accidents, particularly when windy and if it ever happened to rain. When Solomon next visited the Red Cross compound he told his tenants that the water and sanitation service had again promised to include the emptying of their pit-latrine when money was available. Harry was especially grateful for the assurance. He'd cleaned no toilet since fagging for older boys at their otherwise pristine boarding school. He'd often wanted to do some cleaning during his twenty years in the Far East, though more often in this country whose comparatively very few latrines encouraged customers, especially Harry, to find a convenient, much cleaner, less smelly hideaway in which to squat.

When Belinda next phoned he described his daily routine in graphic detail, minus the squatting stuff, as well as the likely fitting of a water tank tap. to stop her suggesting one. He then asked how she thought she would cope with such a primitive and exacting means of survival.

'I'd relish the simplicity! Have you done any gardening yet?'

'Just weeding. Being so good at it, I'm expecting every weed killer producer worth his poison to come chasing after my blood.'

'Prove your worth in September. The stinging nettles are nearly as tall as you.'

That cheered up Harry no end! 'Yes, I'll be home for my birthday. Tsabo's booked us cheap air tickets and he'll soon be on his way, at last, to becoming a barrister.'

'That's the best news I've heard for a long time,' Belinda chirruped, which set Harry wondering whether it was his imminent arrival, or Tsabo's career progression, that had so delighted his wife. Yet another of my pernickety fads! After all, once a Virgoan, always a Virgoan, and he got on with de-frosting an unappetising lump of dried beans.

In the bath next morning, Belinda tried to recall her nightmare. She remembered climbing a very high ladder that swayed in the wind and was dipping her kettle into the water tank when everything went blank. She phoned Harry, certain that he'd fallen off his ladder, or even into the tank! No reply and still no reply an hour later! Then, bless him, he rang her.

Shopping

Attached to the envelope left with the Red Cross compound's security guard was a hand-wrtten note from Mkwere, the phantom prospector in whose café Harry's leg had been mauled by that dog, asking him to post the envelope in England. How the hell does he know I'm flying there? The envelope was addressed to his cousin, Dermot, at a phoney-looking Oxford post-box number.' Very odd! None of his business, but worth checking.

Next day, Harry had another intriguing surprise at Mavimbi Airport. While Tsabo was haggling over excess baggage, a young woman accosted him and introduced herself as Tsabo's middle sister, Dinea. She said she had come to wave her brother and his friend goodbye. Dinea was quite a spectacle – tall, her hour-glass figure crammed into a bulging blouse and tight mini-skirt, very high heels, tinted braids, loads of make-up, big smiles, lots of talk. Tsabo looked angry and scarcely spoke to her.

Not until Harry was airborne and visited a toilet did he discover a second envelope in one of his blazer pockets and inside this one a letter smelling of perfume.

'Dear Mr Harry. Tsabo says you are a very good man. Be very good to me. Yes? No Mavimbi shops sell hair pomade and black pantyhose. Please find them in England, and a short white frock, also. You and me will like this frock very much. The airport knows the day you will come back. Your new friend, Dinea, is waiting.'

He tore up the envelope and the letter and flushed their remnants down the pedestal's escape hole. He couldn't sleep. He neither knew what hair pomade was, nor where to buy it. All he could think of were black pantyhose, short white frocks, and how to extricate himself from another female's scarlet talons. First Arrabella, now Dinea! His cheap ticket was non-transferable, so to ask the airline to change his return flight would be pointless.

He and Tsabo bade farewell in a Heathrow baggage collection hall – Tsabo to retrace his first journey to Oxford. He and Jill hadn't met for almost three years, though they'd phoned each other and corresponded. Harry slunk through customs with just his cabin bag, over-tired, despondent and in no mood to rush into Belinda's arms, yet did his best to look full of the joys of a wet and windy morning. The closer they got to the Cotswolds, however, the more relaxed and cheerful he felt, despite those wretched stinging nettles awaiting his well-proven skills. By the time they reached home, Dinea had also been sucked down that pedestal's escape hole. It was all over and done with! Or was it? But having to hunt round women's clothes shops for black pantyhose and a short white frock appalled him.

The neighbours, also members of the choral society he'd sung with, threw a party in the barn between their lodge and his. Both were renovated farm workers' dwellings. With a glass of Pimms in one hand and a prawn sandwich in the other, he described his and a young American's well-received recital at a gathering of Kolokuana diplomats. Belinda's muted reminder that he'd told their neighbours about that sing-song during his previous leave was, fortunately, lost in the noisy arrival of more guests and several were quite keen to hear of his African exploits. But a bright young spark repudiated the whole concept of humanitarian relief as interfering colonialism and Belinda's arm-tug meant an early night.

In the bath, she praised his slimness and suntan, though on their bed, his vigour set her wondering whether he'd been practising with somebody. Afterwards, they laughed it off! But when he turned over, a beckoning Dinea-image on the wall made him turn back over, to check whether he still had a wife. On waking next morning he daren't look at that wall.

After breakfast he walked to the village and posted Mkwere's envelope. Not trusting African clippers, he hadn't had a haircut since he was last home. The barber would be moving on soon. Like the pub across the road, not enough customers to keep him going. He hadn't heard of hair pomade, but phoned a chum who said he'd had several jars of the stuff for donkey's years. It didn't sell because it contained arsenic. Oh! thought Harry. He called in later, bought three jars and went to the hospital. Belinda had booked him health, dental and hearing checks. Then, hacking out stinging nettle roots absorbed the remaining daylight hours. Still, Belinda had prepared a slap-up, romantic, candle-lit dinner beside a blazing log fire. Since their daughter and her family were on holiday, Belinda suggested he visit them on the way to Heathrow, and if he took the train, she'd have the car to take the dresses she had designed to a prestigious fashion show that promised to be extremely lucrative! How could he *not* agree? After showing his inattentive wife how best to stack the new dishwasher he'd bought her, he added an eternity ring to her sparkling array.

Next morning something made him retrieve a pomade jar from his cabin bag and read its label: 'Pomade prevents and restores receding hair.' More than a few African women had receding hair. He read on . . . the formula had just a trace of arsenic – a pity or lucky?

With the garden looking trim, and any weeds he'd missed hidden under leaves, he set about redecorating the guest bedroom. He also had to redecorate an attic bedroom in case Tsabo and Jill weren't sharing a bed, Belinda said. Wasted effort, Harry reckoned.

That weekend they celebrated Tsabo's and Jill's engagement, Harry's 49th birthday – and his new hearing aids. Tsabo and Jill gave him an album of photographs Jill had taken of his and Tsabo's College. Belinda's gift, a trip for two to a male-voice choir concert in South Wales that came a fairly close second to their love for each other, re-expressed on the railway platform, where two days ago they'd bade farewell to Tsabo, Jill and a black kitten – their belated engagement gift. 'Oh what a gorgeous little pet!' Jill had exclaimed. 'We've always wanted one, haven't we Tsabo.' Nodding unconvincingly, he'd picked up the cat basket, handed it to Jill and checked their luggage.

More birthday presents! From his daughter and her husband, a year's subscription to a magazine for the *over-sixties!* From his grand-daughter, an album for her Grandpa Africa to stick lots of photos of lots of animals in. From his grandson, now walking, but talking a version of Chaucerian English, two pairs of long white socks to hide the scars, when wearing shorts. Having reciprocated with four book-tokens and stayed the night, Harry had to keep promising his grand-daughter at breakfast next morning that he'd come back to see her soon – before sadly mooching off to the nearest women's apparel emporium.

An obliging West Indian assistant chose an off-the-peg short white frock, conforming to Harry's guestimate of Dinea's vital statistics, four pairs of black pantyhose to fit a 30-inch inside-leg and also a jar of the lightest shade of Afro-makeup that the assistant used. With this hurdle cleared with surprisingly very few embarrassments, the next awaited him at a checkout counter, the only one manned or womaned, hence the queue. When his turn eventually came to be served, a middle-aged female cashier with badly bleached blonde hair spread out his purchases, scrutinised them and then winked at him.

'Takin the girlfriend somewhere nice an cosy?'

'I'm buying them for my sister's husband,' was the only reply Harry could think of.

'In ter drag is 'ee? Me favourite's Danny La Rue. I'm in 'is fan club.'

'They're for the husband's wife.'

'They all say that darlin. Me friend's goin out wiv a fella who likes dressin in kinky bras and panties. Ain't in ter them? Course not! When I saw you comin, I thought, 'eres a *real* gent, 'ansome, loadsa money . . . Ain't wunner them quality inspectors, are yer?'

'Get yer finger out Mable,' the male queuer behind Harry indelicately suggested.

'Darlene!' Mable shouted to the West Indian assistant. 'Open the uvver till luvvie . . . Now, let's see . . .frock, four tights, makeup, have-a-nice-day card, an pink ribbon. Cash or credit card?' He inserted his card and keyed in his PIN number, while she gift-wrapped a parcel. 'Put the makeup jar in yer bag darlin. It might break an spoil the frock. An write 'er name in this card, 'ere's a biro.' He wrote: 'For Dinea Mashedi.' After tying the card to the parcel with pink ribbon, Mabel read what he'd written.

'Anuvver wunner them foreigners, by the looksa things.'

'She's an Egyptian mummy.'

'Getting on a bit, is she? Me mum's always sayin she's past it now. Never mind, 'avva smashin time, an don't do nuffin me friend's kinky fella won't do.'

With her raucous advice ringing in his ears and cursing his stupidity, Harry slunk into London's obscurity. The three jars of pomade and the makeup one started clinking in his cabin bag whilst heading towards the underground station and thence to Heathrow. He stopped the clinking in case passers-by rebuked him for being an inveterate alcoholic.

He was still cursing his stupidity when, early next morning, a jumbo-jet delivered him and his cabin bag to Mavimbi Airport and too soon afterwards, very reluctantly, into the gleeful presence of Dinea – this time crammed into her nurse's uniform. He bought her a coffee, which she didn't drink. She just sat there, sulking, then shot off to the toilets. He left the jars and gift-wrapped parcel on the table with the have-a-nice-day card wide open so that she couldn't miss her name and watched from amongst the crowd. She returned to the table, picked up the card and Harry disappeared through the departures entrance.

He was about to buy some duty-free tobacco, when an announcement summoned him to an information desk telephone.

'Where are you?' Dinea asked, plaintively.

'Queuing for my flight to Kolokuana.'

'The presents are lovely! Stay with me and fly tomorrow.'

'I've got to run. The queue's hurrying out to the aircraft.'

Phew! His lungs emptied with relief and he went back to buy the tobacco. He had at least two hours to fritter before take-off. Maybe Dinea knew that. She was smart but not that smart, surely. Removing both his hearing aids, to prevent him hearing another summons to the phone, he sat on a toilet puffing his pipe till his backside went numb. While stretching his legs he heard that chinking sound in his cabin bag. A tobacco tin was chinking against the make-up jar – he'd left Dinea only the three jars of pomade.

The lightest shade of Afro-makeup made his albino accountant, Pinkie, look pinkier! Pete, his press officer, and his clerk in the next-door office were delighted to share a set of *Pride and Prejudice* videos. Speedy wasn't thrilled with the mouth organ that he could clamp round his head and blow when beating the bongos. Fags for Jack. Belinda had sent Fuzzy much-needed money. She and her daughters had moved from the Ocean View cell to a hut Jack had found them on a black charlatan's property. In addition to the exorbitant rent, Fuzzy had to cook and serve meals, clean the man's bungalow and do all the laundry and gardening for nothing, except the privilege of living in close proximity to himself and two girls of dubious social standing. Harry had discovered all this just before flying home when he'd given Fuzzy the cash for her daughter's school fees. The charlatan had agreed, under duress, to reduce Fuzzy's rent and employ some happily married women as maids.

Harry called on Suleiman to find out what had been happening during his absence, and to ease his conscience! He said a suspected prospector, Mkwere, had asked him to post a letter in UK.

Pulling one his uglier faces, Suleiman ushered Harry out of his office. Then out of the compound, to a patch of scrub. Harry looked around, no tree to hang him from! But when Suleiman did speak, his secretive tone of voice demanded Harry's undivided attention.

'You will recall me leaving you and Uncle Bill at Mabela, and probably noticed that the civilian helicopter flew towards the border with the neighbouring country. Mkwere is a prospector, an employee of a reputable London mining company. After landing, I was taken to meet a white African who handed me a bribe and I gave him copies of my letters to the cartel, which had banned the mining of this country's diamond deposits. You might recognise the white African. His dog, not a police dog, mauled your leg. Look, Harry, I know you're keen to find your grandfather's grave. I'd feel the same in your position. But it was very foolish and possibly highly dangerous to let Mr Mboko read that note, even though its directions to some old mine workings are vague. Who else has read the note?'

'You obviously have. And the British police adviser somehow obtained a copy.'

'We'd better stop there. I must insist that you never repeat to anyone what I've told you. Just forget it Harry.'

How could he just forget it? And how the hell did that snooping police adviser get a copy of the note? He'd asked himself that thousands of times!

'Not long ago, automatic data processing revolutionised tedious though vital activities. Now mobile telephony is transforming society and communications,' Harry reminded colleagues. 'An

Oxford graduate has designed a World Wide Web. Soon we'll be able to network computers, here. The cabinet has so far approved the purchase of five hundred cell phones, manufactured in Mavimbi, and one hundred of Jurek's solar panels to re-charge cell phones for users without access to electricity. Every headman of isolated communities, key district officials and relief workers in the southern province has a cell-phone and a solar panel. More high priority users will have both, as soon as practicable. Since radio-coverage in the south is restricted by mountainous terrain, wind-up wirelesses will improve communications even more, if funds are available to buy and service them. Moreover, a new and cheap process that converts suitable garbage into fuel pellets will be welcomed, putting it mildly, by the many southern communities without wood, cardboard or dung to burn for sterilising water and cooking food. But garbage converters have to be bought, serviced and repaired. Volunteers will also have to be taught to show people how to make fuel pellets and keep the converters working. Meanwhile, all communities in the northern province must be told that they will get a cell-phone and other new equipment when production and finances allow. We must avoid protests by envious northerners.'

'Who are servicing and repairing cell phones and solar panels?' Sonny asked.

'Dave, the Yorkshireman you met at Jurek's factory, has set up skills-centres in all six southern districts, where he teaches cell phone and solar panel users to maintain them.'

'Improved communications down in the south.' Suleiman said, 'will make it much easier to keep tabs on the hordes of so-called, internally displaced persons moving north to Kolokuana, which the UN still refuses to classify as refugees. So I'm going it alone, like most senior UN representatives based here! From today, everybody fleeing the south, due to drought and/or poverty, will be classified as refugees and will get UN assistance to find and pay for sanitary housing and a safeguarded water supply. All children, not just the under-fives, will have regular weight and growth checks. They, but also pregnant women, who are under nourished or acutely malnourished will get extra rations or a high-protein diet. Moreover,

I recommend that free medical care and free education both feature in the government's medium-term strategy.'

'Where can I get the money for all that?' whinged Mboko – now a confused, fatalistic loner. Jenkins Makimbo and Sonny Floors called all the shots.

'I'll draft a medium-term strategy,' Harry offered. 'It will align Suleiman's grass-roots projects with our disaster management guidelines. Proposing a national development plan will come next. Then we'll circulate a handbook, briefly summarising the plan in Kasodi, Gwato and English. Is that agreed?' Nods from Jenkins, Sonny and Suleiman.

The new army commander, a massive impeccably turned out brigadier-general, who'd just returned from a senior officers' course in Britain, pledged his soldiers' loyal support. Modestly attired, Solomon Khami spoke for the Red Cross and other non-governmental organisations involved with drought recovery and national development, when endorsing Harry's proposal. Punter Bryant, Save the Children Fund's local director, had this to say:

'The disaster mamagement guidelines have addressed the requirement for a nutritional surveillance system in the south. An efficient nursing sister, qualified to oversee public health, should manage the system. Since there is only one hospital in the south, and while stressing that more are very urgently required, the guidelines also emphasise the need for hospitals to maintain ready-to-move accident and emergency teams, equipped and trained to give on-the-spot assistance. We further recommend that the disaster management plan is approved and its guidelines adopted, as quickly as practicable. Lawrence Kwawenda's experienced consultants, currently reviewing hospital care, can then give regular refresher training to all accident and emergency teams, and to all hospital staffs. We agree that the army should train sufficient policemen to help implement the necessary measures.'

The police commissioner threw a wobbly. 'No member of my force will be trained by the army or enter a barracks!'

'By training together, the police and army will gain each other's confidence and also co-operate more effectively,' Sonny countered.

'Given time and goodwill, it should be possible to form a combined cadre of expert instructors to work here and in all districts.'

'First you confiscate my fire services. Now you impose this, behind my back.' The grossly fat commissioner waddled off in a peeve, closely chaperoned by the even fatter Mboko, both hugging briefcases which were almost certainly empty and with heads that were most probably full of reprisal plots.

Jenkins Makimbo summed up: 'Suleiman will treat every person fleeing from this drought as a refugee. Harry will draft a medium term strategy. Our disaster management plan will need revising after today's discussions. All your inputs are much appreciated.'

Dr Solomon Khami collected Harry from the rondavel and drove down to the Anglican Cathedral. The bishop proudly showed them a mountain of used-clothing sent by shipped containers from the twinned-diocese in England, then took his place beside the pulpit and Solomon and Harry took theirs in a churchwarden's pew halfway along the packed nave. The cathedral resembled the Methodist chapel, where the Welsh male voice choir had so enthralled Belinda and me, Harry reckoned. Here, the mixed choir arrayed itself on the balcony above the altar. The blind cantor hummed a note, beat a rhythm with brief hand movements and an anthem joyously flooded out in neck-tingling harmony. Prayers and hymns followed, in Kasodi for those in the congregation from the north and in Gwato for southerners. The bishop concluded his sermon in English, by praising 'the many kind people who have sent so many such useful things for our needy.' Children took collection bags to the bishop who blessed them and then thanked everybody present for their very generous offerings. The national anthem closed a simple, meaningful and moving service.

After Sunday lunch in Solomon's house with his wife and her parents, he drove Harry beyond Kolokuana's shanty-suburbs, where lay hidden a haven for lost souls, castaways, broken minds and bodies. This Red Cross orphanage, which the locals called Lourdo, had begun its blesséd life as Lourdes and would likely have kept that name had it been in francophone Africa. It was here that

Harry came across an un-named orphan, whom he decided to call Happy Samuella, Ella for short, a substitute for Happy Sam. Ella's thin, feeble body had fallen sideways on a bench, rolled and hit the ground. Gently lifting Ella, he propped her against a pillow, but still she didn't look secure or comfortable. Although Lourdo provided security, Ella would never feel comfortable. Never be able to stop her head lolling so far to one side that her scrawny, twisted neck might snap. Never be able stop the saliva dribbling down her chin and onto the clothes Lourdo had provided. Never know if the day was cloudy or the night starlit, nor see the man who'd helped her or thank him, only hear and touch him. Solomon brought more pillows and thought her age could be eleven or twelve. She'd been found, or left, outside Lourdo's gate earlier that morning.

One of Speedy's many pals made a folding wheelchair and when Ella took possession he adjusted its head clamp and cushioned tilt. With a similar seat in the land-cruiser, she went for a ride from her bench and back – at first tautly nervous, soon supremely excited.

On their first outing together Harry imagined a beaming Happy Sam pushing Ella around Berney's Bazaar and carefully placing his heavy plastic on the footrest below her sandals. For Harry, Saturday shopping would no longer be a chore now that Ella accompanied him.

A fortnight later, a puppy found its way from the land-cruiser onto Ella's lap. Sammy made a mistake on her gymslip and a glimmer of amusement crossed her vacant stare, but nothing as piffling as puppy pee would stop her clinging to such a soft cuddly thing that she could smell, touch and love. Then a miracle happened at Lourdo! A strangled screech suddenly came from Ella's twisted throat: 'Sam . . . mee!' With the puppy looked after by another orphan and Ella and the wheelchair secured in the land-cruiser, on the way to town she shrieked 'Har. . .ree!' A week later, she strung together: 'El. . .la, Har. . .ree, Shop. . .ping!'

By leaning over Harry's desk Speedy could read the mail far easier and could answer the phone when it rang. It did! 'Hullo. Speedy here . . . . . . I'm his driver. Who's speaking? . . . . . . She says she's Dinea and wants to know where you are.'

'Tell her I'm at an orphanage, helping nurses change nappies.'

'He says he's at an orphanage, helping nurses change nappies . . . . she's gone!'

'What's your next question, Speedy?'

'Who's Dinea?'

'A nappy seller.'

The phone rang again, and this time Speedy let Harry take the call. Dinea had passed her nursing sister's and public health exams, and was managing the southern province's nutritional surveillance project. This stunned Harry – quadruply so, when she asked him to come to her nice flat in Mabela. 'Only you and me will be there,' she silkily drooled.

He slashed his trips to the south and held most courses at Kolokuana's army barracks, but Dinea kept on phoning him and he kept up his quasi-polite hostility.

He could have done without globetrotting Jinky flying in from New York, to do this year's performance reviews. After his, she suggested he show her 'a bit of the sharp end' – a startling expression in his agitated state and she found his discomfort highly amusing.

'Show me where it all happens, daarling. I'll rephrase that, too! Drive me down south to meet with some of your students and this Uncle Bill you're always on about. Maybe I could also visit the Polishman's solar-panel factory.' So off they went to Mabela.

Jinky's constant travel was not merely about seeing, but being seen, with no shortage of admiring glances or intrigued stares – wherever her perfume and penetrating questions infiltrated male company. Even the odd lecherous leer, as she hip-swayed on Manhattan skyline heels to her next goggling victim. Yet the fact that she'd been doing the same job for so long and so successfully, without mishap apparently, said as much for her bravado as her crafty ingenuity.

While moseying round Uncle Bill's drought operations centre, Jinky took his arm and inquired: 'When will the nutritional surveillance project hit your districts, honey? Where will you locate the sentinel sites, and who will collect each and every site's information?'

Jinky's show of affection jellified Uncle Bill – her questions forced both of his palms to plead for help. 'Do you know the answers Miss Mashedi?' Of course Dinea did!

'All health-posts and clinics will collect information. The nurses and midwives know the reports they will send me every month. A few have telephones, most will post reports, but this is very slow. I want staff, also, to copy and send their reports and the reports from Mabela Hospital to the health ministry. If Mr Harry buys some fax machines, I can start.'

Dinea pouted, glanced at Harry and smiled sweetly . . . *Coquette* seemed to him a fitting description of his unflagging pursuer.

Waiting outside the Mabela Hotel, her face was a picture when the glamorous blonde elegantly alighted from Harry's land-cruiser. Jinky praised Dinea's briefing, even invited her to dinner that evening, leaving Harry to fend off a blue-uniformed tigress.

'I came to meet *you*, not a *film star!*' Her pick-up truck disappeared in a cloud of dust.

Uncle Bill arrived first, sporting a new tie and an ancient safari-suit. Jinky next, in a classy black two-piece that would have deprived a Wall Street banker of a week's bonus. Finally Dinea entered, modelling a short white frock, which left little to the imagination. Rather than conceal her prominences, it displayed them outrageously.

'You look *faboolous* daarling!' Jinky drawled, giving Dinea a frosty twice-over. 'Say, where did you get that gorgeous frock?'

'Mr Harry gave me a present and I made it fit better.'

Jinky's piercing blue eyes focused, unerringly, on Harry's blinking brown ones. 'How long have you known Dinea?' She didn't add the customary daarling.

'I've known her brother several years.' Not convincing, but at least it was honest.

Latest fashions dominated the female dialogue during dinner. But Uncle Bill conjured up the odd question, some *very* odd, while Harry polished off the wine. When a waitress began clearing the table Jinky went to her room, Dinea to the ladies, the men to the gents.

'What have you been up to, Harry?' inquired Uncle Bill, as they directed their piddle into a groove between wet floor tiles. 'A youngster with a body like hers can kill you.'

'She's Tsabo's middle sister, in case you don't know, and I'm a family friend.'

'And that American? She's got what it takes! But she'd kill me, too, if I could stop her talking . . . I'll buy your coffin tomorrow.'

Harry was trapped in the foyer. 'We go to the disco, yes?'

'Not me. I'll be the only one of my shade there.' Dinea's sharp talons steered him past the crowded bar, where he should have hidden, towards the brain-numbing din.

Stealthily removing his hearing aids, when inside the dimly lit cave he tried his best to emulate her writhing contortions and warn her when the frock appeared unlikely to serve its minimal purposes. But all his clumsy attempts to exhaust her failed, and he retired to a chair, his pipe smoke layering the gloom, hoping the guy with a red bandanna around his head wouldn't put on a smooch, and plotting his escape. While Dinea jived with a group of females, Harry made a stealthy exit.

The town and track to his bedsit were deserted – no vehicle-highjackers on the prowl! While mulling over that evening's events, an engine destroyed the silence. He knew what would happen next. No need to wait for her knock, all he had to do was unlock the door. He hid under his bed! The door was knocked, knocked several times, louder and louder. At last the engine started, its noise faded and he stealthily emerged from his funk hole.

Jinky remarked over breakfast in the hotel: 'Such a cute girl! You're extremely lucky to have a nurse as a close colleague, but I'm sure you've appreciated that already!'

Harry grunted. His sleepless night had been tormented hell. Sometimes wishing he'd unlocked the door and let Dinea in. Far more often, overwhelmingly thankful he hadn't.

At St John's Mission where Harry held local government courses, the rest he held in Kolokuana, Jinky quizzed students about the usefulness of disaster management training and if syllabus changes were necessary. To defer being quizzed, Harry went to find Father Patrick, smiling as ever, in a cassock and sunhat, on his knees, not praying, planting seed potatoes.

'No Jameson's in Berney's Bazaar. Will Vat 69 do, Father?'

'It'll do very much better than this cold tea, don't you know.'

He unscrewed the bottle cap, filled it to the brim, gave it to Harry, poured himself an overdose in his emptied tea mug and Harry offered to fetch some diluting water.

'Medicine is best taken neat! I've just heard from young Patrick. He's still walking out with an Oxford anthropologist and within a year he'll be a full-blown barrister. The Lord has truly shone His light upon him, and all the Mashedi family, for that matter. How's life been treating you, Mr Harry?'

'Keeping reasonably fit in body and soul but always rushing off somewhere! I've now got to take an American to a solar-panel factory.'

'I've been there. A wonderful place with wonderful people doing wonderful things.'

So re-energised with solar power and feed back from Jurek's enthusiasm, Jinky started calling Harry daarling again. She said her superiors had approved the admirable disaster management plan, at last! Nearing Kolokuana, he diverted to Lourdo and there, among all the orphans, he saw Jinky in a totally different light. Gone were the mirror-preening, the celebrity-swagger, the shallow superlatives. In their place, caring gentleness. She washed Ella's face and hands, spoon-fed her, told her no clouds were in the sky, what she'd been doing that day, stroked Sammy, her puppy. She wept in amazement when Ella shrieked: 'Sam . . . mee . . . stay . . . here . . . Jink . . . kee . . . Har . . . ree . . . El . . . la . . . Shop . . . ping!'

Ella returned to Lourdo, ecstatic, with things she could smell – scent and body-lotion; also a big sunshade she could touch, sit under with Sammy and feel a cool shadow.

Miffed at not being allowed to drive Jinky, a real cracker, Speedy had nevertheless sat at Harry's desk, answered his many phone calls, sorted and read all his mail. Now this self-appointed jack of all trades had to surrender Harry's chair to its rightful owner.

'Belinda rang,' Speedy said. 'She's been to America to see her parents and wants you to ring her in England. Tsabo's writing's on this envelope. I'll open it for you.'

'No thanks Speedy. I'm quite capable of doing that. Hop it and I'll phone my wife.'

'Nothing's wrong,' Belinda assured him. 'I helped my mother pack up our family's home, not exactly a pleasant chore to have to do. But it's far too big for just the two of them. My father hopes moving to Florida will cure his arthritis. Going to the States meant I couldn't be the maid of honour at Tsabo's and Jill's wedding. I say this, because you'll be sure to hear from Tsabo, and knowing you, you'll chide him for not inviting me.'

At least Belinda said chide, not castigate. 'Why the rush to get married?' Harry asked.

'They've been living as husband and wife at weekends, so why wait?'

With Belinda's and his lovey-dovey farewells exhausted, Harry shouted: 'Speedy! I could see you listening outside the door!'

'I was stopping the others listening . . . All okay Harry?'

'Ten out of ten for message-passing, minus ten for snooping.'

'All we've gotta do is find out if Tsabo's okay.'

Having recognised the handwriting, Speedy eased the unopened envelope ever closer to Harry and then, as always in such trying circumstances, they both fell about laughing.

Tsabo's news: 'Married last Saturday in Jill's native Cumbria. Best man, Dermot. We greatly missed Belinda and you. No honeymoon yet. Been defending a bystander caught in a Belfast republican rumpus. Heard you bought my errant sister some oddments. Now Jill wants black pantyhose and a short white frock. In <u>both</u> senses, I'm off shopping!'

In the Wet

It didn't rain, it bucketed down, persisting for most of October. Lap-top time!

Harry completed a development handbook, comprising four pages of simply worded, single-line checklists, interleaved with diagrams. The first checklist set out drought recovery targets; the second, disaster management targets. The next two summarised development plans in guideline-form. Sonny's preface – 'The contents reflect the country's capabilities to solve its problems' – featured on the front cover, below the national flag. Key phone numbers and addresses were listed on the back cover, headed: 'To be used in emergencies only.'

The handbook was translated into Kasoldi for northerners and Gwato for southerners. In the Gwato version, press officer Pete replaced all the diagrams with amusing cartoons, because his tribes-people liked pictures that made them laugh.

With the handbook printed and distributed, the sky reverted its normal azure-blue. A Huey helicopter flew south from Kolokuana with Punter Bryant and Harry on board, and landed at Mabela, to pick up Uncle Bill and Yorkshireman Dave. Uncle Bill urgently needed to investigate recent cattle rustling and sheep stealing in his southernmost district. Dave had to inspect solar panels and cell phones all over the place. Punter was happy to fly anywhere, provided he got back! Harry unrolled his map that still showed the route taken on his helicopter trip soon after arriving eighteen months ago.* The pilot opted for the same route, did all his checks and then rivalled, indeed outshone, a spectacular Cape Canaveral lift-off. His passengers were *not* impressed.

They returned to Mabela overwhelmed by all the fast-flowing rivers, cascading water-falls, recovering wetlands and pasture, women hoeing and planting, children waving as they flew past, the impact of cell phones and solar panels, even though they were too

---

*　　Page 68. The sketch-map shows the route.

few and too far apart. The cattle and sheep thieves had been hung before Uncle Bill got there!

They were also disheartened – not just by the lack of dams, which had been expected – but the almost total absence of plumbing to conserve the prolonged rainfall, which had rapidly transformed a yellow-ochre semi-desert into palest green wasteland. Rainfall now mostly benefiting both neighbouring countries. They had seen very few grazing livestock; even fewer tractors or draught-animals ploughing. A great deal more rain was needed, yet southerners had failed to grasp the necessity to trap water in every practicable way. Many chiefs and headmen had said the handbook showed them what to do and how to do it. But none had done it! Not more trainers wandering the outback, Harry gloomily conjectured. And where were the grants made to all six districts? Money which ought to have paid for gutters, down-pipes, water tanks and other essential plumbing. Just one guess would have sufficed. The grant money was lining Kolokuana's corrupt civil servants' pockets – Uncle Bill wasn't alone in going bezerk! The helicopter pilot repeated the circuit the following week and Suleiman re-assessed the problems, Sonny began to solve them and Jenkins Makimbo gave every chief another grant, in ready-cash, and a receipt they had to sign. The corrupt civil servants and their accomplices – in prison-sackcloth – did a lot of unpaid plumbing, which they had to complete to Uncle Bill's satisfaction, before he let them eat. He also summoned every chief and community headman to palavers held throughout his province to make sure, in inimitable fashion, that they not only understood what the handbook said and what its pictures explained, they had to *do* it all, before the next palaver.

Sonny and his water and sanitation group, together with Punter and his agriculture and food security group jointly agreed a revised plan encompassing – plumbing, the building of small community dams, more and larger reservoirs in Kolokuana and Mabela, as well as more irrigation. Their plan relied, like so many other development projects, on World Bank funding, but the co-operation of its well-heeled bureaucrats, whose lengthy stays in a Mavimbi luxury hotel, interspersed with brief chats in Kolokuana, achieved very little, apart from procrastinating promises.

Eighteen months ago, some Japanese businessmen had offered to help the country. The former chief secretary had favoured promoting tourism, ignoring Glen's pleas for small community dams to be built. Having toured both provinces, the businessmen had said their money and expertise would be far better utilised by improving water-catchment in drought-prone areas. Unimpressed by the then chief secretary, they had withdrawn their offer of help. Now, on their second visit, they detected a realistic government attitude and agreed to improve water-catchment in all six southern districts within the next ten years.

Two of Harry's commercial contacts also paid off. An American genetically modified foodstuffs producer and a German engineering company signed up to a large-scale cash-crop/irrigation/tractor project on potentially fertile tracts of the Mabela plain. Both firms would equip and train the plain's larger-scale farmers, which met with fierce opposition from subsistence farmers who grew their own food, and in good harvest years, hoped to sell any surpluses. Peace reigned when donors agreed to fund all farmers direct and not via the country's agriculture ministry. But the ministry vehemently objected to the use of genetically modified crop seed – peace was restored only when the American firm agreed to replace its GM varieties with conventional sorghum, white maize and pulse seeds.

For Harry this meant drafting more guidelines, more contingency plans, and stretching the limits of logistic reach still farther. For all unemployed farmers and hungry families it could mean self-sufficiency and eventually prosperity, or was that another pipe-dream?

For Jurek the new project meant, hopefully, more solar panel sales. For Uncle Bill his lofty vision of persuading a go-ahead donor to attract foreign customers by creating a huge superstore in Mabela's "city" centre took several paces forward, but far more than several paces back among Mabela's many bankrupt traders.

Professor Matanya, the vice chancellor of Kolokuana University – also Tsabo's admirer ever since her tour of Oxford's "Top Ten Gems" – had kept on to Harry for months about telling her staff and students how they could help as many as practicable of their nation's

286

drought victims. What with one thing and another, they had never got round to fixing a date. With the end of the academic year in sight, and a welcome lull in Harry's activities, he sent her copies of the development handbook for circulation within the university and suggested he talk for no longer than half an hour, leaving plenty of time for discussion.

After coffee with students about to graduate, the professor introduced him to what she called her "throng" which, judging by the throng's size, was a fitting description, though judging by the throng's comments, a description neither lacking frequency nor earning universal approval.

She began by saying: 'At last, Mr Burke deserves his Obang-wato praise name, the bringer of rain. He came to our country nearly two years ago and helped to plan and co-ordinate drought relief. And then, for most of the past year, he has advised our government on drought recovery and disaster management. He is now helping to promote development and has produced a development handbook, which I hope you have all read! His efforts remind me of a truism that you would do well to remember. People who can, *do!* People who can't, *teach!*' The laughter threatened to bring the assembly hall's ceiling down.

Harry described the impressive and disheartening aspects of the current situation in the south, illustrated by the screening of a selection of aerial and ground-level coloured photos he'd taken during the helicopter trip. There were no questions, just relieved gasps.

'If disaster strikes the whole or various parts or one part of a country, the overriding requirements are speed, effective action and the assessment of victims' *needs!* Not what they would like. What they need to *survive!* Natural and man-made disasters can strike with or without warning. Parliament has passed an Emergency Powers Act and approved a disaster management plan. Their enforcement should enable the government and non-government relief agencies to react, automatically, to emergencies. Rapid, decisive action greatly depends on the calibre, experience and training of all those, whose duty it is, to respond to a natural or man-made disaster, to prevent it spreading and worsening, thereby threatening many more lives and livelihoods. As shown on the screen, good legislation and preparation are essential in every disaster-prone country. Also essential are accurate information, sound planning, firm control, and constant checking that all relief activities are working efficiently. Relief activities must be co-ordinated, must be flexibile and must be improved or replaced if they are not satisfactory. Relief activities must be publicised, so that everybody knows what they are and what they provide. All relief workers must be trained, if necessary re-trained, and adequately protected from bribery, other corruption and aggression, including armed aggression. All relief aid, water, food, etcetera, must be protected. This diagram on the screen shows how these key functions blend together and how government ministries, relief agencies and volunteers co-operate. Copies of a precis in both your nation's languages, with diagrams, are on tables near the doors.'

'Are you implying that only foreigners like yourself have the knowledge and experience to deal with this country's many emergencies?' asked a Mboko replica spread across two seats in the front row. Heckles and boos farther back.

'Very few people would question the competence of Jenkins Makimbo, your health minister. During severe drought it's all hands to the pump. The water pump!' Applause.

A studious-looking young woman asked: 'The development handbook describes top-down direction and bottom-up participation . . .' Loads of wolf whistles.

Harry couldn't stop himself, he had to laugh. So did almost everybody else.

'I'll define both terms in a moment. Is that acceptable?'

The young woman nodded politely and sat down.

'Let's go through these functions on the screen. Why is accurate information vital?'

'Nothing can be properly done if the information is wrong,' a nearby student replied.

'Weather forecasts, communications, warn people, get help,' were called out.

'Exactly right . . . Now planning. I daresay many of you think of thick, boring books when planning's mentioned. The drought relief plan and drought recovery plan each have only two pages, listing brief guidelines that suggest action, not dictate what must be done. Action is usually suggested top-down. Decisions about the most appropriate action are usually made bottom-up, with those people who will have to take the action participating in decision making. When possible, the people who need action to be taken, ought to take part in decision-making. If you need help, you prefer to be asked what help you need. If you are helping people, you want to be sure your help is appropriate. Too often, too much has been decided in your capital, in provinces or in districts, where not enough is known of the needs and the circumstances of people and livestock trying to survive or recover from drought and other natural disasters, like heavy snowfalls, floods, tornadoes, or man-made disasters, like fires and accidents. Go and find out what is actually needed, before deciding how to help. Get information, bottom-up. Then use it, top-down. The wider your consultation, the greater the chance of your plans being accepted by all those who have to make the plans work. Workers must feel a sense of ownership and, whenever necessary, recommend changes. Bottom-up participation is essential, though it can result in too little being done, or too little help being given. It can also result in too much being done, or too much help being wasted. Because there are often too few helpers, it is important to avoid doing unnecessary work. Therefore top-down planning, direction and co-ordination are just as essential. 'Does that answer your question?' Harry asked the young woman.

'My question was going to be, why haven't our politicians worked bottom-up and visited all of our far too many needy people?'

'Because they think there aren't any,' a chirpy voice sang out. Lots of clapping.

With the clock diagram* that stumped Mboko on the screen, Harry explained how the disaster impact, response, recovery, mitigation, readiness and warning sequence worked. Another transparency showed the composition and functions of the six drought recovery working groups. He also suggested how students

---

*   Page 259. This describes the clock-diagram.

and lecturers might assist with making the country less disaster-prone and hoped they'd help in their spare time or permanently.

Having done his best to do justice to a barrage of challenging questions – mostly about cell phones, solar panels, irrigation and training – Harry left the assembly hall festooned in a gown and hood, the professor must have run out of mortar-boards, masquerading as an honorary doctor of economics. He'd read medieval European history at Oxford.

Over a sandwich lunch in the senior common room there was no shortage of subjects to discuss or interesting ideas to explore farther, one of which led to Harry persuading Sonny Floors to persuade cabinet ministers to introduce a work-experience scheme.

On the professor's recommendation, two students set about computerising Jack's back-of-a-fag-packet food and fodder stock control system – a title it had yet to live up to. The young woman who'd asked the top-down, bottom-up question took on the daunting task of preparing a report on the drought and all relief efforts. Gabriella, a disguised nun and accomplished rural development research student, had intended to return to St John's Mission. To the mother superior's indignant alarm, but with Father Patrick's ever-smiling blessing, she joined Punter Bryant's Save the Children Fund staff. With Punter's wise counsel and a stack of copies of Harry's diaries, minus all of the personal stuff, Sister Gabriella created a post-drought report which would surely prove of immense value to future disaster relief efforts, not just in her home-country, throughout Africa and beyond.

On Saturdays she helped to care for Lourdo's ever increasing number of orphans. Sundays were given over to prayer in the Catholic Cathedral. At the other end of Kolokuana's main street, Solomon Khami, his wife and often Harry sat together at Matins in the Anglican Cathedral.

But having seen countless drought victims suffer and die, Harry's belief in God would remain fragile until, one weekend, yet another miracle happened at Lourdo! He and Sister Gabriella heard Ella screech 'Gab . . . bee!'

Although Gabby had greatly enjoyed and benefited from her five years at university, as well as her three months working with

Punter and too many others to name, her calling took precedence. Back at St John's in her nun's habit, she helped to teach Harry's combined disaster management and development courses held at the Mission which even policemen attended – their commissioner had been replaced by his deputy! The ever-smiling Father Patrick had urged Gabby to devote her many talents to the less gifted and now the Mother Superior acquiesced, albeit hesitantly.

Professor Matanya led weekend processions of students and staff towards the busses, lined up outside the university's assembly hall that took them in various directions and to a variety of places to help many drought-stricken communities recover their livelihoods; to assist the too few doctors and nurses; to repair paths and tracks; to carry water to fields or however best they could relieve the hardship and suffering of many drought-disabled people. Far too many of them were physically or even mentally disabled and still needed help, despite the recent rains and the support they'd received during the emergency.

Work Experience, whereby jobless young people helped poor families recover from drought, became so worthwhile that the cabinet extended the scheme to government work, whereupon civil servants, whatever their status or seniority, staged a mass walk-out. Most of them had only bothered to *walk-in* to pick up their pay and catch up with all the gossip, before being drastically culled, following Lawrence Kwawenda's overhaul and reform of the civil service.

Protected by policemen, protesters with placards condemning "Unpaid and Untrained Employment" blockaded the capital's main street. After two hours of ugly pandemonium, soldiers tore down the barriers. Shops and offices re-opened, traffic flowed again, in spite of constant police harassment. Although a more serious outcome had been avoided, yet another nail had been hammered into the coffin of dwindling army-police co-operation.

Rumours condemned Mboko and the country's sacked police commissioner for instigating the protests, and with the protesters' efforts thwarted by soldiers, they were intent on stirring up more trouble. Men in black suits and shades – the Benzi tribe – patrolled the town in expensive off-roaders again. To prevent them and their cronies meeting in the former UN club bar, which they'd re-opened, armed soldiers patrolled its fenced compound.

With irrefutable evidence placed before the court, the police commissioner was found guilty of gross dereliction of duty and misconduct. Having blamed Mboko, who'd disappeared, for inciting the civil service protests and police brutality, his thirty-year prison sentence was commuted to twenty years "work experience" in drought-stricken areas. For undisclosed reasons, the British 'high commissioner was asked to terminate the police adviser's contract, but due to the adviser's valuable contributions to security, Richard Riddington refused the request – a decision he would soon profoundly regret!

By relentlessly championing the cause of all disadvantaged and suffering Obangwatos, Sister Gabriella became a saint in all but name, a folklore heroine, a steadfast enemy of the tokolosi, evil spirits and much else of worthless suspicion. Whenever called upon, she would be *there*; her time was always *now!* Riding miles to visit the poor, the seriously ill, the malnourished, the AIDS-afflicted, and to placate mourners grieving over the loss of a loved one or their livelihoods – while remaining corruption's vibrant foe, an unshakeable pillar of justice and a tireless improver of disaster readiness training.

After much painstaking orphanage care and encouragement Ella was received, through Sister Gabriella's benevolent offices, as a novice nun at St John's and Sammy, almost a grown dog, would also greatly flourish there. Ella loved all the singing, tried her best to join in, conducted imaginary choirs, and Sammy towed her wheelchair to wherever she'd most like to go.

Gabriella – 'Gab . . . bee' in Ella's ever-increasing vocabulary – drove her back to the orphanage in a St John's delivery van for Dr Solomon Khami's monthly check-up and then they went 'Shop . . . ping.' When Dr Khami, the country's Red Cross director, heard that a train was about to arrive in Mavimbi with eye-specialists and their equipment on board, Ella's name joined his long waiting-list, prioritised according to need and available funds. Her multi-disabilities weighed heavily in Ella's favour and she went by bus with Gabby, other adults and children to a Mavimbi hospital, where they'd stay until called forward. All of them hoped for a miracle! Miracles had happened on that train, elsewhere. Most patients returning on the bus to Kolokuana had had cataracts removed – Ella overjoyed to be able to see with one eye – the other not repaired yet. Gabby phoned Dr Khami and he and Mr Harry were waiting at the orphanage.

'We were all overcome, Dermot, now that Ella can see what everybody looks like. The rest is left to your imagination. I'm too emotional to finish this diary. All the best, Harry.'

King of Katama

Fozz, the accomplished Foster's and borehole sinker, and Marge, both from way down-under, already had seven daughters. The seventh, born a year ago, he'd named Cyril, after his old man in Queensland. With Marge yet again in the family way, Fozz expected a son – to put it mildly – an expectation demanding a renewed spate of F-words.

'Gotta make do with what I can get these days,' he confided to Harry. 'There's me and a (blinking) torch in bed, having another go at reading the best bits of *Hot Dinkum*, when Marge kicks me up the (painful) jacksy and hollers, turn that (confounded) light out and let me get some (wholesome) kip.' The bracketed substitutes Harry's diary invented later.

Fozz-anecdotes and profanity-substitutes over-freqently infiltrated Harry's diaries, not only because they shared similar pool challenges, but were also ardent rugby and cricket fans. Tanked up with Foster's, Fozz was forever having a go at the (villainous) Poms and Harry always did his damnedest to retaliate, but had his alcohol intake been more "down-under" he might have held his own more convincingly. His height, and now his slimness, enabled him to dispense with the rest when the pool ball he aimed to hit was too distant. Diluted whisky also made it much easier to hit the ball. Whereas Fozz, a foot shorter, was further impeded by a Foster's paunch, and the later it became, the less sure he was of the whereabouts of the (pesky) balls, let alone hitting the right one! So Harry came out on top in the pool stakes – no matter what the score was in Pom versus Aussie rugby or cricket. Then even when England played South Africa, New Zealand or whoever, Fozz doggedly rooted for England's opponents. After losing at pool, yet again, the following Friday he poured Harry a couple of *un*-diluted whiskies *before* they played pool and the Pom took a (thorough) thrashing! Fozz was still celebrating his first victory when Marge came out to their shed, which housed his pool table, to lug him off to bed. Her eighth bun in the oven must have slipped his pickled memory. He was last heard asking Marge to let him have another go at fathering a son, or words to that effect. Her reply was (inaudible).

Fozz had been persuaded to turn his talents to supervising rural airstrip construction. The firm he now worked for had converted the Akroyd's former bungalow into offices, Harry's erstwhile cottage into Fozz's spare-parts store and earth-moving equipment filled most of the fenced compound. The firm had also taken over the flying doctor service. Its three Cessnas had flown back from the town just across the border to be based again, as well as efficiently serviced now, at Kolokuana's airport. On a Cessna's outward flight, to pick up seriously sick or injured people, were patients from Kolokuana's death-house of a hospital returning to their isolated homes. The aircraft also dropped Fozz off at a remote airstrip building site, avoiding many miles of driving – then riding when the track became a path. If a Cessna couldn't pick him up on Fridays, he set off home earlier and thumbed a much slower lift back to the pool table, where his even more rapid Foster's intake than usual quickly put him to rights. It also recharged his lack of cue prowess.

Few airstrip building sites were accessible to vehicles so, on completion of a runway, donkeys humped dismantled equipment from site to site; lighter gear and tools were moved by temporarily unemployed, seat-less Cessnas. Fozz's map showed the airstrips planned, those already built and one almost ready to accept aircraft.

'That latest one's near Katama, Tsabo's home-village,' Harry pointed out.

'Its headman's snuffed it and Tsabo's old man's got the (rotten) job,' Fozz said.

'That's news to me,' Harry had to admit. 'The headman must have died suddenly.'

'Quicker the (flipping) better when yer (nasty) numbers up.'

'I hope the provincial governor will stage an apt headman's installation ceremony.'

'The piss up's next Saturday.'

Back in his office, Harry phoned Uncle Bill, who said Tsabo and his wife would arrive on Thursday, a Cessna would fly them from Kolokuana to the new airstrip. Tsabo wanted their visit to be a family surprise. Unable to go to Katama, Uncle Bill had told only the chief they were coming and to organise everything. When Harry rang the flying doctor service, the duty officer said there'd be room in the Cessna, that happened to be dropping off discharged hospital patients for just the two passengers from Britain, who'd otherwise have to travel by taxi to Mabela, then ride to Katama, after an overnight flight. Keen to keep on good terms with the flying doctor service, Harry said he understood, completely, and assumed that Tsabo hadn't phoned him in order to surprise *him*, as well as his family.

Uncle Bill had told one of his food-for-work supervisors, Tsabo's brother-in-law, to ride with Harry to Katama who might have guessed Dinea would be accompanying them. She was all smiles upon realising they would be sharing each other's company. Most men who'd seen her at Mavimbi Airport would have been stirred up by her figure. The short white frock he'd crazily bought in London, which she'd made "fit better" and worn when Jinky invited her to supper at the Mabela Hotel, had grossly accentuated that figure! His self control and willpower had always worked before, though he no longer trusted either.

Speedy could drive him back to Kolokuana but on the way south Speedy had smuttily enthused about a forthcoming weekend in a Mabela Hotel air-conditioned bedroom with Princess, his middle-aged beauty, whom Harry had been allowed to glimpse from afar. Anyway, there was no way he could possibly miss Fred's crowning as King of Katama!

Tsabo's brother-in-law, Bhapello, whom Harry had first met at the track-building-site way out on the Mabela plain, and had come across quite often since, now oversaw dozens of food-for-work sites throughout the south and many more in the offing. A short, sturdy, young man, whose shyness belied proven strength of character, Bhapello had hired horses for Harry, Dinea and her youngest sister, Palima. Now teaching at a mission school in the central highlands, Palima had spent most of the previous day in an overloaded bus. Safety in numbers, Harry hoped – not least because there were reports of leopards en route.

Bhapello led the line on his own horse; Palima and Harry followed on docile steeds; Dinea, typically mounted on a stallion, kept watch at the rear. They each placed a stone on a shrine to lost riders and drank tepid water from Bhapello's gourd at that sharp bend in the track, where Tsabo had told Harry: 'This is as near as we can get to my village on four wheels.' Here the track became an even steeper path, which zigzagged towards the notorious high peaks. Some three hours after leaving Mabela, they rested at the summit of a pass, near the cell-phone pylon, perched on the more easily identifiable dome-shaped pinnacle. While they and the horses took on more water, the midday sun relentlessly beat down on their perspiring everything, tempered by a buffeting gale. The long, treacherous descent along an endless succession of narrow ledges high above ravines, whose depths the heat-haze mercifully hid from Harry's momentary glances to right or left, proved far more intimidating than driving alongside the monster canyon on that hazardous highland track, shortly after arriving in the country. He had felt in control, then. Not so, now, when the docile steed ignored his frantic tugs on the reins, stepped perilously close to the edge of a precipice, shuddered to a petrified halt and nearly threw him into a dark chasm. He'd ridden since infancy, but this was a *new* challenge! An experience, he preferred to call it.

The shadows cast by massive rock outcrops were lengthening and beginning to fill the eroded gulley down which the slightly wider path meandered. Then, suddenly, the village across the gorge came in sight. The village Tsabo had told him so much about, the former chief's home, his unfairness to his Kataman clan, the seven torched rondavels, the fights, the dilapidated church, the midwife's clinic, Tsabo's sisters' school, the rowdy shebeens, that village's tokolosi infestation. Harry had imagined some sort of wild-west place, yet it looked like a run-of-the-mill highland village. The hamlet on a steep mountainside across the gorge he identified on his map as Katama, the only other settlement between Mabela and the border with the neighbouring country . . . Round the next corner, standing aloof on its very own oblong plateau, lo and behold, a runway. Cell phone time!

'Can you see me waving Fozz? Are you coming with us?'

'Can you see that Cessna circling? The pilot won't land in this (howling) gale, unless there's a (fluttering) windsock, and mine's (blown) off! Keep riding mate.'

Dinea now led the line. The path took them over the gorge's rim, twisting and turning until it finally reached the bottom. Dinea fell back, and while their horses drank from the stream, she asked Harry if riding down the many steep and narrow paths had scared him. His casual headshake should have sufficed, but she stroked the dust from her sweater and jeans, smiled and said. 'Tell me tonight. Yes?' Then she galloped off through loose scree, causing loads more dust, standing barefooted in the stirrups, one hand on the reins and the other beckoning him. Bhapello shouted, Palima held her breath and Harry was even more alarmed to find himself praying for Dinea's safety. Visibly delighted to have shown off her fearless horsewoman-ship, she cockily led the riders up yet another tortuous path and this one scaled a cliff-face! . . . It was almost dark when a boy ran to greet them.

'Did Father Patrick say you could leave the mission school?' Bhapello asked him.

'My grandfather asked to take me home, and I rode with him from Mabela four days, before.'

'You speak good English,' Baphello said. 'Sekiso is my firstborn son,' he told Harry. 'He studies at St John's mission school nine months, now, and eight years come to him, soon. I am very proud of him.' Baphello had done well too. His English had improved out of all recognition since Harry first met him – then the foreman of the food-for-work gang building a track way out on the Mabela plain.

Baphello's wife, Matashaba, of matronly build and much shorter than her sisters, hugged gracefully slender Palima, then reached up to kiss lavishly endowed Dinea lightly on the cheek, coldly Harry thought.

'Welcome, Mr Harry,' she said in Gwato. 'My brother Tsabo speaks well of you. My father and mother speak well of you, also, and they rode to village across the gorge, two days before. My father and mother will ride back to greet you, very soon. This I hope.'

'Your parents and Tsabo speak well of you, also, Matashaba. I am very happy to ride to this place, and to meet Sekiso. You have three more children. This I know.'

'The baby sleeps, now. They are twins.' A little boy and girl were staring at the white-man – from a safe distance. 'You will eat mealie-meal, before, and drink tea, after?' their mother asked and beamed when Harry thanked her.

She hurried down the slope to the village's cooking fire, where Palima was preparing food, returned with a bowl of water, washed the twins and laid them on a sleeping mat, beneath the blanket that kept them warm at night. Kneeling at their feet, she sang a prayer, kissed them and said: 'The white man is your new uncle.' They glanced at their new uncle and then clung to each other. Not the smoothest of starts, Harry reckoned.

'My parents live in that rondavel.' Matashaba pointed to the one next door, higher up the slope. 'My sisters will sleep there, also. My husband will take you to an empty rondavel. Many are empty, many villagers are late, and many go to Kolokuana in the very bad drought. The rains come one month, before. It is very good, after, and I am happy, now.'

Bhapello came to say: 'A herd-boy took the horses we rode from Mabella to find good pasture. My few cattle, sheep and goats will stay in a corral tonight, with the ponies, and a herd-dog will guard the rondavel where you will sleep.' So, unless the dog and Dinea were old friends, she wouldn't be knocking on his door, Harry tried to convince himself, while he and Bhapello warmed themselves beside the village's cooking fire.

'When will Katamans, also the people in the village across the gorge, get fuel pellets?' Bhapello asked. 'Many ride or walk far every day, but they find no dung, very often.'

'Until more people are trained to work and grease the pellet-making machine,' Harry explained, 'only those living in towns use pellets, because very few of them have dung to burn. Wood and cardboard are very scarce and expensive. Katamans will have a machine, as soon as possible.'

'I will teach them how the machine works,' Bhapello said. 'I will teach them how to grease and mend it, also.'

Matashaba brought tin platters and Palima served mealie-meal, which they ate with their right hand. This reminded Harry to find out where the latrine was. If there were one! With so few in the south, Harry was used to squatting in the open and kept a toilet roll in his rucksack. To most Obangwatos who'd seen a toilet roll, it would have been regarded as an un-affordable luxury. They wiped themselves and infants with their left hand, then threw the rag or whatever away! Some washed their hands after squatting. Scarcely any did so during bad drought, increasing the risk of contracting ksolli – chronic diarrhoea and typhoid. Tsabo had never given up criticising so much lax hygiene, had condemned the government for never improving sanitation, as well as its lack of readiness to combat far too frequent drought, which he'd likened to Europe's medieval plagues that had just about halved its population. Now AIDS was decimating the northern tribe, more and more people in the capital, fewer of his tribe thus far, and threatening to outdo the worst man-made scourge humankind had known. Yet this AIDS-scare proved the scourge also afflicted the innocent, Harry reckoned – then had to haul his thoughts back to the present. Dinea had fried him an egg and persisted in hanging around until he'd eaten it.'

With the moon and Harry's torch the sole streetlamps, Bhapello led the way to a patch of rocky scrub where the villagers went when they wanted to squat, though Harry could only pee. Taking utmost care not to tread on other people's left-overs, they retraced their steps to the cooking fire, to wash and clean their teeth. Harry's nose told him to wash his boots, as well. He'd trodden on lots of leftovers! With all that behind him, Bhapello took him to the empty rondavel and told him to stay inside, until he took away the dog next morning. Harry didn't need telling twice – his canine bodyguard looked blood thirsty.

He unrolled his sleeping bag on the dirt floor, welcoming its warmth, while listening to the eight o'clock World Service News on his portable clock/radio . . .

It woke him eight hours later! Despite often riding to outlying places, his body was unusually stiff and the inside of both legs chafed by yesterday's riding exploits. But with washed face and hands, a mug of hot tea, and a liberal helping of Palima's mealie-meal, he could face whatever came his way. He watched Matashaba milk a cow, the twins play, and Sekiso ride down into the gorge to fetch two gourds of water from the stream. Dinea, now in brief shorts and an even tighter sweater elegantly displayed herself, perched on a rock outside her parent's rondavel, mirror in one hand, perfecting her make-up with the other. In case she beckoned, he tore off to help Bhapello drive his livestock to pasture.

'Has there been much stock theft in this area?' Harry asked him.

'Some. But everything is stolen in *all* areas! Keeping food-for-work equipment safe is my biggest problem. The bad drought killed my cattle, sheep, pony and donkey. My goats stayed strong. Most thieves steal cattle and sheep. I have bought more cattle and sheep, and must have more herd-boys, but many went to the towns to find water, food and jobs.'

The sky resembled a vast dome that all too quickly would lose its blueness to the heat. The massive boulders behind, above, around Katama, poised to roll and crush all within their path. To the west the high peaks, their glowing pink jaggedness sharpened by the crystal-clear sunlight; deeply eroded gulleys dark mauve; pasture still burnished brown. Women in eye-catching rainbow colours toiled in fields, no larger but much steeper than gardens, hacked out of the mountainside generations ago. If it rained again soon, at least there'd be some maize and maybe beans to harvest, unless that rain washed the soil, now fertilised, down into the gorge, taking with it more rocks and scree. But no fields had fences to stop unguarded livestock ravaging whatever few crops the women managed to grow. The Gwato version of the development handbook had publicised the seed and fertiliser banks set up in all six southern districts, with Pete's cartoons showing how best to prevent or stem erosion. Its guidelines stressed, inter alia, the urgency to build fences.

They must have trudged all of three miles before Baphello's whistles paid off. His herd-boy responded. The horses ridden from Mabela were grazing high up a re-entrant. 'Seven years come to me,' the boy proudly told Harry, 'and to my friend Sekiso, also. My dogs stay close by me, all the nights, and no leopards come.' But

Harry couldn't help noticing that not only were the boy's gumboots far too big, they had two right feet!

Bhapelo provided the answer with learnéd gravitas: 'They are his grandfather's boots'.

The herd-boy drank just a mouthful of the water and gobbled up half the mealie-meal Bhapello had brought him. His dogs then drove all the animals in his charge to where the grass was greener. He might well have grumbled, gazing enviously across the gorge, that the grass was always greener on the other side! The north-facing pasture around Katama, where the villagers' were allowed to graze their livestock was on the sunny side. But *not* across the gorge, where pasture for the most part and much of the day, basked in the high peaks' shadows. There were so many locally imposed, jealously guarded, grossly unfair, land-use rights, which the national development plan's implementers were determined to eradicate. They would also need to enforce the new Enclosure Act's provisions, allowing the fencing of fields to protect crops from marauding tame or wild animals. However, no parliamentary legislation would protect crops from hordes of fence-climbing baboons and burrowing vermin, nor from the still far too prevalent roaming thieves.

Because a windsock blew away, the Cessna spent the night parked on Mabela's airstrip – Tsabo and Jill parked in St John's Mission. Father Patrick welcomed the happy couple and blessed their marriage at a rapidly arranged service, attended by all available pupils and nuns. Tsabo's very first teacher, Sister Marie Louise, then took Jill on a tour of the school's dormitories, classrooms, library, even the pig and chicken sheds. After supper in the refectory, Jill slept in the nunnery – Tsabo in his "old bunk", Sister Marie Louise had called it. Jill wished she hadn't commented that Tsabo would have kept it much tidier.

After breakfast next morning, she and Tsabo shared the Cessna's floor – its back seats had been removed – with three discharged hospital patients. Before take off, the fourth, a young woman, had to be re-suscitated by the pilot, a *Médecin sans Frontière* charity's doctor, and an ambulance took the woman from Mabela's airfield to the local hospital. To add to Jill's worries, when airborne she noticed that the instructions on the crate, which also shared the Cessna's back floor, demanded urgent delivery of the crate's fire-fighting equipment to the new airstrip where Tsabo had said they would land. She made him ask the pilot if the airstrip had caught fire. Having dutifully spoken on his intercom, Tsabo told her that the equipment was being delivered in case the airstrip *did* catch fire.

Two days ago their chief sent a message to Fred, asking him and his wife to ride to the village across the gorge, but hadn't said why. Before they arrived the chief assembled the villagers to tell them two visitors were coming, though only he knew that Tsabo and his wife would give them money to build four pit-latrines. Imagine the scene when Tsabo's parents saw him. *And his wife!* They recognised Jill from the wedding photos, Tsabo had sent them. His mother tried her best to run, so that she could kiss them. His still hobbling father won the race to hug his son, shook both of his son's wife's hands and introduced her to the chief, who introduced her to the assembled villagers and reminded those who didn't know who her husband was. Tsabo explained what pit-latrines were, and then said: 'When four pits are dug and the latrines are built, you will no longer have to squat in the open. After the chief had thanked Tsabo and Jill for their great kindness you may also be able to imagine, especially if you happen to be a Gwato-speaking female, how raptuous a reception they received. Tsabo had told Jill what he was going to say before their arrival.

When they reached Katama, riding horses the chief had lent them, their reception was even more rapturous, even though no villager other than Tsabo's parents knew what was in store for them on the sanitation scene. For Matashaba, meeting Tsabo's wife and their homecoming felt like heaven. Her family were all here, after much long waiting! She asked her father to give the mittens she knitted to Jill, as a present of welcome, and all the Mashedi family – except Dinea – had many hugs, and many happy tears, also.

Because so many villagers swarmed round Tsabo and Jill, it took quite a while before Harry could get a look in, and Fozz was hacked off because the (wretched) Cessna pilot hadn't brought the (umpteen) Foster's six-packs Fozz had asked him to bring.

A babbling crowd now assembled outside the café, Katama's only shop, which Harry was pleased to see had a solar-panel fixed to its corrugated-iron roof. When the Mashedi family came, men bowed, women and children stopped their chatter. The young chief and an elderly priest had ridden from the village across the gorge, apparently with a hideous-looking witchdoctor in tow.

Wrapped in a coarse threadbare grey blanket, bare-footed Fred emerged from the café and the priest invited him to be seated. The witchdoctor set fire to the twin-headed, four-limbed tokolosi effigy she'd brought with her, blew smoke at Fred, leaped about on bent knees, yelping and grunting, bare-handedly ripped the flaming effigy apart and then strew its remains in front of Fred. Not a murmur within her respectful audience.

The young chief removed Fred's blanket, replaced it with a finely-woven and multi-coloured one, placed a lethal-looking spear in Fred's right hand, a shield in his left and a tiara of white anemones, the national flower, around his bare head. Someone muttered something which prompted the chief to put the sandals on Fred's feet.

'This is your headman!' the chief proclaimed.

'God blesses him,' the priest intoned.

Following the national anthem, sung in harmony and with great gusto, Fred addressed the gathering: 'Peace be with you my friends. I will work, all the days, to bring you water and food, and good pasture for your animals, also. This I hope. We have a solar-panel, before. We have the airstrip, now. We will have . . . what are the words?' The prompter muttered 'fuel pellets' and Fred nodded. 'We will have fuel pellets, after. You are my big family, now, and Katama is our home.' He glanced at Tsabo. 'And my kind son will stay in this place when I am late. This I hope, also.' Harry had acted as Jill's interpreter.

Everybody applauded their now beautified headman, but there was no way that Tsabo could welcome the prospect of living here, permanently, nor did Jill fake happiness. Yet, he must fulfil a promise he'd made while still at school. After congratulating his father. he said: 'Many years, before, I saw a good chair, to sit on, when squatting comes to me, and a hut for the chair, and a pit, under. I come from far with my wife to greet you, and to give your headman money, and to ask Kataman men, also, to build four very good pit-latrines,' – which he described. 'I ask Kataman women to clean them, also, and put new paper close by them, every day. I ask the men to empty them, every week, and I ask my father to tell the men where to dig four pits, and how to build four latrines, and where to empty them, also. All this I hope.'

'All this I *know!*' said Fred. 'Yes, Yes,' the villagers chanted. But Harry noticed that some men were scowling, probably because they hated change or more probably because they couldn't stomach the thought of pick-axing pits in their mountainside's solid rock.

Fred rose from his chair. 'A white man comes to this place, and this makes my family and me very happy. Mr Harry, you are our brother and we will welcome you *all* the days. Fred stooped, picked up something hidden from under his chair, removed the string round a large parcel and unwrapped the newspaper-enclosed contents. 'This blanket comes from the hands of my wife. This stick comes from my knife. This hat comes from Mabela.'

Fred left his chair and placed a brown trilby hat on top of Harry's head, amidst much hilarity. The hat was several sizes too small – or Harry's head was several sizes too big! More excited chanting of 'Yes, Yes,' loads more hand-clapping and Harry stood rooted to the spot – flabbergasted, fighting off emotion, lost for words.

'Unlike you to be lost for words,' Tsabo joked, too loudly. Harry hoped it was a joke.

'Thank you headman and brother,' Harry replied in Gwato. 'Thank you many brothers and sisters, also. You are my other family and Katama is my other home, now. All this I know.'

Fred handed him the walking stick, draped the multi-coloured, multi-patterned blanket round his shoulders and just as it was being fastened with a pin, Harry's eyes met Dinea's. She smiled and blatantly blew him a kiss, clearly wanting it to be noticed.

No stretching of Harry's trilby's interior made it fit better. So Jill took some photos of him holding it in one hand, the stick in the other and wrapped in his blanket fastened with a large pin. Moving closer, Jill examined the pin, but then unfastened and removed it. Her verdict: 'It's heavy enough to be solid silver!'

'My Aunt Dinea said she bought the pin in Kolokuana,' young Sekiso revealed, in all innocence.

His Uncle Tsabo gave Harry a withering glare, leaving him legless, as well as hatless.

When their chief, Fred and the village elders had done whatever they had to do inside the café, the new headman's feast could begin outside it. Bhapello and Palima had carried most of the food from Mabela in their saddlebags. The village women served their chief and the Mashedi family first, the priest, Harry and Fozz next, and the rest had to queue. The elders opened casks of home-brewed beer, which soon got everyone singing and dancing. Fozz had obviously stopped pining for his six-packs of Foster's and was in his element. No sooner had he sunk one mug of the beer, than another was thrust in his hand. His standing as the local airstrip-builder had gone to his head, not only down his gullet. Just a sniff of that oily grey liquid turned Harry's stomach.

Fozz had stood beside Mkwere during the ceremony, but the mystery man rode up the steep escarpment behind them, before Harry had a chance to speak to him.

'Where's he off to Fozz?'

'Dunno mate. My job's making (windy) runways.'

'Mkwere's workers will make a track up there,' Bhapello chipped in, 'and a pipe from the high waterfall, also. The track and the pipe will go to the village across the gorge, and round the top of the gorge to Katama, and to the mine at the end of the gorge, close by the the next country. Soldiers guarded the mine, many years, and many guard it, still.'

Having mentioned, in strict confidence, his grandfather's grave to Baphello, over-excited Harry less quietly asked him: 'Shall we ride to the mine tomorrow?'

'No people must go there. Soldiers will shoot them. They will shoot us, also.'

Dermot's bound to know, too, but why had he called his chief handler his *base* and his under-cover mates his *circle*? Just proves that even devout Christians can get away with being economical with the truth, but suppose it's all part and parcel of our trusted security apparatus whose intelligence can be dodgy. He'd never read newspapers at home, in case he threw a wobbly. 'What's a wobbly? he could hear his Southern Baptist wife ask. 'It's a paroxysm,' he heard himself say, but that left Belinda struggling as well, even though her handy Oxford dictionary scarcely shut itself. Oh, happy times. Happier than now! Dinea had seen to that, through no fault of her divorced Mashedi family, who ever since they'd known Harry had never failed to regard him as one of them, the twin's new uncle mused.

That evening, Harry related Bhapello's gobsmacking revelations in a hastily scribbled note, which he'd post in Mabela to Dermot, but then recalled Tsabo's warning that if he was caught snooping for his grandfather's grave, which might be near to some old mine-workings, things could get tough, very tough. Tsabo had again said that he didn'tknow where the old mine-workings were. Then Mkwere had wanted an envelope addressed to Dermot posted at Heathrow and Suleiman had said, later, Mkwere was an employee of a London mining company. Though he chose not to reveal for almost a year why a civilian pilot had flown him in a civilian helicopter to the town just across the border where he'd exchanged envelopes with an Afrikaner intent on stealing diamonds, to help stop Mandela's election as South Africa's first black president – diamonds mined near Katama Bhapello had now disclosed. Nor had Suleiman revealed that the British police adviser, who'd been present when the envelopes were exchanged, had sworn that the mine hadn't been re-opened.

Joining Harry beside the cooking fire, Tsabo seemed keener to walk, rather than warm himself, and suggested that Harry should accompany him. After praying by torch-light beside his grandparent's, his friend Mueketso's and his pony's graves, Tsabo gazed at the galaxy of bright stars, almost within touching distance, and said to Harry: 'By the skin of its teeth this tiny hamlet and its fewer people survived that punishing drought, but with terrible suffering, pain and anguish. Deserted rondavels, empty corrals and a bigger burial ground all stand testament to that.'

While they strolled on, it seemed to Harry that ever since Tsabo had told him so much about Katama, he'd been destined to visit this remote place, which he'd hovered over in a helicopter almost two years ago, during his first tour of the southern province. He'd bring Belinda here and spend the rest of their lives here, or was that just another of his Virgoan fantasies? Whatever it was would be shattered by the question he'd been expecting Tsabo to ask and had willed him not to.

'Are you and Dinea having an affair Harry?'

'What makes you think that?'

'Just a hunch.'

Now perched on a ledge high above the gorge, Harry peered into the darkest depths of that crushing question for what felt like an age until he and Tsabo couldn't stop shivering.

Climbing back up the bridle path they by-passed a few silent rondavels, some forsaken and already derelict, others with folk sleeping peacefully inside. Simple, honest folk, who might well be dreaming of owning a magic cell-phone.

While warming themselves as near as practicable to the cooking fire's embers, Tsabo said: 'Jill's and my flights were a wedding present. The proceeds from my book on tribal history paid for all the ventilated, improved, pit-latrines. VIP latrines!' he added, with a touch of irony. Harry described the helicopter tour of the south after the good rains came, mentioned the grant-money stolen by corrupt bureaucrats and outlined the contents of the development handbook that most government officials, chiefs and headmen had failed to read or to ensure that rainwater was trapped and conserved.

'Will they never learn?' Tsabo muttered resignedly, tossing some bits of dried dung on the fire. 'By the way, Jill had dearly wanted Belinda to be her maid of honour, though she was in America, helping her parents. Maybe you don't know this.'

'I *do* know that! And *you* have known for quite a few years that Belinda and I couldn't be more happily married! Living apart for this long hasn't been easy for either of us and we're both greatly looking forward to enjoying a wonderful Christmas in Cape Town.'

'Bang goes my lousy hunch about you and that minx of an errant sister.'

Tsabo thumped Harry's back and they laughed so much their breath ran out. Had such frivolity occurred within their hallowed Oxford College, it would have surely generated consternation. All their laughter achieved in Katama was to make dogs bark. They made for the corral farthest from inhabited rondavels and urinated against its stone wall, both competing to create the most realistic outline of Oxford's Radcliffe Camera and giggling like a couple of varsity tykes out on the town.

'I'm a crusty old incontinent professor who frequently wets his pants,' croaked Harry.

'I'm a plastered undergraduate who's been sick all over his shoes,' chuckled Tsabo. 'Ron, the King of Oxford scouts, retrieves the shoes from under the undergrad's bed, then sniffs around the room for other similarly soiled objects. Great memories! Which reminds me, are you still producing copious diaries for Dermot's book?'

'Your minx of a sister fleetingly featured in several, but there was nothing untoward, so you needn't worry.'

'I'm not worried. She deserves all the pithily degrading publicity you can dream up.'

They went their separate ways. Torch-lit Harry trying to avoid cats chasing rats – the size of cats! A vulture flopped down, on a dead something or other, giving him a hellava turn! Then Bhapello and the frothing at the mouth guard-dog suddenly appeared from the shadows! With Harry safely inside the locked rondavel, he watched Bhapello through its de-grimed window tie the mastiff to a post beside the door, before making doubly sure the leash was secure.

Harry kept on his anorak, body-warmer, plus several layers beneath, and both pairs of trousers. He was frozen, and they might provide a modicum of protection from another leg-mauling, or whatever that particular dog fancied, were he taken short during the night and had to run to the squatting or standing up place. He'd do whatever he had to do in his emptied rucksack. Wearing the extra clothing severely tested his squeezing-into-a-fleece-lined-sleeping-bag skill.

He seemed to be forcibly dreaming about all manner of scandalous behaviour when he heard Dinea knocking on his door. A surreptitious glance through the window identified Bhapello, waiting to give him a dawn mug of tea. Harry assumed the tea would be given to him and not to that menacing beast. A bolder glance revealed an absentee guard dog.

Although he'd enjoyed last night's meat supper, indigestion accompanied his return to the cooking fire, where the Mashedi family noisily welcomed his arrival – notably Dinea, who fried him an indigestion-intensifying egg, though hindered its reluctant consumption with flauntatious activities that had long impeded Mashedi family harmony. Her mother, Palima and Matashaba shook their heads in disgust – Bhapello took Sekiso to saddle the horses – Jill waylaid Tsabo's wrath by complimenting Dinea's figure – headman Fred's pacifying speech lasted all of a minute. One of those televised soap operas couldn't have done any better, Harry reckoned. After all the kisses, cuddles and handshakes were in his camera, he expected more drama would follow. It was just a matter of deciding how and where to stage the finale. No decision was needed! To ensure that he wouldn't get caught short within range of Dinea's eyes during the ride back to Mabela, he helped Tsabo to fill the bucket now displaying its convenience behind a nearby empty rondavel. Having been kept on tenterhooks far too long, he repeated one of many questions posed during the past two years by voice, fax, phone or letter. 'Have you discovered the old mine-workings yet, where my grandfather's grave might be?' Silence! After the second time of asking, there was no Jill to blow out his still burning fuse. 'For heaven's sake, Harry, how many more flaming times do you need telling? If you're caught snooping things could get tough, very tough.' As before, he didn't say where the old mine workings were, maybe because of his concern for a snooper's safety, but must have known its whereabouts by then.

Before re-joining the others, he told Tsabo: 'I'm taking with me the blanket, trilby and walking stick your father gave me. The blanket pin, which may be silver, I've given him.'

The remainers and riders said their sad farewells, with Dinea a noticeable dissenter. The precarious ledge where Tsabo and Harry had sat side-by-side, now occupied by a baboon, looked far more precarious in daylight. At the foot of the gorge, Dinea fell back from her place at the head of the riders to cross the stream beside Harry. All wide-eyed and smiles, she said: 'You will stay with me in my very nice flat in Mabela tonight. Yes?'

He rode on in silence – strong-willed, self-satisfying silence – wishing he'd got some indigestion tablets, and still wondering what Mkwere and Fozz had been talking about.

Ever since that doctor raped her on his office floor, Dinea had hated African men. All the times she asked to go to the nursing sister's course in Mavimbi, and all her pleads for UN sponsorship, and all her tears, made no difference. She threw his files at him. And when she picked them up, he raped her again! He signed the form and said he would burn it, if she told anyone. She unlocked his door and stood outside the UN health office, angry at him and the bosses who let him work for them. She rang his secretary, many times, and asked her to tell the doctor she was pregnant, but he was too busy to speak to her, always. She rang his secretary from the nursing school in Mavimbi, also, and was told the doctor had gone. What could she do? She had no money to send the secretary to buy his address.

She hated African men even more in Mavimbi. Everywhere she went, they praised her big breasts and bottom, her small waist and long legs, and wanted her to go with them to a hotel. Jealous classmates said she used her body to get men's money, but soon, her pregnancy made her wear loose clothes and she was very scared her figure had gone, forever.

After the baby came, she bottle-fed him. She did exercises, and went swimming, every lunch-break. Her waist was slim, again. Her curves quickly grew much bigger and firmer. The hairdresser massaged them, every week, but wanted to massage much more, also! So she massaged her curves herself, washed and braided her hair and left her baby with nuns while she studied at the nursing school. The nunnery priest christened her son: Moitlamo Elvis Mashedi. She called him Elvis, always. The American pop-star's name! So many black men, some were her teachers, asked her to walk with them in the dark to the beach, close by. She never went. She wanted a rich white man who will make her a film star.

When Tsabo came to the workshop in Mavimbi, he visited her, and was angry to find she had a baby. She begged him not to tell their family. He said she flaunted her body to get what she wanted. No wonder the doctor raped her! He was angry at Mavimbi airport, also, and said she flaunted her body, again, when she talked to his married good friend.

Harry was tall, like her. He had a very nice face and smile, and a very nice beard, also. When he flew back from England, after Christmas, he left her lovely presents on a table at Mavimbi Airport. She asked him to stay a night with her, but he flew to Kolokuana. She went to Mabela, after her public health course, and her parents loved Elvis, their fifth grandchild. They never asked who is his father and welcomed him to the family. He lived with them and she paid his carer. Her father bought everything Elvis needed.

She managed the southern province's nutritional surveillance project, now, but when Harry came to Mabela or they both went to meetings, he talked about work, only. He liked that blonde American, Jinky, much more than her, and after the disco, he didn't open his door when she knocked. And when she phoned him, he didn't want to come to her nice flat in Mabela. When she phoned him, again, his driver said Harry went to the orphanage to help nurses to change nappies. But she knew he was there and didn't want to speak to her. She must find a good way to trap him and keep him for herself.

While all that was going on, Harry had felt increasingly vulnerable to Dinea's myriad wiles. The British high commissioner had expressed his concern to Suleiman about the affair a highly rated expatriate was having with a young African woman. Having stared at Suleiman in bewildered amazement, Harry firmly denied any such transgression, but left Suleiman's office feeling hopeless!

After next Sunday's Matins, Solomon Khami looked uneasy and took Harry aside. He explained that a well-qualified nursing sister had contacted him and several other doctors alleging that a Mr Harry Burke was having sex with her and asking for treatment to help her to get pregnant. Now Harry felt hopeless and brainless!

'I didn't believe Miss Mashedi's allegation,' Solomon generously said. 'Knowing that my general practitioner son in Detroit needed a surgery sister, I phoned him and a week later the lady in question flew with her young son to America.'

Harry's wobbly body suddenly felt strong enough to withstand Solomon's hug and his wife drove them home for the best Sunday dinner since Belinda's feast, before he'd returned to Africa. But that voice inside his head never failed to correct him: 'Before you returned to Africa stupidly without Belinda!' Harry nodded so vigorously, Solomon probably wondered if the cruel allegation had caused him brain damage, though Solomon just topped up Harry's wine glass, turned up his voice volume, and proposed a toast: 'To absent friends, whoever and wherever they are!' His wife's smile blended love with admiration, even more so when Solomon sang *The Old Ruggéd Cross*.

Then, after another glass of wine, Harry warbled the first verse of *Land of Hope and Glory*, the only verse he knew.

He penned that evening 'I shall never be able to thank you adequately, Solomon, not only for standing up for me, but also for pulling off that amazing Detroit-miracle. You are a true Christian – a truism needing not an atom of substantiation since our first meeting. Please pass on to your wife my appreciation of her culinary arts and for such kindness in comforting an adult man who had been made to squirm like a prodigal boy.'

Business As Usual Until . . .

In Harry's defence, the over-long lack of marital love life was not why his faxed diaries had suggested a lapse into adulterous adventures. Nor was he a philanderer, who always fell for attractive, curvaceous, enticing women – however impellingly his somewhat over-developed male instincts might well have tempted him or unintentionally commandeered his perpetually wide-open, ever-eager, female-orientated eyes, ever since our schooldays. Excusably a far from abnormal trait among most growing or grown males.

Should Belinda's frequent, lucrative dress-design-sales travels geographically coincide with Oxford and her ardent clock-watching permitted, she had diverted to my College study to read Harry's latest diaries; secretively bereft of those passages a philanderer would likely term the juicy bits. The King of Katama expurgated account caused Belinda to lapse into prolonged ecstatic raptures, morphing into hysterical giggles upon coming to the mention of Harry's trilby, causing her to exclaim. 'He simply *must* wear it while we're holidaying in Cape Town . . . but only if I make it fit better!' I asked her when they were going there, temporarily overlooking that the most recent diary had highlighted their fast-approaching Christmas reunion. My vision had accidentally focused on the young woman Dinea's ill-fitting short white frock again, a vision so persistent, I was compelled to invite Belinda to dine at The Randolph and sample the hotel's latest menu, also its most expensive.

We agreed the date for my next visit to Belinda's Cotswolds lone hide-out – hopefully with my wife, Wendy, due an overdue release from her *homo sapiens* archaeology project in East Africa. Belinda's attention now re-focused upon Harry's diaries to my alarm! Had her deft detectival talents rumbled my Harry-protective and diary-expurgational efforts?

'Ever since we married Harry's always been in such a rush to do the things he wants to do,' Belinda said. 'I get the same impression reading his diaries. Never ending rush, rush, rush! It spoils his literary style he's always banging on about. Are his too rambling, rather sing-song efforts helping or hindering completion of your book?'

'Very much helping! Diaries tend to be pacey and Harry's have consistently reflected the urgency to get so many crucially needed things done, and done effectively. They also reflect what many others are doing to help end, and if practicable to help end once and for all, his host-country's seemingly never ending disaster continuum.'

'Thank you for saying that. You've made it easier to accept that Harry's long absences have been worthwhile. But I find some parts of his letters and diaries intensely disturbing, especially when brutal conflict threatens the lives of helpers, as well as the helped.'

I badly wanted to re-assure Belinda by reminding her that local soldiers and policemen were readily at hand to quell disturbances and stop brutal conflict, but recent reports from my 'Base' had far from re-assured me, nor others within my 'Circle', that all was well in that country, particularly in Kolokuana where army-police enmity had moved on apace.

Our government will never shrink from its bounden duty to extricate Harry, and every other British expatriate, *before* any trouble starts in the unlikely event of trouble starting, I'd wanted to say, but that would have meant lying and Belinda, more than likely, would have read me like a book, much like she'd eventually be reading my un-expurgated book.

'Will our government pay the ransom if a British expatriate is held hostage?'she asked.

'Unless paying the ransom meant putting more British lives at risk, the option would be given urgent consideration.' I shied off adding that extrication also crucially depended on the availability and proximity of the means of extrication, since that may well have urged her to query whether there were handily reliable means of extrication and what they were.

I wouldn't have been at liberty to disclose that.

While walking to her car Belinda caught me off guard, again. 'I was surprised Harry's latest diary didn't mention Tsabo's sister. Jill phoned me when she got back from Africa, brimming over with vivid descriptions of Dinea's vital statistics and how kind Dinea had been to give Harry a solid-silver blanket pin, blah, blah, blah! I *hate* saying this! What's the betting they're having an affair?'

'Ten-to-nil against!' I blurted out, but Belinda looked totally unconvinced. With her unusually frigid farewell echoing louder with my every step and my hitherto unshakeable certainty of Harry's marital loyalty severely dented, by the time I'd reached the college and collapsed on my bed, unshakeable certainty was ten-to-nil against and serious doubts the favourite! Yet, the longer I laid there, the stronger my conviction became. Women were notoriously envious of other women's figures, because they were much slimmer or more curvaceous than their own. Neither Jill nor Belinda had struck me as falling in the envious category, though serious doubts now stood in the winner's enclosure – until I reached for my bible, opened it at Chapter 14 of St Paul's Epistle to the Romans and re-read: "Who are you to pass judgement on servants of another? It is before their own lord that they stand or fall. And they will be upheld for God is able to make them stand." Even so, not a restful night!

Suleiman's quarrel with his UN superiors over his treating internally displaced persons as refugees and also funding their re-housing had intensified when he'd insisted that all five UN agencies with offices in Kolokuana must move into the long-vacant Central Bank's six-storey, now refurbished building. The local UN food, health, childcare and agriculture supremos threatened to resign on the spot, yet Suleiman unflinchingly stood his ground.

Jinky flew in from New York, waved a light-blue UN Peace Flag, and flew back with a forthright message: 'The move under one roof should go ahead, right now!' One of her bosses, having afforded the highly complex matter due consideration, reluctantly concurred, but then another tricky issue cropped up. If Kolokuana's new UN building kept its present name, Central Bank, that country's government would expect the UN to provide long-term financial security, plus a short-term means of ridding itself of its enormous budget deficit. Moreover, such a dangerous precedent would have far-reaching ramifications far beyond Kolokuana, a prospect so disturbing that all of Jinky's bosses set about setting up a steering group. Faced with more procrastinating delay, Suleiman threatened to resign.

The steering group set up a probing committee – with wide-ranging expertise and multi-ethnic representation – charged with recommending a new name before Friday 26th November. A firm day-remit being so uncommonly stringent within UN headquarters, the chairman requested a 14-day stay of execution and his committee requested him, as chairman, to act on its behalf. On Tuesday, 23rd November, a full three days less than the original remit, and surprised by how easy the whole exercise had been, he came up with two choices: *The UN Centre Kolokuana* or *Democracy and Freedom Tower*. The steering group rejected the first, on the grounds that the acronym TUNCK failed to convey the desired image and unanimously accepted the second, which sounded great! – even though the present Central Bank's six storeys hardly constituted a tower by New York standards. The steering group's superiors happily voted for *Democracy and Freedom Tower* – then an inferior pointed out that DAFT also had its drawbacks and suggested *The New UN Office*. This was approved, but only after two recounts, and all Suleiman's superiors duly informed him by fastest fax that he would have to like the name or lump it.

He lumped it and got on with his tricky issues, such as obtaining agreement on which floors the UN food, health, childcare, agricultural staffs, his development planning staff, the now integrated budget and administrative staff, as well as a new UN clubroom would occupy. With this settled, the childcare supremo complained that his lowest floor denoted lowest relative status. Suleiman said that childcare deserved easiest access! The childcare supremo's objection to sharing the floor with a *clubroom* was overcome by providing two separate, prominently signed ground-floor entrances. Exasperated by so much absurdity and by far too many new UN this's and that's, Suleiman re-renamed the building *The Hub* and kept his far too many superiors in the dark

The "crunch" came soon after men in black suits and shades, crookéd civil servants, bent senior policeman, shady traders, gangsters, pimps and such like, were individually or collectively barred from entering the new clubroom by armed security guards who asked to see their UN pass, personally stamped and signed by Suleiman. If they had one, it was faked or forged! The annual audit of the former clubroom's accounts had already exposed theft of its bar takings, master-minded by the black-suited secret service director. He, the police commissioner and sundry others were charged, in absentia, with embezzlement of UN funds. Now the fighting and torching started – and it began right in front of The Hub.

Solomon Khami's car was overturned and set alight. He escaped uninjured, but Jack his passenger was beaten up, left for dead in the street, and in his broken arms a tokolosi doll labelled: "Welcome Dr Khami and Mr Tsamanchimone to the New UN Clubroom's First and Last Committee Meeting!" With Jack still breathing, Solomon rang for an ambulance on his cell phone and within twenty minutes Jack, his stretcher, the tokolosi doll and the label were in the army barracks' medical centre, his arms in plaster, his head bandaged, a fag between his lips, held by a corporal medic while Jack puffed it. Within an hour, Solomon had assembled a team of doctors and nurses in the medical centre, and sent the tokolosi doll and label to Suleiman. He locked both in his office safe, intending to phone Sonny Floors, then realised he had no secure means of communication. 'You'll have to fax him, Harry, and keep him and key others briefed,' Suleiman said. This looks like an all-night job.' Hence Harry's much briefer than usual record of events – a "log" in military jargon. But, before starting the log, he faxed Sonny to ask if he'd heard about the fire outside the Hub and its consequences. He also knew about the tokolosi doll and label.

6 Dec: 1850. The Hub's 3 armed guards patrolling its compound report burning car + fighting in street outside. 5 hooded men broke in + trashed committee room, but got away. Suleiman (**S**) cancels committee meeting on his cell phone. Harry (**H**) briefs Sonny Floors (**F**) by fax + requests

immediate dusk-to-dawn curfew + cabinet review of situation at 0400 7 Dec.

1900. **F's** faxed reply: '24-hour <u>daily</u> curfew will be imposed, except for soldiers, police and other essential workers. All must show official passes – copy below.' **H** shows fax to **S** + the major in his command post on roof + to all Hub's armed guards. **H** inspects security. 2 armed guards start barricading doors + windows from bottom floor up. Other 7 armed guards searching offices, told to lock all files, laptops + valuable equipment in Hub's cellars.

1918. Solomon faxes **H** from army barracks, describing incident outside Hub + Jack's injuries, his arms need specialist attention. Ambulance with 2 armed troops taken Jack to Kolokuana's hospital, avoiding town centre. Too few doctors + nurses in barracks med centre, lots more blood + med supplies urgently needed.

1920. Major plus **S** + **H** agree codewords re: Hub security + exchange cell phone nos. Major says armed troops now patrolling town centre. Tokolosi dolls nailed to doors of many looted shops in town-centre + most suburbs.

1922. **H** faxes **F** re: shortage of blood + med supplies, also widespread looting. **S** faxes Diane: 'Trouble expected!' Her reply: 'Come home.' His reply: 'I must stay put, so must you. Hide everything important.'

1930. Soldier finds ultimatum stuck on **S**'s car + **H's** truck in Hub's parking lot: 'Drop <u>all</u> embezzlement charges and give clubroom passes. If this is not done we will come to get <u>both</u> of you.' Major shows ultimatum to **S** + **H**. Ultimatum faxed to **F**. **S** briefs major on UN security plan: State Green at present, but ultimatum suggests upgrading to State Orange. Then all UN expatriates living or working in Kolokuana must stay indoors + prepare for evacuation to Mavimbi. UN area wardens will get orders by cell phone. If State Red declared, all UN families + individuals hurry to assembly points + board bus company's buses. Major given addresses of UN area wardens. He says 2 armed troops in disguised army truck will tell all area wardens to report problems + progress on army secure radio whenever possible.

1947. Major informed – soldiers overstretched. **S** declares State Orange. **H** faxes bus company manager: 'State Orange. Prepare to send buses to assembly points. Faxed reply: 'Every bus immobilised last night by hooded gangs.' Major sends 2 armed troops in truck to all UN area wardens' homes with **S**'s typed message: 'State Orange. UN families and individuals living or working in your area of responsibility must lock all doors and keep watch for strangers acting suspiciously. You must report <u>soonest</u> hostile incidents on secure radio, if practicable.' **H** faxes copy of message to **F**.

2015. **S** + **H** now on 2-hr shifts. Hourly briefing in Major's comd. post + hourly situation reports faxed to **F**.

7 Dec: 0445. Major, his comd post + armed troops overstretched all night, sporadic rifle fire, no infiltrators in Hub or compound. Explosions heard. 10 armed guards now patrolling Hub – 5 on alternating 2-hr shifts.

0600. **H** wakes **S** – both revived by hot soup while briefed in comd. post. Major's wireless switched on. Radio Kolokuana News: 'Soldiers caused last night's protests in the town centre by torturing innocent civilians. Soldiers executed eight policemen, also. Mr Tsamanachimone, who had saved hundreds of thousands of his Obangwato tribe from starvation, bled to death, after many beatings with soldiers' rifles. The weather today . . .' Phonecall in **S**'s office: 'Good morning Mr Suleiman Al Rashid and Mr Harry Burke. I hope you heard the news. Have a nice day. See you soon.' African voice, but not local accent. **H** faxes texts of news headlines + phonecall to **F**. Major tells army commander on secure radio. Fax from **F**: 'The army commander will collect Suleiman and you at 0700 and bring you both to a cabinet meeting in his armoured car.' **H** tells **S**, then goes to comd. post to inform Major + other key allies on secure radio.

0612.   Message from UN area warden on an army truck's secure
        radio: 'UN food, health, childcare and agriculture directors
        drove their families to Mavimbi last night. All other UN
        dependents know they must lock their doors and watch out
        for strangers. Please send soldiers to guard all remaining
        people and other UN wardens. **H** tells Major who informs
        army commander (**AC**) on secure radio. His reply: 'Hello
        two. Sunray speaking. Tell warden no soldiers available.
        Hope to send some soon. Out.'

0618.   Fax from Jenkins Makimbo (**JM**): 'Explosion at president's
        palace, looting + violence in main street, police raping
        women + girls, army commander on way to bring you and
        Suleiman to cabinet meeting – now delayed till 0730.'

0625.   **AC** arrived. He knows meeting delayed + will take **S** + **H** in
        his armd. car to main street. He spent most of night there.
        Now 20 plus armed troops (**ATs**) stop approx 30 police
        raping women + girls. Some freed by (**ATs**). Others driven
        off by police (**PCs**) in brown van. 11 **PCs** + 4 secret service
        agents captured + guarded by **ATs** – then driven to army
        barracks in 3 red mail delivery vans. **S** + **H** help load rape
        victims on stretchers into 2 ambulances which return for
        14 **ATs** wounded + 3 **ATs** killed by **PCs**. Near chaos here.
        0710. **AC** takes **S** + **H** to Kolokuana's hospital. More chaos,
        stinking wards, many corpses + groaning casualties on bare
        bedsprings. No nurses. **H** asks ward's doctor: 'Where's
        Mr Tsamanchimone?' Doctor's reply: 'After I'd treated
        his injuries, an ambulance took him to the army barracks'
        medical centre about five o'clock this morning.'

0730.   Only **JM** + **F** in cabinet room; 7 ministers overseas; rest
        sick-lame-lazy. **JM** says: 'The secret service director,
        Sanguekku, phoned me. God knows how he knew I was
        here! He demanded the release of his four agents and also
        the eleven policemen, all arrested by soldiers in the main
        street an hour ago. He's phoning at eight o'clock. If all
        fifteen have not been released by then, he said Mboko will
        die. **AC** says: If they are released, all my soldiers will go
        crazy. Three were killed by policemen or secret service

agents.' **S** asks **JM**: 'Didn't you say, after Mboko fled to London, he asked to be placed in house arrest? **JM** replies: 'He still is. I delayed our meeting and phoned him there.' All present agree Sanguekku bluffing. **JM** to refuse release. Conference-call facility in cabinet room will broadcast what's said.

0800. Phonecall: 'This is Serenity Sanguekku. Your answer, Mr Makimbo?' Same voice + accent as phonecall to **S** + **H** at 0600. **JM** says: 'No policemen and no secret service agents will be released.' Sanguekku replies: 'Drop all the embezzlement charges immediately or Mr Rashid's and Mr Burke's drivers will die. What a shame. Farewell.' Horrified silence – then frantic planning. **AC** says: 'Ten soldiers have patrolled the diplomatic compound and twenty have surrounded the president's palace since the 0615 explosion there. Soon afterwards, Sanguekku and the British police adviser were seen entering the palace. No reports of them leaving. The drivers could be there. It is getting even more difficult to impose the 24-hour curfew with fewer troops. I have requested military assistance.' **JM** says: 'The UK will provide appropriate military assistance later today and police assistance as soon as practicable.' **S** desperate to check if Diane's safe. Their house is near palace. **S** + **H** also desperate to find their drivers. **AC** will take **S** + **H** to **S's** house in armd. car + they will plan rescue there. **JM** + **F** agree – both will stay in cabinet room.

0825. **AC** briefed on armd. car's secure radio: '**ATs** still patrolling diplomatic compound. Sanguekku's black off-roader parked behind palace. No pigs (secret service agents) seen. **AC** says on radio: '**ATs** to guard road to Mr Rashid's house and to guard Mrs Rashid in her house.'

0830. Diane safe + packs case. **ATs** take her in their armd. car to barracks. **S** + **H** will go to palace in her pick-up truck to negotiate drivers' release. **AC** will observe from hidden armd. car with machine-gun cocked. **ATs** surrounding palace will observe + fire weapons when ordered. **S** + **H** to cell phone **AC** every 10 mins. If unable to speak, dialling tones will bring help. **H's** typing finished + **AC** safe-keeps his laptop.

Thus ended the first part of the prosecution's case two months after the above events. The testimonies made on oath by three of those involved, as well as Harry's log and a re-typed record of his laptop entries of relevance to the trial, all featured prominently. As did the written statements signed by four men, described as wearing brown balaclavas, shirts and slacks. They were exempted from appearing in court, for security reasons, and were referred to as **M1**, **M2**, **M3** and **M4** in the evidence now summarised below:

Seven armed men in matching black suits and shades, obviously secret service agents, emerged from the president palace's front portico and surrounded Diane Rashid's pick-up truck. One of them, described in the evidence as the gaoler, who died later that day, asked Suleiman: 'Why you come?'

'We want to speak to Mr Sanguekku. Mr Burke and I are UN officials . . .'

'You and him I see many days. Walk after me.'

Suleiman and Harry were led through the portico, down several steep steps, searched, their watches, wallets and cell phones confiscated, then locked in separate cells. The note describing directions to the possible site of his grandfather's grave, Mr Burke must have removed from his wallet. It would subsequently be found in his Red Cross rondavel.

'Welcome Suleiman al Rashid and Harry Burke!' Sanguekku's voice boomed from the ceiling of both cells.

'Why does Makimbo not release my agents and the policemen?' Sanguekku asked.

'*All* cabinet ministers must agree to release them, but some are overseas.' Harry heard Suleiman reply.

'So you, Mr Rashid, must drop *all* the UN's embezzlement charges. If you don't, you and Mr Burke will go to the interrogation room, where your drivers will greet you.'

'Blackmail!' Harry shouted.

'Whitemail, Mr Burke.' Sanguekku's mocking laughter faded into the distance.

The windowless cell was too narrow to turn round, so Suleiman sat on the stone floor, with his back against the door and a stinking bucket too near his feet. A key turned in the lock, his collar was grabbed and he was pulled out through the door; then dragged along a passage. His manhandling was brutal! Though nothing compared with what awaited him in the interrogation room. His driver, a broken corpse, blood seeping from it spreading across the floor. Suleiman thanked God for Tuwabo's so many years of loyal service and prayed for his widow and family. Harry's driver naked, unconscious, dumped in a corner, Harry kneeling beside him, yelling 'Water?' A masked man failed to stop Harry using a tap. Harry's cupped handfuls of water cleansed Speedy's wounds, his body still bleeding, his arms and legs limp. Groaning, he gulped down more handfuls. Suleiman heard Harry say: 'Don't move Speedy. Try to stay awake.'

The gaoler's and the second man's masks had two heads with bulging, yellow eyeballs and toothless grins; the same as, or similar to, the tolokosi masks Suleiman and Harry had seen, earlier that morning, all the rapists wearing in Kolokuana's main street.

'Mr Enemy Rashid is next,' Sanguekku boomed again. 'I will see you undress.'

'I'm not undressing!' Suleiman shouted back. 'Let me speak to the president?'

Sanguekku laughed. 'He is keeping many tokolosi very busy. I am president now!'

Both masked men tore off Suleiman's clothes and Harry tried to stop them. The gaoler slammed a fist into Harry's stomach and face twice, and also stamped on his back when he fell. Only to be kicked into helpless submission, then kicked across the floor and left for dead, beside Speedy. Both masked men threw Suleiman's naked body onto a hideous-looking rack in the middle of the room and the gaoler tied Suleiman down. The torturer wound a handle, stretching Suleiman's arms, legs and body ever closer to breaking point. Suddenly, the torturer slumped on Suleiman and the gaoler collapsed.

M2 and **M3** inspected their prey, before releasing Suleiman from the rack. Six soldiers stretchered him, Speedy and Harry out through a cellar door, returned to put the driver's, torturer's and gaoler's corpses into body-bags, then carried them through the same door.

Two ambulances, protected front and rear by armed soldiers in trucks, took the three casualties and three body-bags to the army barracks' medical centre. **M1**, **M2**, **M3** and **M4** searched the palace for Sangeukku, the British police adviser and others involved. Only four secret service agents were found. They were manacled, marched at gunpoint to an army truck and guarded by armed soldiers, while **M1**, **M2** and **M4** did a second search of the palace and **M3** installed bugging devices. **M3** also found that the two cells, in which Sulieman and Harry had been imprisoned, both had microphones protected by steel grills embedded in their ceilings. The doors of three cells had been bricked-up; the rest of the cellar's cells had been destroyed by the explosion at the palace earlier that morning.

M1, **M2**, **M3** and **M4** were driven in an army truck to the British high commissioner's residence and took over one of his garages. That truck and its armed soldiers returned to Kolokuana's army barracks. **M2** and **M3** bound and blindfolded the four captured secret agents and took them at gunpoint in the back of **M4's** requisitioned grey van to the army barracks' guardroom, where **M4** separately photographed and interrogated the captives.

M2 and **M3** returned to the palace in **M4's** van, but failed to gain entry to the three cells with bricked-up doorways. Inside the many cells destroyed by the explosion, earlier that day, they found no explosive devices, only broken and scattered corpses, which they photographed and subsequently gave this evidence, with the locations of the three cells with bricked-up doorways to the British police on their arrival, twelve days later. Before dusk, **M1** and **M4** searched the palace and surrounding area. No unexploded devices were found that day, but several were defused within the town centre later that week.

Post mortems helped to identify the torturer and gaoler, both secret service agents, who were cremated. Suleiman's driver's corpse was blessed by the Anglican bishop, before being most honourably buried in Kolokuana's public cemetery.

Two of the army's three larger helicopters had flown the soldiers wounded in the main street to a Mavimbi hospital. After Speedy, Suleiman and Harry had been checked at the barracks' medical centre and made as comfortable as possible, they and Diane were flown in a third Huey to the same hospital. There the three casualties were X-rayed, given essential treatment and sedated before that evening's overnight flight to Heathrow."

Thus ended the second part of the prosecution's case.

Diane phoned Belinda, but a recorded voice said ring back later. She checked the number with Harry. No luck, again. He knew his Oxford college's number off by heart and asked her to ring his cousin, Dermot Macausland, who said he would meet them at Heathrow.

Later that evening the casualties were re-checked and re-sedated, three stretchers and Diane were driven in ambulances to Mavimbi Airport, and there, an immigration official checked Diane's passport and also Suleiman's that she'd hidden within her person before leaving home. But the bossy African official refused to let the African casualty, Speedy, fly without a passport.

Suddenly, greatly to the official's and Diane's surprise, the re-sedated body on Harry's stretcher blurted out: 'I've got no passport! Speedy's flying with me!'

Redemption

That evening my 'Base' faxed the name and location of the London clinic where I should take the casualties in two ambulances that would arrive at Heathrow at 0430. Being near my London flat, I knew the privately owned clinic deserved its widely acclaimed medical and nursing reputation. I left Oxford shortly after midnight, to avoid being caught in the early morning traffic, drove to Heathrow and collected the buff envelope my 'Base' had told me would be at Terminal 3's information desk. Inside the envelope, addressed to D. Macausland, the enclosed faxed note read: 'Hope you get this in time! Am praying that all three casualties get there alive. Very, very, best wishes to every one. Jinky at UN HQ.'

My faxed reply: 'All arrived at 0500, heavily sedated. Suleiman in bad shape. His wife flew with him. They left in first ambulance. Speedy also in bad shape; Harry not too bad; we were in second ambulance. Arrived at clinic 0525. Staff totally on ball! So grateful for all kindnesses. Your very best wishes reciprocated. Dermot Macausland.' In such a rush, I had to go back and thank the clinic's receptionist for the use of her fax machine, before anxiously waiting outside X-ray booths and then in a corridor near the operating theatres.

By six o'clock the casualties were in the clinic's recovery ward. Speedy noisily awake, all four of his plastered limbs strung up on taut wires, suspended from hooks above his bed. Suleiman re-sedated, his wrists and ankles encased in plaster. Harry dozy, his neck in a brace. The nurse monitoring his low pulse rate sympathetically informed him: 'Your ruptured spleen has been repaired, all your broken ribs will repair themselves.' Diane was spooning porridge into Speedy's ever-open mouth. Everyone, bar Suleiman and Speedy, then huddled round the ward's TV set, more than anxious to know what was happening in Kolokuana and elsewhere in the country. Part way through the seven o'clock BBC News, Jenkins Makimbo's face, looking very grim and drawn, appeared on the screen. Peeved at not being able to see the screen,

Speedy yelled: 'Can't hear!' Diane turned up the volume and swiftly confirmed that her husband was still unconsciously sleeping off his injuries.

'You described last evening, minister, the tragic bloodshed, raping and looting in your capital. Has the army restored stability?' the interviewer asked Jenkins Makimbo.

'Uneasy stability. The army has commendably enforced the state of emergency, which the cabinet declared yesterday. But our government and our nation cannot rest until every guilty criminal is behind bars. Regrettably, most of them are still at large, but the army is confident its extensive search will quickly succeed.'

'You said earlier this morning that three seriously injured UN employees have been flown to a hospital in Mavimbi and then overseas. Are you able to say, where, overseas?'

'All I can say is, less than an hour ago we heard with great relief that they survived the flights and are receiving excellent treatment. We wish them a full and speedy recovery.'

Speedy managed to produce a cheer. 'Did you hear that minister mention my name?' Harry groaned and Diane came out with an overdose of her impeccable 'Strine: 'Good on yer cobber! You're as famous as the koala that bit off a Pommie backpacker's wotsit.'A nursing sister was *not* amused, *nor* by Speedy's response: 'What's a wotsit?' She checked the wires above his bed and found they needed tightening – ever so slightly.

'Thanks, Dermot, for laying on those ambulances,' Diane said in more understandable English. 'Any contact with Belinda yet?'

'One of her friends thinks she's selling dresses, somewhere in Europe,' I replied. 'Her mobile-phone goes wherever she goes, but may have become accidentally switched off.'

While a ward assistant served cups of tea Belinda rushed in, tearfully brimming with concern and affectionate sympathy all round, profusely apologetic for being delayed by work commitments in Paris, a newspaper tucked in the front of her raincoat. A friend had phoned the fashion display receptionist who'd told Belinda to get to this clinic as rapidly as possible. Diane outlined, over a couple of calming cups of tea, the main events of the past twenty-four hours, over-embellished by Speedy's and Harry's descriptions of all the pain they'd suffered and were still suffering. Belinda's attention seemed so distracted by Suleiman's unflinching unconsciousness that she neglected her husband and chose to sit by the inert body's bed. Now upgraded to "walking wounded" Harry took his wife to the privacy of the patient's lounge. Belinda never kissed him in public! But, instead of letting him show his affection, she removed the newspaper from inside her raincoat and showed him an article, blaming Suleiman and himself for helping soldiers kill so many women and children who tried to save the lives of all the policemen hit by so many army bullets in Kolokuana's main street.

'Lying bullshit!' Belinda's hand stopped him further offending several cocked ears.

'I knew it was darling.' She gave him a *really* big kiss, right there, in public, ignoring the nurse who wanted to check his pulse rate. He asked to see his grandchildren. She said they and their parents were spending Christmas and New Year with *her* parents in Miami.

A British broadsheet carried the government's response, written by Sonny Floors. He refuted the accusations as scurrilous untruths – also praised Mr Suleiman al Rashid's and Mr Harry Burke's many achievements. "Both are highly rated UN officials who, with Mr Morebo Takeshi, have earned the gratitude of the nation they have very bravely served."

With his fame growing daily, Speedy wished to be known as "Sir" Morebo Takeshi in future. His constant laughter became a tonic for everybody around him, including young nurses who more than frequently caught his attention and vice versa.

'Laughing might detach the drip from your nose,' the sister kept on reminding Speedy, fruitlessly. He'd always had the broadest smile and loudest laugh in Kolokuana, now his irrepressible mirth filled the room. His joking kept Suleiman going and lifted spirits that might otherwise have sunk to the depths of despond. Whenever his duties as a recently conferred barrister allowed, Tsabo brought presents for the three casualties, Diane and Belinda, himself and me, to give to the clinic's professionally diligent staff. With my wife still *homosapiens*-ing in East Africa and having spent two weeks in our London flat, I returned to Oxford tutoring, but kept in close touch with the situation in Kolokuana, the army commander, trusted cabinet ministers and officials, and several undisclosable others.

After another week of expert treatment and observation Harry was discharged from the clinic. Belinda drove him and Diane to the Cotswolds, but Diane hadn't wanted to leave Suleiman and Speedy, yet she badly needed a respite break! Although her encouragement had never flagged, she'd borne too much of the brunt of extracting the casualties from the claws of near-certain death, and once she'd achieved this, insisted with candid resolve that their clinical and nursing care had been, and remained, second-to-none!

` Over coffee at a motorway service station, Diane said her husband must have a career-change, when he'd fully recovered. Belinda sympathised and said her husband would not be returning to Africa. Christmas in Cape Town could wait! Harry had to sit and listen.

Punter Bryant's letter awaited his cheerless homecoming – cheerless because as much as he loved being home, he'd also hated leaving Suleiman and Speedy who'd been such loyal friends for almost two years. Punter wished the three "invalids" (his word) a full and swift recovery. His *mixed* news very soon found its way into, what Harry had been forced to accept, would be (might be) his final African diary. Punter had this to say:

'Restoring stability to Kolokuana – and to those parts of both provinces inflamed by recent events – will take greatly more than soldiers, however well-trained and competent. People looked to the government for disaster protection but what they mostly saw, before Jenkins grasped the reins, were squabbling cabinet ministers and parliamentarians; scores of bent chiefs and their cronies; widespread corruption, underhand rewards, greedy perks, bloody scams and an almost total absence of sound leadership – all set against opaque or non-existent accountability. We, Harry, favoured a bottom-up approach. Ronald Reagan had considered the eleven most terrifying words in the English language were: "I am from the government and I am here to help." Jenkins has started ironing out some of the wrinkles top-down. Both local political parties unanimously elected him, a non-party independent, to lead their nation to political, economic and social stability. Then to prosperity? Your forecast would likely be much less cloudy than mine and let's hope justifiably so.'

'Sonny has drafted a bill, that parliament enacted, appointing Jenkins as the country's first prime minister, with a firm mandate to eliminate bureaucracy and corruption, while introducing accountability and improving efficiency. But, under pressure from the chiefs, parliament added a rider – 'Traditional laws and tribal customs must be preserved.' The cabinet has been reduced from eighteen to six: Jenkins and Uncle Bill, both Obangwato Catholics; three Kasodi Anglicans from the northern tribe; and Sonny who, like me, has non-conformist tendencies. I trust you're well enough to cope with this updating stuff!'

'The prime minister will also oversee the army and police rejuvenation. The foreign minister was a successful UN diplomat. The education, employment and welfare minister had distinguished herself as a civil rights campaigner. Kolokuana University's professor of criminal law will head up a re-vamped and re-staffed justice ministry. Two more new ministries are in being – Uncle Bill's combines water and sanitation, health and nutrition, agriculture, food security and transport – Sonny's combines finance and across-the-board, long-term planning. The cabinet will frame policy. The nation's elected representatives will approve it. Provincial governors will direct it, district administrators will implement policy. Every chief and community headman will attend quarterly "Palavers", chaired by district administrators, who will decide who else to invite – a carbon copy of the set-up Uncle Bill and you installed in all six southern districts. Jenkins then went *bottom-up!* He has directed all district administrators and principal chiefs to join provincial governors and cabinet ministers at half-yearly progress meetings held, turn-and-turn-about within a northern or a southern district. Jenkins will chair these meetings.'

'One of the cabinet members you are unlikely to know is the foreign minister who, if the local press is anything to go by, had to be dragged kicking and screaming from his plush UN office in Geneva. He's a skilful aid negotiator, I'm reliably told. We all live in hope! The other is the education, employment and welfare minister who defeated the so-called "Shredder" at last October's general election. Lawrence Kwawenda has succeeded Sonny Floors as the government's chief secretary, now re-titled the cabinet secretary, also with responsibility for drastically reducing and reforming the over-bloated civil service, as well as hastening the devolution of good governance to and within every district of the northern and southern provinces. The justice minister's post is unfilled – a retired British judge its temporary overseer, until the university professor can take over the post. If all that pleases you, not so by what I'll now impart.'

'The explosion in the president's palace was followed, soon after you left, by four in the town centre, *without* loss of life! The secret service, now a hunted rump, has recruited gangs of scare-mongering teenagers to spread havoc and creep round in the dark nailing tokolosi-dolls to people's doors, especially elderly and infirm people, ignoring the dusk-to-dawn curfew imposed by inadequately few soldiers. Several shops have re-opened, but Berney's Bazaar is nothing more than a burnt-out shell. In trying to restore stability, the army has a monumental task that must continue until Sanguekku, his sidekicks, renegade policemen and so forth, are apprehended. Rewards to their capturers have been offered.'

'What's the form health-wise? So many strangers, as well as your numerous friends, remain very anxious to know this. And how are Suleiman and Speedy? Regards, Punter.'

Harry replied: 'Thanks a hundred-fold for such a newsy letter – a heartening keepsake!

All the government innovations you mentioned cheered me up. Although I'm wondering whether the diamond mining embargo will .be lifted, in order to fund the raising of living standards, pay off the country's crippling foreign debt and assure a more disaster-free and prosperous future. Suleiman and Speedy are recovering steadily. Having left the clinic, they expect to leave a rehabilitation centre just before Christmas. I go for the prescribed, lengthening, daily walk and Belinda drives me to the local hospital once a week. Pass on my bestest wishes to Jenkins, Sonny, Uncle Bill, Jack, etc., and thank Brigadier-General Thaklomo for all he and his soldiers did to rescue the 'three invalids' as you pertinently described us. Keep punting – you'll win a million yet! Your efforts to keep me briefed are very much appreciated and valued. Please keep the news, good or bad, flowing. Very best wishes, Harry.'

Harry raised his wine glass. 'Happy Christmas and a Healthier New Year,' a toast echoed by everyone. Replete after Belinda's bumper, all-in dinner, they sang "Auld Lang Syne" and pulled crackers – Speedy and Suleiman needed help to pull theirs! Then, in colourful paper-hats and well wrapped up, they set off in freezing drizzle to the nearest pub – Harry pushing Suleiman in a wheelchair; followed by Diane and Belinda pushing Speedy. Gathered round a blazing log fire, they joined in with the other customers' carol singing that could have done with just a meagre smattering of Madam Thelma's rasping contralto to offset the surfeit of Harry's over-dominant tenor contributions.

On Boxing Day morning Suleiman dictated a letter to Jinky, tactfully addressed to her New York home, which Belinda typed on her laptop – Harry's was still in Kolokuana!

'Our profound gratitude,' Suleiman began, 'for getting us so rapidly to London and booking three poor old and young souls into such an excellent clinic. I have informed our superiors that I have accepted the chairmanship of a London-based think-tank, which is researching the pros and cons of foreign aid to least-developed countries and other important topics, such as how least developed countries can better look after themselves. African and expatriate colleagues, too many to name, would certainly join with me in expressing our indebtedness to you, especially for your prompt professional advice and assistance, always so readily given. Harry has also tendered his resignation – reluctantly it must be said. His work is done, and done exceptionally ably. We both, together with Speedy and my wife, Diane, send you our belated thanks and very best wishes.'

Meanwhile, Harry's cousin Dermot had driven his wife, Wendy, plus Tsabo and Jill, from Oxford to savour Belinda's curry lunch – sambals and a lot more else. Leaving the women to natter, the men saw out the afternoon leisurely patrolling a few Cotswold lanes. Suleiman and Speedy both comfortably ensconced in wheelchairs, Dermot and Tsabo propelled them, with Harry navigating. The exercise would prove sufficiently exhausting to warrant some pre-supper beer, but before long Dermot steered Harry outside the pub.

'Tomorrow, I'm off to Kolokuana University on a six-month sabbatical. Will you lend me your remaining diaries?'

'There's only my final diary! I left my log of the two last days' events with the army commander . . . You'd be *crazy* to go there, Dermot. Brutality is likely to re-start very soon.'

'Their professor of criminal law's now the minister of justice. I'm her stand-in.'

'And I'm *speechless!* Does Wendy know how risky it's likely to be? Is she going with you? . . . Bloody hell, I can't get my head round all this.'

'Wendy's supervising archaeological-digs in Crete throughout next year. She's happy for me, repeating what she said, to do my thing while she does hers; our modus operandi.'

'Belinda wasn't happy while I was in Africa, with justification as it turned out.'

'There are reasons, which I cannot disclose, why your diaries were and remain vitally important, over and above their value to me, in terms of writing a book. Yet, there were times, when I couldn't forgive myself for being involved in sending you to that country. And heaven knows how I felt when learning of your recent, terrifying ordeal. Those same reasons now apply in my case, but I'm confident the protection promised will materialise and suffice.' Saying more would jeopardise my security cover.

After supper Wendy drove back to Oxford, dropped Tsabo and Jill at their flat, then returned to our London flat. Before turning in, I re-read Harry's final diary and a copy of Punter Bryant's letter, faxed them to 'Base' and next morning received an encoded reply.

'An armed shadow will meet you at Mavimbi Airport. Means of reaching Kolokuana unknown as yet. Your codename, Hornpipe. Your shadow, Bullway, 24, 6ft, slim, closely cropped brown hair, fresh-faced, maroon shirt, slacks and trainers. Destroy after reading.'

Harry's letter to Dr Solomon Khami described where he'd hidden the note about his grandfather's grave and asked him to send it with his belongings. A month later, a metal-bound crate came containing his clothes, bedding, a few bits of crockery and cutlery, his locked briefcase complete with his passport, cheque book, fountain pen, all his pipes, Belinda's latest letters and key documents. Solomon had also sent the rondavel's fully paid-up rent receipt; kindness personified and thoughtfulness so very typical of him! Like that fateful evening, with casualties pouring into the barracks' medical centre, Solomon had found time to apologise for missing the new UN club's first committee meeting, with his car burning outside The Hub!! To cap it all, he rang to ask if the crate had arrived, to save Harry having to ring him. 'I've returned to the cabinet,' he said, now as Uncle Bill's deputy, looking after health, nutrition and food security. Jenkins Makimbo makes a fine prime minister. Koklokuana's hospital has been cleaned and its re-trained staff strive to shake off its death-house image. Worryingly, Sanguekku and most of his evil parasites remain at large and, tragically, there's been more looting, arson, rapings and funerals in the capital. So many of us want you to come back and help. But please stay at home!'

Harry congratulated him on his re-promotion to the cabinet, thanked him for sending the crate so promptly and for his letter, bade farewell, replaced the receiver and wept . . .

He went for a walk, sat on a stile, smoking an indoors-banned pipe – yet still couldn't free himself from that interrogation room scene. That driver's corpse, its blood spreading across the floor. Speedy lying helplessly in a corner, limply fighting for his life, bleeding from cruel wounds, those handfuls of water. Suleiman stretched on that rack withstanding terrible pain, inflicted by two merciless brutes in hideous tokolosi masks. The two silent gunshots, then that immigration official's refusal to let Speedy fly without a passport.

Next day there were more reminders, when a policeman came to record Harry' sworn statement describing the palace-cellar incidents. Suleiman and Speedy had made theirs.

Belinda sold all the dresses she'd designed, which her team of seamstresses had produced, at lucrative fashion shows. She did most of the household chores, all the shopping, and gave her husand 'a cute little number' – she still spoke American – the book's title: "How To Find Your Way Round Your Home."

Harry re-joined the back row of the local choral society. He'd visit his grandchildren and reclaim his seat on his eminent old school's equally eminent governing body as soon as possible. He electrically mowed and cut the lawn-edges dead straight; manually lined-up cutlery and wheeled the rubbish bin to the road on Fridays. But no weeding, loading or unloading the dishwasher, window-cleaning or room-decorating. Too much bending and using ladders were forbidden, though she allowed 'my hero' to follow her upstairs to bed. He didn't deserve to be called that! But telling her risked expulsion to an attic single bed.

Footholds

Before leaving Oxford I re-read Harry's final diary, the copy of Punter Bryant's letter and memorised the encoded note my 'Base' had sent me, and before burning it, repeated: 'An armed shadow will meet you at Mavimbi's airport. Means of reaching Kolokuana as yet unknown. Your code name, Hornpipe. Your armed shadow, Bullway, 24, six feet, slim, closely cropped brown hair, fresh-faced, maroon shirt, slacks and trainers.' While waiting at Heathrow and then airborne, I did more revision.

Back in early December, after the sickening brutality erupted in Kolokuana, my 'Base' had gathered in members of our 'Circle.' Some of us had been monitoring circumstances within the country and particularly in the capital for several years. Primarily, because the foreseeable illegal mining of that country's rich diamond deposits could very well result in subversive elements seizing the mine and trading diamonds for weapons, or whatever. The likelihood of this occuring significantly increased three years ago, with Sanguekku's appointment as the government's secret service director, despite warnings that he'd been a diamonds-for-weapons kingpin in a central Africa.

Last year, with drought crippling the southern province, it became essential to reopen the mine near its eastern border, which had been closed and guarded for almost a century. The sustained efforts of Suleiman, the then UN chief of mission, to get a mining embargo lifted had failed. So, the country's diamonds couldn't be sold, to help fund humanitarian assistance or help to reduce the government's colossal budget deficit. White mercenaries, engaged by Mavimbi's government, made several defeated attempts to seize the mine.

Later in the year, Suleiman and the British police adviser had thwarted an Afrikaner-extremists' plot to re-open the mine and sell its diamonds for urgently needed money to help stop Mandela becoming South Africa's president. With his highly probable election only three months away, the extremists were unlikely to try again.

Mboko had already taken it upon himself to ask a London-based company to reopen the mine and pay some of the country's debts. Some six months ago, the country's army commander ordered the company's employee, Mkwere, who'd managed the mine since its re-opening, to stop work, lay off his staff and more soldiers guarded the mine.

Soon afterwards, a defector from the Amboini gang confessed to using the president's name, Amboini, to bolster drug sales. The president hadn't been seen in public since his installation, four years ago, alledgedly because of continual poor health. In fact, as the defector disclosed, the president had been imprisoned in the palace and tortured. The defector also disclosed that the British police adviser, Mr Trimble, had been Sanguekku's adviser since the secret service director's arrival three years ago and all that time Trimble had been posing as a 'Circle' informant, feeding us and unsuspecting others duff leads.

Last November, Mboko fled to London and pleaded to be placed in house arrest. He had admitted to owning brothels, but denied being party to a palace-plot to seize the mine, nor knew where Kolokuana's many most-wanteds were hiding. He thought the president who had kept him under constant pressure to fund the palace's extravagances might have died. Neither Mboko nor any other cabinet minister had spoken to the president for two years.

On 5th December, British special forces, propitiously training in that country's central highlands, were placed at immediate readiness to help restore law and order in the former crown colony – also to assist local soldiers with protecting the mine and mined diamonds.

On 6th December, a four-man special forces team covertly moved to Kolokuana and next day helped rescue hostages held in the president's palace. Later that day, my 'Base' had received a faxed report stating that one hostage had been murdered. Suleiman, Harry and his driver, Speedy, had been gravely injured and were about to be flown to Heathrow.

I had been involved in sending Harry there, and would never be able shrug off partial responsibility for everything he'd suffered and was still suffering. To say that I'd prayed a lot might have been misconstrued as a selfish attempt to ease my guilty conscience.

The army commander had co-ordinated the hostage rescue operation and had assured us that only thoroughly vetted local officers and soldiers of proven reliability had worked with M1, M2, M3 and M4 – the codenames he'd given the special forces team members.

Subversion within the capital, principally involving secret service agents on the run, sacked policemen and unemployed youths, continued to stretch the army commander's limited resources to near breaking point. Soldiers had to enforce the daily dusk-to-dawn curfew in the town's centre and its sprawling suburbs – as well as search for, capture and question dissidents, with precious few trustworthy police to help them. The situation soon deteriorated to such an extent that a twenty-hour curfew had restricted access to banks, markets and communal water pumps to four hours per day. No shops were open or public services functioned. Cabinet ministers and key officials, sleeping in their offices, also had to be guarded round-the-clock. With military resources stretched even tauter, all foreign nationals living in or near Kolokuana were evacuated by car or bus to Mavimbi and the cabinet requested additional British assistance.

On 16th December, two civilian helicopters flew six more special forces teams from their central highland's training area to the mine, close to the country's eastern border.

By 20th December, sufficient detectives from London were covertly active in the town centre and an increasing number of armed, uniformed British police officers patrolled its streets.

Local soldiers redeployed to the suburbs, where youths were still terrorising residents by nailing grotesque tokolosi dolls to doors, setting them alight and burning down homes. They wore tokolosi masks to further terrify their victims into supporting anti-government, anti-army protests while brutal violence and mindless atrocities continued unabated.

Reports from the special forces teams, deployed along the country's eastern border, indicated that armed white men in camouflage kit, thought to be foreign mercenaries, had been spotted approaching the mine. The neighbouring country's government had refused to embroil its soldiers, but would permit an area twenty miles deep by fifty miles wide on its side of the border to be swept only by Kolokuana's best trained and disciplined troops.

A liaison officer arrived at the army barracks there, his map showing the area to be swept, and would keep his headquarters in Mavimbi briefed on progress or problems.

With the arrow on the cabin-screen's map still above France, a glass of water helped me swallow a sleeping pill – when woken while approaching Mavimbi, I'd missed breakfast, dammit! Another reminder: 'Your code name, Hornpipe, the armed shadow's code name, Bullway, twenty-four, six feet tall, slim, fresh-faced, closely cropped brown hair, maroon shirt, slacks and trainers.'

While easing a luggage trolley through the crowd I'd bought a pizza-look-alike and was about to taste it when, suddenly, a voice behind me muttered: 'Hornpipe?' Having, verified what the voice looked like, I replied: 'Bullway.' He enjoyed half my pizza before buying a couple of coffees.

'No civilian flights to and from Kolokuana since the trouble started three weeks ago,' he confirmed. 'Nobody wants to go there, but loads of murdering bastards want to get out, pronto! Now no military aircraft can land at this airport. Right, let's get moving.'

With my cases locked in a taxi's boot and my briefcase between us on the back seat, without asking where to go, the African driver sped off and joined a main road signposted "To the South" which threw me. Kolokuana was to the west! In twenty minutes we'd left the city, with a mangrove-fringed ocean on our left, forests stretching up towards hills on our right, overloaded lorries and buses foot-down in the opposite direction to Mavimbi's shops, offices, factories, dockyard or wherever.

'Is your radio still on broadcast?' Bullway asked the driver.

The driver nodded. 'You can record his reply . . . Acorn to Pulpit. How do you hear me, over.'. . 'Okay, over.'. . 'ETA four-zero minutes, same place, over.'. . 'Roger, out.'

Bullway laughed. 'Even a chimpanzee could copy roger out! No jokes, please.'

Ten minutes later, Acorn turned off the main road onto a much narrower one, passed maize fields, climbed a seemingly endless zigzagging track to a forest clearing, parked under some trees, unloaded my cases and gave the taxi's keys to a man who drove back down the track.

'Who was that man,' I asked and Bullway pointed to four more among the trees.

'They're all Mavimbi's British embassy hoods who've guarded this landing site.'

A distant hum rapidly grew louder and soon a helicopter landed in the forest clearing. Bullway checked his watch. 'Bang on time. Me and Acorn will carry your cases. Follow us.' We ran to the helicopter, ducked under its whirling rotor blades, I scrambled aboard with my briefcase, and Bullway shoved the cases inside. With Acorn in front beside the fellow-African pilot and Bullway beside me on the back seats, in less than one minute the helicopter was airborne. Buckling my seat belt and getting my head into a helmet I found far easier than working the intercom, but with Bullway's help, I could hear him. 'You've got about two hours to swot up what came yesterday.' He delved into his sweater and handed me an envelope. When opened, I expected to read: 'Eat before dying.' With one eye on the storm clouds ahead, the other decoded a torrent of need-to-knows.

'Base to Hornpipe. 4-man special forces team flown into Kolokuana night 6-7 Dec. All British nationals, marksmen and parachutists. Specialisms stated below. Playfare married, 3 children. Remainder single. Team notifies casualties soonest. Base contacts next-of-kin. Team in one of British high commissioner's garages. Security guards patrol compound's perimeter. You eat and sleep in high commissioner's residence. Report your arrival.'

'Playfare, 34, 5ft 10ins, burly, short fair hair, scarred forehead. Team leader. Ordnance warrant officer. Defused bomb in president's palace cellar 7 Dec. Seven more improvised explosive devices (IEDs) defused that week in town centre, three more since in suburbs.'

'Draper, 28, 6ft 3ins, well-built, black curly hair, parents Fijian. Team medic. Artillery sergeant. Neutralised torturer in palace cellar 7 Dec. Organised casualty evacuation.'

'Bullway. Description already stated. Team electronics. Infantry corporal. Neutralised gaoler in cellar 7 Dec. Installed bugging devices in palace same day, elsewhere later.'

'Gilby, 23, 6ft, slim, long fair hair. Team linguist. Durham Univ & Sandhurst. Cavalry subaltern. Father British, mother Afrikaner, farmed in South Africa, now in Mozambique.

'Richard Riddington, 52, 6ft, thin, greying hair. British high commissioner. Refused to leave with his office staff. Told he must stay in the residence's secure compound.

'Brig-Gen Moses Thaklomo, 46, 6ft 7ins, heavily built. UK-trained, army commander. Current emergency postponed his London Royal Defence Studies College attendance.

'Mkwere, 37, 5ft 9ins, stocky, black curly hair. Born East Africa, now British national, employee London-based company & diamond mine manager.

'Serenity Sanguekku, 43, 6ft 2ins, shaven head. Angolan. Lisbon Univ. Then priest in Angola. Cuba-trained, post-colonial subversion agent & diamonds-for-weapons kingpin.'

'Reg Trimble, 64, 5ft 10ins, greying hair, retired UK chief constable, country's police adviser, proven turncoat informer, Sanguekku's adviser, philanderer young African females.'

With the storm clouds skirted, the sky was clear and visibility good. Mountains to the south, many buildings way below us. 'That's the town nearest the border,' Bullway said. I borrowed his map. It's the town where an Afrikaner extremist's dog mauled Harry's leg and he ended up in the local hospital having a *risky* blood transfusion. One of his diaries had described the fight in a café owned by Mkwere, before its seizure by the local police.

Under an hour later the pilot informed the back-seaters on his intercom: 'Five minutes to touch down.' Acorn followed this up with: 'Hope to meet up with you both again. How about coming for a beer in the officers' mess with both of us this evening?'

'Sorry, we'll come some other time.' Bullway's reaction was far swifter than mine.

We landed in Kolokuana, beside a river, unloaded my cases and Bullway helped lug them up a path towards a palatial residence. 'That's Mr Riddington's shack,' I was told.

A security guard checked my ID card, before unlocking the gate in a fence reinforced with barbed-wire. At the top of the path Bullway said: 'This idle bastard's Draper.'

Draper nodded and grinned, made light work of carrying my two heaviest cases to the residence, through its back door and up to a third-floor bedroom. I carried the lightest one and also my locked briefcase now containing the encoded notes I'd read while airborne. On the way down, my briefcase and I bumped into Richard Riddington, who hurriedly welcomed me, glanced at his watch, said we're late for the daily briefing, marched me out to one of his garages and inside we sat side-by-side on a camp bed. Draper relaxed on another, a sergeant content to let a corporal take charge – in British special forces' teams expertise and experience counted more than army seniority.

'It's strictly code names from now on,' Bullway announced. 'Mr Riddington, you're Congo. Mr Burke's, Hornpipe. Secret service agents, Fancies. This country's soldiers, Jacksons.'

'Congo is too *un*-complimentary. May I be something else?' Richard asked.

'Orders are orders!' Bullway spread out a large-scale map on our bed. 'Just after 0100 two nights ago, me and Draper spotted three Fancies entering a Red Cross orphanage hut. Here!' He pointed to some long huts just to the south of Kolokuana, ringed on his map.

'We know they're after hostages. We nobbled two, the third fled in an un-registered car we'd been tracking and tried to flatten us. We flattened two of his tyres and he headed back towards the town-centre, swerving with loads of sparks. We radioed some Jacksons, described the car and they said they'll watch out for it. So, we start again tonight, with very little help from the local police. They're mostly in clink or effing Fancies still on the run. The UK rozzers and sleuths in the town centre said they're too busy, but will back us up shortly, whatever that means.'

'Aren't there four in your team, to share the load? Where are the others? I asked.

'Not far away.' Bullway's reply earned Draper's grin and nod of approval.

'The two we nobbled the other night,' Bullway resumed, 'are shackled to their bedsprings in separate cells below the army barracks' guardroom. Gilby will have a few kind African words with them tonight. Playfare wants to collate intelligence and plan ahead at midday every Sunday. Okay, that's the lot for today. See you both tomorrow, same time.'

I imagined Playfare, the bomb-defusing team leader, looked cool and ruggéd, whereas Gilby, the long-haired cavalry linguist, was probably laid back, yet equally on the ball.

With no questions to answer, Bullway asked: 'Any grub going?' Congo hurried off, presumably to find his cook. Perhaps he would slow down when Trimble, the police adviser, was nabbed. Admiring Trimble's professed efforts to arrest Sanguekku, Congo had refused to sack the suspected, later confirmed, turncoat. A decision he still profoundly regretted, hopefully.

Back in my bedroom, after transmitting 'Hornpipe to Base. Foothold,' I re-mugged up the need-to-knows, incompletely mugged up in the helicopter, then burnt the lot.

I was shaving when Richard – I balked at calling him Congo – hurried in, sniffed and asked if I was a smoker. 'I had to burn some paper.' He checked if I needed anything. An uninterrupted rest, I was tempted to say, but he had to make do with a weary headshake.

'Should you need anything,' he persisted, 'press that button beside the bed and a bell in the basement will summon my butler. Press the next one and my cook will come up.'

'How do you rate the risk of your staff blabbing about the armed men here?' I asked.

'The reliability of my butler, housekeeper, cook, chauffeur and the rest of my staff is unquestionable! My housekeeper, three maids and a gardener are cleaning the president's palace. That will take *months* to complete!'

There was an unexpected note of humour in Richard's harassed tone of voice. Without another word, he hurried away – maybe to re-assess his trusted staff's reliability.

If the security situation permitted, Kolokuana University's Easter term would start in a month's time. Until then, I was available for other duties, which suited me. As I gathered later that afternoon, it also suited ebullient Bullway and grinning, nodding Draper.

An elderly, bearded Indian in a red turban and white frock coat buttoned upto the neck trotted into my bedroom. 'I am Amar Singh, sir, his excellency's butler. I am giving very good service to many British high commissioners in many sundry places. His excellency is greatly welcoming you to an aperitif, at seven-thirty p.m. I shall serve dinner, at eight p.m. May you kindly indicate the pyjamas you are sleeping in tonight and also the clothes you are wearing in the morning. I am wanting to take them down many stairs to press them and to return them all to you in a jiffy, very shipshape. I am also wanting to polish your shoes. May I please remove them from your feet, sir?'

I removed a dirty pair of black brogues. Having run my en-suite bath, Mr Singh trotted off with a dark green bush shirt, matching shorts and the brogues – but not my pyjammas.

Had I asked Ron Simpson, my exemplary and long-serving college scout, to press my pyjamas it would have caused quite a stir down in the back-quad's shoe-cleaning room.

There was enough water to sit in, though the cup of tea left on a shelf above the bath went down well. I was glad I didn't ask what to wear for dinner, because the butler would have surely said black tie! Such regalia had been farthest from my mind while packing in Oxford. I'd filled one case with documents which might be needed while teaching law, another with suits and academic apparel, a third with scruff-order stuff which was now stacked on the table. My dressing gown had been hung behind the bathroom door and my highly polished shoes the butler had already brought back and were under the table. After so much travelling the bed looked inviting! I'd press the bell button to summon the butler and ask him to convey my apologies to his excellency for missing dinner, but all I'd eaten that day were Bullway's pizza -leftovers. No alternative, I must put on a suit.

The butler trotted in with four candles, put a matchbox beside them on the mantelpiece and hung my immaculately pressed green bush shirt and shorts on hangers to air by the open window. 'For many weeks those electricity-buggers are not working,' he said. 'I am wanting you, sir, to carry a lit candle when you are descending two very steep staircases and also to push the cook's button, when you are wanting her to bring very nice cakes from the kitchen.' I assumed he meant her push-button near my bed.

At seven-thirty, I was sipping an iced aperitif in a grey pullover and matching slacks. Richard wore a maroon velvet jacket, white shirt and Etonian black and white striped tie.

'Are you any good at collecting chicken eggs and growing vegetables?' he asked.

'I did a fair bit of both as a young Ulster lad. Why?'

'No shops are open, the border's closed and nothing's coming from Mavimbi.'

The butler banged a gong, announced 'Dinner is served' and holding a lit candle too near his turban, preceded us from Richard's study, through swinging double doors, along a narrow passage to a spacious kitchen. The smiling and rotund African cook, slaving over a single-ring paraffin stove, transfered the contents of her frying pan onto a silver salver, which the butler accurately positioned in the centre of a scrubbed wooden table, adorned with silver cutlery, two starched napkins neatly folded to resemble a pagoda and two ornately carved wine glasses. An ancient-looking mahogany chair stood at each end.

Richard sniffed the delicacy. 'What's this Matilda?'

'The same as always, sir. Fried eggs and vegetables.'

'Curried fried eggs and assorted vegetables on Saturday evenings,' the butler corrected her. 'May his excellency care to taste the Chablis I am bringing five minutes before from the watertank most nicely hidden down in the nearly empty and very cold wine cellar.'

Richard complied. 'Excellent! Just half a glass for me. Then pour some for . . . What shall I call you? Doctor Macausland sounds somewhat out-of-place, very much like these two heavy, Victorian, chairs the butler pushed from the dining room. This residence was built during her reign. The reception chamber has many excellent, period-memorabilia.'

'Call me Dermot,' I suggested with a mouthful of the cook's excellent fritter. After the meal and just one glass of Chablis, I excused myself and hastened to bed.

I was woken at nine o'clock next morning when the cook brought an un-curried boiled egg and mug of coffee. She secretively let slip that the butler drank the rest of the wine.

At the team's Sunday get-together, Gilby's laid-back posture measured up to my expectations, but he almost certainly had deadly quick-on-the-draw reactions. Apart from his forehead scar, Playfare looked calm rather than ruggéd. A convincingly top man!

Then he and Gilby were summoned by radio – two suspected IEDs in the town centre! Gilby was Playfare's Number Two. In layman's English, an unexploded bomb searcher and go-fetcher.

Bullway outlined that night's anti-hostage-taking, secret-service-snatch plan involving Draper, himself and four hand-picked Jacksons. 'Local armed soldiers,' he reminded me and opened a map. 'Now the security situation near the diamond mine. Friendly force's operating areas are ringed in blue. Ringed in red are the last known locations of around forty armed white mercenaries. Two SAS teams are in ambush positions a mile beyond the border and on both sides of the only motorable road between the mine and the nearest town across the border. The neighbouring country's scrubland nearer the mine is being swept by three of our teams. A battalion of Jacksons still guards the mine. More infantry, combat support and logistic reinforcements were sent there a month ago.' This was the first time since I arrived that special forces, a collective and often more secure title, were referred to as SAS, Special Air Service, of which Bullway was a justiably proud member.

Next morning Playfare, the team's leader, asked Gilby to tell Congo and Hornpipe – alias Richard and me – what the interrogated secret service agents had said.

'The first one, a cowed, slimy specimen, would only give his name and age, his wife's name and age, but not where she lives. He was shown snapshots of several of his secret service colleagues and one of Sanguekku and Trimble together. He said in Portugese he'd never seen any of them before, and when captured, he was taking food to hungry orphans. The second agent spoke good English and was keen to co-operate. Genuinely keen, I had no reason to doubt. He gave me the addresses of three young women and had often driven Trimble to visit them. All three live in the town-centre and are probably shop-girls.'

'Sounds like he's the kinda guy who came out of a woman and now wants to get back into some much younger ones,' Bullway chirped.

Draper nodded and grinned, I try not to, Playfare pretended to cough.

'Lucky Trimble,' Gilby chuckled. 'When I asked the agent to help find Sanguekku, he said many days he also drove Sanguekku who lived in a hut near the Catholic Cathedral. I've also been told that he used to be the organist there, until he played with a choirby.'

The laughter almost brought the garage roof down. Wiping his eyes, Playfare got us back on track. 'We know Sanguekku was a Catholic priest in Angola, maybe he'd twisted one of the Cathedral's staff's arm or whatever, who found him a funk-hole.' Having spoken to Sunray, the army commander, on his radio, Playfare said: 'Our RV is the seminary's refectory behind the Catholic Cathedral at 1630. It's now 1557, sychronise watches, get your gear together and ease springs in a decent toilet while you've got the chance. We'll go in Gilby's van and collect the co-operative secret service agent from his cell in the barracks' guardroom on the way. His code name will be Hacker and we'll take him to the RV with us.'

I knew RV was army speak for rendez-vous and assumed 'us' included me. I was a lone user of the residence's ground-floor, marble-clad lavatory, re-appearing outside the team's garage in the steel helmet and flak jacket Richard had lent me. I was also the lone steel helmet wearer and quickly dumped it inside the garage.

En route to the RV, Gilby's van was waved down by Sunray and after a conflab with Playfare, he welcomed me and I found myself in his armoured car. He was gigantic! All of six feet seven and built like a super-heavyweight boxer. Shortly after our arrival at the RV, Gilby's van appeared, now with Hacker, the co-operative secret service agent, in the back being watched over the rest of the team. Playfare had planned the operation. First, Jacksons were to surround, search and patrol the seminary's ten long thatched huts. Next, Playfare would establish a firm base in the seminary's refectory from which he and Gilby would search the area for IEDs and defuse those found. After that, Draper and Bullway accompanied by Hacker, would storm the hut wherein they hoped to find Sanguekku.

Sunray's binocular-observations, his comments, the sporadic encoded commentary on his armoured car's radio and my eyesight kept me abreast of progress. Jacksons captured three suspected secret service agents in the seminary hut nearest Sanguekku's funk hole, which was in a gully. Outside the door Gilby found a booby trap which Payfare defused, but all they could see through the only window were a sleeping bag and tokolosi mask on the bed, and nailed to a wall a placard announced: 'Sorry! Gone to Choir Practice!'.

'Bugger!' Sunray aptly cursed and told his radio operator: 'Monitor the command net, Hornpipe and I will walk to the hut.' He told his machine-gunner: 'Stay ready to give any or all of us covering fire.' His armoured car driver said: 'I'll keep the engine running.'

A loaded magazine clicked home in Sunray's revolver. Handing me a rifle, he asked: 'Have you used one of these before?' I nodded, but without Draper's grin. Protected by four Jacksons, they walked to hut and Playfare showed them where he'd defused a booby trap just inside the hut's door. Bullway had dismantled a bugging device found under the bed and fetched a large plastic sheet and plastic bags from the van. Wearing gloves, he was wrapping the sleeping bag in the sheet and would put all the other items left in the hut into the bags. Hacker was escorted back to the barracks' guardroom in an army truck. Draper didn't say what he'd been doing. If killing the torturer in that palace cellar before the torturer killed Suleiman is anything to go by, he wouldn't have been idle. Bullway had killed the cellar's gaoler. They were a pigeon-pair, Bullway near the audience, Draper backstage. Had I asked them what their real names were, the curtain would drop.

While Sunray toured the area, guarded by Jacksons, and Gilby continued his search for IEDs, I returned to the garage in the front of his van with the sealed plastic bags and the large sheet containing the sleeping-bag wedged between me and Bullway, who somehow managed to drive reasonably well. Draper was in the back, guarding the three suspected secret service agents captured by Jacksons. With the plastic-enclosed evidence inside the team's garage, Bullway locked it and handed me the key. He and Draper returned to the seminary and Gilby got his van back. Richard's chauffeur marched the three captives at gunpoint into the other garage and locked the door from the inside, justifying Richard's reaction when I'd questioned the reliability of the residency's staff. When we next met, I apologised for my scepticism which he waved aside and said his chauffeur was a sergeant on loan for the duration of the current emergency from a British training unit.

I was contemplating how best to spend my next two days, gathering evidence from the three captives and from all the items locked in the garages, when Richard dashed back. 'A security guard phoned me from the front gate. My housekeeper, who is supervising my three maids, who've been cleaning the president's palace, had parked her car outside the gate and wanted to speak to me. The British policemen searching the palace had told her to drive my maids back to the high commissioner's residence and stay there. She was told to give this envelope to me and to burn it if anyone stopped her car. He cautiously opened the envelope and scanned a sheet of paper before letting me read what it said.

'Sir, I shall report to you at 10 p.m. tonight, as usual. In the meantime, you should be aware that two of my officers, while searching the palace cellars, found three corpses in a cell with a bricked-up doorway. This country's chief justice has identifed the corpses:

1. Mr Amboini, the former president. The corpse had been severely mutilated.
2. Grace Chanaba – apparently nicknamed "The Shredder" – the information minister, until defeated in last year's general election. The corpse bears the signs of repeated physical abuse, including brutal rape.

3. Sephele Mozimbo, the former police commissioner, a suspected Sanguekku ally, and convicted last year for embezzling UN funds. His naked body had been hung from the cell's ceiling, with a piece of cardboard pinned to it, on which had been written: "Nobody Double-Crosses Your Secret Service!"

The SAS gave us photos of every corpse found in the cells destroyed by the 7 Dec. palace explosion. None of these fragmented corpses have been identified. We will send them to our London forensic experts, but a conclusive outcome is unlikely. I expect to have the results of more palace searches by tonight's meeting. Yours respectfully, Inspector Fry.'

Clearly distressed, Richard said: 'I never met the president. He was always indisposed which may well have been invented. The other two I met quite often and considered them untrustworthy. Even though that opinion was shared by colleagues with whom I worked closest, locally, nothing can excuse such ghastly, brutal and unforgiveable crimes. You should photograph both letters, Dermot.'

'I must keep the letters and photos as evidence of how you became involved.'

'Why did you say how I *became involved*?'

'Look, Richard, I'm duty bound to warn you that, because you refused to dismiss that British police adviser, there are people elsewhere who regard you with suspicion. One of my tasks, albeit tasteless, is to prove whether they are right or wrong.'

'Fair enough!' With that, Richard hurried off to re-inspect the compound's security.

Bullway and Draper stepped up their nightly hunts for Sanguekku and his gang. Given a welcome pause on the IED front, I saw more of Playfare and Gilby. One planning more hunts and following up leads, the other using his linguistic expertise while interrogating the three captured secret service agents. He also helped me search the hut and the items found there, such as hairs left in the sleeping bag, in the tokolosi mask, on Sanguekku's presumed belongings. I also meet Inspector Fry when he briefed Richard about his police officers' town-centre searches, regrettably in vain so far – and were joined by the British detective inspector whose assistants were searching Kolokuana's sprawling suburbs. Both of them and Sunray's deputy attended Playfare's Sunday-meetings to collate intelligence and plan ahead. On the downside, because no potential evidence was found in the hut or on its contents, the items taken from the hut were despatched by air to the London forensic experts.

Twice a week Sunray and I updated cabinet ministers. After today's session he invited me to accompany him on 'a jaunt' which required me to sleep overnight in the officers' mess and join him just before dawn in the army barracks' helicopter hangar wearing my camouflaged gear and jungle hat. On arrival, Sunray let me carry his unloaded rifle.

We flew east to the diamond mine and a mile or so beyond the border the helicopter pilot landed precisely on the white cross the SAS team had staked to the arid scrubland. Sunray jumped out, followed by Mavimbi's liaison officer and me, intent on keeping our heads beneath whirling rotor-blades. We crawled through a cloud of choking dust, thrown up by the blades, towards the mound marked on Sunray's map. The roar of the helicopter lifting off was replaced by the din of rifle fire, spurring my determination to get behind the mound. Had we expected such a hostile welcome, perhaps we'd have stayed airborne. But I'm not a soldier! While crawling and keeping as low a profile as humanly possible, a shout pierced the battle-din: 'Over here!' I'd crawled past the mound. Mavimbi's liaison officer was crouching behind it and Sunray lying on top, his binoculars observing events. After about half an hour of taking turns with the binos a helicopter – a Huey I was told – larger than the one hopefully coming back for us, landed about a mile east of our mound, took off and headed west back towards the border. Sunray cursed the lack of radios in his army. After our helicopter arrived, this time they both followed me under those whirling rotor-blades. Our pilot told us on the intercom: 'The Huey's flying to Kolokuana's barracks with seven captured Panters.' White mercenaries, I was able to recall. We also landed there and Sunray took me to the guardroom, where tri-lingual Gilby – English, Afrikaans and Portugese – broke off from interrogating the white mercenaries.

'They hoped to steal diamonds,' he told us, 'then sell them and get money to help stop Mandela's election as South Africa's first black president. They belong to an Afrikaner Broederbond gang, based in the nearest town across the border. By tonight, I aim to find out where their hideout's situated and how many of their chums are also there.'

Gilby returned to the cells beneath the guardroom and we rejoined the liaison officer who wanted to tour the town centre before phoning his Mavimbi headquarters.

I'm 6 feet 2, the same height as my cousin Harry, though my waist measures slightly less than his! Yet, sitting next to Sunray in the back of his armoured car, I was dwarfed, as well as reminded that Brigadier-General Thaklomo was 6 feet 7 tall and probably 46 inches around his middle. Nevertheless, his fast crawling without puffing to and from that mound, had amply proved his physical fitness, plus his acute sense of self-preservation.

'My biblical name's Moses. What's yours Doctor Macausland?' he asked.

'My Irish name's Dermot, You should also be aware that I'm not a *medical* doctor.'

The huge body crushing me against a steel bulkhead shook with rumbling laughter.

'Professor Matanya must be very pleased you're a lawyer and not a medicine man.'

More rumbling laughter and my right hand's all but shaken off, much like it had been when we'd first met.

'Moses is delighted Dermot is with us, here, and to renew his acquaintance. Sixteen years ago you lectured our UK staff college course on post-colonial justice in Africa. It remains as important now as it was then . . . Correction, it's far more important now!'

'I remember that well. My latest talk there was on West Africa's conflict diamonds.'

'That was very good, also. London sent me a tape recording of what you said, with a copy of your CV.'

Oh-ho! My 'Base' would not have sent him my CV. It must have been that Whitehal mandarin, forever over-anxious to get involved, interfere, take the lead, create a cock-up.

The armoured car halted, a crewman unlocked the rear door and Moses leapt out, I stumbled out and thanked Moses for taking me. The liason officer phoned his Mavimbi headquarters giving to whomever he was speaking a detailed report of the incidents and their outcome. Relieved that he didn't mention my name or presence, and confident that the armoured car's engine had drowned Sunray's and my conversation, the liason officer hopefully still believed I was a medical doctor, but wouldn't ask what my non-medical skills were or what they ought to be.

Next day Mavimbi's liason officer flew back from the town just across the border and informed me that *his* country's soldiers had found the mercenaries' base and had captured all the remaining white mercenaries. At Playfare's next Sunday meeting the neighbouring country's soldiers were, with Bullway's unblushing aplomb, codenamed Wobblies.

While attempting to flee from a funk-hole in Kolokuana's town centre, Sanguekku was caught by Hacker, the secret service agent turned informant, and Gilby drove Sanguekku to the town's top security gaol. Then Bullway and Draper nabbed Trimble, the police adviser, leaving a girlfriend's home soon after dawn. Gilby and the British detective inspector joined me at the gaol. While Gilby and I interrogated Sanguekku, the detective inspector was similarly employed in Trimble's cell. After reviewing that tape-recorded interrogation, I questioned Trimble.

In early February Sangekku faced trial for multiple crimes – Trimble for abetting two of those crimes, occassioned largely by Sanguekku blackmailing Trimble's philandering.

Pastures New

During March, Suleiman took up his new post as chairman of a London-based think-tank, researching the pros and cons of foreign aid to least-developed countries, plus other key topics – such as how those countries could better look after themselves. Loving London, Diane returned to the catwalks, modelling slightly more mature female attire, interspersed with monthly trips to further afield fashion shows with Belinda – to parade the two-piece costumes, dresses and sometimes rather naughty bathers Belinda had designed. However, with Suleiman still in a wheelchair and his office conveniently near to their ground floor flat, his full recovery remained Diane's top priority. They would also share the delight of providing a more permanent boarding-school-holiday-home for their son and daughter.

By April, Speedy was fit enough to come top on a hairdressing course: an integral part of his rehabilitation. In July, he and a shapely blonde nurse who'd worked in the London clinic – no chance acquaintance, very much a love-match – were married close to Laura's home on a Scottish island, so remote only her parents witnessed their wedding. She sent Belinda a wedding photo and another of herself rowing a boat with the caption: 'Speedy's pointing to where he wants me to row. I won't let him walk far yet. Rowing's forbidden!'

The newly-weds moved into the flat above the village's vacant barber's shop. Harry paid the rent, business quickly thrived and Laura was delighted to find two bongos going cheap, which she knew Speedy badly wanted, but now banged too loudly every evening.

'I was crazy to give Speedy those bongos,' Laura confided. 'All our neighbours keep complaining and don't believe me when I say, banging bongos helps his recuperation.'

'I banned his blessèd bongos, when he banged them in Africa. Why not do the same?' Harry suggested, and then re-phrased it, to sound much more sympathetic.

Most weeks, he strolled to the village and posted his very latest treatise on foreign aid or whatever, plus his bill, to Suleiman's London office, and always called at the barber's shop for a chat and loads of laughs with Speedy and all the customers awaiting his proven expertise. Even so, Harry never let Speedy cut his hair or, greatly riskier, trim his beard!

Shut away in his attic most days, doing all the things *he* wanted to do, Belinda accused her husband of reverting to his inconsiderately boring pre-Africa routine.

'I'm just finishing this new development handbook.'

'You're always *just* finishing *something!* Why not finish the weeding? And if you stay rooted to that computer, you'll never recover and put back on far too much weight!'

He promised to do better in future, and after she'd gone, resumed typing Part 1 of the new handbook, headed: 'Bhoddo Mantholo (Sewage Disposal).' Part 2 would be headed: 'Khlema (Hygiene)' but had yet to decide what to call Part 3. He must also decide which of his many apposite photographs would best illustrate his simply phrased Gwato advice.

His next chat at the barber's shop revealed that Speedy had also had a 'bollocking', as he put it, and had promised to beat his bongos only during opening hours when he had no customer. In return, Laura had promised to go on a midwife's course and after the birth of their baby she would get a job and pay the rent. 'Okay, Harry?' 'Ten out of ten' Speedy!' 'You gave me ten-out-of-ten only once before.' They both fell about laughing, as they'd often done in Africa, but most of Speedy's body wished he hadn't. Harry's slow-mending stomach muscles thought exercise and pain were the same words.

While polishing Belinda's shoes he asked her: 'Did you know Laura's pregnant?'

'If you didn't spend so much of your time typing, you might have noticed her bump.'

The front door bell rang and his wife's wave of the head had him dashing to answer it. A form and a biro were thrust into his hand: 'Recorded delivery. Sign there,' the postman demanded, before handing over a larger than foolscap-size, stiffened envelope. Having politely thanked the postman, he paused in the hall to open it and pulled out all manner of booklets headed: 'Central Chancery of the Orders Of Knighthood.' For services to weed control, he assumed.

'Who was it?' The question came from the kitchen and presumably because he hadn't returned there, Belinda sped to the front door and picked up a letter, headed: 'The Most Excellent Order of the British Empire.' It was addressed to 'Henry Donal Burke!' Having read it, she exclaimed: 'You've got a *medal!*' Such was the quality of her emotion, Harry was compelled to gasp: 'Hold on! You jolly nearly suffocated me.'

After he'd got to reading the document and every booklet, up in his attic sanctum, he discovered amongst the small-print that he could take three guests to the Buckingham Palace investiture, yet no date when it would happen. Belinda agreed that they would take their daughter and grand-daughter. Then another letter arrived from London, suggesting an investiture date, very disappointingly not until December. Still, she'd have six exciting months to decide what to wear, design and make everything, as well as buy appropriate shoes, gloves and hat, while ensuring that Harry, their daughter and grand-daughter knew what to wear.

Since qualifying as a barrister last summer, Tsabo's law firm had confined most of his court duties to the Oxford circuit, enabling him not only to live with Jill, but also to move from her flat. After investing in a long-term mortgage, they purchased a two-bedroomed Cotswold cottage with roses round its front door – close enough for them to drive to his Oxford office and to Jill's college, where she held most of her anthropology tutorials. He'd hated leaving his college three years ago but relished re-meeting the provost, tutors and many fellow-students at functions, taking Jill with him to the increasing number that were unisex, as well as accompanying her to her College's functions. Yet his best friends were missing – his former law tutor, Dr Dermot Macausland, and his retired scout, Ron Simpson. Dermot had decided to take a sabbatical at Kolokuana University. Ron was in a nursing home just outside Oxford. On his and Jill's first visit, after a reunion that brought tears to their eyes, Ron, now aged 87 and bedridden, said: 'I've still got all them picture postcards from all them gen'almuns I scouted for. An that chief's

blanket you gave me, Mr Tsabo. It keeps me legs an feet warm!'
The picture postcards, which had covered one wall of Ron's former
one-room digs, now festooned two walls of his nursing home room;
with its own bathroom and a bell to press whenever he needed help
or consolation.

With their cottage a handy distance from the Cotswold village
where Harry and Belinda, now Speedy and Laura, lived meant that
Tsabo and Jill could enjoy Belinda's delicious Sunday lunch, Laura's
pregnancy commentary, Speedy's and Harry's banter, and also the
extraordinary antics of the black cat that, when an adorable kitten,
Jill reminded Belinda and Harry, they'd given her and Tsabo as their
engagement present eighteen months ago.

Harry recalled Tsabo's grimace on being given a kitten – when
he and Jill had given him those splendid photos of his college as his
49th birthday present. The tables were turned, however, when Tsabo
asked Harry to look after the cat, while Jill visited her parents in
Cumbria and he went abroad for a month. Harry's instant vision of
chasing such an uncontrollable gambolling moggie caused him not
to ask where Tsabo was off to. Then, regrettably, Belinda sealed the
cat deal by promising Tsabo: 'Of course Harry will look after your
much-loved pet. I'll buy a lead and he can take her for lovely long
walks, while smoking all those harmfully disgusting pipes.'

To rid his vision of a tugging mouser on a lead, Harry was about
to do some weeding or more accurately some pipe puffing behind
the garden shed when his attic phone rang. It was Dr Solomon
Khami. 'You'll never credit this, Harry. My general practitioner
son in Detroit has just rung to say that one of those giant American
football players has married Miss Dinea Mashedi and also adopted
her son. Our gracious Lord can certainly move in a mysterious way,
His wonders to perform.'

'Magic!' Harry gasped, but that smacked of witch doctors and
would offend a devout Christian. 'Apologies, Solomon, I meant to
say *holy* magic.'

'You should have said *devious* holy magic. I'm rushing a bit and
will ring again soon.'

'Look forward to that. And great thanks for telling me Miss
Mashedi's news!' Another exciting chapter had ended in Dinea's

adventurous, vainglorious life and Harry reckoned she deserved everything she was undoubtedly going to get.

Long before qualifying as a barrister last September, whether to practice in Kolokuana or in England had been a question Tsabo had kept on shelving, waiting for Jill to decide. It would be answered for them, when the managing partner of a London law firm, who had been impressed by Tsabo's performances in court, offered to take him into the firm – a far too handsome offer to turn down. The managing partner happened to be a white South African of British descent whom an Afrikaner dominated government had expelled due to his anti-apartheid activities. With Nelson Mandela's election as South Africa's president seemingly a shoe-in, he wanted to re-open his Johannesburg office and asked Tsabo to fly there to defend a white couple, arrested for contravening segregation laws by providing a home for black orphans. Many vehement protests had hit the global media's headlines. If Tsabo's determination to exonerate the couple proved successful it would accelerate the re-opening of the Johannesburg office. The managing partner also hoped that he would agree, in the longer term, to managing that office and expanding the law firm's renewed presence within post-aparthied South Africa.

That was how Tsabo found himself in Johannesburg and greatly surprised that his firm had been able to book him, a non-white man, a room in a luxurious whites-only hotel!

Within a week the imprisoned couple, the owners and the principal carer's of the black orphans' residential home, were found not guilty and returned to the home, far more than relieved to find their black staff and particularly every orphan were still there.

Friday evening's news, travelling this vast country's airwaves, held few surprises. More inter-tribal killings, more inter-racial violence, more promises to build low cost housing, schools and clinics for black people, to provide water, sewers and electricity for them, to crack down on appalling crime and carnage, *if* they voted for a white man, not Mandela, in the presidential election next month. Tsabo switched off the rented car's radio, only to hit the usual peak hour traffic jam and cursed the South African police, with not a copper in sight to bring at least some semblance of order to such chaos. Fellow drivers, many in gleaming gas guzzlers, most in rusty rattletraps, responded to their twice-daily challenge by crowding the hard-shoulder and/or repeatedly switching lanes to force their hazardous way nearer the head of the long queue, somewhere in the polluted distance. When, at last, he reached the motorway exit, there it was, in all its gruesome glory. Yet another pile up! Shattered, burning vehicles, mangled bodies, streams of blood boiling on scalded tarmac, yet no ambulance in sight . . . nor any within miles most likely. With his intention to stop and help thwarted by the constant hooting behind his car, he was compelled to keep pace with traffic now leaving the motorway. With his mobile phone unable to pick up a signal, he stopped at some shops, found a public call box. Tried another. That didn't work either. But a security guard, handcuffed to a shoplifter, promised to ring the emergency services.

A uniformed, black youth unlocked and indolently lifted the barrier, to allow Tsabo to activate gates set in high walls, topped with razor-sharp broken glass, and gain access to the hotel's compound, then to its underground garage. A lift deposited him conveniently near to the hotel's reception desk. He told the uniformed white receptionist that his local business had been completed three weeks earlier than expected, so he would be booking out tomorrow morning and flying to England. The receptionist said: 'A Mr Macausland phoned. He wants you to call him as soon as possible and left his number.'

Tsabo used one of the hotel foyer's long row of readily available telephone-cubicles.

'Great to know you're still alive Dermot.'

'So you've heard about all the problems. Thanks for calling back. I'll come straight to the point. We need your assistance urgently.'

'In what way?'

'I can't say anymore, other than suggest you come for a chat. I'll be at the airport.'

This announcement greeted Tsabo's arrival at Mavimbi Airport: "All passengers going to Kolokuana must come to the information desk." Having asked his name and checked that it matched the name in his passport – reminding him of his very first arrival at his Oxford College – the receptionist took him to a room, where he was greeted by Dermot, barely recognisable in a camouflaged flak jacket, matching trousers, army belt and boots.

'What's going on, Dermot? I thought you meant you'd be at Kolokuana's airport.'

'I couldn't say which one on the phone. Follow me.'

I led Tsabo out of the terminal building, across the tarmac to a helicopter, we climbed onto the back seats and the army major said to Tsabo: 'I'll fit your intercom. The pilot's flown you before and said you know how to use it. He'll fly us to Kolokuana. My call sign on the intercom is Acorn. The pilot's is Vapour.'

When airborne, Vapour said: 'I flew you, Mr Burke and Mr Tsamanachimone to all of the southern districts soon after Mr Burke arrived. Do you remember that blizzard we had to land in and all the snow we had to clear away before we could take off next morning?'

'And you told Mr Tsamanachimone not to shout when using the intercom. You're the army captain who also flew us to that safari lodge in the northern province.'

With his intercom switched off, Tsabo asked me: 'Why did you phone me Dermot?'

'The secret service director, Sanguekku, and the British police adviser, Trimble, were interrogated separately by a British detective inspector, by another person, mentioned in the interrogation record you can read later, and by me. As a result, Sanguekku faces trial for multiple crimes and Trimble for abetting some of those crimes. You've probably read about their capture in the British press. But ever since then, there's been a media blackout imposed by the government, principally because Sanguekku-sympathisers, secret service agents still at large, and uncaptured, errant, local policemen, have committed more arsony and brutal atrocities in an attempt to free both of the alleged criminals. A forlorn attempt, hopefully, because the prime minister and the army commander have confidently assured the cabinet, also parliament, that every soldier and the rapidly increasing number of loyal policemen will very soon stop the turmoil before it spreads, and before victims and loyal protesters start reprisals. All civilian flights between Kolokuana and Mavimbi have been banned for several reasons. Paramount is Kolokuana's and the country's security. That's the background. So, why did I phone you? It's essential to get Sanguekku's trial over and done with quickly. The longer the delay, the greater the likelihood of even more turmoil, dissidence and subversion. The prime minister greatly looks forward to meeting you this evening, as well as asking if you will present the prosecution's case at Sanguekku's trial.'

'Harry told me Mr Makimbo's now prime minister. I used to work with him when he was the country's Red Cross director and very much look forward to congratulating him. But there are experienced lawyers in Kolokuana more suited to this kind of brief than me, and they're in touch with the problems.'

'They may well be in touch. Maybe too much in touch! There's no lawyer who can be trusted to be impartial. Most are in cahoots with errant policemen, crooks and such like. Others would most probably bend in whichever direction bribery dictates. Therefore, it's crucially important that a non-local barrister presents the prosection's case. The fact that you were born and bred locally weighs heavily in your favour.'

'How long is the trial likely to last? I have other commitments in three weeks' time.'

'If necessary, your London law firm will be asked to extend your stay in Africa.'

Tsabo spent the rest of the flight keeping me posted on our whereabouts. When we'd crossed the border into his home-country's airspace, he exclaimed: 'Look how green it all is! So totally different to the arid landscape I left. There must have been oceans of rain.'

'Some heavy snowfalls are expected in the southern province, but not in your village. Search and rescue operations, aided by army and civilian helicopters, have been planned.'

With Sanguekku sentenced to life imprisonment, Kolokuana's media blackout lifted and Tsabo's masterly prosecution acclaimed by the local press, radio and television, he flew back to England.

Sanguekku was extradicted to face trial for similar crimes commited in his country, Angola, before the now murdered president of the country made him secret service director!

Trimble's corroborated evidence was founded on the proven fact that his philandering had enabled Sanguekku to blackmail him into abetting just two of the Angolan's crimes – advising him how to steal diamond's from the mine near the country's border – and lying to the British high commissioner to avoid being dismissed from his police adviser's post. Having pleaded guilty on both counts, he was sentenced to three year's imprisonment in Kolokuana's top-security goal which, on appeal, was commuted to working for five years as an unpaid nursing assistant with a team of British eye specialists curing blindness and removing cataracts, but *elsewhere* in Africa. He also forfeited his British police pension.

Now cleared of suspicion, Richard became far less hurried and much more talkative. Having enjoyed three of his cook's egg and vegetable fritters, and several glasses of his butler's best Chablis, he took me on a tour of his residence's spacious reception chamber and introduced me to its masses of Victorian memorabilia. Then, while Richard or maybe his butler polished off what remained of the Chablis, I escaped upstairs to bed.

With the captured secret service agents and sacked policemen serving sentences, commensurate with their crimes, the hunt continued for the fewer still at large. Any evidence gathering that fell my way, I could do at weekends, leaving me free to start tutoring law at Kolokuana University. I'd met its vice chancellor, Professor Matanya, after Tsabo and Jill had introduced her to their "Top Ten Gems" and before I presented her, on behalf of Oxford's temporarily absent vice chancellor, with an account of our university's history. Despite the professor's demanding workload as the country's justice minister, we spent one evening per week during the remainder of the Easter Term and throughout the longer Winter Term in what she called her temporarily vacated study, reviewing my previous week's endeavours. With that done, she refined my next week's intentions.

Before leaving Kolokuana, I was driven to Mabela where, at last, I would meet Father Patrick. Seven years ago, Tsabo had spent

Christmas with my wife and me in our London flat and I'd shown him some photographs that my father had taken, when governor of the southern province – of Mabela, the surrounding area, and even one of Katama which had dumbfounded Tsabo. He'd told me that a white man's bequest had funded his Oxford scholarship, and ever since then, I'd wanted to find out more. After showing me round St John's mission school, the nun took me to her priest's room. One of Harry's diaries had led me to expect to be greeted by a semi-invalid who always called Tsabo, Patrick, and who'd have difficulty getting up from his chair. Now in a wheelchair, the ever-smiling bearded giant was still wearing a faded brown cassock. His amusing reminiscences kept me enthralled for over an hour, but I eventually managed to explain that I'd been Tsabo's Oxford law tutor and that my father had lived in Mabela while governor of this province until the late 1960s. Father Patrick's reply would now go far beyond dumbfounding *me!*

'Then it was your father's bequest that paid for young Patrick's scholarship. We often met. He and your mother were special people and great friends. I also heard on the radio about Patrick's wonderful prosecution of that murdering maniac. His Obangwato mother laboured long to bring forth such a fine son.'

Nelson Mandela's Xhosa mother must also have laboured long to bring forth her fine son. Born in 1918, in what was then South Africa's Cape Province, now the Eastern Province, his birth name, Rohihlahla – a Xhosa word meaning 'troublemaker' – presaged his life-long dedication to freeing his country of apartheid. A political system that favoured South Africa's white citizens, while cruelly penalising and oppressing its black citizens, the vast majority of the country's population. Among the objectives, Nelson Mandela shared with fellow campaigners were equalising civil rights and installing a democratic government. The millions of black citizens who shared these and similar objectives were keen to go to great lengths to achieve them, including armed conflict and retaliatory armed conflict.

The black-dominated African National Congress, embracing the leading opponents of apartheid, adopted The Freedom Charter in

1955 – its opening words: "We, the people of South Africa, declare for all our country and the world to know that South Africa belongs to all who live in it, black and white, and that no government can justly claim authority, unless it is based on the will of the people."

Sentenced to life imprisonment in 1964 and released in 1990, Nelson Mandela and his country's Afrikaner president, Mr FW de Klerk, were last year jointly awarded the Nobel Peace Prize for their admirable efforts to reconcile their political and other differences.

Now, in April 1994, South Africa's black people had voted for the very first time and, as the world's television screens were still testifying, they had joyfully queued at polling stations, together with white people, peacefully. The outcome – elected representatives of several black-dominated political parties will comprise the new "Rainbow Nation's" first democratically elected government, with Nelson Mandela its elected leader.

'Madiba will soon be South Africa's first black president,' Tsabo enthused, relaxing in one of my college study's armchairs. 'We should celebrate. You must have bought some drinkable wine by now!'

'Only the rather cheap tutorial sherry I offer students. Let's go to the Randolph Hotel.'

I wasn't a drinker, nor was Tsabo, and neither of us were Randolph frequenters. The last time I went there was with Belinda, shortly before Harry, Suleiman and Speedy were set upon! And I was pretty sure Tsabo hadn't been there since his graduation lunch with Harry, Belinda and Jill seven years ago. How time flew! Yet, quite apart from assisting Tsabo celebrate, I owed him at the very least a slap-up dinner for prosecuting Sanguekku at such short notice, and with great aplomb. I had to also confess, that being a tad miserly, menu prices, rather than food quality, counted prominently while selecting eating places – a throw back from my student days – and at the Randolph, food quality matched prices, in my limited experience of such matters. I hadn't bargained nor bugeted, however, on Tsabo's choices: a monster rib-eye steak, plus all the trimmings, as a main course, eased down with the hotel's most expensive red wine. I had made do with a touch larger than the prescribed helping of the angels-on-horseback starter and a glass of fizzy water. With Tsabo clearly replete, we walked off some of his over-eating by going, on his insistence, for a chat with Jill in her College study. I was now feeling a trifle bemused!

After we'd sat down, Jill said: 'Tsabo's law firm has made him a junior partner, he'll manage its re-opened Johannesburg office, and I've got an anthropology lectureship at a nearby university. So, we'll be moving to South Africa, when Tsabo's firm has found us a house. Also, Dermot, I'm pregnant and we'd both be delighted if you'd be a godfather.'

'It will be a great honour, but wouldn't it be wiser to move *after* your baby's birth?' I warn, with the gravity of a prospective godfather and the naïvety of a childless husband. Although Wendy and I had pined to have children, all too sadly, none ever arrived.

'Neither Jill nor her doctor has any qualms,' Tsabo said. 'If you're free on Saturday, Dermot, why not come with us when Jill breaks our news to Harry and Belinda. Speedy will keep us amused, while Laura gives Jill lots of useful pregnancy tips. There's another reason for going. Before I flew to Africa and helped at Sanguekku's trial, Harry kindly agreed to look after Jill's belovéd cat and I've never had time to go and collect it.'

'What's most worrying,' Jill said, 'is that Harry offered to take Blackie for long walks on a lead. She's quite lively and likes to roam freely. I'm afraid Harry may have lost her.'

Unsure how best to react, I offered: 'Harry always does his utmost to avoid diasaster.'

Not the first time I'd had to spring to his defence! The trickiest had been, shielding him from Belinda's suspicion that he might be having an affair with Tsabo's curvaceous sister. But the opportunity to witness Harry taking a cat for a walk on a lead didn't crop up every day of the week and with Wendy supervising archealogical excavations in Crete for the next several months, my weekends were mostly spent preparing for the following week's student tutorials. Needing to inject variety into this somewhat humdrum routine, I readily agreed to accompany Jill and Tsabo – and might even see Harry taking a cat for a walk on a lead.

The best laid plans of mice and men, but this time they didn't work! Next morning the manager of our former scout's nursing home phoned Tsabo, who'd visited Ron Simpson earlier that week. Ron had died in his sleep the previous night! Telephones, including the one in my college study, received and passed on the tragic news. The Union Jack above the front entrance now fluttered at half mast. The provost's secretary gathered as many tutors and members of staff who knew Ron as she could muster, in our chapel, where the chaplain thanked God for Ron's long life and almost a lifetime of loyal, conscientious service to our College. Everyone present, some in tears, echoed the chaplain's Amen.

Afterwards the provost told our College's governing body, which included every tutor: 'The service in our chapel will begin with the words "Old Soldiers Never Die, They Only Fade Away" – a tribute to Ron's army service during the Second World War. The choir will sing an anthem and two rousing hymns. Tsabo Mashedi will choose a poem to recite. You, Dermot, will give the eulogy. I will read the lesson. After the cremation, the ashes will be scattered in the back quad's rose garden, near to Ron's shoe-cleaning room, which reminds me of a record I heard, many years ago, of somebody singing about somebody who'd worn brown boots to a funeral. Ron had invariably worn the same, whilst ensuring that the countless gentlemen, for whom he had diligently scouted, maintained the highest sartorial standards he had set them, and had always worked consistently hard to achieve.'

'When's the funeral?' the collage bursar asked, impatiently.

'Next Tuesday at noon!' With that dealt with, the provost's hyper-protective secretary targeted me. 'Will you or shall I tell Mr Mashedi about choosing and reciting a poem?'

'I'll phone him. He's working in London this week.'

I also told Tsabo that Harry would attend the funeral, bring Blackie in a cat-basket and had promised to leave them in his car, until after the service. Mentioning such a relatively minor detail when we and many others were feeling so sad was out of place, yet I knew how relieved he, and especially Jill, would be to know her treasured pet had not been lost.

With the chapel full to overflowing, the coffin, borne by four sturdy undergraduates, had draped over it the chief's blanket Tsabo, before going down from Oxford, gave his scout. Ron's war medals and his brown boots shared pride of place, resting securely on top of the coffin. The college's butler, preceding the cortege along the aisle, bowed to his right and then to his left: the masses of picture postcards Ron had received from innumerable students, ever grateful for his help and friendship, had been transferred from two walls of his nursing home room to four display panels on both sides the nave. All college scouts and members of the governing body solemnly followed. Before the coffin passed everybody stood, if they weren't standing already, and bowed their heads. Such was the great respect and gratitude Ron had earned during his sixty-years of exemplary service to a college he had respected and been so grateful to serve. Indeed, as Tsabo recalled, before reciting a moving poem: 'After visiting Ron's one-room digs and strolling back together to what he always called home territory, he said in his memorable brogue. They'll better 'av plenty'a cart horses to get me coffin outta 'ere. The best college in the 'ole worl. 'Tis yer know. Oh, yes! So you remember that. I shall never forget those words or forget Ron and neither will all of you, nor will his many friends who are unable to be with us today.'

With the sombre yet uplifting celebration of Ron's many fine achievements during his earthly life drawing to a close, the record our provost had recalled, accompanied Ron's departure to pastures new. Stanley Holloway's cockney hit song about a man who'd worn brown boots to a funeral, resounded within the chapel and through loud-speakers to the back quad where the overspill congregation had heard the service and sung the hymns. The record's finale typified Ron's unstinting generosity: 'Brown boots, I ask yer. Brow-ow-own boots. We didn't ask, 'ee didn't say, 'ee giv'd 'is uvver boots away.'

Katama Awaits

Punter Bryant's latest letter began: 'October's most welcome rains have saved countless Obangwato lives by quenching their own and their remaining livestock's over-long thirst – also converting the southern province's landscape from a dispiriting parched brown to a more encouraging light green. With more rain since then, that paler shade of green has become yet more encouragingly darker – an enlivening backdrop for those tending maize and other plants in their invariably rented fields. Many more fields than in previous years were fertilised before planting and each southern district has a seed-and-fertiliser bank to help kick-start recovery. In an increasing number of villages, worst-hit by the prolonged severe drought, small dams are being built, gutters and downpipes fitted to suitable roofs to catch and conserve rain, paid for by the Japanese businessmen who, a year or more ago, had promised to fund similar improvements within Kolokuana's extensive slums and shanty suburbs.'

'Last year, Harry, you will recall that an American foodstuffs company had promised to set up co-operatives, whereby subsistence farmers could join forces with larger-scale farmers to substantially increase crop production and improve the marketing of their produce. A German engineering firm, having agreed to repair the southern province's precious few tractors and ploughs, has now provided an impressive array of second-hand agricultural tools and earth-moving equipment.'

'All longer-term water supply and food security initiatives need to be supported by effective crop-irrigation. China's ambassador, having undiplomatically supplanted his Taiwanese counterpart, announced his government's intention to irrigate all the southern province's fields, so that every farmer and family could grow cash crops, mainly fruit and nuts, as well as their usual maize and bean crops. Outwardly welcoming these intentions, this country's cabinet ministers inwardly regarded them as extra ways of strengthening China's political and economic footholds, already firmly or being eastablished in several other African countries. Apparently inadequately funded, cabinet ministers suggested a combined irrigation project, with Chinese expertise and sufficient money, but with local labour and supervision. The impasse awaits Beijing's response and then joint resolution.'

'Jurek hopes solar panel sales will increase when people have more money, when the UN has provided all the promised cell phones, and when the country's government has provided the resources to enable the nationalised electricity company to supply more homes, all community headmen, factories, hospitals, health posts, schools and so on. Had Jurek not been a born optimist, he would never have started assembling solar panel kits. Nor would he have convinced those Polish entrepreneurs that their financial backing and subsidised materials would eventually pay dividends. For the present, however, he'll have to make do with striving to become successful. Yet there are on-going developments that may well, in the not too far distant future, turn his dreams into reality, among them: solar powered radios, fridges and cooking facilities that might save the thousands of lives and homes lost every year in fires caused by candles and paraffin or kerosene stoves.'

'Not to be outdone, Richard Riddington has gained British government agreement to fund and help construct sufficient ventilated-pit-latrines in southern communities, thereby substantially improving people's hygiene standards. Your latest development handbook with simply described, trilingual sewage disposal, hygiene and disease-control advice, as well as illustrations that even I can understand is proving its worth throughout this country.'

'On becoming prime minister Jenkins Makimbo had immediately enforced HIV-testing within Kolokuana and persuaded the UN's local health supremo to devote more attention to combating AIDS, a scourge threatening to destroy the nation. By delaying his drive to reduce the government's huge deficit, he had funded hospital staff training and provided AIDS treatment facilities among the best in an African region where the UN, donors and charities were struggling to grasp that killer-nettle and discover effective remedies. He would have banned prostitution, particularly rife in the capital, but parliamentarians with vested interests convinced sufficient colleagues that the sex-industry's vital contribution to national prosperity must not be sacrificed. Nor must hard working men and women be deprived of one of the very few, real pleasures in their long-suffering lives and Jenkins's initiative, backed by all cabinet colleagues, was rejected.'

'As too often happens when a country begins to recover from a catastrophe, parliament became embroiled in lengthy, rather puerile debates about how to reconstruct the nation's capital, especially a town centre torn asunder by last December's bomb explosions, arson attacks, also the fighting between secret service agents, policemen and soldiers. Yet every fanciful idea peddled by parliamentarians, contained a detectable element – "What's in it for me?" The sinners among them, professing saintliness, sought without scruple or regret to protect their perks, some legal, some illicit, rather than project their electors' interests.'

'Jenkins, now progressing the reconstruction of the nation's police force and instilling effective police-army co-operation, has set up a judicial enquiry – its terms of reference aimed at eliminating, once and for all, corruption within government and the country as a whole. He also obtained cabinet approval to postpone re-building the town centre until professional advice and funds are available. The urgently needed housing improvements in all the capital's slums will go ahead, financed by selling the Katama Mine's diamonds, despite the cartel's renewed refusal to lift its self-serving, macro-punitive embargo.'

'Meanwhile Sonny Floors, the finance minister and across-the-board long-term planner will devolve good governance to the lowest appropriate level – whilst strictly enforcing adequate transparency and effective accountability at *all* government levels. The overhaul of the monolithic civil service which Lawrence Kwawenda, now the cabinet secretary, completed last year has produced substantial financial savings and the transfer of surplus human resources to an encouraging number and variety of private enterprises.'

'Uncle Bill, the water and sanitation, health and nutrition, agriculture, food-security and transport minister had been greatly relieved to welcome Dr Solomon Khami as his deputy responsible for health, nutrition and food-security. Also, yours truly, on part-time loan from Save the Children Fund, is Uncle Bill's chief of staff, the appointment title the army commander suggested. Uncle Bill now has a simpler title – development minister – in his words, everything nobody else wants to do! Under his eagle eye the local Red Cross society continues to help improve health care, including children orphaned by drought, AIDS or other reasons. Uncle Bill is equally supportive of Save the Children Fund, which now concentrates its water and food supply efforts in the capital's slums, with Caritas, a Catholic NGO, similarly employed in the predominantly Catholic south, as well as many local charities.'

'You will be delighted to read that your macro-pessimistic ally, Alistair Croft – whose performances as the water and sanitation group's chairman continues – has at last enlisted the WaterAid charity's advice and assistance to find springs, deepen boreholes, protect wetlands and train people to service and repair the increasing number of water pumps the UN's provided. The Red Cross will also become responsible for the housing and care of all children orphaned by drought, AIDS or other causes. Oxfam has re-started the school-children-feeding/crop-growing project the previous government cancelled.* All five UN agencies based in Kolokuana with their staffs co-located within Suleiman's masterpiece, the Hub, now share a common drought recovery/ development mission, a unified budget, integrated administration and flexibly responsive procedures. ** You asked what is being done to help the multitude of poor, hungry, thirsty and sick Obangwatos who fled the south, hoping to find in Kolokuana paid work, food, water and medicines. As you know too well most found only unsanitary, unlit, rat-ridden shacks, but the then-government failed to provide the succour they sought and deserved. Now, rather than permanently returning to the south – which could be all too soon re-afficted by drought and maybe by heavy snowfalls or whatever – the radically new government, together with donors, UN agencies and charities, strive to fund and to provide refugees with decent shelter, piped water and mains electricity. All jobless people fit enough to

---

*   Page 136.
** Page 316.

work, temporarily return to the south, are housed in tented camps at many work sites, and earn enough money to buy food, medicines and other necessities; not only for themselves, but also for their relatives and friends who refused or were unable to leave their drought-stricken homes.'

'The police reorganisation and recruiting reforms promise to revolutionise army-police co-operation, recovery/development training, law and order enforcement, yet many more solar-panel-re-chargeable-cell-phones. are needed, not only by the army and police!'

'Sonny Floors is trying to get the UN to approve a revised cell phone cost-sharing deal. Catholic Uncle Bill has declined the cabinet's invitation to stand at August's presidential election, though he resolutely heads the list of senators, members of parliament and chiefs who have all nominated the Anglican bishop. Does this impress you?'

Harry faxed a reply: 'It certainly does impress me! The bishop was very largely instrumental, with Professor Archer of England's twinned Anglican diocese, in providing fuel-pellet-producing machines, wind-up wireless sets, used-clothing for drought victims, remotely located clinics and wood-lots with sadly too often too many dead or dying trees. Here's hoping the recent rains have given all wood-lots a new lease of life.'

Next morning Harry drove to Oxford with his copy of Punter Bryant's long epistle and another for Dermot. Having discussed the contents, Harry confirmed that copies of his development handbooks had been sent by Suleiman's think-tank staff to least-developed countries, advising their governments to re-produce them in their languages and provide copies for their communtiees. Suleiman's request for a hand-book explaining the disease-control measures essential for detecting HIV and for preventing or curbing the spread of AIDS, Harry had left to qualified authors. He needed no reminding of his AIDS scare!

After lunch in their college Hall, Dermot disclosed in the privacy of his study: 'I'd like to update you, Harry. You'll recall that Mr Mboko fled to London, where he'd pleaded to be placed under house-arrest. My interrogation of him there, and an exhaustive review by members of my 'Circle' of his ministerial performance in Kolokuana, had proved that the deceased president had compelled him, during the past four years, to fund the presidential palace's extravagances or Sanguekku's and his cronies's extravagances! Furthermore, Tsabo had proved during Sanguekku's trial that the president had appointed him secret service director without Mboko's or the cabinet's approval. When Mboko was allowed to return to Kolokuana, he sold the Horseman's Rest, donated the proceeds to charity and vowed under oath not to indulge in any form of corruption. Every parliamentarian has vowed the same under oath and the secret service has been banned. Mboko's now sports minister.'

'I hope he's in the cabinet,' Harry said, 'where other ministers can watch him closely.'

No Commonwealth electoral commission was needed to confirm August's polling result, Bishop Ebenezer Maphuso being the sole presidential candidate. On television and radio he thanked everyone who voted for him, whatever their religious or political beliefs, for electing him to support all of them. 'I will also support our elected government, the army, police and civil service which now employ Kasodi, as well as Obangwato people.'

August would lay claim to another auspicious event when Jill's and Tsabo's daughter, Amora, arrived a month early, avoiding birth abroad and qualifying for a British passport. Standing round the font in Tsabo's and Jill's local church, Dermot, Belinda and Jill's sister vowed to be caring god-parents – Harry, Speedy and Jill's parents were witnesses. Speedy's wife, Laura, had to take Buster their boisterous son outside and they also missed the tea party afterwards. Tsabo flew to Johannesburg a fortnight later, with all the luggage, followed at the medically prescribed pace by raring-to-go Jill and carry-cotted Amora.

The dress, hat, shoes and gloves that Belinda wore at Harry's wonderful Buckingham Palace investiture earlier in December had their second outing when Monica – Angela Akroyd's very best friend – changed her surname to Riddington and married Richard in the cricket pavilion of a renowned South African school, now multi-ethnic, in Kwa-Zulu Natal – near the house Dennis and Angela bought before leaving Kolokuana. Richard had vacated his palatial high commissioner's residence and would share Monica's bungalow at her farm, exercise her horses, rear foals and sell them to the highest bidder. Monica would continue teaching Obangwato women how to make tapestries, which had sold so well, she'd been able to employ more women, as well as many girls, whose parents couldn't afford to send them to school. Richard also told Harry: 'Two of your old friends, Frank, that Australian, otherwise known as Fozz, and Dave, the Yorkshireman, had received recognition for their invaluable contributions to drought relief, post-drought recovery and development.' Harry expressed his delight, but failed to conceal his too visible delight when Richard recalled that, during the investiture, Fozz had urged him in a very audible, rather raucous accent: 'Come on, mate. Don't muck about! Why can't Queenie hang her gong on me?' Looking disconsolate, Richard moaned: 'I hope he did say *muck,* though it sounded like his notorious eff-word! I also very much regret to add that his wife, daughters and most of the audience applauded whatever he said!'

'Perhaps they were applauding all his achievements,' Harry said, instead of letting himself laugh.

Belinda and Harry stayed overnight with the Akroyd's, or to be precise, they stayed part of the night in one of their beds. Reminiscences, laughter and a glass or two had kept them awake. Dennis's engineering business had taken a turn for the better, though he still found time to produce many admirable paintings and continued selling red Pinotage. Having created an equestrian club, Angela taught multi-coloured children how to ride.

Next morning Dennis drove Harry and Belinda up into the Drakensbergs, a high range of seemingly unsurmountable mountains dominating the skyline behind his garden. Dennis had opted to drive Angela's far more reliable pick-up truck, rather than his cantankerous vintage Jaguar. After satisfying a South African border guard that they had passports and were exporting nothing of worth, the pick-up truck heroically began its steeply hazardous climb, via innumerable acute bends that separated the sheer rock-face-clinging track from ravines of increasing depth, while edging its way ever-upwards towards the Kingdom of Lesotho, also known as the Kingdom in the Skies and formerly Basutoland.

Ever since childhood, Harry had yearned to surmount the Drakensbergs, particularly the track, renowned by countless highland adventurers as one of the best Wonders of the World which would safely, he hoped, enable him to reach the summit of the famous Sani Pass! Meanwhile, he had cling to the spare wheel in the pick-up truck's load space, also hoping that Belinda and Dennis in the cab weren't feeling altitude-dizzy. Now they had caught up a lorry overloaded with maize sacks, seriously slowing their upward progress and reducing their engine noise sufficiently for Harry to hear Belinda in their truck's cab shout at Dennis: 'Don't you *dare* overtake it!'

Having eventually reached the track's summit, still obediently behind the overloaded maize-carrying truck, a border guard admitted them all to Lesotho and Harry could at last savour his first sight of southern Africa's highest mountain – the almost 12,000 feet high, rounded grandeur of Thabana Ntlenyana! However, it wasn't long before he also caught sight of the terribly eroded, barren, arid countryside, dotted with small thatched huts; and then several pitiably thin, ill-clad children hurrying towards the white strangers, hoping to receive just a coin to give their mothers, grandmothers or carers – but if they had no carers, to buy a handful of maize to cook mealie-meal – if they could find dung to burn on a fire!

So many reminders that day had re-whetted Harry's memory of his two years farther north in Africa, though no reminders were needed of the plight of the continent's millions too many tragically deprived children. Rarely a day passed without him recalling Happy Sam's face after his blanket had been stolen; nor his beaming smile on being given a note instead of the usual coins to buy a replacement. Nor would he forget the equally young boy crouching among the barbed wire round a distribution point shack full of food aid, with a ration card clasped to his chest, having lost his way trying to find that shack. Given a sack full of food, he had bravely set off, hoping to find his way back to his sick mother and probably hiding from the many roving thieves constantly on the look out for sack carriers, regardless of their plight or age. Whenever reminiscing about similar memories, two images never failed to cause him far more sadness than many others. An emaciated girl, aged eleven or twelve Solomon Khami had estimated, although propped up by pillows, falling off an orphanage bench. Her delight when given a puppy she could touch, smell and love. She never knew if there were clouds in the sky, nor what people looked like. She could hear them speaking, but had never spoken herself, and any moment her twisted throat might stop her breathing any more. Then that miracle had happened. She shrieked: 'Har . . . ree' and soon 'El . . . la' . . . 'Har . . . ree' . . . 'Shop . . . ping.' Even though Ella could now joyously see with one eye, their first meetings would remain in his memory forever, nor would he and everyone else who knew Ella forget what that train's eye specialists achieved. His other persistent image – the inscription on the cross marking Happy Sam's grave with the words: 'Died on his pavement home clinging to a tee-shirt.' Belinda had always wanted a son and the possibility of adopting Happy Sam had so thrilled her. The inscription, the cross and the grave she understandably insisted on seeing on reaching Kolokuana. 'Visiting the grave will be harrowing for us both, but especially for Belinda,' muttered Harry, obeying her beckonings and returning to the pick-up truck.

After an uneventful return journey, a good night's sleep and a breakdown-less ride in Dennis's Jaguar to Durban Airport, Belinda and Harry flew to Port Elizabeth, where she sunbathed, he watched cricket and next day drove a rented camper-van via a succession of scenically spectacular coast roads to a Cape Town hotel to celebrate Christmas in style.

By mid-January they had visited the Cape of Good Hope, Cape Point, where a baboon stole Harry's bag of delicious apricots, soared in a cable car to the top of Table Mountain with its breathtaking views across Table Bay – including Robben Island, where Nelson Mandela was imprisoned for so many years. Early next morning they flew to Mavimbi, and then on to Kolokuana. Tsabo had intended to meet them at the airport, but had to go to Katama. He'd arranged for them to be driven from the airport to the Horseman's Rest, where he'd booked them a rondavel, to be driven at one o'clock to meet the president and at five o'clock next morning to be driven to the army barracks to be flown by helicopter to Katama, where he would await their arrival. It had to be that early, because they must be back at Kolokuana airport in time to catch the noon flight to Mavimbi and the evening flight to Heathrow. Their cheap air tickets were not interchangeable and the day after they returned home, Belinda had a lucrative fashion show commitment. Harry had preferred to visit Katama during their next African holiday, but Belinda insisted on meeting Tsabo's parents, his eldest sister, her family and visiting Tsabo's birthplace. A government car took them from Kolokuana Airport to the Horseman's Rest. The driver parked and then took them to a conference room, where Harry introduced Belinda to President Maphuso. 'He's also the Anglican bishop,' Harry had told her.

She'd met some of the guests during her previous visit: Jenkins Makimbo, Uncle Bill, Lawrence Kwawenda, Jack and their wives; also an even fatter Mboko. Others she hadn't met before: Sonny and Sticky Floors, Dr Solomon and Mrs Khami, Punter Bryant, a huge brigadier-general, the army commander and more, whose names the noise had drowned.

Fuzzy, who'd asked Belinda for one of her rings, arrived with Pinkie, the accountant, and Pete, the press officer had shyly stayed in the background. Belinda could have a far quieter chat with them. Harry had already told them about Suleiman, Speedy, Tsabo, their wives and their children.

The president concluded his warm welcome, by saying: 'I have read that George the Fifth, a King greatly admired by his millions of British and Commonwealth peoples, as all recent monarchs were or still are, once admitted that he didn't like abroad, because he had been there! Whenever you, Mr and Mrs Harry, wish to venture overseas you will be heartily welcomed by everybody within this country.' The president produced a bunch of anemones. 'A revered national flower,' he said and gave the bunch to Belinda. But before she could thank him, he unwrapped a bulky parcel, draped a multi-coloured blanket round Harry's shoulders, placed a baseball cap on his head and explained to Belinda: 'This is an Obangwato principal chief's blanket and the Bringer of Rain praise name, sewn on the front of the cap, are this nation's far more than grateful thanks for all your husband's hard work. The anemones are an equally grateful tribute to his wife, for letting him come here six years ago. I must ask you, Mr Harry, to take this parcel to Mr Suleiman al Rashid and that other one to Mr Morebo Takeshi who is also, I'm reliably told, very widely known as Speedy.' There were cheers, a few inaudible quips and some laughter amid the applause!

With her husband over-preoccupied with adjusting his blanket, Belinda thanked the president for his kind words and both generous gifts, but then thought she should add: 'In one of Harry's very many diaries he typed, during his relief work and all his adventurous travels in your country, he mentioned that a village headman, the father of our very good friend Tsabo Mashedi, had given Harry a chief's blanket, a walking stick and a trilby.'

'This Bringer of Rain baseball cap fits much better than that trilby,' Harry remarked, and the president's smile confirmed his appreciation of the compliment – but why had he left in such a hurry? Then, the Anglican bishop wheeled in the Catholic priest, Father Patrick, under Sister Gabriella's watchful supervision. More applause! When the president and his guests had said their farewells, Harry's reunion and Belinda's first meeting with both new arrivals would warrant a diary entry, typed that evening on his re-possessed laptop. Kept secure by the army commander since the palace cellar tragedy, its record of those events had provided crucial evidence at Saguekku's and all his fellow-criminals' trials.

'After enjoying mugs of tepid tea and what remained of the beetroot sandwhiches, my favourite filling, Sister Gabriella – Gabby, as she had always liked being called – drove Father Patrick, his wheelchair, Belinda and me in a van to Kolokuana's public cemetery: the Place of Rabbits in Gwato. Gabby had often visited street-boys' graves while working in or around Kolokuana, and Father Patrick wanted to go with us. Belinda courageously recited a prayer beside 'my darling little boy's' grave – just a rain-caused quagmire. We scraped the mud off the concrete cross, then Belinda laid the anemones she'd been given below the now readable inscription on the concrete cross, devastated by the words: 'Died on his pavement home clinging to a tee-shirt.' The tee-shirt she had given him! Father Patrick consoled her, recited the 23 rd Psalm and

Belinda tearfully thanked him. On the way to the Horseman's Rest where Belinda and I were staying, Gabby said the same train and eye-specialists had returned to Mavimbi. A bus would bring Ella, now able to see with both eyes, and other treated patients back to the Red Cross orphanage. Gabby would collect Ella and drive her to their nunnery in Mabela.' I couldn't believe what she'd said and asked her to repeat it. Happiness tears were still in our eyes when the four of us bade our farewells, promising to meet again soon, and for Gabby to drive her cherished priest, still unmissably the white-man-who-smiles, back to his treasured St John's Mission.'

With their waves lost in traffic, Belinda and Harry crossed the main street to the burnt-out shell of Berney's Bazaar, now being rebuilt, as was the British Council's library.

An army helicopter delivered them at six o'clock next morning, not to Katama, but on a flat hilltop, above what Harry took to be the diamond mine —piles of rock, many cranes, lots of earth-moving equipment and a tented camp.* Awaiting their arrival were Tsabo, a priest in a brown cassock, a soldier with a bugle and Mkwere of whom Harry had always been suspicious – but Suleiman had said was an employee of a London mining company. Mkwere had also owned the café where a dog mauled Harry's leg. Then there'd been that mystifying envelope, addressed to Dermot's Oxford post box that Mkwere had wanted Harry to post in England. Now Mkwere said: 'Nearly two years ago, Tsabo asked me to tell him if any graves were found in this area, and recently, some soldiers found two. This one has a wooden cross stuck in it, the date and name are August 1904 and Donal Henry Burke. Tsabo said he was your grandfather Mr Harry?'

Belinda had stopped Harry falling over and calmed him down enough to listen to the priest's prayers. After the soldier had sounded *The Last Post* on his bugle, Harry shook Mkwere's hand but all he could croak was. 'Very many thanks for such kind persistence.'

---

*   Sketch-map of the funeral and guarded sites near Katama on next page.

SKETCH MAP : KATAMA AREA
(approx 2 ms to 5 miles)

N

Dome-shaped
Pinnacle

High Peaks

Waterfall

Airstrip Plateau

Village Across
the Gorge

Track from
Airstrip to Katama
and Guarded Site

Katama

Gorge

Guarded
Site

Funeral Service

——————— Army-built Dirt Track

- - - - - - Bridle Path over the
High Peaks to Mabela

—I—I—I· Steep Path from Funeral Service

—x—x— Barbed - Wire Enclosure

—xx—xx— Border with Neighbouring Country

∿∿∿∿ Stream from Waterfall, down gorge and across border

8 - 10 500 ft in altitude

The Katama area, guarded site and funeral site

'I'll send you and Dermot photos of your grandfather's grave, of us all praying beside it, and of the soldier blowing his bugle,' Tsabo said. 'I'll phone Dermot this evening after his student tutorials and spill the beans!'

Mkwere led them all down the remains of a steep zigzagging path to a gate in the lofty fence topped with razor-sharp barbed wire. An armed soldier checked Harry's and Jill's passports, unlocked the gate and they passed a small brick-built office – on its door: "Mr Mkwere, Katama Mine Manager".

Meat stew for a hurried breakfast in the miner's canteen, cooked by Tsabo's mother, served by his eldest sister and shared by his father, headman Fred, everyone who'd stood by the grave and some miners. Time to leave! Fred begged Harry and Belinda to visit again soon, they both followed Tsabo to another gate, which an armed soldier unlocked, and outside the fence climbed into the helicopter.

The flight to Kolokuana Airport with Tsabo – their cases were already stowed in the prop-aircraft. Au Revoir to Tsabo at Mavimbi Airport. He flew back to Johannesburg, to Jill and their precious daughter, Amora. Belinda and Harry slept that night in a jumbo-jet. By underground train from Heathrow to London to deliver Suleiman's parcel, which also contained a principal chief's blanket woven in England, then train and taxi to Speedy's barber's shop – in his parcel, a fleece-lined anorak and matching gloves, made in Mabela, his home town. He gave the gloves to Laura, his adorable mid-wife wife and the loving mother of their son, Buster, pestering to bang the bongos. So much rushing had worked! Missing lunch, Belinda drove the dresses she'd designed and seamstresses had produced to the fashion show, which had regularly proved lucrative, while Harry began reading the latest Economist – a newspaper that every week since reading medieval history at Oxford had urged him to improve his knowledge of practically every fact and opinion under the sun, rain or snow – or the lack of them. He cut out a statistical quotation highlighting the wicked financial impact so much lipstick-buying was having on poor people's water and sanitation, pasted it on cardboard and propped it up within easy-reading distance:

"Americans spend $8 billion a year on cosmetics, Europeans $50 billion on cigarettes, yet the world cannot find the $9 billion needed to give all people every-day access to clean drinking water and decent sanitary facilities."

Economist, 19th September 1998

On second thoughts, he hid the extract in case his wife read it and banned even out-of-doors pipe smoking, but he had to admit, only to himself, that he had never totted up his tobacco burning consumption, nor its cost, however hard he had tried to attempt to do so. His attic phone rang: 'Hallo Grandpa Africa,' his ten-year-young grand-daughter, Emmy, chirped. 'Thank you for more photos of where you used to work, but you didn't send any of you shooting all those hungry leopards you told me about when we went to my school?'

'Sorry darling! Next time I come, you'll be eleven and I'll buy your present.'

'I'd like a nice white frock please, if that's okay.'

'Grandma will help you choose it. I'm no good at doing those sorts of female things.'

She giggled. 'My mum said you always took your African girlfriends nice presents!'

'They weren't girlfriends or presents, they were things some people badly needed.'

'Love you Grandpa. Tell Grandma I love her too. See you both soon.'

'Not as much as we love you,' but Emmy must have gone before he could tell her that.

Her Grandpa Africa now had plenty to worry about – Dinea had wanted a short white frock. Just another coincidence, he hoped, and phoned his gossip-prone daughter.

'It was only a joke!' she jocularly assured him.

'I'd rather do without jokes of that sort.' And all she said was: 'Don't be so sensitive!'

While sneaking a weeding-break to enjoy just a few pipe-puffs behind his garden shed, he kicked himself for not demanding to be told who else, in addition to Emmy, and probably Belinda, their otherwise belovéd daughter had shared her witticism with!

After more than a few pipe-puffs it dawned on him that he'd not phoned Dermot about their grandfather's grave. Having described the helicopter flight and landing, the scenery, his and Belinda's reception, who were there and his version of the revelatory moment, he asked Dermot: 'Has Tsabo phoned you? He also said he'd send you photos of the grave.'

'I've been away. Great news! Where did you say the grave and mine were?' I had to ask that, even though I'd visited the mine twice. But they were under-cover visits. I'd also enlisted Tsabo's help, soon after Harry had arrived in that country, to advise him neither to search for our grandfather's grave nor the old mine workings, but without telling Tsabo the mine's hereabouts.

All round, it couldn't have turned out much better – the country benefited from legal diamond sales, and instead of having to leave home and family to work elsewhere, most of Katama's men and also its women had jobs at the nearby mine.

For the rest of that winter the blanket Tsabo's father had given Harry, reinforced his and Belinda's bedding. His principal chief's multi-coloured blanket which, like Suleiman's, had been woven in England, he had to wrap round him himself when braving that year's southern African winter – while helping Lesotho's government and the disaster management and development agencies working working with it to implement the recommendations in his hand books.

Belinda never ventured from their rented room without wearing her super-thick duffle coat and woollen hat with ear-flaps. Why was she here? Have a guess. Simple! There was no other way of ensuring that Harry would return home when his three months' leave of absence expired. He would find something else to do and she would have ended up here, anyway, helping him find a leopard or a tokolosi to shoot – now that, after all the fruitless enquiries and thwarted searches, his grandfather's grave had at last been found.

Reference Index

Novel's Narrator, Dermot Macausland (university tutor)

293-316, 318, 323-8, 330, 332-3,
335-6, 338, 355-9, 362, 365-7, 369,
373-6, 378-80, 382, 384
Hornpipe (Dermot Macausland) 334,
337, 340-1, 343, 347, 349

I

Inspector Fry (British police officer) 351

J

Jacksons (local soldiers) 343, 347, 349-50
James, Dr Arrabella (UN official) 211-17
Jill (anthropology postgraduate) 38-9,
41, 43-4, 155, 269, 271, 283, 302-3,
305-6, 308, 310, 316, 333-4, 357-9,
363, 365-7, 374, 382
Jinky (UN official) 167-8, 170, 188, 232,
241, 279-82, 296, 312, 327, 333

K

Kasodi (northern province's tribe and
dialect) 276-7, 374
Katama (Mashedi family's village) 3,
5-6, 8-10, 12-16, 18-19, 29-31, 36,
46, 72, 88, 96-7, 101, 103-6, 110,
112, 123, 237, 294-7, 301-6, 308-9,
314, 364, 371, 377-8, 380, 382, 384
Khami, Dr Solomon (paediatrian and
health minister, later local Red
Cross director) 193, 263, 276-
7, 290, 292, 312, 318, 334, 358,
371, 377
Kolokuana (country's capital) 18, 26,
28-9, 32, 34, 45, 47, 51-3, 57, 59,
63, 67, 73-6, 78, 84, 86, 93-5, 102,
104-6, 111, 114, 117, 123, 127, 131,
136, 148-9, 158, 160-1, 163-4, 167,
172, 179-82, 184, 186, 188, 191-4,
198, 201-2, 209, 211, 218, 221, 224,
226, 230, 236, 240-1, 253, 258,
261-2, 264, 266, 273, 275, 281-2,
284-5, 290, 293, 295-6, 299, 306,
312, 315-17, 319, 324-5, 327, 329-
30, 333-4, 337-41, 343, 359-63,
369-70, 372, 374-5, 377, 379
Kwawenda, Lawrence (management
consultant, later government

official) 218-21, 233, 241, 246,
250, 276, 291, 332, 371, 378

L

Laura (Speedy's wife) 355-6, 358, 366,
374, 382

M

Mabela (southern province's capital)
6-13, 18, 24-6, 28, 30-2, 35-6, 38,
45-7, 65, 80, 96-7, 102-11, 121, 124,
132, 135-6, 149-50, 186, 190-2,
194-9, 203, 221-2, 224, 226, 230,
234, 241, 259, 274, 279, 284-6,
296-8, 301, 305-7, 310, 312, 363-4,
380, 382
Macausland, Dermot (university tutor)
33, 233, 326-7, 357
Madam Thelma (Suleiman's secretary)
58, 62, 66, 173, 176, 225, 235, 333
Makimbo, Jenkins (charity official) 132-
3, 136, 147, 160-2, 188, 199, 233,
248, 250, 257-8, 261, 264, 276-7,
285, 288, 321-2, 327-8, 335, 378
Marge (Fozz's wife) 76-7, 294-5
Mashedi, Ngabo and Ma (parents) 6-7,
9-11, 16, 30
Matashaba, Dinea, and Palima (Ngabo
and Ma's daughters) 7, 25-6, 28,
30-1, 40, 86-9, 99-105, 107-12, 169,
237, 241, 269-70, 272-3, 278-81,
296, 298-301, 303, 305-8, 310-12,
314, 316, 358, 383
Matilda (Richard Riddington's cook) 346
Mavimbi (neighbouring country's capital)
32, 47, 51-2, 60, 75, 82-3, 85, 91,
95, 100, 112-14, 123-5, 135, 138,
146, 148, 157, 169, 194, 197, 214,
221, 228, 232, 236, 252, 261, 275,
292, 311-12, 319, 321, 328, 339-40,
346, 353-4, 362, 377-8, 380
Mkwere (phantom prospector) 121, 123,
226-7, 269, 274, 306-7, 311, 338,
342, 380, 382
Monica (workshop and stud farm owner)
207, 210, 217-18, 228, 249, 251,
374-5

U

Uncle Bill (government official) 71-2,
136, 150, 185-6, 191, 196-204, 222-
4, 230, 246, 250, 258, 263, 274,
279-80, 284-6, 295-6, 331-2, 335,
371-2, 378

W

Wendy (Dermot Macausland's wife) 48,
314, 333-4, 366

Printed in the United States
By Bookmasters